SHATTERED
NIGHT

SHATTERED
NIGHT

Kay Sandiford

& Alan Burgess

WARNER BOOKS

A Warner Communications Company

B
Sandiford

To Charles . . .

Copyright © 1984 by Kay Sandiford and Alan Burgess

Warner Books, Inc., 666 Fifth Avenue, New York, NY 10103

W A Warner Communications Company

Printed in the United States of America

First printing: January 1984
10 9 8 7 6 5 4 3 2 1

Library of Congress Cataloging in Publication Data

Sandiford, Kay.
    Shattered night.

    1. Murder—Texas—Houston—Case studies.   2. Sandiford,
Frank M., 1932–1980.   3. Sandiford, Kay.   4. Women
prisoners—Texas—Houston—Biography.   5. Trials—Murder
—Texas—Houston—Case studies.   I. Burgess, Alan.
II. Title.
HV6534.H8S26   1984   364.1'523'0924 [B]   83-42688
ISBN 0-446-51259-1

C.2

CONTENTS

Authors' Note

This is a true story. However, we have changed various names in its telling because many of the people involved are professional men and women who prefer to remain anonymous. This also applies to those members of the jury who kindly gave us their versions of what occurred in the jury room.

Our grateful thanks are also especially due to Marian Rosen for her continuing help and assistance, to Michael Von Blon, and to our editor, John Cox.

One

THE
SHOOTING

1

KAY Sandiford waited for the red light on the dashboard of her shining, dark maroon Mercedes to flicker out, and wondered how she was ever going to live through that evening.

She turned the ignition key and heard the smooth diesel purr of the engine. Gently—for she was always a careful driver—she reversed out of the double garage, swinging around to skirt the tall cypress trees that masked the walled Italianate garden which at first sight had so attracted Frank.

It was a garden hidden from passersby: tall pines, a lawn, flower beds, a blue-tiled pool. The front of the house, an elegant white facade, overlooked another wide lawn and more pine trees that stretched toward fasionable Del Monte Drive. Set in the heart of Rivers Oaks, Houston's exclusive residential district, the property had appealed to Frank at once, the perfect setting for a doctor of his magnetism, a heart surgeon of his manifest talent and driving ambition. It was strange, perhaps, that a man of Frank's perception should have had no premonition of disaster.

Kay had never seen him make up his mind so fast. Instructions were heaped upon her. "Darling, ring your lawyer Steadman in Baltimore *immediately*; we'll need the deposit transferred from your account. You can arrange the mortgage payments from the same source later."

1

"Yes, Frank," Kay recalled having said. Obedient as a little Chinese wife, she had thrust her own objections into the back of her mind. "I'll get on the phone straightaway, Frank."

Now, six year later, as she nosed the Mercedes around toward the avenue, she realized that that was how the rich, indulgent life had begun. But why—she braked at the intersection to let a polished limousine swirl past—if she had been asked at that moment about her unhappiness, would she have denied its existence?

Her reason? It was simply her lack of success with Frank, her failures, that made her feel upset. But she would improve. Of course, she must improve, and then happiness would come. She was, as anyone would tell you, one of the luckiest and most envied women in River Oaks.

Kathleen Sandiford was thirty-nine years old, a pretty woman with an oval face, dark hair, bright brown eyes, perfect teeth, and a wide smile. Her engaging manner was the legacy of a mother born in Baltimore of laughing Irish from County Cork; her stubborn honesty that of a father, also born in Baltimore, of German ancestry.

Kay's parents had been moderately wealthy, and indulgent toward their only child. Her childhood had been happy. She had been well educated, had had money of her own. Her trim, shapely figure was dressed in expensive clothes. After a disastrous first marriage to Newton—even though it had produced her adored son Charles—her second to Frank, the handsome Italian doctor from Rome, was, in the eyes of all her women friends, a coup and a success, and these days in Houston every woman who met the dark, attentive Frank, who felt the clasp of his warm hands, the intensity of his eyes, thought him absolutely divine.

As a heart surgeon, he was equated with Christian Barnard of South Africa—the Sandifords had entertained Chris in their home on Del Monte—and with Denton Cooley of Houston's Texas Heart Institute, where Frank had learned his craft and now earned an income of three hundred and fifty thousand dollars a year.

What more could a woman ask? At that moment Kay Sandiford could not have guessed. Her loyalty to Frank was incorruptible, her anxiety to be a fitting wife to such a fine human being, alternately poignant and embarrassing; her love, however unrequited, simply there for the taking.

That was perhaps one of the reasons why, when she braked and paused, she breathed in deeply and whispered, "No more tears... no tears."

She would "act" this evening; she always felt she was good at acting the happy, relaxed hostess. She would laugh and make entertaining conversation. There was nothing to be terrified about. After all, it was only a dinner at the Doctor's Club in the Medical Center with Bob and Jennifer, and they were as nice a couple as you could hope to meet. Bob was a colleague of Frank's, a cardiologist. They would talk all night about triple bypasses and ungrateful patients and a dozen aspects of their craft, while she and Jennifer compared notes on life. Jennifer, with her soft blue eyes looking out at the world through clear-framed glasses, seemed to have been specifically designed for compassion and comfort. If you didn't have a current problem of your own, Jennifer would bring up someone else's with which to test your ingenuity. The steady arrival of five lovely daughters had deepened rather than lessened her capacity for understanding.

Kay was worried that Frank would, as usual, be uptight that evening. Without interruption, he'd been like that for almost a year now. Their last recruiting trip to Italy three months ago had been, for her, an abominable experience. Their audience with Pope John Paul II, whom Kay thought a marvelous man, had not gone well at all from Frank's point of view. And he had blamed her for that. Kay was well aware that Frank's consuming ambition to become one of the pope's personal physicians might have received a setback. Frank said it was all her fault—women had no place at such functions—and she had anxiously considered what she might have done wrong. Maybe, after all, she was not good enough for him. But God, she had tried. She had tried so hard it hurt. And she didn't really mind when he hurt her. Which he often did.

She eased the Mercedes out into the darkening, tree-lined avenue and switched on the radio. The music was soft and soothing, a broad wash of security to match the elegant mansions that stood in spacious lawns on either side. She passed the Cooleys' white, pillared house, another reason why Frank had yearned for Del Monte: the boss himself only a few blocks away, two elegant cars in the driveway. Why not? Denton Cooley would certainly rate as one of Houston's most prestigious citizens, only preceded by a few short weeks, by Dr. Barnard, for the honor of performing the first heart-transplant operation in history. Yet

Denton never condescended toward her. In Kay's self-effacing terminology, Denton was a real neat guy; she liked him and his wife, Louise, very much.

She crossed the intersection at Kirby, drove past the high towers of downtown Houston, their lights glimmering now in the gloom of that January evening, and presently reached the Doctor's Club.

She paused before getting out, switching on the light and peering into her hand mirror to look at her eyes. They didn't look too bad. Not too puffy from all the crying. Not a bad cover-up job. No one could possibly know how often and secretly she wept these days, how strong were Frank's marvelous surgeon's hands, so strong that when he gripped her upper arm and ground his knuckles deep into her armpit, the pain was excruciating. And he left no marks. Since that first time in Baltimore, Frank had never left any marks. After all, he was a doctor, and doctors knew about pain and healing and bruises and all that stuff.

Later, the lady psychologist from Denver was to describe those four days leading up to that horrendous night of January 29, 1980, as a "reign of terror," but Kay Sandiford, also reflecting on the past, the longer past, thought that the reign had actually begun seventeen years back when the door of that Baltimore apartment belonging to the Harrises—parents of one of Kay's best friends—swung open and there, on the threshold, stood Frank. Doctore Francesco Maria Sandiford from Rome, eventually to be Americanized into Dr. Frank Sandiford of Houston, Texas, an immigrant in the United States for only two months, tall, elegant, arrogant, everything about him shining: the dark hair, the olive skin, the pointed black shoes, even the dove gray of his Italian suit seeming to enhance the glow of the huge bunch of yellow roses he carried as a romantic gift to his hostess.

But it was the eyes that had held Kay. All his personal magnetism was concentrated in those eyes, so dark she could not distinguish pupil from iris—eyes that from that moment on seemed to follow her, haunt her, and, yes, threaten her, even to the last second of his life.

It was warm and intimate in the cocktail section of the Doctor's Club and, as usual, Frank was late. Bob and Jennifer were on their first Scotch, and Bob stood up to kiss Kay, offer her his seat, and excuse Frank's dereliction cheerfully, saying, "We all know Frank. Always late.

These great heart surgeons are never on time, except when it matters, in the operating theater."

"Has he got something big on?" Kay asked.

"Only a normal bypass," Bob answered. "Nothing he hasn't done a hundred times before. Now, what are you drinking? Bourbon and water?"

"Yes, please." Kay sat down to talk to Jennifer while Bob headed for the bar. "How are the daughters?" she asked.

"Any ones in particular, or all five of them?" Jennifer replied.

Kay laughed. "Five daughters. You've really got staying power, Jennifer, and me with only one son."

"Charles is doing all right in boarding school?" Jennifer asked with genuine interest.

"Yes, Connecticut seems to suit him."

Kay saw Frank arrive. Everybody saw Frank arrive. Frank expected everyone to know he'd arrived. He did not glance in her direction or acknowledge her existence, and Kay felt the small, chill feeling settle in her stomach. He said, "Hello, Jennifer," and took Bob by the elbow, steering him back toward the bar. Kay now knew there was big trouble ahead, and her problem was how to deflect or counter it. That knowledge was not going to make for a pleasant evening.

The men returned. They all had a couple of drinks at the table. Frank chatted with Bob about hospital matters. Jennifer talked to Kay about the girls, and Kay smiled and laughed and gave all the correct answers. Sometimes she wondered why she didn't just stop and scream and scream and scream. Then they went in to dinner.

Jennifer told Kay later that she, Kay, had ordered the wine, a Chateau Citron 1966, two bottles of it; that was one of the tasks Frank always left to her. But Kay had no memory of it; she remembered only that he hadn't looked at her once the whole night. He had sat across the table from her and never glanced at her, not once. She remembered being frightened and just a little worried that her voice was getting flustered and was communicating her anxiety to Jennifer, for she had come to understand that eye contact with Frank was terribly important, and recently, more and more, it was as if he wasn't there. Jennifer told her afterward that Frank had ignored them both, simply talked to Bob, and of course that wasn't unusual; two doctors together who'd been working all day and were now comparing notes. But Jennifer also told her afterward that she'd found something very unusual about the intensity of Frank's behavior, this total conversational boycott of both women.

After dinner they got their coats, said good night, and went their separate ways. Kay told the parking attendant she'd pick up the Mercedes the next day. Usually Kay didn't let Frank drive because he was tired, so she went to the driver's side of the car, the pearl-gray Buick, but Frank said angrily, "I'll drive."

She slid across the seat, and as he got in and started the engine she could feel his tension: the almost physical emanations, the vibrations, the build-up of angst. Still, he never glanced at her, his eyes always on the windshield, the hood, anywhere but on her. Once out of the parking lot, he floored the accelerator and they screeched past Jones Library as if they were in a race, zipped through a stop sign, veered right, and roared out along Fannin, the way they usually went home. She didn't dare speak. Abruptly he turned into Hermann Park, which housed the zoo. He was flying around every corner and now she felt she had to speak, and she said mildly, "Frank, why are we in Hermann?"

He didn't answer, just took every bend with a squeal of tires and a lurch of bodywork. When he got to the zoo entrance, he slammed on the brakes and said angrily, "Get out!" Obediently she climbed out and waited. He came around the front and seized her wrist. "Come on," he said, "we're going to the zoo."

This was absurd. He was dragging her and she resisted. "But, Frank, the zoo is closed. Look; the gates are shut. They're always shut after dark."

He paused, glanced at her suspiciously, looked at the locked gates and then back at her. Without another word he got back in the car, and she got back in beside him. "Frank," she said, appealing, "what's the matter with you? Let's go home."

His voice was so choked he could barely speak. "I want to tell you something," he muttered, and off they roared again like crazy kids on a joy ride. In the middle of this screaming chase he managed to get it out. "I want a divorce!" he shouted. "D'you understand that? I want a divorce."

She shook her head, trying to clear her confusion. Frank wanted a divorce? In the first year of their marriage in Houston she'd been the one to ask, and he'd been coldly adamant. No divorce. Ever. Why had he suddenly changed? Nevertheless, she reacted as the patient, obedient, loving wife. "All right, we'll get a divorce," she said. She didn't want to make Frank angry by disagreeing with him. These days she was terrified of making Frank angry. And in this place, in the middle of the night, the thought was chilling. But she was relieved in one sense. Judging from his almost demonic attitude, she had thought it must be a matter of life and death. He had bungled and someone had died on the operating table. He'd murdered Denton Cooley, as he'd threatened he would. But all he wanted was a divorce. They hadn't discussed it for years because Frank had always given the same cold and implacable answer: "Don't think you'll ever leave me alive." And that had been the end of the discussion. Frank had always had this feeling about his reputation as a paragon, the perfect family man; that was why she went on always trying to be the perfect wife.

He was silent for a few moments as they tore through the night. Then he went on angrily, "I want you out of the house by Monday. I want the taxes worked up for the CPA, I want the bills paid, and I want you to go to Reno and get a divorce. I'm going to move my housekeeper in."

Her reaction was muted; she couldn't take it in. He wanted all this done by Monday night? And this was Friday night? As he hurled the car around the bends she appealed to him, saying, "Frank, you don't do things that way. I'll do anything as long as it's done in a reasonable way. There's a lot of stuff involved in a divorce."

She knew that inside she was a wreck. Inevitably these days she was high-strung with Frank. But she tried to rationalize, talk to him in a matter-of-fact way, take the heat off. She wasn't saying, "No, I won't do it," but in her mind she was thinking, *What an impossible request*. There was no way she could get all the tax work done, all the chits and receipts collated, pay all the bills, and go to Reno by Monday.

At that moment she wasn't thinking, *But it's my home too!* She simply knew she couldn't do what he wanted in the time available.

He drove on like a madman, almost screaming: "You do it! You hear me? You do it!"

They reached Del Monte and he parked the car in the drive. Kay unlocked the door. Frank came marching in behind her. Usually she would go upstairs, get undressed, put on her robe, and see what the situation was like—perhaps go into the TV room and see if life would be bearable if he wasn't in too bad a mood. But this night was different; he wouldn't leave her alone.

She walked into the living room and he was only two feet behind her, berating her about her bad character and the fact that she couldn't do anything right. His voice was a hiss of hatred. "You don't look right; you don't act right; you don't have children . . . everything you do is wrong. Look at you; you can't even keep your hair tidy. You look ridiculous now. Why do you always wear those ridiculous clothes?" That was hard to bear because they were clothes Frank had insisted she buy—and which he'd examined; everything had to be brought home for his approval to make sure it was all right. Now he had turned to another familiar diatribe: how he had tried to make a decent wife out of her but she was no good; she did nothing right. If she could have stood back from him and just listened, she probably would have thought it sounded corny or preposterous. But it was hissed at her over and over again, an endless hatred, and it was getting right into her; she was becoming deeply upset. By the minute she was slipping into a panic, like an attack of claustrophobia and she couldn't stand it. He had a way of speaking that was like a record; his voice didn't rise or fall—it was just a constant flat stream of hatred and revilement, a monotone that went on and on. He wouldn't get off her and she'd heard it all a thousand times before.

She ran up to her bathroom to escape but he even followed her there. Never before had he come into her bathroom; until now she could always say she was taking a bath and he'd leave her alone. She'd lie in the bathtub sometimes for a couple of hours and eventually he'd fall asleep somewhere. But that night he didn't. He followed her into the kitchen; she just couldn't get away from him.

She felt herself losing touch with reality. She had to get away, to hide. Somehow she found herself between the refrigerator and the wall, banging her head against the wall; anything to close out his voice, his hatred. She could remember thinking, *If only he'd shut up. Please, Frank, shut up!* She put her hands to her ears but she couldn't stop the sound. Whether she was shouting out loud or only in her thoughts, she never knew, but in her head she was hysterical. She was exploding. She could remember that intensity, almost an inner scream. She thought despairingly, *If he doesn't shut up, my head's going to blow; the top of it's going to come off!* The feeling was terrible. She couldn't remember anything like it in her life. She sank down to the floor, curled in a ball half behind the refrigerator. She heard him say he had tried to help her but he couldn't and he wasn't going to try anymore.

He said she was a wounded animal who should be put out of her misery. She remembered that vividly. That was the thought she carried as she lapsed into a blur of unconsciousness.

Later that night she came to and struggled upstairs. She decided there was no point in continuing to live such a life and decided to do away with herself. She had pills...sleeping pills. She had no idea what time it was or where Frank was. Anything to end the agony. She didn't know if he was in the house or if he'd left. Then she discovered him in the TV room and she took the bottle in her hand and walked over and said, "I'm going to take these!"

She emptied the bottle into her hand, then opened her hand and showed him what it held. Frank, lying on the couch, didn't say anything; he was drinking Petrus out of the bottle and watching TV. She went alone to Charles's room and wrote him a note. Then she took the pills to the bathroom, swallowed them, and went back into Charles's room. She loved Charles's room with its two spartan beds and all his bits and pieces, football and motorcycle helmets and weights for lifting. It was always a haven for her; he was her blood. She lay down on the bed and waited to fall asleep. Then Frank came in, with an afghan she'd knitted for him years before; the only thing she'd ever made for him that he'd really liked. He covered her with it and kissed her on the cheek. Then he said "Good night" and, after a pause, "Good-bye."

She remembered waking with a terrible stomachache. She staggered out of bed and was sick, didn't make it to the bathroom. Then she realized it was morning, Saturday morning. Feeling awful, she decided to try to go on living. But she didn't want to face Frank, she couldn't confront him. She just wanted to get out in case he came back and started in on her again. That was a terrifying thought. So she decided to go up to the lake house. How she drove the seventy miles north up Highway 45 she didn't know, but as soon as she walked into the cottage, she realized she was so shattered she couldn't relax there either. She couldn't sit down. She walked around. She smoked a cigarette. She was frantic and she had a compulsion to talk to somebody; she had to ring somebody up; she had to talk to someone who might help. She thought of the Morises. She and Frank had had them over to dinner, gone out to dinner with them pretty often. Frank liked Paul and Ruth Moris; they were one of the few couples he enjoyed going out with. At one time it had looked as if Frank was going to get on the board of Paul Moris's firm as a director, but that had never worked out. She picked up the phone and dialed. It would be many months, through what seemed a lifetime of agony, before she realized fully how vital that phone call would be.

Paul Moris answered. Ruth was not home; she was out buying a car with their son. Paul was very friendly. He understood that she was upset. "Well, you just come over here and talk to us," he said. Kay replied that she was not in town and it would take her a couple of hours to get back. But Paul was insistent. "No, you come right back here. Ruth will be back by then."

In some confusion Kay turned around and drove back to Houston. She parked at the back of the Morises' French Chateau-style house. Paul had told her to do that; they had a big six-to-eight-car garage. Ruth still wasn't back, so Paul took Kay into the bar and fixed her a drink; she thought it was champagne because Paul always seemed to open champagne. He started talking to her and she thought she told him about Friday night, and definitely about the divorce, and she remembered Paul saying, "Oh, all that's nonsense. Frank's just working too hard; he's under pressure," or something like that. And she told him about being frightened; she recalled that, because Paul seemed to understand that and told her, "You must go out to dinner with us tonight." She remembered protesting, but Paul wouldn't hear of it. He insisted. "You go home and change, and we'll pick you up." She remembered some discussion that if Frank were home she couldn't go, but if Frank weren't home she would. By this time Ruth had come home and was listening. But mainly Kay remembered the conversation as being between Paul and herself.

The end result was that Kay went home and changed into a black cashmere dress and the Morises picked her up. The three of them went to Tony's restaurant; she didn't remember what she ate. Fred Wales, a lawyer, was there, sitting on the left against the wall with his wife, and Ruth said that Kay should contact Fred if she wanted a divorce. So after Fred came by the table to say hello, and they were all introduced, the Morises both said, "Why don't you go and see Fred?"

Kay was still upset and frightened when they took her home, so Paul went into the house with her and checked around. In retrospect she found that a little strange because Paul had never done that before, but perhaps she'd never been that upset before. When they went into the little bar off the living room, she knew at once that Frank had been there. She saw that the couch had been lain on; the little pillows were mussed where someone had put a head; the phone was on the floor; and there was a bottle of Campari on the floor too, so she knew for certain that Frank had been home. But she didn't tell Paul that.

Paul left. It was still Saturday. She didn't remember what she did after that. She thought she probably took a pill and went to bed. Nine times out of ten she took a pill and went to sleep because she certainly didn't want to be conscious when Frank came home. She remembered sadly, "I didn't feel real swift that night because I'd taken all those other pills."

Frank wasn't home on Sunday. At all. Nothing. Sunday was blurred but she knew that at some point she paid all the bills. Because they had to be paid between Friday and Monday. And then she got all their tax stuff together because she had catalogued everything. The only other thing she remembered about Sunday was painful. Frank called. He was at the hospital; he said he'd been there all day and wanted to come home for dinner. She couldn't bear the thought of dinner at home with him; she wanted to go out. He couldn't hit her in a restaurant. Experience had taught her that if he was in a bad mood and she could get him to take her out, things were easier; she had that motivation firmly fixed in her head. She couldn't remember what time he arrived home, but somehow she induced him to take her to the Stables, a restaurant they both liked.

Frank behaved abominably, for the first time ever insulting her loudly in public. Her humiliation was abject. She wept quietly all through the meal, about which she remembered very little. But the waitresses at the Stables remembered Frank's performance and her distress—vividly—and later they wrote her a letter offering to testify and help her in any way they could. She thought that was very kind of them, but did not know quite how to thank them.

They left the restaurant and Frank began to drive her back to Del Monte, but he stopped at the corner of Westheimer and Willowwick and turned her out of the car. "Walk the rest of the way home," he said in contemptuous anger. She slid out into the darkness. She felt very lonely and afraid as she watched his taillights disappear. She never knew where he went. He didn't come home that night either. The house felt cold and lonely when she finally reached it.

On Tuesday, January 29, 1980, thunderclouds moved in from the Gulf, spreading up from Galveston fifty miles inland across the flatlands that lead to the skyscrapers of downtown Houston, and then moving on to River Oaks. The last gray dawn that Dr. Frank Sandiford would ever see filtered slowly through the branches of the pines and oaks and brightened the heavy dew that lay on the wide lawns of Saint Augustine grass along Del Monte Drive. The light moved in between the thin slats of the blinds of the graceful house, touching the ghostlike figure of the woman patrolling the silent rooms with the pathetic intensity of a human being whose mind is balanced on a tightrope of hysteria. On Monday she had gone to see Fred Wales about the divorce, but somehow it hadn't jelled. It wasn't his fault, but she felt she needed a woman lawyer; her antipathy to men was growing by the hour. Now, as always, she was waiting for Frank. She knew only that today was Tuesday and that the term of his ultimatum was over. And that she was terrified. She waited for his key in the lock with the terror of the condemned waiting for the executioner. She knew she wouldn't miss Frank's key in the lock. Frank's arrivals and departures were always high drama. No word needed to be spoken, no glance exchanged, but Frank could fling open a door, accelerate an engine, spin a tire in gravel, or brake to a halt, certain that his actions proclaimed his mood. And now his mood would be black.

Kay had started her patrol before midnight, unable to sleep, unable to settle, obsessed with her problem. She had paced from the kitchen through the dining room and across the hallway—glancing at the front doorway, half afraid he would spring through it—and into the living room, large, square, and elegant with her grand piano in one corner, the Early American furniture arranged tastefully, the carpets scattered on the polished floor. On the wall above the fireplace a single spotlight—which had acted as her beacon through these long night hours—was directed on a large oil portrait of Frank, masterful in a fashionable dark suit, white shirt, and dark tie, and Charles, not quite eighteen, slightly behind him. Charles looked so young and vulnerable that her heart went out to him and for the hundredth time she thought, *Now, what am I going to tell him, what am I going to say?*

She sat down on the settee, lit a cigarette, took a few puffs, and jabbed it out in an ashtray already filled with stubs, then moved off on her familiar rounds, this time taking the back corridor from the hallway to the kitchen. She reheated some coffee, sipped half a cup, and walked off again on her disoriented journey of despair. What did he mean when he said, "I want you out by Monday night. Tuesday I move in with my housekeeper." Housekeeper? What housekeeper?

Had she been rational and coherent—impossible after her suicide attempt—she might have seen that she was doing to herself precisely what other twentieth-century torturers did. The simple weapons of starvation, sleeplessness, terror, and disorientation were inducing a despair close to madness.

As she wandered through the silent house for the thousandth time, she knew she was losing her grip on reality. It was past two A.M. now, and Frank never came after two. Yet she simply had to confide—no, not confide; that was placing too big a burden on a friend—she had to talk to someone, chatter about shopping, clothes, tennis, jogging; gossip, get back into a cycle of reality she understood, and away from this dimension of terror. It was too early; she had to wait for the dawn. Who could she talk to at three, four, five in the morning? At five thirty she glanced through the blinds at the gray dawn. In River Oaks it was still too early for Mexican servants to arrive, too early for joggers to cruise by, too early for dogs to bark. Would it ever be eight o'clock? Eight was a decent hour. But who could she call then? Jennifer? Perhaps Jennifer. Jennifer and Bob had been there on Friday night when it had all started. Jennifer would understand. Yes, she could ring Jennifer at eight. Maybe she could last until eight fifteen and then try to sound normal, as if it were just a social call, as if she weren't appealing for help from this peculiar corner of hell.

And then, Christ...! The key was in the lock, the door banged open, and Frank was in the house. It was a quarter to six in the morning. She was in the kitchen. She heard him run up the front stairs, heard him banging doors and drawers, apparently changing his clothes. Where he'd spent the night she had no idea. He shouted down angrily that he had to be at the hospital at six thirty. A little later he came into the kitchen and swallowed some coffee. He was the same bitter, disdainful man. He did not look at her. He said icily, "I want you out of the house by tonight. I want you out of the house when I come home tonight. The housekeeper will be coming, and I want you *out!*"

The kitchen door slammed behind him; his car reversed; he slammed it into forward gear and roared down the drive. She realized she was shaking, hardly able to move, and felt herself getting "really freaky." She forced herself to wait until eight fifteen; then she picked up the phone and rang Jennifer's number.

2

As soon as Jennifer picked up the phone and heard Kay's voice—
"Have you time to come over for a visit?"—she knew something was
wrong.

"Of course I have time," Jennifer replied. "What time would you
like me?"

There was a little pause and then Kay said hesitantly, "Would nine
o'clock be all right?"

With the sure intuition that friendship engenders and the logic that
never seemed to desert her, Jennifer arrived at five to nine.

Kay opened the door and led her through the house into the kitchen.
Glancing at Kay's face, Jennifer recognized tension and guessed it had
something to do with Frank's attitude the previous Friday night. Kay
poured the coffee and steered the conversation through the shallows of
the weather and "The news wasn't very good, was it?" and then it began
to pour out of her in a flood: the drive back through Hermann Park,
Frank's demand for a divorce, his peremptory order that she leave the
house. But Kay didn't elaborate on her suicide attempt or Frank's reaction
to it; she didn't want to overburden their friendship, but, oh God, she
wanted someone to talk to and to help her.

Jennifer was unequivocal. Frank had ordered her to leave the house.

That was absurd. If anyone was to leave the house it should be Frank. In this sort of situation the man left the house; he had no right to tell her to quit.

The phone rang.

Kay paused and allowed it to ring. Then she tightened her lips and picked it up. Jennifer saw her face soften and break into a smile. "Charles," she said in pure delight. "What's that?" Her smile became a laugh. "You've been accepted at college? Where? Oh, Charles, that's marvelous. That's just great." Jennifer heard the small break in her voice and heard her try to cover it up. "No, Charles, it's just excitement, really it is. I'm so thrilled. No, Charles, darling, there's nothing wrong, there really isn't..."

She put her hand over the phone, listening to her son, and turned to Jennifer, saying, "What shall I do? He knows I'm upset. Shall I tell him?"

Jennifer answered off the top of her head. "He's going to have to know sometime," she answered. She saw Kay's nod of agreement, but then, as Jennifer listened to her friend's stumbling explanation, she began to sense for the first time the real depths of Kay's despair.

"Charles, darling. Your father thinks it better we get a divorce." The long pause, her face breaking up as she listened to his reactions. "No, darling, I'm not upset. Really I'm not upset. It's all right. Don't think I'm upset. Really I'm not upset."

The emotional scene was too much for Jennifer. She moved into the adjoining living room. A few seconds later Kay replaced the receiver, and joined Jennifer. Kay, seated on the divan, hands tightly clutched in her lap, was in deep distress. "Oh, Jennifer," she said, "he was upset. He was so upset."

Jennifer realized that instant reassurance was needed. She sat down next to Kay and said gently, "Kay, dear, it can't be all that bad."

"Charles wanted his father's phone number, and I gave it to him. I really shouldn't have done that. He'll ring him up. Frank hates being disturbed at the hospital. I shouldn't have done that."

Jennifer persevered. "What else could you have done, Kay?"

But now Kay was talking to herself. "He said he wanted to call his father. But I shouldn't have given him the number. I really shouldn't. Frank will be very angry. Oh, Frank will be so angry."

Jennifer's voice was firm and reasonable. "Kay, you're blaming yourself too much. First things first. You say Frank wants you out of the house. That's unfair. If Frank wants a divorce, then Frank's the one to pack a bag and go."

Jennifer talked to her friend for ten minutes, trying to be rational, trying to cheer her. Then the phone rang again, interrupting her words. Jennifer saw Kay's face tighten with fear.

"Oh, no," Kay whispered. She closed her eyes for a second, not daring to answer. When she opened them, she said, "That's Frank." The phone sat on a small table next to the divan, ringing insistently.

Jennifer didn't have the nerve to say, "It could be anybody, a neighbor, a friend." She moved away from the divan to an armchair, as if to give Kay elbow room, courage almost, to pick up the receiver, for she also knew that it had to be Frank.

Kay picked up the receiver. She listened without moving a muscle in her body. Her mouth opened once or twice but no sound came out. Then at last she said, "Frank, I didn't call Charles. Charles called me."

Jennifer, watching her friend's face, sensed her deep humiliation and fear. Kay was listening now, just saying yes and no, yes and no. The conversation was very brief. And when it was over, Jennifer could tell from the way Kay held on to the receiver, then looked at it as if it were something strange and formidable, that Frank had hung up on her.

Kay closed her eyes for a second, wondering how much she could confide to Jennifer. "Frank is so angry. He said I shouldn't have told Charles over the telephone, that I should have waited until tonight and he could have talked to him or gone to Connecticut to discuss it with him." And she reiterated, "Frank's very, very angry." Kay was shaking, mute with despair.

Jennifer, seized with sudden apprehension, said quickly, "Kay, let's get out of here. I know they have a busy schedule at the hospital but Frank might just come here between cases. Let's you and me get out of here. Grab your purse and your coat and let's get out of here. Let's go to my house."

Driving down San Felipe, Jennifer realized that Kay was in a state of shock. She shook all the way to Jennifer's house, about fifteen to twenty minutes away—a constant, uncontrollable shaking.

"What am I going to do?" Kay entreated. "Frank is so upset."

"Charles had to know about the divorce," Jennifer replied. "When we get to my house, maybe you could call the headmaster in Connecticut and tell him that Charles has had this upsetting news and then the headmaster can help him and see that he gets the proper counseling today."

Kay reacted instantly to that. "Yes," she agreed, "that's what I have to do." And then she added, "I'm going to call my father's lawyer, Ernest Steadman in Baltimore, and I'm going to call Ferrie Lee." Ferrie Lee was the Sandifords' black maid.

They arrived at Jennifer's house at about 10:30 A.M. and Jennifer took Kay to a bedroom so that Kay could make her phone calls. Jennifer went to the kitchen to do the dishes and clean up. Kay returned momentarily, slightly buoyed, and said the headmaster was glad she had told him about Charles over the telephone, because when the boys got these phone calls at night, the staff had a terrible time helping them. With telephone calls during daylight hours, Kay said, the school could cope with the situation much more easily because it had many more helpers around.

Kay explained this logic to Jennifer twice, and Jennifer realized that her friend was retelling the story in an effort to blot out of her mind the extreme severity of her problem.

Kay then went back to the bedroom to telephone Ernest Steadman. After a few seconds of conversation she called out to Jennifer: could she pick up the kitchen telephone and join them in a three-way conversation?

Somewhat reluctantly Jennifer obeyed, and heard Ernest Steadman's deep, cultivated voice: "Jennifer, if you're a friend of Kay's I really think she should spend the next few nights at your house. Could you manage that?"

Without hesitation Jennifer agreed.

But then Kay interrupted, saying, "But I don't want to involve Jennifer and Bob in this. I just don't want to involve Bob in this."

The lawyer was gently insistent. "Kay, this is something serious. I really feel that for your sake you should accept Jennifer's invitation to stay with her for a couple of nights, until we get this thing settled. Do you agree, Jennifer?"

"Kay can stay here as long as she wants to," Jennifer said. The conversation ended on that assumption; Kay would stay with Jennifer.

Together in the kitchen, Kay made her first confession: "Oh, Jennifer, I'm so tired. I've been up pacing the floor all night long. I haven't slept at all. All I've done is walk from room to room, drink coffee, and smoke cigarettes."

The other important point to emerge from the three-way telephone conversation was that Ernest Steadman had already been contacted by the Houston divorce lawyer Frederick Wales, whom Kay had been to see on Monday afternoon. Wales had informed Steadman that he understood Kay's dilemma and her desire for a woman attorney and had suggested that she contact a Houston attorney named Marian Rosen. He had given Steadman Mrs. Rosen's telephone number, and Steadman had talked to her. She sounded very competent and nice. If Kay would call her as soon as possible, Mrs. Rosen would set up an appointment.

Recalling that advice, Jennifer said, "Kay, I think you should call her now!"

Kay hesitated, then picked up the phone and dialed. She talked for a few seconds and then replaced the receiver. She sounded worried when she turned back to Jennifer. "Jennifer, do you really think I'm doing the right thing in going to see this lady attorney?"

"Of course. Why not?"

Kay was still hesitant. "I don't want to antagonize Frank. Frank hates Jews and he hates women professionals. Do you really think I'm doing the right thing?"

Jennifer tried to reassure her. "Kay," she said, "I saw her on television a year or two ago talking about some case of hers, and she impressed me as being very knowledgeable. I think you need to get legal advice, Kay, and your lawyer in Baltimore, whom you trust, has referred you to her, so I feel we should go down there. If you don't like her, we can go someplace else."

Kay nodded. "You're right," she said. "Of course you're right."

However, Jennifer was now a bit uneasy herself, because Kay had made it plain to her several times that, although she was immensely grateful for Jennifer's help, she didn't want to embarrass Jennifer. After all, Frank and Bob were colleagues and friends; they were quite close, in fact. If Frank saw Jennifer with Kay and realized they had been discussing his affairs, he would be very angry. A bit of Kay's pervasive fear had now rubbed off on Jennifer, and she was quite relieved to leave the house again.

They drove first to the bank to make a deposit, then downtown,

Jennifer by then showing how adversely the situation was affecting her. "I made every goof there was," she later recalled. She went down Main Street knowing all the time that she couldn't make a turn, and had to go on to Fannin to make the turn she wanted.

Kay didn't help by saying, "Jennifer, I'm so tired. I'm just not thinking straight. I'm tired through, my whole body."

Jennifer fully appreciated Kay's fatigue, but she knew that somehow she had to counter her objections. "I know you're tired, Kay," she answered, "but I really do feel that you need to see Mrs. Rosen today. You need to know what your next step in this should be. You can go home and have a nap after you've talked to her."

Reluctantly Kay agreed, and Jennifer drove on into downtown Houston and delivered Kay to the right office block, then looked for a parking place. She returned and waited patiently in the lobby until Kay appeared with Marian Rosen by her side and introduced them. Then Jennifer and Kay departed.

In the car afterward Kay confided: "She's nice. She's on my side. I can rely on her."

"Did she tell you what to do?" Jennifer asked.

"The same advice that you first gave me. She said to *stay* in the house, but have someone stay with me. Ferrie Lee will stay. I told her. She also told me to change the dual names on my safety deposit boxes to my name only."

Jennifer drove to the River Oaks bank where the safety deposit boxes were housed. She waited while Kay went inside. When Kay came out and got back in the car again, she seemed more relaxed. Almost since the moment they had met that morning, Kay had been talking about what she was going to do when the divorce went through. Now it seemed she had an idea.

"I think I could work in a bank," she said. "Going in there gave me the idea. After all, I've been handling all Frank's and my finances. That's only on a small scale, I know, but I think I could be a bank teller or some sort of small person in a bank."

Later Jennifer remembered: "She was kind of happy that it had occurred to her. We also discussed the possibility of her hiring a detective agency or someone to stay in the house with her that night and I said, 'You are sure the maid, Ferrie Lee, can stay with you?' And she said, 'Oh, sure. Ferrie Lee can stay with me. Ferrie Lee will stay with me in my room. I know that.' She thought about it again and then said, 'Jennifer, do you think I ought to hire a man to stay in the house with me tonight?' I said, 'I think that's a good idea,' and added, 'Did you discuss this with Mrs. Rosen?' And she said, 'We discussed contacting a detective agency to send over a man.' She added, 'The man could stay in Charles's bathroom and if Frank came home Frank would never know he was there.'"

Thinking about it much later, Jennifer realized that it was not the normal sort of conversation a couple of friends have when they go shopping. The whole episode was tinged with an aura of apprehension and unreality. Jennifer also realized that Kay was more exhausted than she had ever seen her before. Her eyes were tired-looking and black lines had appeared under them. Jennifer asked when Kay had last eaten, and added, "Do you want me to fix you some lunch?"

In spite of herself, Kay smiled. "Jennifer, you know I don't eat lunch."

"When was the last time you ate?" Jennifer asked.

Kay hesitated. "Well, I don't know," she said. "I think I had three bags of Fritos yesterday."

Jennifer knew they wouldn't have helped much. But her mind had moved on to something else they had discussed. Kay had said she was concerned about guns. Frank had two revolvers in the house and Mrs. Rosen had told her to hide the guns. Jennifer reminded Kay now.

Kay hesitated again and then answered shyly, "You know, I'd like to unload them but I really don't know how—because I have never handled a revolver. I really would like to unload them," she continued, "but I'm afraid I might... you know... I'm not familiar with them, so I don't think I'd better."

Jennifer knew all about Frank and guns, because she knew how her own husband felt about the subject. Bob didn't believe in guns in the house, and he used to joke about Frank's habit of going out to shoot squirrels. Naturally conversation at River Oaks dinner parties often turned toward security and the need for weapons, but certainly her friend Kay was not into guns. One gun lover in the house was enough.

Jennifer dropped Kay off at the house on Del Monte around four o'clock. They kissed each other on the cheek, and Kay squeezed Jennifer's hand and thanked her for all the help. Jennifer assured Kay that eventually everything would be all right.

Jennifer returned to her own home, picked up two of her teenage daughters, and took them shopping at the Galleria. At first she was haunted by worry, but she forgot it as she walked around the huge complex of shops, boutiques, ice rink, cafes, and restaurants that make up Houston's most elegant shopping center. They returned home around eight o'clock.

Doing another good deed, Jennifer now telephoned another friend to volunteer to supply dinner to her family because the friend had to visit her son in the hospital. She finished the conversation and glanced at the clock. It was 9:05.

Within a few minutes the telephone rang, and the nightmare began.

It was Kay, her voice filled with horror, a shrill cry of near madness: "Jennifer! Jennifer! Come over here as quick as you can! Don't wait, don't wait!"

"Kay, listen to me... Kay... Kay."

But the connection was cut off.

Jennifer knew now that the disquiet she'd felt since the phone first rang that morning had scaled to some terrible climax. Her dread communicated itself to her two daughters, who stared at her gravely. Not bothering to conceal her fears, Jennifer said, "Something terrible's happened. I've got to go to Mrs. Sandiford's."

"How do you know it's terrible?"

"I just know. I know!" She told her daughters that she had to leave at once. Daddy should have been home by now, but as soon as he arrived they were to tell him where she had gone. Then she tried to telephone Brenda, another friend of hers, who lived no more than a block away, and see if Brenda would come with her. Brenda's phone was busy. Well, Jennifer would try and pick her up on the way, for she could waste no more time. She drove straight to Brenda's and rang the front doorbell insistently. Brenda answered. Jennifer explained the situation. Could she come at once with her to Kay Sandiford's house? She felt certain something terrible had happened. How did she know something terrible had happened? Brenda asked. Jennifer couldn't waste time on arguments. She didn't know how she knew, but she knew! She had to go.

"Wait," Brenda said, "wait! My husband called five minutes ago, and he's on the way home and he's got Bob with him. If they don't arrive within five minutes, I'll come with you in your car."

Three minutes later the men's car pulled into the drive. Jennifer rushed out alone. Bob was surprised to see her. She had no time for explanations. "Get in," she snapped. "Get in."

Bob did as he was told and she drove away. "Now, Jennifer—" he began, but his wife cut him short.

"I've just had Kay Sandiford on the phone, screaming on the phone, really screaming, that I've got to get across there now. Now! 'Don't wait,' she screamed, 'don't wait.'" Bob protested reasonably, but Jennifer wouldn't hear it. "I've been with Kay all day, Bob. She's terribly upset. I've never seen anyone so upset in my life."

"Okay, dear, okay," Bob answered mildly. "But you might be making a big fuss over nothing."

It was a journey of tragic banality. As they reached the railway crossing, the lights were flashing and an endless, rattling stream of railway coaches rolled by.

Bob tried another soothing stall. "Now, Jennifer, don't worry..."

"Bob, if you'd been with Kay all day you'd have the same feeling I have."

Bob, needing his dinner but being a patient husband, said, "But if she screamed loudly at you over the telephone, she can't be in all that much trouble. You know about these fights, these marriage tiffs..."

"Bob, I know in my bones..."

Bob allowed himself a hint of disagreement. "But I've just been talking to Frank at the hospital! He's just given me a salami... dammit, I left it in the other car. I mean, Jennifer, come on..."

The train passed, blowing its sad salute into the night. Jennifer accelerated away. It took them five more minutes to reach River Oaks. The streets seemed as quiet, dark, and peaceful as ever. But as they came to the corner where Mockingbird intersects with Del Monte, they saw the line of police cars, their lights flashing, the grim, dark figures of police officers, many with flashlights, prowling around the grounds and standing at the open front door. Now there was no more protest from Bob. Both of them froze into an incredulous silence. Life stood still.

Jennifer parked the car opposite the house, leaped out, and started running for the front door before Bob had time to move. Two policemen barred the way. "My name is Jennifer Sutton. I'm Mrs. Sandiford's friend. She just telephoned me. Can I go in?"

The policemen were polite but adamant. "No, ma'am, you can't."

Bob came up beside her and held her hand.

There was no time for further conjecture or conversation, but the dreadful scene that followed remained indelibly stamped on Jennifer's mind. The front door was open. From inside the house came hysterical screaming and weeping, a despair that grew louder as two hefty policemen emerged from the doorway, strong arms hooked under each armpit of a woman they were towing backward between them. Hair disheveled, face convulsed, she was struggling helplessly as her heels dragged and bumped along the ground. A further grotesque, almost obscene indignity inflicted upon her was the fact that her hands appeared to be handcuffed or bound together inside a plastic bag.

Jennifer's breath caught in her throat as she realized with a jolt that the woman was Kay—sweet, gentle, respectable, lovable Kay—and they were treating her like a wild animal. The final stunning shock came as, pitifully, Kay, seeing Jennifer as she was dragged by, screamed despairingly, "Jennifer, I've shot Frank! I've shot Frank!" Her sobs trailed away as Jennifer, scarcely crediting what she had seen, watched Kay being brutally bundled into the patrol car.

Marian Rosen, looking much younger than the forty-odd years to which without a trace of coquetry she freely admits, is very feminine, slender, and pretty, with brown eyes and pale gold hair, usually held back by a clasp. Her beauty camouflages her extraordinary perseverence and strength, as well as her encyclopedic knowledge of the law. Marian is a shrewd, tough divorce and criminal lawyer, though after talking to her for five minutes one wonders why she chose law instead of facing an audience as Portia in *The Merchant of Venice*. But if ever the heavenly authority who arranges these things dropped into Marian's lap a case for which she was uniquely equipped, it was the case of Kay Sandiford.

Immediately, a real and affectionate bond had sprung up between them. The moment Kay entered her office, Marian had recognized someone suffering from a scarcely containable hurt. With a practiced eye she had noted the expensive, "sensible" clothes: the white silk blouse, the brown tweed skirt. There were shadows under Kay's eyes, brown eyes, from her mother's side, as Marian would ascertain, giving a clue to her ancestry, eyes one can often glimpse among the elegants at the Curragh races, or staring out over the white walls of peat-burning cottages in Galway. But they were eyes also clouded with pain and bewilderment.

Gently Marian had said that perhaps they could chat generally. Could Kay give her some idea of what was troubling her? Marian remembered thinking that, had she known Kay Sandiford better, from the very look on her face and the tension running through her body like an electric current, she would have advised Kay to seek psychiatric help. Indeed, one of the subjects Marian had warily begun to skirt that day was whether Kay had ever been in counseling. Quite quickly it had come out that Kay fundamentally disbelieved in "that sort of thing." Still, she clearly needed help. Something was terribly wrong.

Thus, with the intuitive perception of a good criminal lawyer, Marian had returned to her ranch-style house, where she lived with her tall, laconic, easygoing Texan husband, Freddy, and where they had raised their now grown-up son and daughter, with a slight but nagging worry scratching at the back of her mind.

She wasn't altogether shocked therefore when, soaking in a hot bath at nine thirty that night, she was interrupted by her husband calling through the door that a message relayed from the office answering service indicated an emergency call from a Mr. Steadman in Baltimore. Marian jumped out of the bath, grabbed a dressing gown, and rushed to the telephone, whereupon Ernest Steadman, his agitation plain, shouted, "Kay Sandiford has just shot her husband! Can you get over there immediately?"

Marian "threw on a few clothes," a description that rarely prevents her from looking as if she'd just emerged from a fashion house in the Place Vendôme, and sped in her Mercedes to Del Monte Drive, ten minutes away. She parked behind the line of flashing police cars, dodged interfering police hands with the agility of a quarterback, and raced to the leading vehicle. Kay was in it crouched in the back. Marian banged on the window. She thought that Kay Sandiford recognized her even though Kay was weeping hysterically, and Marian knew that somehow she had to try to make contact with her, give her hope, give her instruction . . . so she yelled at the top of her voice, "Don't make any statements! Don't make any statements!" Even as the words echoed off the window of the departing police car, she thought, *Oh, my God, what am I saying? Famous words from your attorney as the police car rushes off! This must be a movie!*

That thought disappeared from her mind as she turned and raced for her car. The expensive German automobile proved its reliability and speed, for as Marian explained: "I tell you I moved so fast that when the group of police guarding Kay got into the elevator going up to homicide on the third floor, boy, I was right in that elevator with them!"

The Houston police were neither amused by her appearance nor cooperative with her intentions. They were familiar with criminal attorneys appearing like genies out of magic lamps—but usually *after* the event. This dame was practically waiting beside the body.

They made their disapproval plain. They didn't like her at all. What the hell was a defense attorney doing arriving on the scene practically as the shots were fired and certainly not more than a minute or two after the police arrived. Something very odd was going on. As a result of their suspicions they would not allow Marian to talk to Kay; they had their own priorities—which Marian knew included photographing and fingerprinting—and Marian's interview did not figure among them.

Marian, unable to prevent Kay's being hustled out of the room, still wildly hysterical, sobbing and screaming, now made her presence plain. She had a right to be there helping her client. Where was the officer in charge? No one seemed to know. Well, if she was not put in touch with the officer in charge immediately, it was unlikely he would be the officer in charge in the future. She made her point. The officer in charge, recognizing a determined attorney, led the way to the back room where Kay was being booked.

Marian was horrified by what she saw. There was a small table at one end of the room and Kay was beneath it, curled in the fetal position, looking like a small hunted animal trying to hide from the entire world. Marian helped them tug and entice her out of her hiding place. Kay's face was drawn, blotched with tears, her hair a tangled mess; she looked as if she was out of her mind, and nothing coherent emerged from her lips, simply a stream of hysterical wailing: "I've killed my husband. My wonderful husband. But he was beating me. He was coming at me with a tennis racket."

"Now, Kay, Kay," Marian said, trying to make contact. "Listen to me...listen to me..." But Kay Sandiford was not listening to anybody; her grief and hysteria had engulfed her. The two arresting patrolmen, Rosencrantz and Williams, approached Marian to talk with her, and she found them to be decent, reasonable men who were anxious to help—and anxious for Marian to help them. They had tried to inform Kay of her rights under the Supreme Court's ruling in the *Miranda* case—that is, her right to seek the help of a lawyer and to refuse to make any statement whatever until then. But Kay had been too far gone even to understand what they were talking about. They had got absolutely nothing out of her, except the oft-repeated and dizzyingly incriminating statement that she'd killed her husband. Rosencrantz took Marian to one side and said forlornly, "I've just got to get some information, some details, for my report. I know her name is Kathleen Sandiford, but what is her date of birth and the rest of the stuff?"

Marian promised to help him as soon as Kay calmed down, and little by little the police officers, realizing that Marian Rosen was not as uncooperative as they first supposed, became more friendly. Another officer wanted permission to do a metal trace on Kay's hands, and Marian said she had no objection. It was obvious to Marian from the very start that, with Kay yelling to the world that she had just shot her husband, there would be very little point in contesting the fact that Kay had fired a gun.

Sometime after midnight the police told Marian that they were transferring Kay to jail for the night. Except for staying behind to contact a bondsman and arrange bail, in order to get Kay out of jail first thing in the morning, there was nothing more Marian could do.

The last scene with Kay was almost as emotional as the first. Several of her friends and neighbors had arrived to see if they could help: Jennifer and Bob, Dr. Williams and Mike Ackerman, neighbors who lived a few doors away. Kay, still sobbing and distressed, did not appear to recognize anyone until her maid, Ferrie Lee Potts, appeared. The police had brought Ferrie Lee to the station to make a statement, as she appeared to be the only other person in the house at the time of the shooting, and the only possible eyewitness. When Kay saw her, she threw herself, crying hysterically, into Ferrie Lee's arms, wailing over and over again, "Oh, Ferrie Lee, Ferrie Lee." With some difficulty the police pried Kay away and took her down to the cells.

Marian went back to her car and drove home. It was two A.M. when she wearily unlocked her front door. Freddy woke up as she entered the bedroom. "What happened?" he asked.

Marian had only the strength to answer, "It was terrible, just terrible."

Freddy knew his wife pretty well and didn't ask any more questions.

From the moment she heard Frank Sandiford's feet on the stairs and turned to see him on the upstairs landing, her tennis racket raised in his hand, his sibilant voice grating "I'm going to get you," life and memory jarred to a halt for Kay Sandiford—not with a sudden lowering curtain, but with a flickering, whirling, confused kaleidoscope of jumbled scenes. After that her mind occasionally lifted toward bemused clarity, a shock of apprehension, a feeling of justified uncertainty. *What am I doing here? What's going on? Who are these people? What do they want from me? What are they talking about? Are they all mad?*

But she hadn't the faintest memory of what had actually happened.

She remembered, as in a fevered dream, being in the kitchen with Frank. He was lying on the floor. She kept saying to him, "Frank, what are you doing lying on the floor like that? Why don't you get up? Please, don't act like that. Stop lying on the floor. What's the matter with you? Get up. Get up. . . ."

She recalled her utter panic when she suddenly realized there were policemen everywhere, that they were chasing *her*, and that she was trying desperately to escape. And, as in every nightmare, she knew she couldn't escape; somewhere, somehow, they were going to trap her.

She remembered racing up the front hall stairs, away from the policemen, who were screaming at her and screaming at each other. "It's a crazy woman with a gun! She's up the stairs! Double around! Cut her off!"

The noise, the threats—they all gathered into a rolling cloud behind her, threatening her like a great storm, and she tried to make her feet run faster, fly faster, away from them. Into her bedroom. No place to hide there: under the bed, behind the chair, under the coverlet. No, no, no. Into the dressing room toward the bathroom. But they were coming around through Charles's room, through his bathroom, cutting her off. *Oh, God, give me somewhere to hide, to hide . . . on the floor. Curl into a tight ball.*

Then the black legs were coming through all the doors directly toward her, standing around her like great polished black logs. She tried to squeeze into the texture of the carpet, but she couldn't get any lower.

And now there were black shoes glistening like polished armor in her face. There was a light in the ceiling, and they were lifting her up, trying to wrap her in newspaper like a dead fish. . . .

Then, somehow, she was in a car, and Marian's face was at the window.

Later, she remembered, they hustled her into an elevator, which took her downstairs. They stood her in front of a wall, and she realized they were taking her photograph. Then they took her hands and pressed them against an inky pad and spread her fingers on paper. What they were doing all this for she had no idea, but she didn't like it. But when one of the women there demanded her wedding ring, she reacted immediately. She told the woman indignantly that it had never been off her finger from the day she was married and it wasn't coming off now. She shied away, protecting the ring with her other hand. The woman yelled at her, and someone grabbed her, and rough hands caught hers, forced open her fingers, and pulled off the ring. She began to weep then, and she let them take her gold Rolex watch without resistance. Why were they doing all this to her? What had she done? Why would they be so cruel as to steal her wedding ring? Then the woman looked at her and said angrily, "You've killed somebody! You're a criminal."

Kay stared at her in utter amazement, thinking, *What are you talking about? What are you talking about?*

They pushed her into another room, and there were the eyes of a man in a doctor's greens tracking her around the room. He was about thirty-five and he had red hair. There was no desk in that room, only an awful surgical table, and the man kept saying, "Lie down on the table." She wasn't going to do that. No way. She'd been that route before. There was no way any guy in green was coming near her that night. But he followed her around and around the table, and she knew she mustn't lose eye contact with him—that was vital. If she lost that, all control was gone. She didn't look for a door. All she did was circle the table, staring at him as he followed her, just like cat and mouse. And then, when she knew she couldn't go on with the game any longer, she stumbled against a chair, collapsed into it, and shouted, "Don't you dare come near me!" And he just left her alone.

She remembered that they sort of picked her up out of the chair. She didn't think she could have walked two steps more that night. Then she was in an elevator again and there was Marian looking so concerned and gentle. Marian kept putting her hand on her face and saying gentle things to her. She was wearing a purple suit, and they'd put purple dye on her hands and somehow the purple dye from Marian's suit had got on her hands. It was very puzzling.

And elevator took her somewhere and stopped. They took her out along a dark corridor with cells, and women in the cells, and a stench of alcohol. Then they shoved her into a cell, and there were a whole bunch of women in there, and she was frightened. It was all dark, very dark, and they were all marching around—eight or ten women. It was noisy—shouting and clanking of doors and locks—and it smelled horrible. There were bed bunks and she sat on one of them, crying; she thought she was crying quietly to herself. Then suddenly there was a woman coming at her. She had a triangular face and wild eyes and a bush of black hair, and she pulled Kay onto the floor, thrashing away. The others shouted at her to stop. Apparently Kay had sat on her bed. It was madness. Kay stayed down on the floor, all curled up. Then the cell door banged open and she was dragged out. She was terrified.

They led her somewhere and put her in another cell, a long thin cell, this time made of iron and concrete, with a light bulb blazing in the ceiling. She had a gray blanket and a pillow with black stripes on it. Everything was dirty and there were cockroaches on the floor. She remembered looking out of the cell and seeing some people at the end of a hallway and an office. She could see a desk and a TV set and two women sitting in front of it.

They took her into another office, and a woman in long pants wanted her to take some pills but she refused. Then another woman, who had a piece of paper, said she had to sign it. But she remembered Marian saying, "Don't sign anything, don't sign anything." So she didn't sign it, and the woman got so mad she shouted, "Then you'll rot in jail till you do sign it!" Then they turned her out.

Suddenly, outside, there were other women around her, being sweet and kind and saying, "It's your first time here. It's all right. It's all right. You're going to be all right." These women sat her down on a bench, crowding around and saying, "Don't cry. You'll be all right." One sat on either side of her and one sat down on the floor at her feet, and they were all so nice, so concerned, so warm, and their arms were so comforting that she just couldn't help going on crying.

Then they came and put her in the elevator again and took her to another cell, with a mattress, and she lay down and fell asleep.

Early the next morning Kay was awakened and sent down alone in the elevator to the ground floor. Apparently arrangements for her release on a bail bond were being made there. But she didn't really know what was happening. She just did what she was told. The door of the elevator opened and she stepped out into half darkness, a long, dark corridor of a place, and it frightened her. She stood with her back against a wall, not knowing what was happening, vulnerable and helpless. From an office near an exit about twenty yards away a head poked around and shouted rudely, "Stay there until you're called!" Apparently some item uncompleted in her bail bond had to be rectified.

Now she was aware that there were three other people in the corridor with her. Two black men and a woman, all apparently elated because they were about to be released. The woman and one of the men walked toward the office singing and jiving, making a diversion that Kay understood only later was to cover the advances of their friend. He approached Kay, not pausing for a second, his hands groping, pinning her against the wall, calling her a white patsy. It was the final degradation. She was crying again. She didn't have the strength to scream. She had nothing left. . . .

Only the stentorian shout from the office—"Kathleen Sandiford! Come through!"—stopped him. He pulled away, shrugging, grinning, as if it had all been part of the night's entertainment.

She walked through the office and out into the daylight. The man who had acted as bondsman smiled at her. She didn't smile back. He opened the door of his Buick Riviera, the same sort of car that Frank drove, except that this one was brown and Frank's had been gray. He drove her into town and took her up to Marian Rosen's office.

They might even have passed the car driven by a young woman on her way to work at a local hospital, who heard her program of pop music suddenly interrupted by a news flash. It reported that famous heart surgeon Dr. Frank Sandiford had been shot dead by his wife in their River Oaks home. The news paralyzed her. Hardly conscious of the car horns blasting behind her, she swung over to the side of the road and braked to a halt. She let her head fall forward on the steering wheel and began to sob as if her heart had broken.

3

A T 8:30 A.M. on Wednesday, January 30, 1980, the phone rang in
Jennifer Sutton's house. It was Marian Rosen, telling her that she
expected the bondsman to be bringing Kay Sandiford to her office around
9 A.M. and asking if Jennifer could be there, that she would be a great
help. Jennifer was there on the dot, having received an assurance from
Bob that he would be available should he be needed.

Jennifer remembered: "When they brought Kay into the office, she
was very distraught, very disturbed. She recognized both Mrs. Rosen and
me, and she wanted to know what was happening. 'Why did they keep
me in that place with all those prostitutes last night?' she cried. 'Why
are you all here? Why isn't Frank here? He should be here. Why isn't
Frank here?'"

How to explain to a hysterical Kay Sandiford that her husband was
not present because she had shot him to death the night before was not
beyond Jennifer's comprehension, but Jennifer was far too distressed and
compassionate herself to wish to tell Kay what had happened.

She observed Kay closely. She could see that Kay was not psychotic,
but that she was very, very agitated. She seemed to be with it one minute
and gone the next, as if she was drifting in and out of reality. And she
kept on demanding to know where Frank was and why he wasn't there

to help her. Jennifer became increasingly worried. She needed no medical training to understand that Kay was suicidal, and looking around Marian's office, which had big wide windows on the twelfth story of Houston's Zapata Tower building, she knew that a way out for Kay was easily available. And Kay kept looking at those windows. By now Dr. Williams had also been sent for, and Jennifer passed the word to the telephone operator at the hospital to ask Bob if he could come at once. She knew her friend needed a lot of looking after.

Marian Rosen was in her adjacent office attending to the many legal chores that Kay's new status entailed. Ferrie Lee Potts had also arrived and recorded her eyewitness account and certified statement as to what she remembered about what had happened; it was of fundamental importance if it was to corroborate or counter the statements the police had obtained a few hours earlier.

Marian remembered that Jennifer had come on the phone from the other office. She was anxious, saying, "Marian, you must come in here and tell Kay that Frank is dead. She keeps saying, 'Where's Frank? Why doesn't he come and help me?' And I just don't know what to say to her. And you've got these big glass windows in this office. I'm really scared that Kay might try and jump out."

Marian went straight in and immediately saw what Jennifer meant. Kay was weeping and very close to hysteria again. Marian knew she had to take a strong, possibly cruel but necessary line. Eventually Kay had to understand and come to grips with what she had done. Marian took Kay's hand and sat down on a chair and said as gently as she could, "Now, Kay, you must understand. Last night you shot Frank. And he's dead. He's dead."

Kay's reaction was frightening. She started crying and screaming, "It's not true! It's not true! I left Frank at the house. Why isn't he here with me? Why isn't he here?"

The whole scene was very distressing to all of them. Jennifer closed her eyes, hardly able to watch Kay. Kay began to wail, "He was the most brilliant surgeon. It should have been me, not him. I should be dead. He should be alive. It should have been me."

Dr. Williams and Bob arrived and tried to calm her down. Both agreed, in consultation, that she was definitely suicidal and must be kept under supervision. They had to get her into a hospital if only for her own safety. First they tried Saint Luke's, where Frank had worked, but Saint Luke's had no ward for the mentally ill.

"And as soon as they used that description we knew we were going to have a difficult time," Jennifer recalled. "Then we tried another hospital, Saint Joseph's. No room there either. Then Marian thought of a psychiatrist friend of hers, Dr. Claghorn, and she rang him. Yes, he thought he might get Kay into a central hospital in Houston. It was a pretty tough place, but if they thought Kay was suicidal it was really the only safe place for her to be."

Marian remembered: "Bob and Jennifer offered to take her there and I watched them leave with a great deal of anxiety. Already I knew this was not a normal client-attorney relationship. I kissed Kay's cheek and held her tight; she was so vulnerable, so wiped out by this disaster. In some strange way I also knew that she'd left her life in my hands."

The elevator arrived and Kay and the Suttons stepped in. Jennifer caught Bob's eye and his nod of sympathy. She drew a deep breath. This was going to be very difficult for both of them. But it had to be done. There was no way they could take Kay back to Del Monte, where she had killed her husband, and who knew what sort of scene remained?

Kay was muttering to herself now: "Frank had so much to give to the world. He had so much good to do. I can give nothing to the world. Here I am alive, and he's dead. . . ." She turned to Jennifer. "He isn't dead, is he, Jennifer?"

"Yes, he is," Jennifer said.

Kay's weeping increased. "Here I am alive and he'd dead. I've shot the world's greatest heart surgeon."

Jennifer put her arm around Kay's shoulders. Only Bob's firm hand on her own shoulder prevented her from joining in Kay's desolation.

In the car they sat on either side of Kay, and they could feel her anxiety increase as they neared their destination. Jennifer had never heard of the place before. It was a tall red-brick building, flat-faced, inconspicuous, anonymous. Kay didn't like it either. Jennifer felt her shiver as they walked up to the desk to complete the formalities.

Now Kay was becoming increasingly suspicious. She knew she wanted to go home and she knew she didn't want to go to this hospital. They gave her a form to read. She tried to understand it. It said it gave the doctors and staff the right to do anything they liked with her: to give her any drugs, any sort of treatment. She could hear the voices of Bob and Jennifer pleading with her:

"It's a nice little hospital, Kay, and you won't be here long."

"It's for your own good, darling. That form doesn't mean anything."

Somehow Kay knew they were acting, that they were trying to tell her everything was going to be fine, and she could feel a rising wave of panic. But she was so confused, so exhausted, that she wept and signed her life away.

Later, when reason and life returned, Kay remembered her state of mind at that moment: "I had this awful feeling that I was isolated, really isolated. I can't explain it, but I felt that they were going to put me in there one way or another, all my friends, with a smile on their faces. I suppose it was unfair of me to think this way; I didn't know the trauma I was causing everybody. But I resented even Jennifer acting as if this was fine and okay and everything was going to be hunky-dory. I wasn't crazy. And even now I don't believe it was the right way to behave toward me, toward any patient. I admit I didn't know, or didn't want to know, that I had shot Frank, and had pushed it deep down in my subconscious, but in my terms I surfaced every so often, and I thought angrily, *What are they doing to me?* Then I suppose I'd get frightened again; the darkness would crowd in again and I'd shrink back inside my skull.

"I don't think you should lie to a patient. I know they had to make a quick decision, and perhaps they wanted me in that place for legal reasons. But they should have said, 'Kay, it's for your own good to spend a week or a month in this institution, and after that we'll talk about it.' As it was, all the talk about 'It's just a sweet little hospital and everything is going to be all right,' and when I questioned them about signing that paper, 'Oh, don't bother about that; it doesn't mean anything,' introduced me to a second nightmare. If you go into an ordinary hospital you have the right to check out any time you want to. But once you sign into a mental institution, you have no right to check out until *they* say so. And that fact by itself is enough to make a sane person insane. You see, it wasn't happening to *them*, it was happening to *me*. I wasn't crazy—that's the whole point—but people were treating me as if I was coming off the wall. I was a desperate human being who'd done something dreadful, and I needed someone to put their arms around me and be straight with me, not treat me as though I were a mad woman who had to be locked up. I know if you shoot your husband dead, and then go crazy with hysteria and shock, people have every right to think you must be out of your mind. But at that moment treating me like a mad creature who had to be manipulated for her own good drove me deeper into the darkness. Yet still I kept coming out of oblivion into a sort of sanity. And it was terrifying; a nightmare feeling that my friends, my dearest friends, with great cunning were conniving to trap me. And even those who weren't conniving, like the guards and attendants at the hospital, didn't seem to care whether I lived or died. To them, it seemed to me, I was just another hunk of flesh."

Kay's nightmare intensified as she said good-bye to Jennifer and Bob, and two attendants in white uniforms took her firmly by each arm and led her inside. Kay saw that there were attendants, or guards—she thought of them as guards—everywhere. The two escorting her led her up to a door; another unlocked it. She was led through. Another guard relocked it. Another door was unlocked and suddenly she was thrust into a big circular room, an arena, almost like a bullring. It was brightly lit. The floor was polished linoleum, bare brown linoleum. And it was full of people. Mad people. Her mind froze. She turned back to the door. There was no handle. She was locked in.

Terrified, she cringed with her back against the wall, the only security she could find. She looked around. Raised up out of harm's way in the center was a sort of watchtower from which five disembodied heads looked down. She counted them: three white heads, a black head, and a yellow head all scanning the activities of fifteen to twenty inmates, men and women in dressing gowns, nightgowns, pajamas; barefoot, shoulders hunched, heads bent, shuffling around in a circle like circus animals at exercise. Other inmates were just sitting; still others were running and screaming; one was urinating on the floor. A young woman who seemed lost now approached. She was thin, with big black eyes and long, stringy black hair. She wore a white blouse and a dark skirt, and Kay had a terrible feeling that she must have been an inmate for a long, long time. She sidled up to Kay and touched her with gentle fingers, then drifted away and came back again and touched her with the same gentle fingers; then she moved back into the procession.

Kay did not understand until later that she was in the maximum security section of the asylum. She had been slotted for the "suicide watch"—no razor blades, pins, needles, knives, forks, bottles.

During those first few terrifying minutes only one awful, compelling thought filled Kay's mind. *Oh, God, am I mad? Is this what it feels like to be mad?*

Five minutes later two white-coated attendants approached her, not looking at her, talking about her as if she didn't exist, but discussing where she was supposed to sleep. By this time Kay had noticed that little bedrooms, or padded cells, opened at intervals off the arena.

The two attendants led her into one. It was very small. There was a mattress on the floor and a bathroom and lavatory off to one side. There were no windows. The atmosphere was claustrophobic. Kay was terrified. She'd die without air. "Please, I can't sleep here," she appealed. "Please put me somewhere else." Then she understood that, as far as they were concerned, she *truly* didn't exist; she was a thing, an animal that one cajoled or coaxed into its kennel. They ignored her, leaving and locking the door behind them.

Exhausted and fearful, she crouched on the mattress. She must have fallen asleep, because she remembered dreaming and feeling constricted, and then she woke up and realized where she was and went into absolute panic. She was locked in a padded cell, trapped, suffocating. She plunged the three steps to the door and banged against it with desperate small fists, screaming at the top of her lungs, "Let me out! Let me out!" She banged and banged incessantly until an attendant opened the door. She crept out into the light. The other inmates were still shuffling around. The attendant left her. She cowered against the wall and watched them. Maybe half an hour passed, but she'd lost track of time.

Then a woman inmate suddenly went berserk, yelling and screaming, shouting insults and striking out randomly. Three big male attendants—known as "the team"—began to chase her and caught her after a mad scramble. It took all three of them to hold her down because she was wild, and when you're wild, Kay knew, you've got extra strength. The woman wasn't all that big, but for Kay, the whole thing was a pretty scary scene.

Shortly after this episode an attendant approached Kay again and led her toward a different sort of cell, a room about six feet by four containing a small table and two chairs, again with no window and the same sense of dreadful claustrophobia. After the attendant locked her in, Kay could feel her screaming point getting closer. If she wasn't mad then, they were going to drive her mad. A few minutes later the door was unlocked; a man came in and the door was locked behind him. Her first thought was, *God, they've trapped me with a man!* Even later she lamented, "If only they'd said, 'A doctor is coming to see you,' or even, 'A man is coming to see you.' If they'd said anything. . . ." But suddenly this strange man was in her cell, and men had been chasing her, holding her down, dragging her from place to place, trying to rape her, for the past twenty-four hours. She was scared to death of men. For Christ's sake, they were treating her as if she didn't have a brain. Maybe she didn't!

She'd been in the clothes she was wearing for what felt like forever. Nobody had said anything about washing her hands or combing her hair. She was used to being *clean*, and they wouldn't even give her a comb. Her hair was wild; she was still wearing the brown corduroy pants and burgundy turtleneck sweater and loafers. In her terms, she had been in that filthy jail, in that filthy cell, in the same filthy clothes forever, and she was filthy, disgusting!

The man looked at her and smiled. He was in his forties. He wasn't wearing a white uniform. He said, "My name's Jim Claghorn. I'm your psychiatrist. Marian Rosen retained me." Kay glared at him. She hated all men. She hated them because she was terrified of them.

Jim Claghorn admitted quite openly that, although he regretted the necessity of placing Kay in that hospital, at the time he had had no alternative. He was gravely concerned because she had exhibited a marked suicidal bent. He was ordinarily very reluctant to place people in the "closed" section, known as Level One, because it was primarily intended as a facility for people who were simply not able to fend for themselves, or who might take their lives if they were not constantly supervised. He knew it was a terrible place; he also knew that it had probably increased Kay's distress. But at the time there had been no alternative; it had been absolutely essential for her safety.

"Sit down, Kay," Claghorn said, taking the nearer chair.

Warily Kay obeyed, and had the feeling that perhaps this man was as apprehensive of her as she was of him. She also had a feeling that he was just sizing her up.

"I'm here to help you, Kay," he said, "and to start with just a few general questions—you know, height, weight, schooling, family. Can you give me those details?"

Kay said she could.

"Now, about your education," Jim said.

Kay went into her normal spiel: Quaker school, Vassar, Johns Hopkins University, where she'd got her master's in Russian history. Then she stopped and thought about what she'd said.

"I'm lying," she said. "What I'm telling you is not true."

Jim Claghorn didn't seem surprised. "Well, tell me what is true."

"The part about the Quaker school in Baltimore is true. But then I went to William and Mary College in Williamsburg, and I left because I hated it. It was two years before I went back and got my degree at Johns Hopkins in Baltimore. And although I was accepted at Vassar, I never went there."

"Why did you lie?" Jim Claghorn asked softly.

"Because Frank always told me to tell it that way. He thought it sounded better."

Jim Claghorn didn't pursue the matter further but went on making notes. Eventually he asked, "What do you remember about the shooting?"

"Nothing," Kay replied, "nothing at all, except that I remember seeing a black ball, and a smaller yellow ball on top of it. D'you think that could have been the shooting?"

He said, "The black ball could have been the barrel of the gun as you fired it, and the yellow ball could have been the explosion of the cartridge."

Kay Sandiford didn't note how long the interview lasted. But, however long, it didn't make her feel any better. If anything, it made her feel more weary. She didn't feel she had established a rapport with this man who had asked her questions.

When Claghorn left, the attendant came and led Kay back into another padded cell. The door was locked behind her, and she saw, lying on the floor, the very woman who had earlier gone berserk. She was motionless but moaning softly. The "team" had obviously given her a shot. There was a mattress against the wall and the attendant had tossed in a blanket and a pillow. Kay was so tired now that she could barely stand. She sank down on the mattress, past caring, almost past living.

The evening after the shooting Marian Rosen arrived at the hospital. With her were Ernest Steadman, who had flown down from Baltimore, and Charles, who had been collected from school in Connecticut by the Sandifords' kindly Houston neighbor Mike Ackerman. They were questioned and admitted, and then furnished with a private room in which to talk to Kay. They saw at once that Kay was still in a highly nervous and neurotic state. If she could have explained adequately what she had been through, they might have understood her plight better.

Charles was eighteen, not much more than a boy. He himself was in shock, confused and distressed, and as soon as he saw his mother, he cried, "Mom, why did you do it?" Marian saw the agony on Kay's face.

"He was trying to beat me, Charles! He came at me with a tennis racket! I'm sorry, Charles." She was weeping. "I should have killed myself instead."

Charles was adamant. "No, you shouldn't, Mom, no, you shouldn't. And look at this place, Mom, it's awful, it's absolutely impossible. I'm going to get you out of here. There's no way you're staying here. I'm getting you out of this place—now!"

Kay never forgot Charles's words. She couldn't answer his questions about why she'd killed Frank, but at least her son didn't talk to her as if she were a screwball. He didn't think she was off her head. He talked to her as if she was his mom. And she loved him for it. Charles wasn't going back to school, he said, until he'd got his mom out of that place and she'd got back on her feet.

At that moment none of them appreciated the main fear infesting Kay's mind. Sure, they were all going to get her out—that's what they said—but how did they know they could do it? Didn't they understand that she had signed herself in and given the hospital what amounted to a blank check? They could lock her up, give her electric shocks, drug her into insensibility if they felt like it.

Kay was now intent only on survival. She'd seen the three big guys in action. She'd come from the civilized world outside and the contrast between that and this was paralyzing. Marian, Ernest, and Charles were all going to leave and she was going to be left behind. Suppose she started a screaming fit, saying the place was terrible and how she hated it, and then she was left behind? What would the staff do to her then? She couldn't even reveal her fears to Marian and Charles in case she was overheard. She was obsessed with the terror the guards might inflict.

Marian sensed some of this. She knew that Kay was still in a state of shock, crying almost constantly. She knew that Kay was suicidal. And she realized that somehow, no matter how long it took, they had to convey to Kay that she needed gigantic courage and conviction to climb out of her deep pit of despair; that suicide was not the answer; that Charles needed her; that she had to go on living and face the future no matter what it brought.

About Kay's present need—moving her out of Level One—Marian was not in doubt. It had not been difficult to arrange, and the change, to Kay, was the difference between night and day. Suddenly she was in the elevator with Marian, Ernest, and Charles and they were going up. As soon as they emerged the whole atmosphere changed. The place was light, airy, furnished. There were young nurses around. They smiled at Kay. They showed her to a room that had a window, a bath, and a real bed, like a small hotel room, and Charles nosed around, saying, "Not bad, Mom, eh?"

She could have her bath in private; a sweet little nurse gave her a sleeping pill. The others kissed her good night. She climbed into bed. At last she could sleep.

However, there were still difficulties and hurdles to be overcome. Kay remembered the young woman, thin, narrow-faced, and tight-lipped, who banged on her door the next morning, saying she was from the downstairs office. Her manner, like her face, was brusque and unfriendly.

"I've got this paper from the district attorney's office. You've got to sign it. Here's a pen."

Kay was disturbed. "I am allowed to read it, I suppose," she said.

"Yes, you can read it and then you must sign it."

Kay read it through slowly and carefully. It was a release of all her hospital records to the district attorney's office. A small red light winked in her brain as she remembered Marian's caution about signing anything.

"I'm not going to sign this," she said quietly.

The young woman was annoyed. "Well, you've got to sign it. You've got to sign it within two hours."

"I want to make a phone call to my lawyer."

"You're not allowed to do that."

"So I sign away all my hospital records without even referring to my lawyer?"

"The DA's office insists that you sign this paper. And they're only giving you two hours to make up your mind."

"They can give me ten years," said Kay. "I'm not doing it. Just take it away."

Kay watched the young woman flounce out of the room, banging the door behind her, and although she felt nervous and a little upset, she also felt excited. For the first time—perhaps in her entire life—she had said no to something important. She had said no on Frank's behalf a thousand times, but this was for herself—for *herself*.

She hung on to Marian as a fishing vessel in choppy seas hangs on to its buoy. She relied on Marian implicitly; she needed her counsel and advice for everything. Not signing that paper had scared her stiff. But she'd done it. The woman had not intimidated her. Marian had said "Don't sign anything," and, well, she wasn't going to sign anything.

Reflecting on that period in the hospital, Kay knew that she "wasn't right." She knew even in the relative "peace" of the upper floors that she wanted to go home. For the first few days she crept around constantly, trying all the windows to see if she could find one unlocked so she could jump out of it and run home. She doubted if the fact that she was on the twentieth floor would have deterred her.

As the days passed and she got a firmer grip on reality, she found herself an onlooker in an unreal world, and she felt deeply sorry for the people incarcerated with her. Never before had she realized that behind the facade of that building, that plain, brick-fronted, nondescript building in the heart of Houston, existed so much abject despair. She had passed it a hundred times and never guessed. Now she knew. Now she knew that if the breaks were wrong, once you went up in that elevator you went straight to hell.

Every day began bleakly. It took a week for her to screw up enough courage to join a few of her fellow patients and take the elevator down to breakfast in the cafeteria. Marian brought her clothes from home: silk blouses and tweed skirts, the usual "uniform" that Frank had insisted she wear. And slowly she learned that if you wanted to get out, you had to conform and "behave."

That first experience in the "big room" had terrified her. On this upper floor it was different: people could find refuge in their own private rooms, sort out their anxieties, and perhaps discover a fragile, if temporary, security; and they could relate to the other patients. Everyone wanted to get out, get back to the world, return to normality. Among all of them a shy camaraderie existed. No one asked why you were there. During all the "activities" no one asked what had brought you there. Yes, they found out, but even then they were deeply concerned with their own problems, the point they had just reached in their own bewildered journey.

Kay found the boredom endless. Up at six thirty, constant medication, childish games, hours sitting around, a few paperbacks to read, a TV set, a pool table that didn't have all its parts.

The hospital had a pool upstairs, but the patients weren't allowed to swim lengths, only to splash around for fifteen minutes, then be hauled out. There were no real physical activities like tennis or gymnasium work. Nothing on an adult level. Sure, Kay discovered that some of the patients were sicker than others. Most of them had had a breakdown, a psychological problem that needed to be ironed out. But they were adults and a lot of them were highly intelligent, and they were all treated like children.

The hospital staff seemed to take it for granted that if a patient had any mental hang-up, it ruled him or her out of activities. Yet it was plain that many of the patients could approach wide areas of experience with adult minds. They were hemmed in and judged by a set of ludicrous, juvenile criteria. They were judged as to whether or not they were fit to re-enter so-called civilized society by how they participated in the juvenile games invented by hospital society. There they were, under the stress and strain of whatever had brought them there, and they were treated like children. And if they didn't react and perform like children in these absurd classes, down on their report card—or Kay's report card—would go: "Kay did not perform well in music class today." That report went to the relevant psychiatrist, and that nonsensical summing-up might make the difference between getting out or staying in. So they had to learn to be docile, obedient, and devious. Kay didn't like that.

Charles helped. He came every day and brought magazines. Kay thought that was splendid because Charles, probably without knowing it, brought her all the feminist magazines. She'd never read any of them before; she'd never even been into or attracted by that scene, but Charles had plainly decided to take her life in his hands. Marian tried to visit Kay every other day. Ernest Steadman stayed for a few days and then had to return to Baltimore. Jim Claghorn visited her every day.

On the day of the funeral Jennifer and Charles collected Kay at the entrance to the hospital. Kay, dressed in a black suit and white blouse, sat demurely in the back seat crushed between the two of them. At the funeral home their feet crunched on the gravel path as they approached the chapel and joined the procession of mourners passing the open casket. Charles and Jennifer pressed in a little closer as if, Kay thought, to protect her from the other mourners—in her mind, a parade of wraiths and shadows. She recognized Frank's sister. Should she go up and talk to her? Say, "I'm sorry, Maria, that I shot your brother"? But Maria had turned away, giving not the slightest sign of recognition.

When Marian had brought up the question of Frank's funeral, and whether or not Kay should attend it, Kay had tried to think about it seriously—seriously because, privately, she still could not grasp the fact that Frank was dead. If Frank *was* dead and there was going to be a funeral, then most certainly she should go. It was her responsibility to attend. And Charles should attend also. Would Marian, who had already brought her various changes of clothing from the house, see that she wore the right outfit?

Marian worried about the funeral for different reasons. If the press heard about it, it was likely that photographers and reporters would be there in droves. Most certainly she did not want Kay in her condition besieged by newspapermen. Marian could form a mental picture of the front page: "Accused Murderess Sobs at Husband's Graveside." Not that they were "burying" Frank in the sense that they were going to inter him in the ground—there was still some indecision about what should be done with his body. Should it be buried in Houston? Should it be sent back to Rome for burial in the family vault?

Jennifer and Charles led Kay up to the bier. Frank was laid out in his coffin in a dark suit, a white shirt, and his favorite black-and-red-striped tie, his bleached white face restored by the skillful undertakers to the muteness of stone and the texture of marble. His eyes were closed, and Kay was relieved by that. If they had been open, she would have known from the black, sightless gaze whether it was really Frank or not, known that he was staring back at her from some private corner of his own self-created hell. But this way she could still harbor doubts. She could believe it wasn't actually Frank. They'd stitched up his head, and she knew they were not Frank's stitches. Frank would never let any patient leave his operating table stitched up like that. Frank's stitches were as neat and beautiful as a skilled seamstress's. Frank would have hated those stitches.

Jennifer and Charles led Kay back to her place in the pew, and as soon as they sat down Kay began to twitter into Jennifer's ear like a small bird perched on her shoulder.

"Jennifer? Is that Frank?"

"Yes, Kay, it's Frank."

"It really is Frank?"

"Yes, it is."

"I really did it. Did I do that?"

"Yes, you did, Kay."

Kay sat still and quiet after that. And they did not leave and get into the car until all the other mourners had departed. But now as they drove away from the cemetery, another bloodbeat of anguish was added to Kay's guilt. They had told her Frank was dead. She had seen Frank dead. Now she had to accept the evidence of her own eyes. She had killed the very man she had tried so hard to love, to whom she had given all the love she possessed in every shade and dimension. She had killed a talented man, a brilliant surgeon, a man who had saved hundreds of patients from pain and death, a man for whom scores of his Italian patients fell on their knees and tried to kiss his hands, even his shoes, and called him a saint. He had tried to mold her into something worthwhile, to shape her into a strong and useful partner at his side, and she had failed him. Worse, in one moment of mindless terror she had destroyed him. She had to face the insurmountable horror of what she had done. And now she was not certain that she could do that. There was no box of darkness small enough into which she could creep to hide away from the light and the noise. Now she had to face the responsibility. And now she was not certain she had enough strength and sanity to do it.

Of course, she could go on pretending. She could go on living one day at a time, keeping the guilt buried inside, trying to reconcile life with the coterie of patients at the hospital: the woman bullied by her husband, the nurse who'd had a breakdown, the young man with multiple sclerosis whose wife had fled with their young baby the moment they learned he had the disease, and Bill the cowboy, who wore cowboy boots and hat and jeans and whom she thought a really nice fellow. Kay never knew what was supposed to be wrong with him. They all kept most things tightly wrapped inside themselves. Everybody was in there for his or her own reasons, sheltering secrets inside themselves. They'd chatter at meals: who's leaving and who's coming; who's getting out today; oh, that doctor never lets his patients out, and that one gives too much medication; have you heard what happened on the juvenile ward?

All of life revolved around her world in the hospital; did a life outside exist at all? When Bill offered to take her out and show her that it did, she could hardly believe her good fortune.

As Bill was going to be discharged shortly, he had a pass to go out for a few hours, and he requested that Kay be allowed to go with him. Somebody said yes. And there she was outside the hospital alone with Bill. Outside, there were trees and cars and the park, and she'd never realized before what being alive was really about, how glorious it could be. She felt reborn. Bill took her to the zoo and they watched the animals. He was warm and considerate, and she saw real people. Then he took her back, and a few days later he was gone, and she never saw him again. But she never forgot him, and never forgot her first day in a real world.

That was the start of "going out." Ernest would pay periodic visits from Baltimore and he would say, "Kay, now I'm allowing you only one drink, and I don't want you to drink any more after that. And what do you think about going into a convent? I really think you should give serious consideration, Kay, to going into a convent. I mean, what are you going to do with your life now?"

She would come back after seeing Ernest and think, *Thank God I'm back in the hospital.* Shortly after that visit she was allowed out practically every night with Charles. And at last, after a month, Marian said she could go home.

Throughout Kay's incarceration, Marian Rosen was acutely aware of Kay's belief that she was a prisoner. But Marian also appreciated that as long as Kay still had suicidal tendencies, she had to stay. Nevertheless it was vital to Marian to have Kay free as quickly as possible. With a trial approaching, a great deal of preparatory work had to be done: witnesses had to be contacted and interviewed, lines of inquiry pursued. Kay's presence was fundamental to all this. She knew everyone; she had their telephone numbers and addresses. There was also the legal necessity of the arraignment, where the defendant appears in court before the judge, who ascertains if a lawyer is representing the defendant or not, and if not, appoints one.

Marian also knew that the DA's office had now scoured the Del

Monte house for evidence and had amassed a collection of data: shattered bannister rails, bullet casings, scrapings from walls and carpets, broken bottles and glasses, fragments of clothing, a cigarette packet, a magazine, measurements of rooms and stairs. Marian had seen to it that the rooms had been cleaned after their investigations: bloodstains washed away, evidence of Frank's violent death removed. But the bannisters scored by the bullets, and the broken plaster where the .357 shells had gouged deep holes in the walls, were still brutal reminders of the shooting.

However, if Kay insisted on returning to Del Monte—and she did insist, desperately—then Marian felt she should go home. Marian concluded that the first few days would inevitably be traumatic and that, if possible, Charles should be there.

Kay had been warned that the police and forensic experts had been through the house, that things had been torn up and pushed aside and the place had been sealed off under twenty-four-hour guard. But even foreknowledge of these events did not really prepare her for what she saw when she walked through the door. It was eerie. She walked up the stairs and saw the splintered bannisters, the bullet holes in the walls. She caught her breath. She thought, *I did that?* She had pulled the trigger that had sent those bullets crashing into that wall, and that had killed Frank. The shock of recognition was traumatic; it chilled her inside. She knew that Jim Claghorn had been giving her sedatives every day, and there were other things they had given her at the hospital. She guessed they all knew she would be upset when she saw the house, and they'd made allowances for that and knew how to treat her. So, accompanied by Marian and Charles, with more pills to send her to sleep, she climbed into the big brass bed and curled up and obediently went to sleep. In fact, she was so highly sedated that she was hallucinating.

In the middle of the night she woke up. She seemed to be floating off the bed and going out the window; she felt physically sick. Her mind was blowing away. It was dark, and suddenly she felt all alone in that terrible house. Panic erupted inside her, a screaming, hysterical panic. She had to get out of the house; it was closing in on her. She had to flee! Barefoot, in her nightgown, hardly knowing what she was doing, she leaped out of bed, raced down the back stairs, cut through the back door, and ran around the house, heading for the front drive and Del Monte Drive. God knows where she was going or what was driving her.

But later she thanked God for Jim Christian, the security guard who'd watched over the house in her absence. He had decided that he was not going to leave her that night. His tour of duty was over but he'd made his own decision to stay... just in case. Duty over, paid or unpaid, he wasn't going. He had seen the shape she was in when she came home and had decided she was in no state to be left alone, even with Charles. He was there when he was needed. Hearing her cries, he grabbed her with big warm arms as she fled by and held her tightly as she cried and screeched and kicked in paroxysms of fear. Then he gently carried her back to the house.

Jim woke Charles, who, being young and healthy, had slept through the whole thing. Then Jim rang Marian, and there was some discussion about what they were going to do. But Jim assured Marian that he wasn't going to leave as long as Kay needed him, and Marian and Kay agreed. Kay stayed awake and managed to survive the night until the dawn came. The next day, with Jim still there and people coming by, she simmered down and was able to cope.

In the hospital Kay had seen Marian every other day, but when Kay got out she was on her own; there was nobody holding her hand. Eventually, of course, Charles would have to go back to school in Connecticut. Marian was often on the phone to her, but Kay had a hard job getting things together. So now it was decided that she should have help in the house to look after her, and she got a housekeeper named Peaches who cost her a cool seventy-five dollars a day and cooked food she couldn't eat. Peaches announced that she wanted to sleep in Frank's room and lie on Frank's settee in the TV room. Kay didn't want anybody in Frank's room, on Frank's couch, or in Frank's chair. Kay didn't want anybody in Frank's bathroom. She was protecting Frank. Later she could scarcely believe what she'd done. She gave poor Peaches a hell of a time. Peaches clearly must have thought Kay the biggest racist in town. Poor woman; without knowing, she had invaded Frank's domain. And Kay was protecting Frank's territory—she was still *his* person. Peaches stayed only a few days and left gratefully. Then Marian decided that if Michael, a twenty-five-year-old law student doing an internship in her office, could live in the quarters over the garage and act as a general guardian, that might help. But poor Michael. Kay gave him a runaround too.

For the first few weeks Charles had been there all the time and Kay recalled that they had terrible fights: she broke dishes, screamed and shouted. It was a horrible time. She'd get up from the table and throw everything on the floor... just crazy... as bad as Frank. She couldn't cook a meal, couldn't even boil water. She burned all the pots and had to get more. If somebody didn't feed her she didn't eat. And that went on for weeks. Charles had to do the cooking; there wasn't anyone else.

In fact, they had to go out to dinner most of the time, and every time they did she lapsed into silent hysteria and wept and wept. She just couldn't be with people. She was sure someone was going to kill her. If anybody approached her table, her eyes widened and she all but shrank underneath it. She thought everyone was condemning her. She couldn't even go out in the yard; it was a physical impossibility. The first time she ever dared to was after Charles had left and she had to show Michael how to turn on the watering system. The fear was awful.

Meanwhile, Ernest Steadman was doing his best up in Baltimore to indoctrinate Kay with his personal "redemption of Kay Sandiford" program. Ernest saw only one way out of Kay's tragic impasse. Calling her constantly, he'd begin: "Now, Kay, you've got your Bible. Open it at the Sermon on the Mount. Now we'll start reading it together...." And off they'd go. "...But if thine eye be evil, thy whole body shall be full of darkness. If therefore the light that is in thee be darkness, how great *is* that darkness!" And then, after finishing the reading, he'd continue, "Kay, you've done a terrible thing. Kay, you'll have to pay for it. Kay, you must find peace...."

Kay knew that Ernest was trying to help her, but she found him intolerable nonetheless. He wanted her to atone, go into a convent. He thought she should immediately go out and work with women who had also been battered, go to their homes, help them, learn from them. He did not seem to understand from the safe distance of Baltimore that at that moment simple survival was all she could handle, that she was no more equipped to help battered women than to fly to the moon. Nevertheless, she listened gravely to every word and believed him. If Ernest succeeded in doing anything, it was to confirm her own opinion of herself as a weirdo.

Nothing could change her belief that she had killed a great man and that she was now a social leper and should perhaps kill herself. And she was prepared to do so if that was what atonement entailed. She did not find the finality of death daunting. After her two suicide attempts before the tragedy (she had also tried to kill herself shortly after she met Frank) she knew precisely the dosage needed to end her life, and the time required to do it. She doubted she would ever live to stand trial.

Moreover, her mind was set in the belief that she would never reveal the truth of her story to anyone, certainly not at a public trial with the whole world listening in. She had always been a very private person, stuffing the unpleasant experiences into the black bag of her subconscious, always indoctrinated by Frank's convincing assumptions: that together they had achieved the unspeakable, that there were intimacies between man and woman that were never discussed, never brought into the light, fit perhaps for the priest but not for the public. And because she was proper and vulnerable and considered the female to be weaker than the male, she had believed him. Therefore she would not speak.

Marian Rosen knew that without Kay's complete cooperation their case was lost before it began. Marian knew that unless she could unhook Kay from her belief in Frank's divinity, and make clear to her that, within the handsome body, inside the nimble brain, despite the masterliness of the surgeon's hands, there existed an ordinary male with feet mired in the hypocritical materialism of his age—quick money, faithless sex, and self-indulgent living—they had no chance of a reprieve.

Marian had already received the indictment from "The duly organized Grand Jury of Harris County, Texas," alleging that on January 29, 1980, "Kathleen Sandiford intentionally and knowingly caused the death of Frank Sandiford with a gun." The felony charge was murder. Capital punishment had not yet returned to Texas, although it would within the next two years and a black man would be executed by lethal injection within five miles of the lakeside cottage Kay had chosen for her sanctuary. Marian Rosen knew that certainly the district attorney prosecuting in the Sandiford case would press for and likely get ninety years in prison, a sentence that would effectively silence Kay forever. Marian also knew that, no matter which judge handled the case, he would certainly, by law, insist that it was Kay who was on trial and not Frank, and that without the stresses Kay had endured becoming known to a jury, their cause was hopeless.

So Marian had to know about Kay Sandiford. And Kay Sandiford had to learn about the real Frank Sandiford.

So Jim Claghorn faced Kay across the table in his office and said gently, "Now, Kay, let's go back to the beginning. . . ."

Two

THE
BEGINNING

4

SHE could remember quite clearly that first day at school. Eighteen months old, firmly clutching the hand of Daddy on one side and Mom on the other as she toddled into the Friends School in Baltimore, a place where she would receive her education for the next fifteen years. Ringlets, a pale blue dress, chubby legs, a bright smile—the tiny innocent off to learn the ways of the world at play-school, because the Quakers believed that it was never too early to shame the devil and plot the upward path toward righteousness, decency, and love. From those very earliest moments Kathleen knew that, above all, you had to tell the truth. If you did not tell the truth, if you lied, you were immediately expelled and never allowed to return. She saw this calamity occur a couple of times to classmates and it frightened her; it was a disgrace too dreadful to contemplate.

From an early age she had difficulty in reconciling God with her sort of reality. God was a man who lived in a cloud high up in the sky, a suspicious place to live if ever there was one, and as far as she was concerned his demands seemed grossly unfair.

Kay's parents—her mother a Catholic and her father a Lutheran— had compromised over their daughter's religious denomination by making her an Episcopalian. Which meant that every Friday evening Daddy handed over her week's pocket money, twenty-five cents, a whole quarter, and each Sunday morning she went off to Sunday school where the transparent unfairness took place. Sermon over, with all the other little girls before she piped her way through the collection hymn, "Praise God from whom all blessings flow, praise God and all his creatures low..." along came the churchwarden with that clinking collecting bag and sycophantic smile and, plonk, in went her whole twenty-five cents because they didn't give you change in church, and that was the end of the mouth-watering dream of one strawberry ice cream and two Hershey bars.

Yes, she knew that Speedy, her father's chauffeur and handyman, could always be counted on to subsidize her visits to the drugstore. But that was not the point. God, posturing as someone who loved little children, was confiscating her treasure. Surely that was not Christian or right. It did not take long for her indignation to boil over. At the end of church one Sunday she ambushed the parson as he came down the aisle. "Why," she demanded with five-year-old indignation, "if God is so good, does he take all my money every week?"

The parson smiled down benevolently at the ringlets, hostile brown eyes, and belligerent, turned-up lip. He had all the answers.

"My child," he said gently, "that is your contribution, your offering to God, who will look after you and care for you and love you forever."

Kathleen didn't think much of that as an answer either. In any case, Daddy looked after *her*, while God was just up there on his cloud enjoying her strawberry ice cream and unwrapping the first inch of her Hershey bar. She never really took to religion. But a happy childhood? Certainly. Like the morning ritual with Daddy in the bathroom; his feigned surprised at finding his small daughter perched on the closed lid of the toilet as he entered in his bathrobe, bearing his mug of boiling water from the kitchen. Entranced, she watched the fashioning of the flocculent white suds and smelled the sweet soap as he worked up a lather on his face; she watched the fitting of the bright new blade onto the prongs of the screwtop Gillette and heard the dry scrape of the razor as it made beautiful pathways down his cheeks and across his chin like the perfect strokes of a mower across a smooth lawn. It was, to little Kay, a sensuous and absorbing experience—so much so that on a couple of occasions Daddy surprised his daughter standing before the mirror, face lathered up to her eyebrows and blowing her round cheeks into the necessary balloons and shaving herself. His cure was simple. If little girls started shaving they would probably grow whiskers, and that would look very strange when she went to school, wouldn't it?

So many memories of childhood and growing up in Baltimore, of pale lemon dawns and rosy apple sunsets, winters when the icicles crackled and frost powdered the woodland paths! In her bloodstream she could feel the pounding of Cherokee's hoofs as she raced her pony through the avenues of pines, ducking the lashing branches, fiercely involved in her deep, personal exaltation.

As she grew up Kathleen Hupfeldt was intensely proud of being American, of being born in Maryland. She knew that the first blood of the Civil War had been shed in Baltimore, when Union troops passing from one train station to another were confronted by Southern sympathizers. Shots were exchanged. Young men died, as many other young men would die during the bitter fratricidal war. Historically that gave it a special place in her emotions. Romantic, decisive things had happened there. Kay, in those days, took sides. There was not a gene in her body prepared to compromise.

She was proud of her father. Both of Herbert Harry Hupfeldt's parents, German father, French mother, had been born in the United States, and while Daddy spoke German, was proud of his German associations, and belonged to a small German literary group that included H. L. Mencken, he was in essence true-blue American. He had inherited all the German virtues of patience, industry, gentleness, a love of music; he was a creature of habit and orderliness, but he was also his own man, his emotions tightly held inside him and rarely allowed to peep out. His small daughter demanded his love, but Herbert found it hard to give in outward gestures.

The French blood in the family probably went some way to explain the wild, gregarious, go-ahead, ambitious antics of Herbert's older brother, Will. Kay loved Uncle Will, especially when he took her down to the cellar and fed her sips of bourbon while he shucked Maryland oysters.

The Hupfeldt brothers were never very wealthy, although just before the crash of 1929, when they were investing heavily in real estate, it appeared certain they were going to become millionaires. But they remained well-to-do; they ran a thriving optometrist practice in Baltimore and could fall back on that, and eventually Uncle Will, through his wife's relations, branched out into a prosperous meat-packing business.

The love affair and marriage of handsome Herbert Hupfeldt and pretty Kathryn Sullivan, the Irish girl from across town, encountered much opposition. To the Sullivans—with brothers in the Baltimore police force, officials in Democratic party posts, and sisters in the hospitals or novices in the Church—Kathryn's defection was considered a form of madness. To the German relatives Herbert's brainstorm appeared to be an abdication of all social responsibility. But Herbert and Kathryn ignored all sage advice. In love, they ran off and got married.

"Daddy, behind that quiet exterior, must have been quite a dasher in his younger days," Kay recalled later, "and Mom was certainly an Irish beauty. I think they were very happy; certainly at first they were very happy. I never heard my father raise his voice to my mother. Ever. My mother used to fuss, of course; she was Irish. But no one reproached her. She looked like a Renoir woman, cherubic, with very pretty skin; always looked much younger than she was, black hair that just shaded gray at the temples as she got older. She was a cheerful person; she laughed a lot and cried a lot and yelled a lot, and she hugged me and sang Irish songs so beautifully. 'Irish Eyes Are Smiling' and 'Danny Boy' and 'Irish Lullaby.' She used to hold me on her lap when I was little and sing. She'd sit in the dark and hold me and it was so wonderful, and I'd hurry through my prayers:

> "Now I lay me down to sleep,
> I pray the Lord my soul to keep,
> If I should die before I wake,
> I pray the Lord my soul to take.

"And she'd pop me into bed and kiss me.

"Later Daddy took over that job because after dinner Mom was always off to see her friends or relations to play cards or dance and talk until midnight.

"You could tell the time of day by Daddy," Kay observed. "Every morning he rose at exactly the same time, bathed and shaved and dressed to the second, then went into the garden in summertime, and the greenhouse in winter, and re-emerged with a rosebud or a bachelor's button in his buttonhole."

Every morning he ate exactly the same breakfast: grapefruit, wheat germ, one boiled egg, toast, two cups of coffee. When the front door opened and Herbert Hupfeldt departed for the car, you knew it was exactly ten minutes past eight and you also knew that as he drove down Charles Street to his office in the heart of Baltimore, he would catch every green light at every intersection with the meticulous timing that measured all his life.

"Daddy always came home between six thirty and seven, every night without fail, and dinner was served at seven fifteen. After dinner I'd go into his study and there he would sit at his desk in the lamplight, and I'd sometimes sit quietly watching him writing his books. I'd been brought up with the German barrier to touching. You never touched anyone. I could never get close to Daddy, whom I really loved, not as close as I wanted. The only excuse I could think of for getting close was to feel his hair, or put a finger on his balding head; it had to be something that wasn't a caress... because he didn't like that. He would sit there reading his paper, but if I sat on the arm of his chair I could touch him, and I wanted to touch Daddy and I wanted him to hold me, and he rarely did. But he was my greatest security. Alice, the maid, always had the bed turned down, and he'd tuck me in both sides very firmly, give me a kiss, put a glass of water on the table, and then he'd go down to the bottom of the bed and listen to me reciting my prayers.

"When they got married, Mom kept getting pregnant, but she kept losing the babies, and they discovered later that Mom had RH-negative blood and Daddy RH-positive. But in those days people were not really into that sort of thing, and they were older—Mom was in her thirties, Daddy in his forties—when they finally got their smarts together and went to Johns Hopkins Hospital, where they should have gone in the first place. They were told all about the antipathy of various blood groups and what could be done about it. Finally they did have a son; he would have been my older brother, but he died shortly after his birth. Anyway, Mom kept on going to Hopkins and they planned for me like you would not believe, and Mom was in her late thirties when she finally had me, and I guess by this time some of the shine was off the shoe. They'd just come back from a visit to Germany, and then Daddy was away at the World's Fair in New York. And Daddy wanted a son. He just wanted a boy."

Kathryn in her unguarded moments revealed this to her small daughter. Yes, they had planned to call him Fritz. And Kay, with the radiowave intuition of a small female, knew that her father was deeply disappointed that she had arrived instead of Fritz. So with grim determination she set out to be Fritz. This, she felt with simple childish logic, would make her father happy, and more than anything else in her life she wanted that. Like a million females before her and a million who will come, she fashioned her life to please the masculine gender.

"I hated being a girl, couldn't stand it. I wanted to be a boy, so I acted like a boy. I remember my two buddies were boys, Billy Brewster and Herbie Fee—there weren't any girls in the neighborhood—and we rode bicycles and roller-skated and climbed trees and did all the things boys do. I decided we should have a Fort Pee Wee, so I got Speedy to find us some wood to build it, and since I'd gotten the wood, I was the chief. We had a blood pact. You take a razor blade and cut an X on your wrist and join wrists. Herbie was the second member of the Fort Pee Wee Gang and Billy was the third. We had a little group of guys; I was the only girl, but I was the chief. Oh, I was a proper little boy. I remember when we went to Atlantic City for vacation in the summer and I won the body-surfing competition among the kids for three years in a row just to show I was as good as any boy."

As soon as she learned to write, Kathleen became a great "writer-down"; her secret places were always bulging with a miscellany of notes, observations, resolutions, stories, and philosophies. Remembering a visit to Uncle Will and his wife, Aunt Lou, Kay, still a small girl, wrote:

"Mom was sick but not that sick. Daddy said that I was to go to Auntie Lou for a bit as Mom would be in the hospital for a little while. Auntie Lou lived in a huge white stucco house. There was land around and a kennel, but that did not matter to me. I really loved Aunt Lou. She always gave me the most beautiful clothes, and was always sweet and smiling. Everybody else in my life would frown and tell me what I had done wrong. Initially life didn't change much because I still went to school, only Charles, the black chauffeur, drove me instead of Speedy and it took longer because we had to cross the bridge. Charles didn't talk as much as Speedy, and Aunt Lou and Uncle Will had three children, my first cousins Billy, Peggy, and Nancy. Upstairs there was a large hall and we all had our rooms off of it. Nancy was my best friend. She had the least attractive room, as it was behind Peggy's and really isolated. She wore braces on her teeth. After I did my homework, I would pass through Peggy's room—she hated me—because she was blonde and really sexy and couldn't be bothered with this piggy little cousin that was me. She was four years older than Nancy and she was always on the phone.

"Nancy would be in her room and together we would extract her braces. How she stood the pain I will never know; she was the first really brave friend I ever had because she was always taking out her braces because the dentist, the beast, had devised braces with prongs which could not be taken out. But I pressed on one side and Nancy pressed on the other and in a countermotion we could relieve her of torture for the night, and she could suck her thumb, which was the reason for all the commotion anyway. After we got her braces out we would sneak down the back stairs to the kitchen. By then the kitchen was closed and we had it all to ourselves. Nancy was overweight and she had a doctor for that too, and he was always trying to starve her to death, and charging her mom for her demise. We were sure he wanted to marry Aunt Lou. My problem was I never ate at dinner because Uncle Will scared me to death, and Billy, my cousin, had told me he took little girls to the basement and ate them alive. He did go to the basement a lot. By ten thirty my stomach was aching and we hit the refrigerator. There were two. In one was all the ice cream, cakes, and sauces. And in the other the veges, meats, and salads. We would have contests as to who could make the best sundaes and we would leave the refrigerator doors open for light as we consumed our delicacies. Saturated, we would climb up the back stairs and usually fall asleep in her bed, because returning to my room meant passing through Cousin Peggy's room and she would wake up. In the morning Peggy would leave early because she had her own roadster, with a rumble seat on the back, and she would pick up her friends on the way to school. Charles only drove Nancy and me. The only room I liked to sleep in was Cousin Billy's. All of us girls had rooms with white walls and ruffles on the bed and dressing tables. Cousin Billy's room was at the top of the stairs next to Grandmother Schluderburg's and, like hers, it was paneled in deep-toned wood with bookcases and looked out on the garden. Each night Aunt Lou would find me after my bath in Cousin Billy's bed, and she would read me *Heidi* and *Little Women*, and I would fall asleep. These were the nights when Aunt Lou was home, but the next morning I would wake in my own bed. I almost liked it better when she wasn't there after dinner and I could sneak into Nancy's room. Nancy liked it better too because we could get her braces out. Everything went along the same for a while. Either Aunt Lou read to me in Billy's room or I went to Nancy's room. I never really saw much of Billy; he went to fight in the war. Aunt Lou let me spend the whole night sometimes in Cousin Billy's bed after she read to me after he had gone to fight in the war. She put a picture of Billy beside the bed, and after reading to me she had me kiss it. I knew that when I grew up I should marry Cousin Billy, as I loved him and I loved his bed. I stopped going to see Nancy and she lost weight. Mom came back from the hospital. Aunt Lou cried when I left."

Speedy came into Kay's life the day she was born. Speedy had grown up on the eastern shore of Virginia; his mother had remarried, and at fourteen he was being kicked around by his stepfather. Uncle Will had a boat, and Uncle Will and Kay's father were fishing from it when Speedy appeared and wanted to work on the boat. Once he started he never wanted to leave. So he worked for one or the other brother from that moment on. He lived at first with Uncle Will and Aunt Lou and then helped in the optometrist business.

"I was supposed to be born at the end of September 1939, but on the ninth, when Daddy and Uncle Will were away at New York at the World's Fair, Mom went into labor and only Speedy was there to drive her to the hospital. So eventually Mom produces me, and there is Speedy still out in the waiting room with a whole collection of husbands waiting for news of their babies, and out comes the matron with me in her arms. Without looking up, she calls, 'Dr. Hupfeldt, you're the proud father of this baby girl,' and she places me in the arms of the man who has come up, and almost drops dead at the sight of the big black man who's got me. Speedy was a tall, good looking young man in those days too. I have pictures of me sitting on his knee when he's in his chauffeur's uniform and I'm a little girl with my curls dancing around. Speedy used to take me everywhere. He took care of Daddy, he took care of the yard, he took care of the house, and he took care of me, did all kinds of things. And he did everything so slowly that he was bound to be called Speedy. His real name was Theodore Roosevelt Greene.

"Speedy drove me to school every morning when I was young, except when I lived with Uncle Will and Aunt Lou. And he put up my train set every Christmas and he'd be Santa Claus. It scared me at first, because I didn't know Speedy with that white beard on, but when I did I'd leave out milk and cookies on Christmas Eve because I knew he was the one who was gonna eat 'em. Speedy was wonderful to me. Speedy said, 'Stay away from them boys. Them boys will only get you into trouble.'

"I should have listened to Speedy.

"Speedy told me to beware of boys. Alice told me the facts of life.

"Alice was wonderful. She was a short little black lady—and I mean lady. If she weighed eighty pounds, I'd be surprised; she was certainly never taller than five-two. She was born in Baltimore; she was a twin but her twin sister died at childbirth. Alice Bernice Johnson was her full name and I don't know how she ever came into the family, but she was just an integral part of my life from the time I first opened my eyes. She wasn't educated; she'd just been born smart.

"Speedy was literally a child when he came to work for Uncle Will, but Alice was a young woman probably in her twenties when she came to work for us. She'd gone through seventh or eighth grade in Catholic school, trained by the nuns, and she lived at the house, cooked and cleaned and took care of me. She had Thursdays off, and a weekend a month off. We were the greatest of friends, and as a little girl I remember she earned her forty-eight dollars a week, and I suppose it went up. I can remember Daddy paying her in the kitchen every time she had her weekend off, and then she'd go home, home being a little room somewhere. But her life was part of our family. I was mean to her sometimes. I was young and spoiled and wrapped up in myself. I remember I'd eat her cupcakes sometimes like a nasty little girl; she had her own special cupcakes which she'd bring as treats when she'd come back from her weekend, and they always looked so good to me I gobbled them up. I remember Alice would reprimand me and say, 'Kay, you ought not to do that.' I never thought until long afterward that it was a terrible thing I did. I just thought, *Gee, they look so good, I'm going to eat 'em.*

"Alice and Speedy used to fuss together. You see, it was Alice's kitchen, and Speedy used to come in for lunch. And she wouldn't make his lunch because she 'wasn't hired to wait on another black.' So big Speedy and little Alice would get sore with each other, and she'd make him cook his own food, and Speedy loved pork chops and fat cheese sandwiches, and he would make a mess! And she would be on to him: 'You clean that up. I won't have you coming into my kitchen making this mess.' And she would give him holy hell.

"These days I sometimes wonder if Alice knew more about me than my own mother did. It was Alice I'd come home to and say, 'Gee, I really hit a great goal in hockey today,' and Alice would want to hear about how I pounded up the wing and outwitted the backs with my skill—and she'd praise me even if she knew it was a lot of hooey. Mom wouldn't be there in the afternoon, and if she was, she'd have her friends and they'd be playing canasta or bridge or having a luncheon or something. I'd hug Alice; she was such a skinny little thing, I'd squeeze her to death. I sure squeezed and hugged Alice. Real black she was. She looked like a rabbit; she wore glasses and had a sweet little rabbit nose. I really loved her. When I had my first period—neither school nor my Mom had prepared me—it was Alice who told me. I'd thought I was bleeding to death. And when Newton, my first boyfriend, tried to kiss me, it was Speedy who read the riot act about the terrible things that happen when you get into cars with boys.

"Alice died in her fifties, and she looked seventy. I think she was sick and never went to the doctor and just didn't tell anybody. She crept backward and forward like a little mouse to her little room in a black quarter of Baltimore. I sometimes wondered why she went, but maybe everyone needs a little place of their own. And the world never knew about Alice, but I did, and though I took her for granted, I loved her; she had such good sense, and she was a good person. She's buried now between my mother and father—in my place.

"All my cousins went to boys' schools or girls' schools—that's on my daddy's side—and all the other kids on my mother's side went to parochial schools because they were Catholics. Mother and Daddy didn't want me to go to an all-girls' school; they wanted me to go to a co-ed. So the only place I could go was the Friends School. I started to wear the school uniform as soon as I was old enough, and I always remember Mom referring to me as 'the child in uniform.' 'Is the child in uniform home yet?' she'd say. And in some tiny way that hurt me. It was a starched blue uniform . . . I used to have to wear them five days a week, and they were made out of a material called Indian Head, a very stiff material, not soft at all—a sort of heavy, cheap cotton. The uniform had a yoke in front and a yoke in back and a Quaker collar that snapped on. Everything was stiffly starched. There were pleats that came all the way down the front and down the back and they had to be pressed. I had to wear fresh collars and cuffs every day, and Mom just hated it if I'd come home and I'd gotten into a ball game and messed it all up. White and blue saddle shoes, white socks, navy-blue sweaters, no hats. I went to school dressed like that for nine years.

"The Quakers believe in service to the community, and all through my school life this was drummed into us. In school we always made scrapbooks for the children in hospitals or we'd gather up canned goods and things for poor people at Christmas and Thanksgiving; even as a little tot you could do something. You didn't have to—it was voluntary—but on weekends you would give service to the community; you'd go down to the poorer section, take care of kids, work in the hospitals, do something like that.

"It was a very proper upbringing, growing up in the upper-middle-class society of Baltimore. You might say I was the end of the white gloves era. When you went into town or to church, you wore white gloves. I had a whole drawer full of white and colored gloves. And Mom saw to it that I took ballet and piano lessons and went to the Peabody Conservatory, where all properly brought up young ladies added to their education. I went to this conservatory from the time I was five in order to learn how to speak, how to sit, how to cross my legs, how to place my feet, walk with a book on my head, carry myself, how to be a lady. I went after school every Thursday at three o'clock... and I still hate Thursdays.

"But I enjoyed playing the piano. It satisfied me, made up a little, I guess, for the emotion I needed in my home life, because I guess as an only child perhaps I needed a double dose of affection. I think I did.

"It wasn't Mom's fault that she wanted to play canasta and go to nightclubs and enjoy herself, but I wish she'd taken me to an art museum occasionally. And, of course, when I was very little and she took me to the Women's Exchange restaurant I was scared to death. I thought with a name like that it was where moms swapped their children if they'd been naughty or they didn't like them, and I was terrified that she'd give me away and I'd have to live with a different mom.

"But I know it wasn't Mom's or Daddy's fault that they couldn't live up to a child's dreams of what the perfect parent is. What parent can? I also know I was a spoiled brat, eating Alice's cupcakes like that. And I remember I went to two dances a month in my teens and I never wore the same dress to a dance twice ever, and they cost forty to fifty bucks each. New dress, new shoes. I twisted Daddy around my finger with childish ruthlessness. It's all very well talking about the responsibility of teaching children values when you have an insistent little plague like me about. No wonder my cousins were envious. I had more dresses than Mother had closets to put them in."

Summing up her school career, Kay doesn't give herself much credit: "I was an average student, a cheerleader, co-chairman of the school bazaar, and rather the average 'girl next door.' Except for one thing: I wanted to go to college."

But, before doing so, she wanted something else. A spring vacation in Bermuda when she was fifteen afforded the opportunity.

"Off I went to Bermuda for the spring break with my very best friend in the world and another school friend. The three of us stayed with Mom's friend Mrs. Randolf, who lived on Hamilton Beach. She and her husband had an inn that accommodated ten or twelve guests, and lower down the beach there were four or five cottages. We girls opted to stay in one of the cottages, but my mom and one of the other moms said that we should stay in the main guest house. So we did. Mrs. Randolf met us at the airport and we were ensconced in the big house, each with our own room and bath. Of course, we had had visions of being on the cliff in a cottage all together, big fire each night, cheap gin, and our friends. As it worked out, we were in rooms that opened into the living room of the big house, so we couldn't P.J. it into each other's room, as there was always a bridge game going on in the living room after our curfew.

"I promptly got sick after two days and suggested that my two friends get sick too. They did so. The response was just what the doctor ordered. Mrs. Randolf invited the next-door neighbor's son, who was on the island for the spring break from Dartmouth, with his two friends for dinner with the cottage guests in the big house. We girls just loved it. Drinks were served first in the bar and we all had our sherry, then excused ourselves and went into the ladies' room to decide who wanted to be with whom. With that decided, we returned to the bar and told Mrs. R. whom we would like to sit next to. Of course, the young couples were put at different tables and we girls ate like birds and the guys ate like Norsemen. But we'd made our splendid plans, because even though we were not at the same tables for dinner, we girls went to bed as planned before the boys had left, a fact I'm sure was most appreciated by Mrs. R. As all of the guests watched, we demurely entered our separate rooms—and frantically showered and changed.

"At the appointed hour we crept out of our bedroom windows and there were our guys with their motor scooters, dressed for the evening. We were all so excited as we crept to the gates and only after a safe distance climbed aboard the scooters and clutched the waists of our Sir Galahads. This became our standard procedure at night. After dinner we girls would retire after coffee had been served, and the boys were always there and the evenings were wonderful. For the next week or so the evenings went on with all six of us loving the rides by the sea and the bars with the blacks where no whites went, and the walks on the beach and the swims at Horseshoe Bay.

After five days we all wanted more, and we girls had a problem because Mrs. R. always brought our breakfast trays in to our room at six a.m. and we just made it sometimes. Alistair, my guy, whose parents owned the property next door, kept wanting us to go to his house, but between the three of us girls, we knew we would never survive if Mrs. R. ever found out. The gods were with us. Mrs. R.'s son, who was in school in the States, came down with pneumonia, and Mr. and Mrs. R. unexpectedly had to leave for New Jersey on the next plane. We were free.

"We girls decided that night that we would lose our virginity. We all made a pledge, one hand down, another slapped on top, the third hand in, then another, until six hands, palms down, formed a firm, warm pile. The die was cast. We knew from the boys' urgency on the beach and while swimming that they'd already lost their virginity. They were eighteen, college freshmen going into their sophomore year, all three from Dartmouth.

"That night after coffee we did our usual thing, but we girls had decided to surprise the boys by saying we could go back to the beach cottage. 'Honeymoon Cottage.' That night, after the calypso band, the Manhattans, and the beach, we said, 'Let's go and have a fire at Honeymoon Cottage.' And off we went. Alistair made the fire and there was this marvelous huge log in the fireplace with a couch in front, and French doors leading from the living room onto the terrace, which overlooked the sea. To the left of the kitchen there was the bedroom. We all danced and listened to records and drank more and more Manhattans and somewhere along the way Alistair and I were alone on the terrace. Before long we were on the couch in front of the marvelous fire, and we were warm and submerged and aware only of the fire. I made up a little poem: 'The pig is in the parlor, the cow is in the lake, the baby's in the garbage can, what difference does it make?'

"It wasn't all that great... it hurt. I think Jessie got off with her boy better than Alistair and me. We knew our third friend hadn't done it, because she didn't know what we were talking about, because if you haven't done it you can't understand. We figured out pretty fast she hadn't done it."

Sex was one thing but falling in love quite another. The first boy Kay fell in love with was Jimmy. Every afternoon after school Speedy would drive her out to Mr. Bentley's Equitation School, and there was Cherokee, her pony, waiting for her, saddled and ready. Mr. Bentley taught her equitation and jumping, and after that, before dark, she would walk Cherokee along the paths through the woods and wonder if she really loved her pony better than Daddy or Mom. There were other stables in the area, and on one ride she bumped into Jimmy riding a little chestnut filly and leading two other ponies. One glance from his crystal-blue eyes, one look at the handsome, suntanned, athletic boy with blond hair, was enough to make her glow. He was a couple of years older than she, but Jimmy loved horses with the same inner awareness that she did. His family was poor. He had a job working at the stables, and he and Kay became great friends because Jimmy knew far more about ponies and jumping than she did. And as Kay progressed, she began to ride in shows in various parts of the country.

"We talked constantly about the shows and who won and why; he was always up in first or second, and when I got a second I was really happy. No one ever told me I rode well. Mr. B. would tell me why I lost first, but Jimmy helped me; he helped me braid the mane and tail and would look over the class and the judge and tell me what position to be in. It was strange because we began to be in the same classes and shows in Maryland, Virginia, and Pennsylvania. And I began to rely on him. Soon I was following him into the ring and following his lead. We began coming in first and second. Weekends were spent at the stables and Mom thought that I had gone horse-crazy.

"One time I was jumping and Cherokee fell into the jump, and the bar came down on me. I was conscious but hurting and Mr. B. was there and wanted an ambulance, but Jimmy was there too in his black coat, hat, and jodhpurs—a big expense for him to have those clothes—and Jimmy ordered me back on my pony and made me complete the course.

I was disqualified but people clapped their hands. Jimmy had been right. I was frozen on that pony, but I will never forget his lesson; he made me get up and finish, even though he knew I was disqualified.

"After that I was not permitted to see Jimmy. During the week, following my lesson with Mr. B., I had to go home and someone else cooled down Cherokee. But we managed eventually. Part of Jimmy's job was to clean the stables, and on Saturday classes would be over by twelve, and we could hurry down to the ponies and clean the stalls, and no one would be there. After that was over we could go up in the loft and talk and talk; he had this super idea that if we had twin ponies we could train together, and be together and win together.

"We heard about these two little geldings. Mr. B. was interested in one of them and I convinced Mom to sell Cherokee and buy the other. Mom was not really convinced, because Mr. B. said that the gelding was a two-year-old and not trained. But I convinced her, and Jimmy and I trained those geldings on lead and saddle, always together. We even got to the point where we rode in tandem and jumped in tandem like twins. It felt so good. In 1958 I graduated from high school and went off to college. Jimmy graduated from high school and went off to trade school. Both ponies were sold."

And Kay had now met Andrew.

5

ALTHOUGH Kay could not remember a time when Newton had not been her regular date, he had not really entered into her dreams. On the contrary, already destined for college, she had become aware of Andrew, a handsome Jewish boy in her class. He also seemed acutely aware of her. They were both absorbed in music, art, and books, and in saving the world, a proposition that to them, at seventeen, in the mid-1950s, did not seem too outrageous an ambition. Andrew was going to be a doctor like his father, and they decided they would live in a cottage overlooking the sea, and while Andrew was out saving lives and the world generally, Kay would keep herself occupied raising the six children they planned to produce.

But such was not to be.

The first strike against Kay and Andrew's romantic plans occurred when Kay set out for her first year at William and Mary in Williamsburg and Andrew set out for his first year at Harvard.

Moreover, Papa Hupfeldt, an old-fashioned man, was not totally convinced of the need to send his attractive daughter to college. No doubt William and Mary was a good place to study. But what was better for the future of a young girl than to get married to a nice young man like Newton, who came from a good and wealthy family. Marriage, home, children—all of it was a conception hard to dismiss. Papa Hupfeldt never said it in so many words, but Kay knew that her future was his primary concern.

Still, she pined for Andrew and Andrew yearned for her. And for a year they managed to appease their desire quite adequately, for she could afford to slip up to Boston every weekend and, as Daddy sent her money regularly and without questions, she had a sneaking suspicion he might even suspect what was going on. Kay stayed at the Brattle Inn in Cambridge, making sure she always had a room on the first floor, because it wasn't proper for Andrew to visit a young lady in her room. Fortunately there was a ladder against a barn just around the corner, and as darkness fell the ladder would poke through Kay's window. "Andrew had to leave early in the morning, before dawn," Kay said, "but it was all very romantic, conspiratorial, and absolutely joyous. It was always cold and we'd snuggle together."

Nevertheless, the long nights between weekends were dreary and Kay decided the only answer was to transfer from William and Mary, which she hated, to Vassar, which she thought was practically next door to Harvard, and no more than a long ladder-length from Andrew. Her application was accepted, and the thought of the next year in Andrew's arms was now an anticipation scarcely to be borne.

But one other thing stood between them and perfect happiness. Daddy had arranged for her to take the grand tour that summer with a friend. The trip included France, Germany, Switzerland, and Italy, and she would be away for nearly three months.

Outward bound, she was undaunted. But before she reached Paris on the return, she wrote to Andrew begging him to meet her in Paris and spend a few days with her there. No reply ever came. No letter, cable, or phone call.

By this time Kay's and Newton's parents had opened discussions to consider the future of their respective daughter and son. The fact that Newton had failed his exams, been sacked from Hopkins, and was idling around waiting for someone or something to give him direction, while Kathleen was playing around with a completely unsuitable Jewish boy, no doubt figured in these discussions. The remedy was plain: Kay would return from Europe and marry Newton. After all, they had been acknowledged as sweethearts—practically engaged—for years. Daddy Newton would set them up in an apartment in New York and find a job with prospects in a stock brokerage firm where Daddy Newton had great influence. Katie Hupfeldt and Newton would live happily ever after. All the parents would breathe easier.

Nor was Kathleen altogether opposed to the plan. Not only was a marriage to Newton safe; she had a lot riding on him.

"I grew up from the cradle with Newton. Our baby buggies were parked side by side while our two nannies gossiped at the market and we gurgled at each other from under our baby bonnets. Our families were friends; we both went to the Friends School, and latching on to Newton was the most natural thing in the world."

And as Kay Hupfeldt entered her teens, it had become even more natural. Her responsibility as cheerleader of the girls who tapped the drums, rah-rah-rah'd in unison, and turned cartwheels along the sidelines to expose saucy lace-trimmed red pants was purely to inspire Newton, captain of the lacrosse team, to victory. Newton was a cheerful, athletic, husky, gregarious young man. They had a puppy love relationship that never went beyond a few kisses and a little petting, but they got on.

Kay said, "I never really sat down and examined Newton. I never really examined anybody in relation either to themselves or to me, until I woke up and found I had shot Frank. But even then I was so busy examining Frank that I had forgotten I'd never considered what drove Newton toward his despair."

It was with a small shock of surprise, then, that when Kay finally got around to reappraising Newton, she realized that behind his facade of worldiness and bravado lurked an insecurity as old as Oedipus's. He believed his mother did not love him. That she had rejected him. She was a Victorian in all her proclivities, had borne her husband a son and considered therefore her wifely duties discharged. One child was enough. Newton's conception, therefore, after a sixteen-year gap, had been a social embarrassment of gargantuan dimensions, hard for her to bear, and she had made that fact plain both in public and in Newton's presence.

Kay nevertheless got on well with Irma. "I called her Little Mother, and in those early years I thought Irma's constant complaining about Newton was due to a mother's concerned love rather than outraged respectability."

Kay also sensed that the blossom on the marriage between Irma and Daddy Newton had withered long ago but that Daddy Newton knew how to have a good time. As a wealthy stockbroker, he used to spend three days a week in New York, where he had an apartment on Park Avenue, and as Kay observed later, "When he would take us out, he knew El Morocco and all the places, so you didn't have to be a private eye to know that Daddy Newton enjoyed himself.

"He was the sort of daddy that in some ways I wish my own daddy had been. He would come up and hug and kiss me and put his arm around my waist and say, 'How's my girl?' and buy me little presents. He was a very warm, likable person. But, of course, with his busy public and private life, Daddy Newton wasn't there very much either, so Newton was mainly brought up by the black maid, Sarah, a wonderful woman, while his own mother really should have been doing the job.

"In a sense Newton was abandoned, an unwanted kid, though, of course, we didn't know it when we were teenagers because we were busy just having fun. If he said, 'I want a new rifle,' he got a new rifle. He had cars bought for him from the time he could drive. I'll never forget the afternoon we borrowed his father's new Packard convertible, a car he had strict instructions not to touch, and we drove off to Ocean City to the beach. It was a marvelous, brand-new, baby-blue dream, with white leather upholstery, spoked wheels, and whitewall tires. We had a case of beer in the back; he's seventeen and I'm fifteen and I can still see us humming down the road, the roof down, the wind in our hair, feeling just like something out of *The Great Gatsby*. We arrive at the ocean, swing onto a lonely part of the beach, and suddenly I feel the rear wheels go down deep into the sand—whoop! And there we were, stuck. But stuck! I had no money; Newton had forgotten to bring his wallet, so we had to ring up Daddy Newton and confess. Then, to make matters worse, the great big steel arm of the tow truck that came to rescue us suddenly collapsed and crashed down on the trunk, leaving a huge dent. I mean we were outcasts. We were not allowed to see each other for at least two weeks. I spent the entire two weeks eating Tastykakes and drinking Pepsi-Cola to console myself. It was awful. Newton only got told off.

"We thought we were pretty wild and pretty clever. By the time they were fourteen a lot of the high school kids were into drink—mainly cans of beer. I mean, regularly we had these parties where the boys would get so drunk, they'd fall in the pool. And they'd drink bathtub gin. . . . They'd get so drunk, you wouldn't believe it. . . . Sure, it was years and years past prohibition, but I guess those gangster associations made them feel grown-up and rebellious—all part of the fifties scene. Newton, when he was sixteen and seventeen, would go off and not be seen for two or three days, and Little Mother would practically have a fit and go into one of her religious manias: 'God has put this child upon me; God is punishing me.' And it was always *me*; she didn't ever seem to consider what drove Newton."

Thus, when Kay arrived back from the grand tour, bitterly disappointed not only by Andrew's inability to join her in Paris but also by his failure even to contact her, she was more surprised than distressed when she found that she was engaged to be married to Newton. She paused only momentarily to draw a deep breath and decided not to protest. Suddenly it was very pleasant being at the center of things, and to find expensive wedding gifts already arriving. If Andrew was ignoring her, then Newton was fine. She liked Newton "really well." All her friends congratulated her on the match. Newton slipped the engagement ring, a slim platinum circle with a beautiful setting of blue-white stones, onto her finger, and it matched exactly the baby-blue Corvette convertible that Daddy Newton already donated as part of his wedding gift. After all, she was nineteen and it was about time she got married, and deep down she knew that marriage to Andrew was not a practical possibility.

The time of the wedding was quickly arranged: an evening ceremony at 8 p.m. on December 27, 1958. She wore a princess gown in white velvet; the veil, all twenty feet of it, made in Bruges by the sisters there. Everything went beautifully. The candlelight touched the tears on her cheeks, and she pretended it was Andrew she was marrying. That was the only illusion she allowed herself.

Afterward she decided that she had to forget her romance with Andrew.

The honeymoon in Bermuda was even better. The physical relationship surprised her. "It was so strange to make love to him. I mean, I had known him all my life; he was like an old shoe. Then suddenly he was supposed to be my husband."

She was delighted to find they were happy in bed. This was an added bonus, for she had applied her mind dutifully to the future. She intended to be a good and faithful wife.

Indeed, when they settled into their new apartment in New York, she began one of the happiest periods of her life. The apartment, which Daddy Newton had provided, had a long kitchen with counters on both sides and a big window, outside of which they kept the Danish pastries they ate for breakfast. The living room was the best room, with big windows on two sides; there was also a little hall and a large bedroom. The bathroom was gigantic, with high ceilings and space to get lost in. They discovered that their next-door neighbor was a prostitute, and that occasionally made things a little difficult, because her callers would sometimes get mixed up and knock on their door. "They'd be a little surprised," Kay said, "to see mousey me standing there instead of her. I'd be in blue jeans, freckles, and bare feet, and you could see from the startled look on their faces that this isn't exactly what they expected to pay for."

Kay was twenty years old. Mrs. Robinson was an "older woman"— in her thirties. Very pretty. She didn't talk much but she was very friendly. Kay never saw Mrs. Robinson in anything but a peignoir and they lived there over a year. Newton realized immediately what she was, but Kay had no idea that ladies "like that" lived in such apartments. Kay decided Mrs. Robinson was always in bed; she just never got out of bed, which was probably the truth.

Kay quickly began to take to the city. She'd get up in the morning and go to the art galleries and the shops. She and Newton didn't spend all that much time in the apartment, and at first they used to get all kinds of carry-out food, especially Hungarian. Later she got deep into cooking and entertaining. She got a roast beef when they had their first "company." It was supposed to be special and it was so tough she wouldn't let the company eat it. Furious, she wrapped it up and took it back to the shop on Third Avenue, plopped it on the counter, and said, "This thing cost me all of six bucks and it was so tough I couldn't serve it." She went on at them so long that they just gave her another one.

Every morning she would make Newton's breakfast and off he'd go down to Wall Street, and every evening she'd meet him somewhere, and they would go to little bars he knew and have a drink. New York wasn't a violent town in those days; they could go anywhere and loved going up to Harlem to listen to jazz. On weekends they went to Connecticut to meet Newton's friends who worked with him on Wall Street, and they stayed with them or at little inns. Every holiday the in-laws arrived with a turkey and all the trimmings, which made Kay a bit uneasy but she got through it.

The first hint of things to come crept into their lives when Newton started coming home a bit later, and for Kay the days got lonelier, so she thought, *Why don't I get a job too?* She rang Mom up about that, but Mom wasn't convinced about such a course of action. In fact, it took a meeting of the four parents plus Newton and Kay at their apartment to get her the necessary permission. It proved to Kay that they both were under pretty intensive surveillance even though Newton was over twenty-one and she was moving toward that advanced age herself.

The job she got was with a brokerage house on Broad Street—ten till five, fifty bucks a week. She was thrilled. She filled in at first for other girls away for their lunch hour, and then, with more experience, she filled in stock certificates and attended to the switchboard. Friday was payday and the guys would always take the girls out for a drink after work. Then Christmas came and she was now one of the girls and she got presents too, all kinds of exciting things. Proudly she'd go uptown, go shopping, and spend her wages. She remembered buying a really expensive umbrella one time, and an alligator handbag. She had had to save a couple of weeks for that.

Newton worked at a firm his father had an interest in, serving his apprenticeship there, the understanding being that eventually he and Kay would return to Baltimore so Newton could work in his father's head office. Newton was also studying for an exam: he needed a certificate to sell stocks and bonds, which took a year to get. Every night he'd go off to night school, and Kay would go with him to take his notes and help anyway she could. After night school they'd go out and have a drink and a sandwich or perhaps dinner, and often finish at the Vanderbilt Hotel, which was right across the street from their apartment at Ten Park Avenue, at Thirty-fourth. The hotel, which has since been torn down, always had a piano player or a guitarist playing soft thirties tunes and Kay thought it was very romantic. She realized she was happier than she'd ever been: she had a job; she felt very involved and useful; she felt grown up; and she loved her man. She was also aware, however, that she'd never be so happy again and therefore should enjoy every minute. She said, "I don't know how you know that some things are too good to last, but you do."

Her idyllic happiness lasted a little more than six months. She could not put her finger on the time it all started, if not to go wrong, then certainly to waver, but she could certainly name the place: the bar at the Vanderbilt.

All Kay wanted when they arrived would be a couple of drinks, a little romantic conversation while listening to the music, and home to bed. Newton needed more. More time, more drinks. As the weeks passed, Kay got into the habit of staying on and on as long as she could stay awake, hoping that Newton would feel satisfied and want to go home with her. It rarely happened. He wanted the night and the drinks to go on forever. So she would sigh, say good night, and go home by herself.

She also noticed in those months when they patrolled the town and found the little bars that the patrons in those places all seemed to know Newton extremely well. The erosion was slow, a slow alteration in Newton's personality: he became a little more morose, a bit more irritable, less understanding.

Like the rest of his cronies, Newton liked to drink and he also played pool like a fanatic: at times she thought he lived only to play pool. Now he renewed both activities—all night long! Now he was reactivating his old bad habits, and that didn't augur well for their marriage.

After that, Kay said, "He'd never get up and go to work. I mean, he was supposed to be at work from nine to five selling stocks and bonds, but he would show up at twelve or one. Then he'd spend an hour or so in the office, have lunch, and, I presume, go off to play pool. He'd disappear for two or three days at a time. I don't know what he did—I never knew what he did—but he'd never come home. I'd go back to the apartment and eat and get up and go to work. It didn't really disturb me; nobody was there to know about it, and I took it in my stride. I've never been nosy. People don't understand that. It didn't really matter. I've always been taught to carry on. If I'd had a fit, gone into 'Where have you been all night?'—what good would it have done? I mean, I might say, 'Goddammit, fix your own breakfast,' something like that, but Newton would never impose on me; Newton would never say, 'I want breakfast.' He'd go into the kitchen and get a doughnut or something."

Kay didn't know what to do. Her mother was on the phone to her constantly, and in moments of crisis Kay reversed the process. Mom, after due reflection, lasting all of ten seconds, thought that the answer to the problem was simple: a baby, a grandchild, which would delight Daddy Newton and her own mom and dad.

Kay wrinkled her forehead. That sounded all too simple. It would be all very well if the honeymoon atmosphere of the first six months had continued and they had stayed as a solid twosome. But the enchantment was over. Now she felt very insecure and isolated. Bringing a baby into the world when Newton looked as if he were slipping out of it would not solve problems; it would create them. She would have to think very hard about it.

Thinking out loud made things no easier. Newton continued his nocturnal peregrinations of New York bars and pool halls and Kay decided Mom must be right. It was not hard to become pregnant; Newton was always a willing and enthusiastic partner. She believes she became pregnant on May 19, 1960. She did not tell Newton until she was absolutely certain, deciding to wait until she had consulted the family doctor in Baltimore. This was easy to arrange on one of their weekend visits. But even with the news confirmed, she was still hesitant about what to say to her young husband. She decided to edge him toward the news of his impending fatherhood by knitting a tiny pair of blue baby booties; she saved them for the Saturday morning drive to see friends in Ocean City. It was a lovely, sunny day.

The Corvette flew along like a bird. She fished in her handbag, extracted the booties, and gently waved them in Newton's direction. She saw his face change. She had barely got out the words "Newton, you are going to become a father," when he slammed on the brakes and screeched to a halt at the side of the freeway. His expression was so cold, his reaction so hostile, she couldn't speak. They both sat there in shock for several seconds. He restarted the car and drove on. She felt the tears in her eyes and closed them to try to keep them from running through her lashes. She felt utterly alone and helpless. The weekend at Ocean City was filled with people and parties and plans for future summer weekends and parties. And at the end of it Newton had not said a word and she was lonelier than ever.

The pregnancy was hailed by family and in-laws, who treated it as a blessing without equal. The blessed couple left New York and moved to a rented apartment in Baltimore. Newton went to work in his father's office, and as Kay grew larger, lunches at the Baltimore Country Club with relatives, and dinners at the Woman's Club of Roland Park, with either Newton's mother or her own, increased in number. Kay joined in the laughter—the successful mom-to-be, backed to the hilt by both sets of parents—but she never felt less like laughing. And Newton was rarely around.

"I didn't try to discuss the trouble with Little Mother or Mom. I mean, we just didn't talk about it. You just did not, in that society, talk about ugly things. You pushed them into the nearest out-tray, marked 'Forget.' Newton's mother and my mother knew very well that Newton just wasn't coming home nights, but they didn't talk about that either. I was scared of having a baby. I remember the night the pains started. Newton and I had been at his parents' home for dinner, and as soon as we got back to our rented apartment, Newton took off on one of his binges. Between midnight and one A.M. I knew that baby was on the way. I phoned the hospital, and they said to come to the hospital with my husband straightaway. So what could I do? I couldn't ring up my mom and say, 'Mom, there's no one here. Newton's out on the town somewhere in Baltimore—help!' I hadn't been brought up like that. You fended for yourself. So I rang for a taxi. It was snowing hard and the driver was a bit surprised, but very nice, and he helped me down the driveway and took me into the hospital when we got there. They popped me into bed and on February third at 11:32 Charles was born.

"I didn't like him much when he was born because I didn't know what to do with him. I thought he was going to break; I was scared to death of him... that little lolling head. And the grandmas were always running around saying, 'Watch his head.' They frightened me to death. I'd never been around babies, but as soon as he started acting as if he wasn't going to break, I really loved him and enjoyed him. When he ate, I ate. When he went to bed, I went to bed, and when he got up, I got up. He was *my* baby."

It was after Charles's birth that Kay's father presented to them a house on the edge of Baltimore, in a green wooded area known as Spring Lake. It was a ranch-style house, three bedrooms and three bathrooms, a kitchen, a dining room, and a huge basement fitted out as a pool room. It seemed to Kay that they had guests every night to play pool and eat and drink, and between the job of entertaining them and looking after the baby, she was exhausted.

"I went to sleep hearing those damn pool balls click-click-clicking all night long," she said. "They didn't get started until ten or eleven... three or four guys drinking beer and playing pool." But then Newton seemed to get tired of playing pool in his own house and started staying out nights again. He wandered in and out at odd hours, and whenever they were together he was glassy-eyed and incoherent. Little Mother knew all about Newton's drinking, because sometimes Kay called her or she called Kay to try and find him, but the subject as a conversational topic was taboo.

Kay said, "I remember the night the police called at two in the morning and said Newton had wrapped the baby-blue Corvette—Daddy Newton's wedding gift—around a tree, and could we come and fetch him? They were quite nice about it. As it was only two or three blocks away from his parents' home, I called his mom and told her I'd pick her up and we'd collect him together. Newton was stretched out there on the grass, out cold, quite unhurt, even though the car was demolished. That's the way life with Newton went on. Newton would take off for weeks. I remember he made seventy-five dollars a week in his father's firm. I would get up early because of the baby and I couldn't get Newton out of bed, and I would nag him. 'Go to work.... Father's waiting for you.' Eventually he'd roll out, nine, nine thirty, ten o'clock, halfway through my day, then he'd dress immaculately. Newton was a super dresser—everything was perfect. His father too was a perfectionist; twice a day he changed his shirt—always white. When we lived in New York we literally had to send Newton's shirts home every week. I used to take them to the post office stacked in a tin that was just the size of a folded shirt. They were laundered by this one maid in his household and Newton would only wear these shirts.

"Anyway, he would get dressed, and I would expect him for dinner, and then I wouldn't hear from him for four or five days—not a word. Why didn't I do anything about it? Well, in the first place I didn't want people to know he was gone. It would upset me, but I was more upset about letting people know he wasn't there than about the fact that I was alone and by myself. Then he'd just show up. He'd been playing pool and drinking; where he slept I didn't know. He'd come back looking like a disaster—bearded, hung over. I'd ask him where he'd been and he'd say he'd been to a pool hall, and he'd never mention who he'd been with; and then a couple of days later some pool shark would show up at the front door and say, 'I've got a pool game with Newton.' A pool shark who played pool for money."

Kay is convinced that the final tragedy, which tipped Newton over the edge, was the sudden death of his father. "I'll never forget that night," she said. "Little Mother, half crazy, running around preaching to the wall in her grief. 'God has taken my husband.' But she didn't provide the dramatic high point of the evening; that was produced by a young, good-looking partner in the firm. I opened the door to him and there he stood joking and smiling and saying, 'The King is dead. Long live the King!' Then he demanded all of Daddy Newton's papers, 'everything to do with the office.' With Little Mother going off her head, and no Newton in sight, I knew this was totally wrong. I told him so, and when he had gone, I collected all the papers I could find and hid them. I was furious at this partner's behavior, especially when you understood how ingratiating he was in front of Daddy Newton, who was so generous and ·gentle, who'd give you the watch off his wrist.

"Newton was left a large trust fund by his father, but certainly Charles and I never saw one cent of it. Once Daddy Newton died there was no need to tolerate Newton in the downtown office; Newton wasn't ever there anyway. So now, for the first time in my life, I had to start making my own decisions. Newton was slipping out of our lives because he came home less and less and deteriorated more and more, and I just finally reached the conclusion that Newton and I were no longer living together.

"I was getting more and more involved with Baby Charles, and I knew there must be more to life than just waiting around for Newton to come home and vent his anger and frustration on us. That's what it came down to... there was anger inside him, anger coupled with deterioration. Now I understand that most of the anger was directed toward himself, but the only way he showed it was toward me. And, above all, I wanted Baby Charles to know happiness. I wanted him to have his chance. I didn't want just to be defending him against Newton. I wanted to get a life together that would work, and Newton wasn't even beginning to try to get it to work."

Kay decided to get a divorce. She didn't tell a soul about it. She knew that neither her family nor Little Mother would help, so she started off by herself. The family lawyer was no help at all. His involvement, he said, would constitute a conflict of interest. So she found another lawyer down the street. It was a painful process; they had to get a detective to follow Newton. It took about a year and a half to get the case into court. Kay became the owner of the house and the furnishings, which her own father had provided anyway. She was also awarded alimony and child support, but was never paid a cent. For the time being her own parents supported her and Baby Charles.

Newton left the house with hardly a word and went to live with his mother. Once he was out of the house he never made any attempt to see Kay again. Little Mother tried to make Newton see his son, but she was never successful. And very soon he slipped away from his mother too and disappeared. Forever.

6

WITHOUT Newton, Kay now had to make the decisions concerning her future. About one thing she was certain: she had to complete her education, and with that in mind she enrolled at Baltimore's Johns Hopkins University to study for a degree in Russian history.

She had planned to take English history at William and Mary, but now she chose Russian because she had become intrigued with the dramatic history of the Romanov dynasty.

Helping and influencing her decisions was her circle of Jewish school friends, for her Quaker school had provided education without any religious discrimination, and this group, which had included Andrew, were warm and companionable; indeed, she found in their company the compassion and understanding she needed. They accepted without disapproval the fact that she was divorced: she could discuss with them such natural hazards of life in the twentieth century in a way she could not hope to do with her own family or in-laws, rooted as they were in conventional Baltimore society.

"I would go over to have dinner with my parents, and they would talk as if Newton and I were still together, as if he were out on a job or something, or working late. They simply would not acknowledge the fact that he was not coming back into my life. Mom would say, 'How is

Newton? Is he doing well?' and I—who hadn't seen him for three months or so, and did not have the foggiest notion of what he was doing—would keep up the pretense by saying, 'I guess so,' or something equally inane."

At night Kay was always alone in the house at Spring Lake but there were helpers around: Speedy and Alice inevitably, and also a maid who worked for Little Mother.

Nevertheless, it was the parents of one of her Jewish girl friends, Nancy, who began to figure quite frequently in her life.

"They started inviting me out when I was left alone with Charles—Alice would always baby-sit—and they would take me out to dinner or to a symphony concert, and there would usually be some guy around to act as my escort. I never fancied any of them in the slightest, until Roger came on the scene. Nancy had these wealthy relatives in New York, who lived in a big apartment on Park Avenue, and Nancy invited their son, Roger, down to Baltimore for the weekend to meet me.

"He was twenty-five years old, Jewish, intellectual, and he wore thick-lensed spectacles; and he had enormous warmth, intelligence, sensitivity, and joie de vivre. I was taller than he was but he didn't mind; I used to make fun of him but he didn't mind. He knew everywhere in New York; we'd go to the posh places, the theater and the opera, and the seediest places too, where he knew all the guys who played in the bands; the jazz was great."

Roger filled an emotional gap in Kay's life, but certainly not a sexual one. She had decided that a platonic affair was all she was ready for. Nevertheless, going to New York every weekend to stay in Roger's parents' apartment was fun. The apartment was huge and luxurious and Roger behaved impeccably.

About him she wrote: "Everything with Roger was beautiful. He would meet me at Penn Station, and then we'd take a taxi to his parents' apartment, and I'd find he'd planned every evening. It would be dinner at a Chinese restaurant and then a show; Saturday an opening at a gallery. When I was with Roger he took care of me. He paid the taxi; he held my arm when we had to wade through the slush of New York. He wanted to know how I felt; I felt he really loved me."

As the months passed, needing love, Kay gradually fell in love with him—or as much in love as she could with someone she liked enormously and felt completely at ease with, and who cherished her, but who could not really fulfill her romantic longings. She had been reared to believe she must tailor her ideals to match actuality, and this she now wanted to do. Roger would be a safe anchorage; he wanted to marry her; he liked the idea of a ready-made family and of being stepfather to Charles. Together they decided that when Charles was old enough, his education would be enhanced by a sojourn at a boarding school in Switzerland; they believed that travel, new countries, different people, other problems, broadened the mind and the imagination.

Roger worked in advertising, a field Kay thought not good enough or suitable to sustain them. Roger's father, for his own reasons, encouraged her attitude; he wanted his son to follow him into his law office. Without protest, Roger switched professions and started a three-year course at law school.

In advertising, Roger had been earning good money; as a law student, he was supported by his father. Since neither he nor Kay wanted to start married life on an allowance from the family, they decided to postpone their wedding until Roger's graduation.

Dr. Hupfeldt grudgingly approved of Roger. Kay knew that deep in his heart her father regretted her divorce from Newton, although he shied away from ever discussing it. Of her return to college he had approved only reluctantly. What did a woman want with so much education? Security for a woman lay in marriage. But Daddy slowly began to trust and like Roger, and they understood he would not stand in their way.

So Kay and Roger went on making plans for their wedding, even though, because of Roger's law studies, it was some two and a half years away. They decided that their honeymoon would be a trip around the world. They discussed where they would live. And neither of them imagined for a moment that someone like Frank was waiting in the wings.

Destiny intervened on July 17, 1963. "It was a beautiful day," Kay recalled, "and I was terribly nervous about going out and meeting a strange man, because, after all, I wasn't even divorced yet and I was already promised to Roger. But the fact that it was Sunday lunch, and the Harrises were the parents of one of my best girl friends, well, that made it all right. Besides, I really wanted to go. Mrs. Harris and her husband were involved with an international visitors' organization; they had heard of Frank through a friend, and, being a warm Jewish mother who adored matchmaking, she thought we could make a happy foursome.

"The big and peremptory ring of the bell startled us all; I had yet to learn that no one expressed his personality more forcefully through his entrances and exits than did Frank. Mrs. Harris hurried across the hall, swung open the door, and even as Frank imprisoned his hostess's hand within his own, bending to kiss, caress, and then gently enfold her fingers around the stems of the roses, his dark eyes swung around the room like a periscope. They locked on Kay's and, after only a few whispered words to Mrs. Harris, he strode purposefully toward Kay, to confront her with a species of male she had never encountered before.

He took her hand and lifted it to his lips. The deep voice, tinged with a discernible accent, murmured: "*Molto gentile, signora.* I am Dr. Francesco Sandiford, from Rome."

Kay was electrified but she managed a bright smile.

Later in their relationship, Frank was quite willing to disclose the secrets of his charm. Modesty in such matters was not his habit. How an Italian held and kissed a woman's hand was an exercise of infinite variety and could convey practically any message—admiration, friendship, interest, flirtation, or lust. There was, of course, an elementary and respectful way of greeting older women, but with the younger ones, the ones with beauty, the brushing of the lips across the hand, the pressures, the caressing—those gestures became an amatory art form. Frank openly laughed at American attempts to imitate this Latin custom. It was in the blood and not to be learned from a textbook.

Frank, incidentally, saved all his charm for women. "American men were not taken in by it," Kay recalled, "because they distrusted the familiarity of the big hug. But women adored it. Frank's physical approach was all-embracing; he would literally take hold of a woman, yet do it in such a way that it was socially acceptable, bring her to his chest so that she could smell him, kiss her hand, press it between his own, speak into her eyes, and captivate her.

"You can hardly do that with a man," Kay said. "Latin men do embrace, of course, but still, there's a degree of distance. Frank would sometimes narrow that distance. It would be acceptable for him to embrace a male patient he'd operated on—especially a Latin one and, more so, if he'd just saved his life. But otherwise this barely acceptable lingering might be thought of as a little off. American men didn't take to Frank. But American women? Heavens! Women would call me up on the phone and say, 'God, Kay, who was the man in your house today?' And I would say, "What man? Oh, Frank! That's just my husband!' And they'd say, 'Jesus! What a voice.'"

At that first meeting in Mrs. Harris's dining room, Kay listened enthralled, hanging on Frank's every word. "I adored every minute of it. I mean, Frank kissed my hand a lot of times that day, and if I had had the benefit of his candor earlier, I'd have known of his intentions very clearly.

"I remember the dress I had on and I remember him commenting on it. It was green, silk tweed, and off-white, and it was nice; I loved it. It was sleeveless, and it buttoned down the front and it was very proper. I didn't ask him, but he told me he liked the quality of the material. But he didn't like the idea that I would go out in a sleeveless dress. That was not ladylike; ladies did not go out in sleeveless dresses. So I received the first piece of Frank's 'constructive criticism' on our very first meeting and I remember very well saying back to him, 'Well, you wear a European suit and you're in America.'

"I was on one side of the table and he was on the other. I can't remember what we were all talking about but he never took his black eyes off me; they held me so steadily I had to glance away. His conversation was always directed toward me; it still gives me goosebumps when I think of it. I've got to admit it was a new and exciting experience. I liked it and I didn't... I was slightly scared of him.

"He told us how he had completed his education in Rome—his father was a professor at the university there—and how he wanted to become a doctor. He said he was ambitious and he didn't think there were enough opportunities in medicine in Rome. So he had decided to emigrate to the United States. He had been accepted as an intern at Baltimore's University of Maryland Hospital. And I thought then he had courage. He was thirty-five years old, his English was poor, his Italian medical degree was worth very little in the U.S., and he still went out on a long limb and emigrated.

"So we went on listening to Frank and then up came the subject of swimming... probably Mrs. Harris had told him there was a pool on the roof of the apartment house where he could go swimming. I didn't want to go swimming. I'd got myself all dressed up. I'd had my hair specially done by the hairdresser and I didn't have a bathing suit. But Mrs. Harris got into the act—'Oh, Kay, you can use mine'—and I got conned into swimming. In those days I was always being pushed around. What people wanted me to do I did.

"We both got into swimming suits, each with a towel around us, and Mr. Harris took us upstairs in the elevator. The pool was not all that big.

"Frank wore Mr. Harris's bathing suit, and I saw at once that he had beautiful legs; I didn't look at him much except to see his face and his beautiful legs. Mr. Harris left us and we dived into the pool, and splash, my hairdo was ruined. He was a very good swimmer; I was reasonable, but one stroke of his would make two of mine. He was very powerful and I liked that—I see things in a person's character when they're in the water. But not only his face and the eyes looking at me— his entire persona overwhelmed me. The way he approached the water also fascinated me; he was in his own element. I remember being impressed with his physical strength. But I couldn't get away from his eyes, and once we were both in the water I had this sense of being intimidated, almost as if I were in the water with something that could eat me.

"His English was very poor, but I've always liked helping people who don't get on very well in the language. We had this discussion about names. Francesca had always been one of my favorite names, I said, but wasn't his a girl's name?

"He was indignant about that. Certainly not! As we splashed around he explained about the endings in Italian: the 'a' ending is feminine, the 'o' ending is masculine. Nevertheless, I think my observation struck home, because Frank didn't waste much time abandoning Francesco Maria Sandiford and changing his name officially to the Americanized Frank M. Sandiford, a decision that I think upset his mother considerably.

"There was no one else up there on the roof that late Sunday afternoon. And suddenly, without any warning at all, it started to happen. I was doing a little mild surface diving, and I was underwater, when suddenly he came up under me like a shark and grabbed me, taking me to the surface. I mean, I'd only just met him and his hands were all over me, and there he was at the side of the pool holding me tightly against him; it was obvious that sex was his prime intention. I was scared and shocked. It was so sudden. So, okay, how do you do it in a pool in bathing suits? But it seemed to me I might not be in mine much longer. Somehow I struggled free and I tell you I got out of that pool fast. Then what do you do next? Scream your head off and rush away crying 'rape'? I was so embarrassed I didn't know what to do. But even then I knew that it wasn't 'me' to make a scene. I couldn't tell Mrs. Harris what had happened. I couldn't tell anybody. Already I was hiding things about Frank. But I was really shaking when I got out of the pool. He had frightened me. And he didn't come up and apologize or anything. So I just got myself together and acted as if nothing had happened. I didn't discuss it with him and I didn't talk to Mrs. Harris about it. I rubbed myself dry and he did the same and we dressed down in the apartment.

"I drove home and he went home. He had my phone number. I don't remember if I gave it to him or Mrs. Harris gave it to him, but he said he wanted to see me again, and I didn't make any objections.

"I felt this revulsion against him, but also this excitement and fascination. I'm not trying to conceal my share of the blame. He was the most handsome, exciting, and 'different' man I had ever met. I was swept along on a tide of events that I couldn't stop to analyze and didn't want to halt. Not for a second.

"He took me to dinner a day or two later, and from there it just evolved. I know I was completely dominated by Frank from the first moment I met him, and I suppose I wanted to be dominated. Soon he was calling me every night and often several times through the night.

"I taught him English over the telephone; we'd chatter for hours. You see, he arrived in the U.S. with an English accent. His mother had taught him first of all and he had also learned from records made by English instructors. His accent was attractive. You could not tell if it was Italian. Some people thought it was French, and as his mother was French, that was understandable. He looked French. His entire parentage was mixed up. His father was born in Italy but his side of the family were originally Dutch—that's where the name Sandiford came from. Even though Frank was born in Italy and educated there, he was still—with a name like that—something of a foreigner. And Frank liked that. It set him a little apart.

"Our relationship started in this strange way. He'd ring up in the middle of the night and call me darling, and we'd just talk about anything; about the black people who came into the hospital and how he couldn't understand one word of what they were saying; how they cut each other up with knives and he sewed them up, and it was terrible. How he hated Max—Max was the Jewish guy who was nice enough to let Frank share his house when Frank first arrived in the States. As an intern, he did the whole lot: women's ward for two weeks, men's ward for another two weeks, private practice for the same period, then on to the emergency wards. It's a rotating internship, so that you get experience in different kinds of surgery.

"At that time, of course, waiting for my divorce to come through, I was not supposed to be seen in the company of gentlemen. I had to be pure and good for two years. Therefore, if my mother-in-law or Newton wanted to be difficult and gain custody of Charles, and they found out I was meeting Frank, they could say, 'She's not a fit mother.' So I was very concerned because Charles was my entire life. I was also disturbed by my parents' continued refusal to even face the fact that I was getting a divorce. So my clandestine relationship with Frank was about the only thing open to me. And it wasn't really open to me at all, because I was now Frank's possession. Sex happened immediately. I can't remember ever being with Frank in those days when he didn't have sex. And that was my feeling from the very first—it was Frank having sex; I was just "there." When we went out, we'd drive to Washington because no one knew us there, and he'd stop on the freeway not once, but twice on the same journey. It wasn't as if I was in love with him, not in the way one normally understands love. He didn't even charm me; he was always much to fast, too intense, too uncaring for anyone's needs except his own. I could never operate on his wavelength; my body and my mind couldn't work together with him—he moved like that and I moved like this. He was a snake charmer with me. But, of course, there it was— Frank was this terribly exciting, unusual man. And there was fear too, though I don't think I ever identified it as fear in those days; that sort of danger point I pushed out of the way. But, hell, when you wake up with your legs and arms tied to the bed, you're scared."

To this day Kay finds Frank's responsibility for the death of her mother both elusive and disturbing. Her mother certainly knew nothing of their actual relationship: "Mother wanted things done in a proper way, and even though Frank didn't care much for my mother, he courted her, flattered her, and she liked it. But she wanted things for me 'properly.' Mother would have had a fit if she'd known I was living with Frank. She was Irish and she would have had the troops out. I mean, zing, she would have had his head."

Kay's house at Spring Lake stood on the other side of town, twenty miles from her parents' home at Aintree Road, and during the first year of their association Frank's phone calls and visits were inevitably nocturnal, scarcely noted even by neighbors. Her mother, naturally, was frequently on the phone, often three times a day, inquiring about her grandson's food intake, bowel movements, and general well-being, and at least three times a week Kay piled Buff and Laddie, the two collie dogs, plus Baby Charles into the blue Ford Falcon station wagon and drove over to see her mother.

This was the period when Kay's mother was at her most uncomprehending about the divorce, even more reluctant to accept the truth than was Kay's father. As far as Mrs. Hupfeldt was concerned, the divorce had never happened. Kay played along, making affirmative noises; it was purposeless to protest against such irrationality.

Her mother's assumption of this attitude made Frank's position crystal clear: Kay was married; obviously Frank could be only a platonic friend. But Frank did not like being only a platonic friend. Unable to charm her mother to the degree he felt was his due, he eyed her warily and viewed her as an inconvenience.

Seven months after Frank entered Kay's life, Kay's mother fell ill. "Mom was often sick. It was a kind of personality thing with her; having headaches and temperatures. It happened every now and then; she was just a bit unwell, and no one was really worried, and Daddy knew all about it.

"Certainly Mom had been pretty sick in the past, especially during the period when she was having all those miscarriages. And once she had a gallbladder operation, which I'm sure wasn't at all pleasant. But I think Mom took out a lot of frustration by saying, 'I'm sick! I'm staying in bed. For a week.' Which she did. It was a sort of therapy.

"So this time when I talked to Mother, I told her to call the doctor; but he couldn't come so, as usual, she simply went to bed. When I got there, I knew she was sick. She was all sweaty, she had a temperature, and naturally she felt rotten. She'd had these ups and downs before— she was diabetic and you really had to watch her. I mean, she loved sweets; she'd hide them, and occasionally we had to have 'search and seize' operations to see where Mom had hidden her sweets. I mean, you'd find this giant box of Virginia Dare chocolates hidden away and half empty. These ups and downs could be dangerous for her as a diabetic, and she also had a heart condition. Anyway, I tried her doctor and I couldn't get hold of him. So I called Frank—after all, he was a doctor—

and I think I said she had the flu; the flu was going around then. And he brought me the bottle of pills, to the house."

Frank told Kay, as far as she can remember, that the pills were from Austin's Pharmacy in Baltimore, but Kay can't remember if that name was on the bottle. The pills themselves were just ordinary-looking pills; the instructions on how to use them were clear: to be taken every four hours. Kay took the pills to her mother's bedside and administered the first dose, leaving the bottle by her mother's bed. Before leaving, she made clear to both Alice and her mother the exact prescribed dose.

The next morning the phone rang at eleven o'clock. Alice's voice was urgent. "Kay, will you come over at once! Your Mom's real sick."

Kay grabbed Charles and drove swiftly across town to Aintree Road. Alice led the way upstairs.

In the bathroom, wearing her nightgown and robe, her mother lay on the floor, her head turned to one side. Without touching her, Kay knew instantly that she was dead. Her own heart suddenly felt empty, as if all the blood had drained away. A surge of sadness so possessed her that she had to close her eyes. She dropped on one knee and gently touched her mother's forehead. It was cold—cold when it was always warm. Sixty-one years old, and looking fifty. So pretty. Kay looked up at Alice and saw the tears on her cheeks.

Winking hers away, Kay stood up and went to the phone. From the moment she said, "Daddy, it's Mom...," Dr. Hupfeldt tried to delay the truth by breaking in and saying, "But I looked in at her before I left and she seemed—" And then he couldn't say any more.

A host of people came in one capacity or another, but Frank was there first. "My feeling," Kay said later, "was that he just flew. He examined Mom and he kept whispering to me, 'Don't let them perform an autopsy. Don't let them perform an autopsy.' I couldn't understand what he meant. An autopsy? I mean, there was no reason.

"Then Speedy and Daddy arrived, back from the office, and Daddy was in a terrible state, hysterical and sobbing, and I had to try and comfort him.

"That evening Frank repeated to me that there mustn't be an autopsy. He said that the pills he'd given me were poison, and because I had given her the pills, I was responsible for her death. Maybe he said it purely for sadistic reasons, just trying to torment me, but I was never certain.

"As the days went by, the chill of what he'd said entered my bones, and for years I really believed I had killed my mother. I'd have dreams about it, agonized dreams asking myself what I should do—should I confess my guilt in a letter to be opened after I died? I just couldn't absolve myself from the responsibility. It stayed with me for all the years that I lived with him. It still does."

During the period of Frank's residency no one knew him better than Kay, and no one but she knew how he was dominating and debauching her even to the extent of trying to make her give up her studies at Hopkins.

"Sometimes he insisted on making love just before I was due at class, so I couldn't go to class. And sometimes when I'd park in the parking lot of Hopkins he was there and on to me. I was taking a bunch of stuff, a lot of history courses, never less than three nights a week. I went to summer school too; I wanted to catch up. And Frank would be waiting for me. He knew where I parked. I'd have a class at five thirty or six, and I'd get there a bit early, thinking I might have coffee with one of the other students or go to the library to look something up, and he'd be there. He'd just grab me and make love with me in the back of the car, and by that time I was so disheveled and destroyed I couldn't go to class, and then he'd leave me.

"I'll never forget my final exams; he knew I was taking my finals and there he was. In the exams I flunked all except one. He absolutely destroyed me that week. Two tests I didn't even take. I was so upset I didn't even go into the examination room. So later, in order to get my degree, I had to make up exams.

"Frank definitely didn't want me to get that college degree. Women didn't do such things. Women didn't compete with men. Especially men like Frank."

Nor did he want her getting out of shape.

"He'd give me pills all the time. I'd either be too fat or too skinny or too tired or too hyped-up or whatever—making love all the time is exhausting; your whole physiology, your body, gets out of kilter. You don't even breed dogs that way. I wish I had pictures of how I looked during that time. Eat, eat, eat, he'd say, and I'd eat, eat, eat. Anything just to keep him quiet. And then when I'd gained thirty pounds he'd say, 'You're too fat; you've got to lose weight,' and that meant more pills to lose weight. Then it would be, 'Why are you tired? What's the matter with you? You need something to make you sleep.' So I'd be taking diet pills and then I'd be taking something to put me to sleep. I mean, I was a pill-head; I took whatever he said. Every time he thought I was pregnant, he'd give me pills to get rid of it.

"In this way, Frank became a constant, and clandestine, companion to me. Sometimes he would appear without a car at the house at strange hours, and always I would let him in, partly because I didn't want the neighbors to think he was there spending the night, partly because—I admit it—I wanted him, and partly because he demanded to be let in. At other times he would ring me and tell me to pick him up, and we would return to the house together. We never went to his apartment, which he hated. Then suddenly he moved in completely.

"For Frank, it was quite an easy adjustment. The doorbell rang, and there he was standing on the front porch with his suitcase in his hand and a smile on his lips. I had to make a quick decision. I either had to make a scene on the front porch, which the neighbors would observe, or I could let him in and make the best of it. I let him in.

"Sex was never ending. And he took this delight in ridiculing American conformity by his sexual behavior. The ladies' powder room, for example... what a ridiculous idea, he said, two lavatories, one for men and one for women. So, to show his contempt, on at least two occasions he waited until the coast was clear and no one was likely to come in, then marched into the women's room and took me then and there."

Certainly Frank had so excelled in carnal knowledge of Kay's body that sometimes she considered herself a mere participant, an aide-de-camp in the bedroom, bathroom, swimming pool, or car. Other times she thought that the number of times he stopped the car on the hard shoulder of the Baltimore–Washington expressway should have qualified him for the *Guinness Book of World Records*. His priapic urgency seemed almost a religious necessity, as if he expected to expire within minutes of the act and needed her testimony to his continuing virility to get him into heaven.

There were two reasons why Kay decided to sell the house at Spring Lake and move back with her father. One, he needed her. Her mother's death had left him bereft, of her gaiety, her chatter, her fussiness and her laughter; the house without her was hollow and empty. Yes, Alice looked after him, sadly creeping around the place, and Speedy did his best to cheer him up. But, still, he needed Kathleen.

The other, equally urgent reason was Frank.

Still clinging to the remnants of Baltimore respectability, Kay was under constant stress during this time, torn between Frank's incessant demands and the belief—which helped to sustain her—that Roger was always available as an escape valve, that within a matter of months, somehow or other, she would be safely married to Roger and this scandalous episode with Frank would end.

Kay knew that, if ever she was to free herself from Frank's domination, her father's need was her opportunity. She was aware that Frank was altogether too happy living in the ranch house situated on old farmland at Spring Lake. He had procured for himself a pretty divorcée, with wealthy-looking parents, and a large house surrounded by a third of an acre of lawn. There was a dining room, with a veranda where he could eat outside in the summer; living room; music room, with a black baby grand Steinway piano; master bedroom decorated with wallpaper of little pink flowers that Kay loved; dressing room; TV room; and, in the basement, a big paneled pool room with a full-sized Brunswick pool table, not to mention the maid's room and bath.

"I suppose you could say there was a certain expediency about our relationship, advantageous to both. I wasn't sleeping anyway, and it was nice to talk to someone, and I helped his English. I was alone in the house with the baby and I was trying to be big and brave, but I'd never been alone before; I'd always had a maid or Speedy or somebody. To be alone, totally, was something I didn't like.

"From Mrs. Harris's point of view, I suppose, I was probably a girl looking for another husband. But from my point of view, I was a girl who wasn't allowed to see another man for a year and a half, until the divorce was finalized, and it was getting pretty boring sitting around for a year and a half staring at the floor."

Frank did not welcome the news that Kay was selling the house and moving back into Aintree Road with her father, and that he therefore would have to find another apartment. But Kay had made up her mind. This was her chance, if not to end their relationship, then at least to keep it within bounds. She had, however, missed one important point. Frank had no intention of ending anything. Kay belonged to him.

Nor was Frank inclined to accept Roger's continuing presence on the scene.

"He simply loathed Roger, for he knew that even for him I was not going to give up my weekends; Roger was my one lifeline to stability and reality. So Frank would deliver me to the station at Baltimore and dear Roger, without the faintest notion of what was going on, would meet me at Penn Station and on Sunday night put me back on the train, for Frank to meet me when I arrived. Frank would take me straight to his apartment to make sure I hadn't had sex with Roger—checking for telltale bruises, always for bruises. He always sneered at Roger because he was Jewish. 'You think you can just get married,' he used to say. 'The Jews just don't do things that way. There'll be an arrangement. The fathers will get together and your father will pay over a dowry, and then it will be all right. You'll just be sold.'"

That made Kay angry because she didn't believe one word of it. Roger was not like that. The idea of a financial settlement, a contract about what was essentially a thing of the heart, was anathema to her.

Sustained by this firm belief, she passed her father's study one night and saw that his light was still burning. He had probably gone to bed and forgotten to switch it off. She went in.

Abstractedly, she looked down at his desk. On the blotter lay a letter typed on stiff legal paper embossed with the heavy letterhead of a firm of lawyers in New York. It was a letter from Roger's father, a letter from one well-to-do father to another concerning the marriage of his son and the monetary and property arrangements—so much for an apartment, so much for living expenses, so much for Roger's finishing his law studies—that therefore should be made.

Kay was devastated. "I just freaked out. I just wanted to cry. I wanted to run. I had a girl friend who was always inviting me up to her aunt's cottage in Pennsylvania. I rang her and she said, 'Sure, let's go up straightaway.'

"I arranged with Alice to look after Baby Charles, left a note for Daddy. We got into the car and drove up to this holiday resort full of bars and dances and parties. I stayed there two weeks and I don't think I slept more than two hours a night. I was a caricature of the film heroine who, abandoned, decides to burn the candle at both ends.

"I remember one night I telephoned Roger, really called out to him for help, but he was out at a concert—and I felt somehow he would be. I spoke to his friend and said I've got to talk to Roger, I must talk to Roger... but I didn't leave a phone number, and I suppose I thought if Roger really cared he'd come flying to Baltimore and find out where I was and come and save me. But Roger really wasn't like that, and he didn't know it was an emergency. He wrote me a letter saying he was sorry he wasn't there, but he would be at the apartment for the next two weeks waiting for me to call. And I didn't. I think it was the way he responded; he just didn't sense my need. It was like that time with Andrew—he didn't come when he was really needed, and it wasn't his fault either."

Kay wanted Roger to save her from Frank, to save her from herself, in fact. But in these days she was bewildered. She was afraid of Frank's domination, but she was also aware that in both her other courtships, the past one with Andrew and the present one with Roger, some small dimension, some assurance of security, was absent.

So, irritated both by her own attitude and the fact that their relationship was never quite right, she started to scold Roger and say little mocking things and be a bit nasty. He'd let her have her way, accept what she said with a smile, try and calm her down. She knew she was being unkind and she really didn't want to act that way. It was such a shame. Both Andrew and Roger possessed what she needed so badly—warmth and compassion—but neither of them quite understood. How could they when she did not understand herself? Her yearnings. The inward tumult. Perhaps latent feminism... a sort of revolt. She sang different songs.

Thus once Frank, direct, assertive, and demanding, was on the scene, Roger inevitably began to fade, and Frank, knowing he'd made Kay pregnant, used his paternity as a weapon, saying that if Kay would give up Roger and agree to marry him, he would perform an abortion. No, they could not be married immediately. It wasn't convenient. He had to qualify professionally first. A baby would only get in the way. That could come later, when they had money and prestige. Kay didn't want to be an unmarried mother, although she wanted the baby. But she could see Frank's point of view. Indeed, she was learning quite quickly to see only Frank's view.

She has sincere regrets.

"Roger was such a nice guy. He sent me letters and I didn't read them; I threw them away. He was probably telling me he loved me. But sometimes you can't carry the burden of what you've done; you just turn your back and walk away, and probably it was the very best thing I ever did for Roger. Now he can hate me. If I'd tried to be reasonable, and we'd talked about it, he might still be in love with me."

7

"SUICIDE never entered my mind until I met Frank," said Kay San-diford, remembering those first years in Baltimore with him. "Meeting Frank was like body surfing, the body riding the waves, and then you get dashed against the pebbles on the beach. He was full of passion and emotion all the time; I couldn't control it. He was always looking for something beyond his reach. And Frank took; he was a great taker. I had never met this in my whole life before. Newton and I were like brother and sister. I'd known Newton all my life; making love with Newton was like going for a swim—nothing extraordinary. I never got angry with him; even when I divorced him, I was never angry with him— just disappointed that he didn't raise the level or the temperature of life.

"It was a horrible time of my life those first years with Frank with all those pills he knew about. I was a real freak-out and I think I was getting near the end of my strength. I suppose it was the orderly person in me that had got submerged, drowned. He was going to marry me, but not then. He was going to marry me when it suited him; and that was when he'd completed his studies. But when would that be? Sure, he knew where *he* was going. But I didn't. Then I got pregnant again, and I really wanted the baby. But I knew Frank wouldn't allow it. So in my confused state I decided to end it all.

"I didn't know where I was or what I was doing. It was two or three o'clock when I arrived at Frank's new apartment. I knew he wouldn't be there. He had to spend every other night on call at the University of Maryland Hospital. I remember putting the pillows on the bed and settling down to study for a Russian history exam, which I knew I'd never take. After about two hours of studying I went out on the fire escape. I guess it was late March, and the sun was setting and the light was beautiful. In Baltimore at that time of year, the evening sky has such clarity, and the silhouettes against it are breathtaking. So that was to be my last sunset. Then I went into the bathroom where Frank kept all of his pills.

"He'd told me what they were: if you want to lose ten pounds, take these; if you want to go to sleep, take these—and as I wanted to go to sleep forever, I took a whole handful. They were big, fat, white pills. And I lay on the bed and just drifted away, and then Frank, for some reason or other, came home. He knew what I'd done immediately and pushed a tube down my throat. You've got to be a doctor to know where the stomach is and he sucked out the contents. Must have been horrible, for sleeping pills have a terrible taste. He made me throw up. He gave me coffee and stuff and walked me around. And then he left. And I stayed there a while. It took me a while to get up. And I thought that I had lost the baby because of all that commotion and I didn't know that I hadn't and I became aware shortly, in a month or so, that I was still pregnant."

Kay wanted the baby. She wanted to get married. She wanted to get on with a real life, and she told Frank about it one night in a Baltimore restaurant. Why not have the baby? What difference would a few months make?

Apparently all the difference in the world to Frank. The child had to be aborted.

She said: "He told me it was a boy, and I never knew how he could do that to his own son. But he did, and I never understood that. I never forgave him for it either. It was the one thing I didn't forgive him for. I still don't."

Frank had it all worked out. Following the proper routine, he had already asked Dr. Hupfeldt for Kathleen's hand, and Dr. Hupfeldt had pushed his glasses up onto his forehead and said disapprovingly, "Looks to me as if my daughter is always going to be a twenty-thousand-dollar-a-year-girl, and you look to me as if you're always going to be a five-thousand-dollar-a-year-man." But he voiced no other opposition. He knew his daughter was of age and that she would make up her own mind. If she was in love with this man—whom he'd distrusted from the moment they met—there was nothing he could do about it.

Frank, having now completed his internship, intended to move on and up. He had also decided that he wanted to specialize in thoracic surgery. His chief of surgery at the University of Maryland pointed him in the right direction by suggesting he contact the Texas Medical Center in Houston, already reputedly one of the three most important medical centers in the United States, especially for heart and chest surgery. He suggested that Frank apply to Dr. DeBakey, a pioneer and one of the world's leading experts in that field, for a thoracic internship. Dr. DeBakey accepted Frank for one year as a fellow in general surgery at a salary of five thousand dollars a year, so Herbert Hupfeldt's prognostication proved right, at least at the start; even though, in the future, Frank's salary would dwarf that figure.

The next step was clear, Kay recalls.

"Now that Frank had his appointment in Texas, he decided it was time to get married. I didn't really want to go to Texas. All I knew about it was that it was full of cowboys and rattlesnakes, but Frank had said that he would only be down there for a year and then he'd come back and go into practice with these two other young surgeons on the Eastern Shore, which was a beautiful part of Maryland that I adored. Frank told everyone we were going to get married at the Church of the Transfiguration in New York, which he thought was an impressive place, but actually we were married in a courthouse on the Eastern Shore, and I remember I supplied the seventeen dollars and ninety-five cents for my wedding ring. We had to get a couple of witnesses off the street, but it was a pretty little place and I loved it. I still have my wedding bouquet of daisies. A week after the wedding we went back to Baltimore, where Daddy laid on a reception at the Baltimore Country Club with all the guests Frank wanted, including his mother and his sister, Maria, who had also married an American and now lived in Washington. It was a champagne dinner with a wedding cake, and what was left of the cake

Alice wrapped up, and on the wrapping wrote in her neat, careful hand, 'Wedding Cake Number Two.'"

It was the suddenness of the attack that really frightened Kay.

"We'd been married about a week when we got back. We went to my father's house. My father was away for the night and we were there together at dinner. In the dining room there's a wall made of glass and when we got up from the dinner table, I looked into the mirror. We turned toward the mirror, and I looked at Frank and I said I felt we looked like a nice couple. I just meant that I thought we looked nice together and he...he...he turned and he...he looked at me and he had these dark eyes, just dark with nothing inside, no feeling, flat. And he started hitting me and I was so surprised. He hit me. He hit me with his fist, and Frank never hit me with his fist. He kept hitting me and I remember I didn't understand why and I...I fell down eventually...I mean after a while. And he started kicking me and I remember I kept thinking, *why is he doing this?* I didn't know what I'd done. I don't know what happened after that; I passed out. I don't remember. After that he carried me upstairs and he put me to bed and he undressed me and he...I remember he went in my bathroom. We were in my bedroom, where I'd slept when I lived in my father's house, and there's a bathroom and he put me in bed...close to the bathroom. He didn't...he didn't have to do that.

"As he bathed my face he told me that every wife needs a good beating to learn authority, to recognize authority. He didn't have to do that. He didn't. I knew. I knew. He didn't have to do it. He really didn't. And it wasn't...it wasn't necessary. I knew his authority; but he was nice. He was really nice after that. That was the only time he really hit me with his fists in my face. My face was a mess."

Kay could remember hearing Frank on the phone to her father that evening—the low, reasoning tones of the professional physician, soothing, explanatory:

"Nothing serious, I do assure you. We'd stopped at the light, and this fool of a driver—No, I don't think he'd been drinking; just inattentive, careless—came straight into the back of us. Kay hit the windshield...thrown forward...face cut and bruised, but don't worry, nothing serious, nothing broken. Plastic surgery? Oh, no, you will see for yourself. Nothing I can't handle. Yes, resting in bed. I'll keep her in bed for a few days. . . ."

Her father had walked into the room, stood over the bed, looked down at her. One of Kay's eyes was blackened and puffed up; but she could focus with the other. She could see the square serious face, the graying hair, the firm mouth that had smiled down at her all her life, the staff of her security and love. And she knew he knew the truth. And she knew as he looked down at her with such sadness in his eyes, at what had become of "his little girl," she knew the ache he felt inside. He didn't even have to read the importuning in her blackened eye to know what she wanted him to do—"Let things pass, Daddy. Don't make a scene. Walk away." But he couldn't do that. He wouldn't make a scene. But he couldn't condone this brutal assault on his child.

He stood at the side of her bed for what seemed an hour, utterly still, absolutely silent, while Frank babbled on about the details of the "accident."

It took Kay years to understand that Frank always believed people believed everything he said. Even his wildest concoctions were delivered in measured tones. And when the listener nodded or smiled or said yes politely, Frank *knew* he was believed. It was self-deception of a very rare kind.

At length, Dr. Hupfeldt turned and faced Frank. He stared straight into Frank's face without saying a word. Frank's eyes were immediately somewhere else as he went on acting his part, perhaps by this time almost believing the story he was inventing, hardly noticing when Kay's father had left the room without saying a single word from start to finish.

Kay's father never forgave Frank. He never wanted to speak to Frank again. Nor would he have, except for the knowledge that if he maintained an icy silence the unpleasantness would only rebound against his daughter. So he answered monosyllabically, never held a serious conversation, choked off argument or discussion as soon as it came up. Frank hardly noticed. He was used to talking to himself; the old man was just not on his frequency. Frank often lectured Kay on her father's shortcomings.

Almost unconsciously, as the light aircraft banked around to land, Kay ran her fingers lightly across the contours of her face, reassuring herself that the bruises that had blackened her eyes and puffed her lips were now barely discernible. Yes, she would arrive at the hotel in Little Dix Bay triumphant, looking and feeling like a honeymoon bride.

Pressing her face against the aircraft window, she could glimpse the emerald ocean breaking against the reef, the sandy beaches cut like white fingernails into little coves, the palm fronds rushing past below their wheels, and, unable to repress her excitement, she shouted above the clamoring engine, "Frank, look! The island *is* shaped like a pregnant woman. That's why Columbus named it Virgin Gorda—the fat virgin."

Weeks earlier, assessing honeymoon prospects, Kay had chosen the Virgin Islands, that extended chain of atolls stretching westward along latitudes where the Caribbean Sea blurs cartographically into the Atlantic Ocean.

Celebrating occasions had always been an important part of Kay's esprit. The Irish half of her made a point of celebrating holidays—Christmas, July Fourth, Thanksgiving—while the German half regularly scrutinized the little green leather book indented with symbols and reminders, the better not to forget someone's birthday. She also commemorated sad occasions, such as funerals, but mostly her ceremoniousness was upbeat, focusing on weddings, of course—and honeymoons. Now, they were something! Especially if it was your second, and the first hadn't been all that exciting.

Frank, slumped back in his seat, eyes closed, head tilted back, his handsome Italian profile damp with perspiration, was conspicuously uninterested in the similarity of their island to a fat virgin, completely indifferent to Columbus's poetic fancy. Tentatively, to soothe him, to show him that she loved him, Kay touched his arm with her small, soft hand, and immediately, with the quick reflex action she was getting to know so well, he pulled away. At once and instinctively she adjusted to the small rejection. It was understandable that he was upset—it had been a long, tiring flight from Baltimore to the islands, and from Puerto Rico to Little Dix Bay. Frank, she knew, was happy flying only when in jumbo jets, with pretty stewardesses patrolling the aisles. He was her husband. She would understand.

The aircraft settled like a buzzing wasp on the grassy runway and taxied around to the flat concrete terminal. A polite black man in white shorts and a peaked cap was waiting to drive them to their hotel, and Kay's intoxication increased with every bend in the road. The contrast between Baltimore's busy, traffic-filled streets and this flower-filled, seabright island was stunning. This was what Frank needed—a change of scenery, ocean breezes, relaxation, a honeymoon!

At the hotel Kay purred with delight at their hillside bungalow. "Look at the view—just look!" She smoothed the hems of the pink sheets laid out on the bed—a specialty for honeymoon couples—observed with fascination the old-fashioned ceiling fan slicing noiselessly through the warm air, rearranged the bowl of flowers, and discovered the complimentary bottle of rum, another gesture of hospitality from the thoughtful management. Frank by now had his suitcase open and was strewing clothes around the room in a delirium of impatience. "Where the hell are my pills? Where are those goddamn pills!" By way of distraction, Kay held up the rum for his scrutiny. "There's ice and a bottle of Coke too," she said.

Like many Europeans, Frank was not a heavy drinker, but now he exclaimed, "Thank God!" and reached for the bottle. He needed liquid to wash down the pills—potions to give him strength and make him feel better. He splashed a generous three inches into a tumbler, added ice cubes and Coke, drank thirstily, collapsed into an armchair, and announced that he felt lousy. By the time Kay had finished hanging her clothes in the closet, he was halfway through the bottle and insisting that there was no way he was going to make dinner. No dinner; he needed sleep.

That evening in the dining room, wearing the dress specially selected for the occasion, Kay picked her way through shrimp cocktail, grilled sea bass, and fruit salad, accepted the headwaiter's sympathy at Frank's indisposition, smiled at the other guests, and returned to the bungalow to find Frank snoring between his pink sheets. He didn't wake up.

They spent the next day snorkeling in the cove and Frank got sunburned. Returning belatedly to the cottage, he announced with frigid abruptness that his skin was too painful to endure being touched. Kay, hurt, didn't reply. Plainly the honeymoon was not going to follow the usual pattern.

Dutifully, in her round schoolgirl handwriting, she wrote to her father: "Little Dix is a small Caribbean gem, clean and civilized. Very British. The compound is situated in a cove on the island, protected, with a pretty beach and a Caribbean blue sea. The focus of the resort cosmetically is the dining room and terrace built in a half-moon design with a thatched roof high above the beach. Red and orange bougainvillea cascades its way from the terrace down to the sea and fragrant frangipani and other brightly painted tropical flowers are everywhere. Once a day the launch from St. Johns comes in and causes a lot of activity; otherwise life inside the cove has a soft tropical rhythm about it. The fish life within the reef is amazing. One loses hours just enjoying the looking and the feeding. Sea urchins, some fire coral, and a solitary barracuda are the only unfriendlies one might encounter. After a marvelous day of Caribbean incubation one is ready for the fresh, fruit-flavored rum drinks and to sit outside the cottage high on the rock and to watch the pinkish cast of day's end come into the cove. After, the waters glitter like small silver coins reflecting against the boats and finally the extensive sweep of complete darkness fills the bay."

On the second day Frank decided they would hire a Sailfish and go out beyond the reef. Kay knew nothing about sailing, but sitting in the stern in her one-piece swimsuit, skimming across the rippled surface of Little Dix Bay toward the gap in the coral reef, she was quite relaxed. Outside the reef it was a different story; she was not quite so happy as they met the swell and the breeze freshened in the open ocean. Frank, however, seemed untroubled, handling their little craft expertly as they leaped and bounced through the waves. Suddenly they had left civilization. The sky was enormous, the land far away, the sea elemental. Kay adjusted to her new perspective and found it exhilarating. They ran parallel to the shore for about half an hour before, with a rattle of sail and a swing of the boom, Frank went about and they surged back along the edge of the reef. They were about three hundred yards from the opening that led back to the cove, and Kay, legs up to her chin, happy to feel the wind in her hair and the sun on her back, was completely unprepared for Frank's violent action—the sudden brutal shove, which sent her sprawling overboard. It was a shock as stunning as a sudden blow. She went under, came up gasping for air, and the boat was already thirty feet away and moving fast. Above the wind she heard him shout, "Swim back! You swim back!"

Kay didn't waste her breath trying to shout. A larger than average swell dropped her into a trough and when it lifted her up again the Sailfish was fifty yards away. She thought—trying hard to believe it, because by now she had experienced Frank's sudden crazy impulses before—*It's a joke. It's one of Frank's nonfunny jokes.* She knew at once that she was seriously in danger. The water around her feet felt cold, and the current was strong. She treaded water. She knew she mustn't panic; she had to relax, keep her head, swim steadily and slowly in the right direction, maintain her distance from the reef, be careful not to gulp sea water instead of air. She tried to lift herself out of the water, craning upward, but all she could glimpse were the crests of the waves. Frank must have turned in through the reef and into the bay. Surely he must be waiting for her there in the calm waters of the cove.

She struggled on, swimming first the crawl, then plowing on for a few yards with the sidestroke. The half hour it took her to reach the entrance to the cove was one of the most distressing experiences of her life. But once she reached the gap, the swirling seas lifted her and gave her buoyancy, washing her through into calmer water. There was no sign of Frank or the Sailfish, but the sight of the distant beach and shoreside buildings gave her courage. She turned on her back, floating gently in the clear water. She was very tired and knew she still had a long swim to shore.

Slowly she swam in toward the empty beach, struggled up through the shallows, and sat, utterly exhausted, on the sand. When she recovered a little, she walked up the cliff to the bungalow, took a warm shower, and changed into a light dress. She found Frank sitting in the bar at the hotel, sipping a Campari and soda. He smiled at her, his suntan accentuating the whiteness of his large, even teeth. Obviously she had passed the test. She was too tired to even smile back.

That evening, after dinner, things changed for the better: they met Mike and Paula. Frank liked Mike and Paula immediately because they provided the means for bigger fish to hunt and deeper diving. Mike, in his early thirties, with close-cropped brown hair, a rugged face, and a bold nose jutting out like a headland between watchful green eyes, was an ex-marine and a trained scuba diver. Mustered out in California, he'd gotten a job, saved his wages, married Paula, and built his boat, the *Reef Runner*, a sturdy little oceangoing cabin cruiser. Together they had decided to opt out of the ordinary and head for the far-off Caribbean, hoping to make a living out of chartering their boat, teaching scuba diving, and selling lobsters and fish to the holiday hotels.

In view of his later remarks, Mike must have watched Frank and Kay set out in the Sailfish that morning, seen Frank return alone and head for the bar, and also observed Kay struggle in from the sea an hour afterward. But Mike was taciturn; words seeped out of him very slowly.

Small, slender Paula, blonde and bronzed, with a snub nose and a wide smile, did most of the talking although she was not exactly loquacious either. Be that as it may, the end result of their meeting was that Mike and Paula would take Frank and Kay lobster fishing in the *Reef Runner* the next day.

The next morning, inevitably, the sun rose in a cloudless sky, but beyond the reef the swells were still large and menacing. This time, Kay decided that no power on earth was going to get her into that water. She felt grateful for the *Reef Runner*: solid, a big engine drumming beneath the deck. With Paula at the wheel pacing her patrols, engine idling but ready to throttle into powerful action should either of the bobbing red snorkels of Frank and Mike appear to to be in trouble, Kay felt secure. Frank was a strong swimmer and, equipped with snorkel, fins, and spear gun, he was quite at home in the pitching seas. With fishing baskets attached to their belts, he and Mike spent the morning probing the steep shelving of the reef for lobster. Frank returned fairly frequently for a rest; he wasn't in top physical condition like Mike was, but he caught his share. Mike returned only to deliver his catch, tipping his bag onto the deck near Kay's feet, grinning at her exclamations of fear, pity, and admiration for the brilliant blue-black spiky creatures harvested from the sea.

Toward dusk they cruised back along the reef, and Kay, weary but content, toasted to a golden brown by the salt wind and the hot sun, compared their peaceful run through the gap into the cove with her exhausting experience twenty-four hours earlier. The sense of tranquility in the cove was therapeutic. Happily they agreed to repeat the expedition the following morning.

It was late in the afternoon of the next day when Mike made his unexpected announcement. He heaved himself back aboard, pushed his mask up on his forehead, and looked quizzically at Kay, who said, "I think Paula's getting a bit anxious about Frank. She's having trouble keeping his snorkel in sight."

"Frank's okay," Mike said abruptly. "I've just left him. He can always take care of himself." Dripping water, he sat down on the gunnel and fixed her with his green eyes. Trying to sound casual, he said, apropos of nothing that had occurred between them before, "You know, when we first met, I didn't think you were a real honeymoon couple at all."

Kay wrinkled her eyes under her sunglasses, not understanding what he was getting at. In Baltimore strangers—well, comparative strangers—didn't make personal remarks like that.

"But we *are* a honeymoon couple," she said. "We were married two weeks ago—June twenty-first, to be exact."

Mike paused, bending to tighten the heel straps on his fins. "I didn't mean it like that," he said, and Kay sensed that he was struggling in deeper water than he encountered in his scuba diving. Then, taking a deep breath, he blurted, "I know you love Frank, but I don't think Frank loves you."

Having got his load off his chest, Mike stood up, picked up his spear gun, and dived over the side. Kay watched him disappear in a flurry of bubbles and fins. She felt vaguely disquieted. She never forgot his words but she didn't mention them to anyone. It was only during the bitter months after the shooting that they resurfaced in her consciousness. Then she wondered how Mike, the withdrawn marine turned fisherman, observing both Frank and herself over such a short period, felt it necessary to deliver his odd warning. Sometimes she wondered if his ancestry, like hers, included a great-grandmother raised in the pale mists of Ireland, who could intuitively foresee the currents of human tragedy and the wrecks that littered the future.

In the future the psychiatrists and analysts would be able to document with pitiless clarity the patterns, inevitable as a Greek tragedy, that began with that first domination of Frank Sandiford over his bride. But for the moment none could anticipate the black tragedy that would strike on January 29, 1980.

The rest of the honeymoon passed smoothly enough. Frank and Kay did not make love. Frank spent a lot of time lying in the bathtub reading novels by Mickey Spillane.

"By the time the six days were up," Kay said, "we were both ready to go home."

8

KAY paid one advance visit to Houston to check out with Frank the lay of the land. They stayed at the Holiday Inn. She hated practically everything she saw. The city was all too spread out, with freeways racing in every direction. You couldn't walk anywhere. As she had suspected, it was all too Wild West.

However, it was now her husband's place of work, and a wife must be at her husband's side, so she was prepared to make the best of it.

As a wedding gift, Kay's father had given them a Buick station wagon, which they used for the journey to Texas. Maria, Frank's sister, who lived in Washington with her American husband, gave them an apricot poodle named Mirabelle.

Kay enjoyed the first part of the journey to Texas, and enjoyed particularly having Charles—on holiday from Switzerland—with them. Crossing the Mississippi over a high bridge was one of the highlights of the journey. Three nights on the road, however, rather dulled her enthusiasm, and they arrived at their destination late at night, tired and worn out.

The precise destination was a racing stable on the outskirts of town, an address given them by a friend of the family whose niece ran the place. She welcomed them as if they were old and close friends, hugging and kissing Kay, and then hugging and kissing her a second time around.

"She was very horsey looking, and she took an immediate liking to me," Kay said. "It just wasn't my scene; I just didn't understand what was going on. There she was continuing to hug and kiss me, and showing us the terribly grubby accommodations and announcing that there wasn't even a shower in the room. Maybe it was just natural affection, but I was very suspicious, as I'd read something about lesbianism, and I thought, *Gee, this is more than I get from Frank.*"

Frank was very cool toward her suspicions, saying it was all in her mind. Kay knew that it wasn't, but she had made up her mind in any case that *one* night was all she was going to spend in that racing stable.

There was, however, one difficulty. She had by this time discovered one of Frank's less attractive characteristics. He never did anything until the last minute; he never allowed enough time for what he had to do, and when he discovered that he didn't have enough time, he flew off the handle blaming nature, his friends, his wife—especially his wife.

Now he revealed that, having arrived at Houston in the late evening, he was due to appear at the hospital and report for duty at seven a.m. This meant he would commandeer the station wagon, and Kay and Charles would be left without wheels and at the mercy of the horsey niece.

There was no way, Kay insisted, that this was going to happen. She would also get up at dawn, deliver Frank to the hospital on time, and then go off in the station wagon and search for some sort of accommodation. It might turn out to be a stop-gap, but anything was better than another night at the corral.

Accordingly, after she delivered Frank, she bought a newspaper, found a telephone booth, and with a handful of nickels began to telephone numbers in the apartments-for-rent advertisements. She found a vacancy in an apartment building that had just reopened after having been condemned. She went to investigate and found that the apartment was awful. But it had to do. Two hundred dollars a month, one bedroom, a kitchen, bathroom and shower. No furniture. So she went through the ads and yellow pages again and discovered a store that rented all sorts of furniture—modern, French, Early American. She drove there, looked around, selected a bed, chest of drawers, table, and four chairs—instant home-making. Charles, having finished his holiday, went back to school in Switzerland and the newlyweds moved in.

As a thoracic fellow assisting DeBakey in the operating theater, Frank worked very hard. He'd work three days in the hospital for every one day out, and then all he wanted to do was sleep. Kay reconciled herself to a situation she regarded as only temporary and sweated it out, sitting in that apartment through the long, baking-hot Houston summer. She had no car; Frank took that every day. There was nowhere to walk; there are no sidewalks in Houston. And no television—Frank thought television a waste of time. So Kay just sat and read one paperback after another. Daddy would occasionally send her money and she'd go up to Baltimore for a weekend. But she knew she couldn't stand this life for long.

Eventually, when Frank came home one weekend, she tried to sound calm and rational when she said, "Frank, this just isn't going to work out. I think we should get a divorce." She knew at once from Frank's face that she had no hope. She'd thought it through camly and rationally from her point of view but hadn't really examined Frank's. He'd lost his virginity in the eyes of the Church; everyone knew they were married, and the last thing he wanted was the stigma of a divorce. She never forgot his thin smile as he said, "There won't be any divorce. Ever. You see, you'll never leave me alive."

What finally saved her life was tennis. She knew she had to get out of the house, knew she must move. So she bought a racket and a can of balls and trudged over to the tennis courts in Memorial Park. The Houston Ladies Tennis Association took pity on the lonely young woman appearing at the side of the court holding a racket and a can of balls and smiling hopefully. Sure, she could join in. She was welcome.

Every day from then on, increasing her circle of tennis friends and improving with practice, Kay would play singles in the morning, at least three sets, then have a cheeseburger or a sandwich with the girls and go out and play a few sets of doubles in the afternoon. At three one of her tennis partners would drop her off at the apartment. She'd shower and hope that Frank would come home. If he didn't—and as often as not he didn't—she'd make dinner for herself, read another paperback, and go to bed. But tennis kept her healthy and gave her an immediate reason for staying alive.

Meanwhile, Frank's ambition to become a heart surgeon had received a setback. With the end of his one year of fellowship approaching, he applied for a residency. If successful, it meant he had to spend only two more years in training before taking his first exam. But that year the Thoracic Examination Board decided that applicants should have a three-year residency in heart surgery before moving on. There also seemed some doubt whether the first year with DeBakey would count, and Frank became very depressed.

Then two developments altered their lives. First, Kay's father, knowing that she was not happy in Houston and that among the reasons was the apartment she lived in, said he would buy the couple a house; she could start looking for one. He also began to provide an income of a thousand dollars a month.

"I had fun looking for the house and getting all excited about it," Kay recalls. "I literally walked the streets around the hospital, looking for some place I liked. And on Wordsworth—this really pretty, tree-lined avenue with pleasant little houses set back from the road—I saw one which just took my eye. A middle-aged woman was gardening and I said to her, 'I just love your house.' She looked at me a little startled at first, then said, 'Well, my husband died a few months ago'—it turned out he was a judge—'and I'm thinking of moving into an apartment.' I said, 'Well, how much do you want for it?' She said, 'I don't know.' I said, 'Can you find out?' She said, 'Yes.' I said, 'Okay, I'll come back tomorrow.' So I went back the next day and she'd talked to somebody and they'd told her to ask twenty-eight thousand dollars. I said, 'Fine, let me see if I can raise twenty-eight thousand dollars, 'cause I really want your house.'

"I called Daddy and I can still hear his voice getting hoarse with outrage. 'Twenty-eight thousand dollars! Jesus Christ, Kay, couldn't you find something cheaper than that?' I said 'Daddy, it's beautiful; it's divine; I've been all over it; it's marvelous. It looks just like an Andrew Wyeth barn.'"

Daddy considered that last debatable point and conceded. He sent Kay twenty-eight thousand dollars.

The second development that turned the tide was an unexpected stroke of luck for Frank. Denton Cooley, one of the most successful and famous heart surgeons in Houston and therefore in the world, had recently terminated his association with DeBakey, and with private funds and on his own initiative, he had chosen that moment to found his own Texas Heart Institute. Cooley anticipated that heart surgery, still in its infancy, would soon become commonplace. He now invited Frank to become his first thoracic resident, and Frank accepted with alacrity.

As a result of these developments, both Kay and Frank were, for the time being, reasonably content. They moved into Wordsworth and Frank took up his responsibilities at the Heart Institute. But there were difficulties.

"If Frank wouldn't give me a divorce, at least we now had a home," Kay observed. "He had a good job with a rising salary. I could play tennis and fix the house. But I wanted a baby—Frank had always said we could have children; I never would have married him if he hadn't—but now his objection was, 'We'll have a child when our finances are secure.' And I was beginning to sense that Frank would never have enough of anything. Despite his salary and the money Daddy gave me and the way Daddy helped us pay our taxes and insurance, we never had any security, and that made me worried.

"At the end of the month, if I had fifty bucks left in our checking account it was a miracle. I literally waited for our monthly five thousand to go in so I could start shopping at the grocery store. Frank spent money as if he printed it himself. Made no difference if we had five thousand or thirty thousand a month—Frank spent it."

Kay's father's evident loneliness at this time also made her unhappy because she was too far removed from him to help, and she knew how deep had been his feelings toward her mother. She knew that even if they had not succeeded in producing a string of babies, which her mother would have welcomed, their life together was rounded and coherent. But now, for her father, there was no pleasure in the present.

"The present was everything to him. What's important is *now*, this *moment*, and that was so important to Daddy, not yesterday or tomorrow. If you take your 'nows' you'll enjoy life. I know people who have to know exactly what they're doing a month and a half ahead or they don't feel secure; we need that tie of 'now' to make life worthwhile, to take away insecurity. Daddy never deviated in his habit of enjoying 'now,' and his primary habit was Mom. She filled all his life. And now she was gone."

Kay heard from Speedy that her father was getting more and more depressed. Alice got him up every morning and saw that he had his breakfast, that his shirts were laundered crisp and fresh, that he set off for the office, the well-loved and respected Dr. Herbert Hupfeldt. But now, it seemed, he did not catch all those green lights on his once-effortless passage to his business in downtown Baltimore; now, with equally expert timing, he hit every red light on his own chosen route to self-destruction. He began to drink heavily. By ten in the morning, when all the clerks were at their desks and the succession of clients were receiving attention, Dr. Hupfeldt was slipping down to the basement for another fortifying glass of vodka. And in the evening, using Speedy as a reliable chauffeur, he would stop off at a friend's house for a glass of bourbon and branch.

He had no one to go home to, and like other men who have no one to go home to, he stayed out. Kay invited him down to Houston to live with them, and he came for one visit. But his grandson was away in Switzerland, he could sense her disquiet with Frank, and he couldn't stand Frank's patronizing or presence. So he went home to die.

After Alice died, he lasted just six months.

Sadly, Kay returned to Baltimore to attend to her father's affairs and arrange for his funeral. By this time Frank was obsessed with heart surgery at the Texas Heart Institute, and was too busy to accompany her. She kept her father's body in the funeral parlor for an entire week because she didn't want to bury it without her husband at her side. Frank flew up for the funeral and immediately returned to Houston. He came back, however, for the reading of the will, and his reactions on that occasion upset her.

They met in Ernest Steadman's office. Ernest read the will, which provided that all of Dr. Hupfeldt's money and possessions be left to his daughter. Before Ernest Steadman could close the conversation or ask if there were any questions, Frank spoke out firmly. As Kathleen's husband, he wanted everything signed over to him: the money, the house, the furniture, were now his. He was the husband, the Italian husband, and that was the lawful and proper thing to do. So if Mr. Steadman would draw up the papers...

Mr. Steadman's lips tightened, and he said very slowly, "But that's not the way we do things here, Frank. I don't think Kay should sign over her money to you at all."

And, as Kay later said, "If he hadn't been so goddamn greedy, just been more restrained about it all, I might have done what he asked. But he came on so strong, forced the issue so self-righteously—it was now *his* money; what were we all waiting for? He was so assertive, and I guess the fact that he'd kept my poor old father waiting for a week in the funeral parlor didn't endear me to his view."

Nevertheless, Frank went on arguing. "He didn't want to give up on the subject. You couldn't *discuss* anything with Frank; when Frank wanted it he wanted it. And always got it. He always flattened me but, of course, he'd found a harder nut in Ernest, who, being German, was just as tough as Frank. It wasn't an edifying scene.

"Not only did he demand that all my inheritance be turned over to him, he also wanted insurance taken out on me. I thought that ridiculous. I burst out, 'Frank, you're the one who needs insurance, you're the wage earner, not me!' But he wanted life insurance taken out on me, a real biggie, two or three hundred thousand dollars, and he said this to Ernest Steadman, very loud.

"Ernest backed me up the whole way. He tried to explain that in America you didn't take out life insurance on the wife; you took it out on the wage earner—the husband—to guarantee the income of the family if the wage earner died. It took a little while for this to register with Frank and then, realizing that he wasn't going to get anywhere on this tack, he began to pretend he didn't really understand the concept of life insurance. But he got more and more furious about the idea of life insurance on him. I suppose that I was a little heated myself at this time, so I said, 'Frank, if you won't take out life insurance, I'll take it out for you!'

"Frank was just reaching forty at that time, and before forty you get a better deal. That's the reason I owned the policy; I paid about sixteen hundred dollars a year for it. Eventually there were several policies on Frank, and for that first one Frank was right there in the office with Ernest and me and that other lawyer. After that he wasn't. I'd call Ernest and say, 'Frank's got another raise and there's no point in my discussing it with him; he'll say no.'

"I'd ask if we should have another insurance policy on Frank. And Ernest would always say yes. After all, he was my financial adviser. So, as Frank's income increased dramatically, from five thousand dollars to three hundred and fifty thousand dollars, we increased the insurance premiums. The point about the whole thing in my terms was not the thought that he might die, but that as his salary increased we still had nothing left at the end of the year. Insurance at least saved something.

By the time we'd paid our bills, we had no savings and nothing left after receiving this huge salary."

Kay's father's death and the sale of his house left her deeply depressed. In her terms, she was now alone; one part of her life was over forever. She was doubly determined therefore to be not only a good wife to Frank, but a successful one, and for the next twelve years no one worked harder than she to make their marriage work. There were good moments and bad moments—probably more bad than good, but she tried to take them in her stride. During that first year living on Wordsworth it seemed possible that things might work out. Frank was not yet on his feet; he was merely one of the surgeons who worked at the Texas Heart Institute and had not yet mastered many of the tricks of his trade.

They got on well with their neighbors. The neighbors realized that Frank had some peculiar habits like cutting the lawn at two a.m., but, after all, he was a foreigner and they were always liable to do funny things, weren't they?

But Frank was also a doctor and that was a good thing to have in the neighborhood. Indeed, Frank had no objections to answering all their questions concerning their aches and pains. Kay always felt that he was at his best as a diagnostician: she knew he was a fine heart surgeon, but as a general practitioner, a country doctor perhaps, investigating the myriad complaints of a large community, he would have excelled. His gift of quick recognition of the symptoms of illness, no matter how simple or how complicated they might be, was brilliant.

During that Wordsworth period Kay took steps to try to keep herself occupied. She was now, more than ever before, aware of Frank's desire to keep her locked in the house all day. This would have driven her crazy, so she embarked on diversionary tactics.

In those early Wordsworth days Kay realized that not only did Frank dislike her playing tennis, he also hated all her tennis friends, referring to them scathingly as prostitutes and whores. This did not greatly distress Kay because by now she was aware that he was likely to dismiss eighty percent of the female population of the United States or any other country with equal vehemence.

When she pointed out to him, however, that if he didn't like her tennis friends, he might like her socializing with the best people in Houston and thus furthering both his reputation and his career, he was deeply suspicious. How did she intend to do that? By becoming a docent, by being a volunteer, by working with the young, to introduce them to the arts, museums, theater, ballet, that sort of thing. Frank nodded his head thoughtfully at this explanation; yes, that sort of occupation might prove useful.

From that moment on the role of docent provided Kay with an adequate excuse for being out of the house. Unknown to Frank, though, she became a docent at the Houston Zoo.

"So I went to my training classes at the zoo and got my little badge to pin on my dress. But one thing I couldn't bear were snakes. Ever since an incident in my childhood I had been terrified of snakes. When I was a little girl in Baltimore, we had a house on the river about an hour's drive away. We kids swam there and you had to watch out for water snakes. The river had a soft, muddy bottom. We played cowboys and Indians in the woods, and Mom made us hot dogs and hamburgers. I was the only girl in our crowd, but I shot arrows and threw crab apples with the gang. One of the gang was Henry, a real little toughie. One day he came up behind me with a milk snake. It's quite a harmless snake, and this one was about four feet long, thick as a wine bottle, and dark colored like a moccasin. They're quite passive as a rule, but he wrapped it around my neck from behind and it was opening its mouth and he kept pushing its head into my face. I could have died. I'm surprised I didn't. I'll never forget it. I have nightmares about it today. Sweet little blond Henry.

"So I told the nice guy at the zoo who was introducing us that I couldn't manage snakes, and he was very sweet and said, 'Okay, don't you worry...take your time.' And after a few lessons showing us Rosie, the boa, he said to me, 'Why don't you just touch her? She likes to be touched. She's feminine and friendly.' So I put out one very nervous finger and touched her, and it was like touching a pretty warm wallet. She wasn't slimy as I had imagined, so I touched her again. Rosie seemed to like me, and after a few more touches she was coiled around my arm, as satisfied as a five-foot kitten. I got very fond of Rosie; she was affectionate and loving and she had been touched and held by many, many children. She was like a favorite old auntie.

"As soon as I was ready, I started my duties. What happened was a team of us docents plus a driver piled into a Zoomobile that carried five or six animals out to various schools. We might take a llama, a pig, and a cat—something children could be familiar with—and a small animal like a lemur, which they wouldn't know about, and a bird, such as a toucan or a parrot. We had a marvelous parrot who could talk. And, of course, Rosie. The kids loved the whole thing, and you just prayed that the animals wouldn't poo-poo in the middle of the classroom, especially the llama.

"Well, this particular day, with Frank thinking happily that I was out at the symphony or the opera recruiting wealthy heart patients, I was doing the thing I simply adored. The Zoomobile went out twice that day and it was on the second shift in the afternoon that things began to go wrong. We were scheduled to go to a small school, about twenty to thirty kids. We'd never been there before, and the driver, a very nice guy, hadn't worked out the time going or coming. We were late getting there and late leaving. So we get into the Zoomobile to come home and we arrive on the far side of town from the zoo. We didn't anticipate all this stopping and starting in the traffic, and we broke down right in front of Foley's, a big downtown department store. We held the traffic up for hours. Finally the driver said, 'I'll have to telephone the zoo and get help.' But no one arrived and he rang again, and no one arrived, and now it had become a crisis, because the zoo had closed. So there we were in downtown Houston in the middle of a traffic jam with five animals in their cages, including a pony-sized llama, which you could hardly get into a taxi, or even walk through River Oaks.

"So each of the team of docents volunteered to take an animal home. The driver volunteered to walk the llama home with him; the others took the cat, pig, lemur and parrot, and I said I'd take Rosie. She was in a burlap sack and she was heavy, but she was snoozing quietly after her busy day and I liked her and I hoped she liked me. The taxi driver must have thought I was a crazy shopper carrying a big bag of potatoes home, and when I got back to Wordsworth—it was quite late by this time—I went in and thought, *Where shall I put Rosie?* I decided the best place was the bathtub, nice and cool for her. So I placed her gently in the bath and patted her and said, 'Be a good girl and go to sleep.' And then I pulled the shower curtain closed and went to bed myself. My plan was that the next morning, first thing, I would take Rosie back to the zoo. No problem.

"I knew Frank might or might not come home, but it was a fairly peaceful time with him then and he probably would use the downstairs bathroom anyway, and he certainly wouldn't take a shower.

I woke in the middle of the night to the most bloodcurdling sound, a scream of absolute terror. I didn't recognize the voice; it was just a nightmare scream—a sound I'd never heard approximated before. I jumped up in bed. Then I realized it was coming from the bathroom, a male voice, and I'd forgotten about Rosie! And it dawned on me! Oh, my God, it's Rosie. It's Rosie! And Frank! I dashed to the bathroom and there was Frank plastered against the bathroom wall. He had his arms glued back against the tiles. He was so flat against the wall that he looked as if he'd been painted there, and his face was the same color as his hospital greens. The sack hung limply over the edge of the bathtub because Rosie had already left.

"Frank had gone into the bathroom to wash his hands, pulled back the curtain and wondered what was in the sack, untied the knot, and Rosie, disturbed by the light and obviously thinking, 'Oh, good, time for breakfast!' had just shot up out of the sack where she'd been curled up for the night, smiling and saying, 'Good morning!'

"I yelled, 'Frank, don't be frightened. It's only Rosie. She's a nice snake!' Though I could imagine his feelings when he opened the sack and a five-foot-long, six-inch-thick boa constrictor glided past, I couldn't quite fathom his terror. I really had to unpeel him from the bathroom tiles. I more or less pushed him down the stairs and said, 'Get a large drink!'

"Then I went to find Rosie. She'd slithered across the cool wooden floor of the upstairs hall and coiled herself into a neat circle of snake in one corner and gone to sleep again. I didn't quite know what to do with her; she seemed perfectly happy. But I picked her up and cradled her in my arms, carried her back to the bath, slid her back into her sack, and she went to sleep again. As I've said, she was a very polite, sleepy snake. I can't remember what happened to Frank that night but I know he didn't come upstairs again. But Frank never forgot or forgave anything."

Being scared out of his wits by the sudden slither of a snake out of his bathtub was a reaction anyone could understand. But Frank had other strange phobias. He was preoccupied with death. And equally preoccupied with the certainty that malignancies were attacking him.

"He would be wandering around the house, or he would have taken a shower, and suddenly I would hear a yell, and it would be a yell with a dimension of terror in it: 'Kay! Quick!'

"I would rush to the bathroom or wherever it was, and Frank would be certain he had cancer.

"'That mole wasn't there yesterday. Look! See, here. I have another melanoma.'

"Frank was always dying of some awful complaint. He was always worrying about heart disease, always taking little capsules of nitroglycerine. In fact, he was always taking medicine—of infinite variety, practically every day and every week. He did have arthritis—I knew that—and he also told me that when he was young, and ill, he was given penicillin, to which he was allergic, and almost died."

Another of Frank's phobias was suspicion. He was often searching through Kay's possessions to discover "things." That riled her. Nothing was ever private from Frank. He opened all her letters. Kay never snooped, would never pry into other people's affairs. Frank never stopped. Bookcases, drawers, suitcases—he was always looking for something. On one occasion he went through her bureau and discovered Roger's old letters to her. She thought they were lovely letters and had kept them for sentimental reasons. Now his suspicions were out in the open. She'd been having an affair. The letters proved it. It was no use her protesting that she and Roger had rarely even kissed. Frank believed in his own paranoia.

Frank also had a habit of fantasizing. He told Kay about terrible things he'd supposedly done—like his prescribing poison for her ill mother, or stealing things, or "pulling the tubes" on other doctors' heart patients at the institute. Kay didn't know what to believe. But she kept Frank's confessions to herself.

By 1974 Frank Sandiford was a successful heart surgeon earning a lot of money. Accordingly, he wanted to move up in other ways than just professionally. A house on the same street as Denton Cooley was a step in the right direction.

In general Kay agreed. Wordsworth was too small to display the few attractive pieces of Early American furniture left to her in her father's will. But she had not been overwhelmed by her first sight of the house on Del Monte Drive. She thought it looked awful, like a sanitorium, its flower borders filled with blue plumbago—a weed with a blue flower—the wood-shingled roof blowing apart, the wrought iron on its balcony broken; it looked derelict. Yes, she could see it had unlimited potential; nevertheless, she harbored grave doubts. Once inside the house, however, she was more impressed. It had been built in 1936 as a wedding gift for Dillon Anderson's wife. Anderson was a lawyer who eventually became a member of President Eisenhower's cabinet. It was solid, yet attractive. The staircase, which led up from the wide center hall, was bannistered and elegant. The rooms were high-ceilinged, large, and elegant. Still, Kay held back. The life-style that the house was designed to impose would be stiff and formal. She wanted a house where she and Frank could have children, a warm, colorful place; she still clung to that ambition.

Frank, on this occasion, surprised her. One of his distinctive traits was to agonize over decisions. She, to be sure, had to be present during the agony, but her role was purely that of a sounding board or aid to procrastination; the ultimate decision would be Frank's and only Frank's. But on this occasion Frank asked her if she liked the house, and though she doubted he would listen to her reply, at least he let her speak her piece.

"I said there were things I liked and things I didn't like. I liked the fact that many of the upstairs rooms could be locked off to form a single unit, which appealed to me, because I was so often alone that it would give me a sense of security. But I didn't like the pretentiousness of the place. I dreamed of the Eastern Shore on Chesapeake Bay—a house with a big open fireplace, and languid Labradors snoozing in front of it, country chintzes...a warm and welcoming home.

"And downstairs was so big; it was a fifty-yard walk from the kitchen through the breakfast room, through the dining room, across the hall into the living room, and beyond it to the elegant little room with French windows, where we put the bar. Above all, it was a house designed for servants; it was an expedition just to go down in the morning to fix a cup of coffee. And the whole neighborhood was super-genteel River Oaks— beautiful, expensive. I wasn't really into the River Oaks syndrome, but Frank just adored it."

River Oaks, situated as it is like a gigantic walled garden among Houston's chaotic swirl of freeways, skyscrapers, slums, and most expensive shops, is without doubt one of the most exclusive, expensive, and beautiful residential areas in the world. In undulating acres closed on one side by the deep, dark, curling gleam of Houston's bayou, and on the others by the wide traffic arteries radiating from the central city, it embraces an area of deep green shade and peace. It suggests an almost pastoral scene, with tall, sighing pines and soaring oaks. Its mansions, set in lawns of lush Saint Augustine grass, reflect the golden architecture of a dozen countries and as many regions of the United States.

"Frank wanted to make an offer on the house on Del Monte Drive right away," Kay said. "After that first urging he didn't listen to anything I said. We stood in the small room at the far end, and George, the real estate guy, who'd been waiting in another room, came in looking expectant. Frank said, 'How much do they want for it?' And George told him. Frank said, 'Offer them five thousand less.' The house was on the market for about two days, and Mrs. Anderson, Dillon Anderson's widow, accepted that first offer. No doubt if she'd waited she'd have got more, but I don't think that money was a great problem in her life."

Kay rang up Ernest Steadman and got the money to make the down payment and then arranged for the mortgage payments. After that, she said, "Frank was happy, at least as happy as he ever could be. And I hadn't been hit once during the transaction."

But that changed as soon as the excitement of the purchase had passed. The abuse was all part of the re-education of Kay Sandiford, or at least that is what she thought. But there were some things Frank couldn't alter. He had to live with those.

"He always said I was physically unattractive. Oh yes, he thought I was awful looking. Everything about me was wrong. My face was terrible. My brown eyes? Common people had brown eyes. And curly hair? That was horrible. And fat legs, and too short, and I bit my nails— only because of him I bit my nails! I was stupid, ugly, unable to understand anything; but, you know, after hearing it for so long, I suppose it just stopped hurting.

"Being beaten up was just one of the hazards of living with Frank— except that it was so unnecessary. The reason he gave for beating me up, at least the reason he gave me *at first*—to prove he was the master— was so dumb. He just didn't have to prove that. I was an obedient, submissive little female anyway. I certainly didn't realize then that this was a continuing syndrome, one that could lead to destruction. All I wanted was *peace*.

"But Frank was always the same; he never changed. I was just an excuse for him to relieve himself. I don't really think I existed for him; he was hitting out at his own frustration and dissatisfaction. I mean, he had to have somebody to beat on—me, him. Oh, yes, he beat on himself in a way, taking all those drugs and drinking and overeating. He never showed restraint in anything he did, except in surgery. That was one place where he had to hold himself in check, but when he went out to dinner, he'd eat like he'd never seen food before, or he'd eat nothing at all; he never had a pace. We'd go out to dinner at Tony's or Maxim's, and he would order shrimp cocktail, vichyssoise, watercress salad, endive salad, a fish, a piece of meat, a crème caramel for dessert, and he'd eat it all; he'd eat enough for three or four people. And if he especially liked, say, the vichyssoise he'd say, 'I'll have another cup.' Where he put it I don't know, and then he'd go home and go into the bathroom and throw it all up, make himself sick with a diuretic and then take Valium. I never knew if it was a deliberate ploy of his—'I'm going to eat myself sick and throw up'—or not. But he pushed his body and every part of himself beyond their natural limits. Other times, we'd go out to dinner and he'd say, 'I'm not eating,' and he wouldn't touch a thing. I'd have to eat alone."

Naturally, after the Rosie incident she had given up her position as a docent at the Zoo; Frank would have assaulted her if she'd even looked at another animal. But settled in Del Monte, she began to attend three-hour classes every Monday morning at the Houston Museum of Fine Arts, to obtain docent status and guide visiting groups round the exhibits. It took many months of lectures and extensive note-taking to collect the material for a thesis, which she would offer to the Examining Board.

One day at Del Monte, forgetfully, she put her pile of notebooks and pads on a shelf in the back corridor. Frank found them. Every pad and notebook was stripped, meticulously torn into confetti pieces and laid out in a neat trail along the corridor. There was no way she could write her paper. Distressed, she rang up the Museum and said she was sorry but events had intervened, and she could not offer her thesis. They were sympathetic. They said, maybe later. She never said a word to Frank, and he said nothing to her.

Kay recalls that in those days she lived in constant fear, although she didn't recognize it as such. "I couldn't relate to the word *fear*, because I thought that was the way you were supposed to feel about your husband when he was this normal sort of male tyrant. And I was the eternal optimist. Things would change. Frank would get to know what a good wife I was, one hundred percent behind him and his career. We'd have those six sons, and I'd live happily ever after."

In River Oaks in the spring, the warm air drifting northward from the Gulf of Mexico, which is fifty miles to the south, infuses the breeze with a silken humidity that settles like a damp bloom on the skin. The weather heats up through April and May, and in full summer the thermometers, displayed high up on bank and department store walls, stick around ninety-five degrees Fahrenheit. Every weekday morning in River Oaks, at the first light of dawn, the hum of lawn mowers can be heard as the Mexican gardeners go about their business trimming the lush lawns. Meanwhile, behind the mansions, chauffeurs can be seen shining and waxing cars of the finest pedigree—Rolls-Royces, Cadillacs, Mercedes-Benzes, Ferraris—all polished to match the brilliance of the Texas sun. Sun is the normal theme, but nature sometimes intervenes. Occasionally, tropical thunderstorms send down bolts of bright blue lightning, violent as an air raid, sweeping floods of rain through the freeway underpasses and rattling the glass in the windows of the stately homes so hard that the numerous burglar alarms jar into action and galvanize the normally peaceful patrols of the River Oaks Private Police Department into hurried activity.

The essence of gracious living in River Oaks is immediately obvious; the adhesive binding the community together is wealth, often enormous wealth. Yet River Oaks is a very private neighborhood. Very often only one old lady, and perhaps a servant, occupies a mansion big enough to shelter a brigade. Privacy is sacrosanct. Often neighbor does not speak to neighbor, and no one walks around much after dark.

But on the whole, life in River Oaks is beautiful, and even in Kay and Frank's case, so it proved to be. Only six years after the Sandifords settled into their exclusive new address, with Frank's salary then approaching four hundred thousand dollars a year, they had become the envy of many of their friends. Socially, the gay young woman from Baltimore and the handsome, gregarious, successful heart surgeon from Rome mixed with the most prominent people, whose incomes were counted in millions, who wintered in Palm Springs or the Caribbean, and who were frequently seen in the glossy magazines. Patently, the attractive couple seemed to be the embodiment of the American dream.

9

In July 1974, scarcely a month after the Sandifords moved into their new Del Monte Drive residence, they flew off on their first recruiting tour to Italy. The Texas Heart Institute had welcomed patients from Europe and Latin America years before Frank was on the scene, but as Frank was Italian, had been educated in Rome, and had many contacts there, it only made sense that he should be used to build up the connection between the Heart Institute and Italy. The trip was funded by the institute, and Kay was excited at the thought of seeing Italy again.

Frank had briefed her on heart operations and the part she was to play: "Obviously the fact that in your sixties you could be given what to all intents and purposes was a new heart, a new ability to chase young girls, drink more wine, and what-have-you, appealed tremendously to Italians, as of course it appeals to all mankind. That, of course, was the business aspect of the trip."

But the prospect that really excited Kay was that of a personal audience with His Holiness the Pope.

Kay was determined to be prepared for all eventualities. She took a crash course in Italian at the Berlitz School, and by the time she got off the plane in Rome she was quite willing to demonstrate her skill by delivering a short, prepared speech to the reporters who were there to welcome the new maestro from Houston.

"I loved Italy. I've always loved it from the moment I first saw it on my 'grand tour' when I was eighteen.

"The Italians are wonderful people; they appreciate you from a distance, and they don't impose. I love Italy: it's warm, it vibrates, whole streets vibrate, the people vibrate.

"And I love Rome, above all; it's my favorite city in the whole world.

"So I said something along these lines to the newsmen, how my husband and I were thrilled at this small reception at the airport, and how I was looking forward to meeting His Holiness.

"For that, however, I had to have instruction, and that's when I first met Father Georgi.

"Father Georgi was a sweet, wonderful, cherubic little man, and I adored him for having so much kindness and humility and down-to-earthness. He spoke perfect English, and he told me, 'You'll be all right. I'll watch you.' And he gave me lessons on what I had to do: go down on one knee and just touch your lips to the ring when he offers you his hand.

"So Father Georgi in his long black robes and his little black beret, his eyes twinkling, picks up Frank and me in his tiny Fiat Cinque Cento from the Hassler Hotel, and off we trundle through the streets of Rome, over one of the bridges across the Tiber, and through the outer gates of the Vatican into the gardens—the gardens set the scene; they're so serene and beautiful—and then, after parking the car, through enormous doors into the Vatican itself with all the Swiss Guards dressed in armor and doublets.

"I myself was dressed in a black dress down to my ankles, black shoes, black stockings, a string of pearls, and a veil.

"Before you see the pope you go through three different offices, all of them above stairs. First, you go up in the elevator and step out into a long corridor, and as you proceed along it's driven home to you at once that you're in an absolutely different world. The carpets, the enormous masterpieces on the walls, the color, the tranquility, the serenity—I mean, you're indoctrinated before you've covered a hundred yards. At the far end you enter the first room and you are asked to be seated, and you perch uneasily on the very edge of your chair—in awe. I mean I was really nervous. By this time I'm having trouble with my veil, because it was only attached to my hair. So Father Georgi is trying to help me stick it on—and adding to his experience, because the poor man's never tried to put bobby pins in a veil in his whole life before.

"The chamber we entered next is really beautiful. It's pearl gray, this soft, almost translucent pearl gray, and again there's this wonderful feeling of peace, of tranquility—and austerity as well this time because of the color. And there are more incredibly beautiful masterpieces on the walls, and these very old and beautiful chairs against the walls. You sit there and a secretary comes out—all men, of course, so you feel a bit lonely as a woman; you feel that women aren't really welcome there. It's a man's world behind those walls and doors—and you feel it's a great honor for you to be admitted.

"Finally we were ushered into the third room, and there's the pope, Paul the Sixth, standing with some other dignitary behind him. I was so surprised; he was such a tiny fellow in his robes and little, red papal booties, a very fragile person about as big as me. The pope extends his hand to me first, and I go into my routine. I had to go down very low because he's such a short guy, and I'm dripping black veil in all directions, so it's all a bit hazardous. Then he invites us to be seated, and he sits down behind his huge desk.

"I was pointed to one chair, and Frank to another, and Father Georgi sat somewhere else. The pope chatted with Frank. Frank told him that his father had met him some years before and we talked about the Texas Heart Institute, and what a wonderful healing institution it was. Then the pope asked me if I spoke Italian and I said no, whereupon he said, 'So, Mrs. Sandiford, you speak English?' and I said 'Yes, Your Holiness,' and he said, 'What is the situation of women in the United States?' Well, my veil almost fell off. I mean, that's a large question on which to engage a pope. But I was ready to tell him—it isn't often a girl from Baltimore gets to sound off to the head of the Catholic Church— and off I went... about how women's position was changing in the United States, and I was going to go on about divorce and then abortion and it was about time the Catholic Church listened to the women in its ranks. I could tell without looking that Frank's eyes were boring bullet holes through me, and of course I hardly managed to get through three or four sentences before Father Georgi, the old smoothie, who knew all about these things, gently intervened. No one wanted me to say anything about anything, and the conversation was directed back to Frank.

"Afterward we stood up like tin soldiers to have our pictures taken. Then you kiss his ring again, and he blesses you and blesses your family, and hopes you have more children. You wait for him to leave and it's all over. I thought the whole experience was wonderful."

Kay and Frank were granted two other papal audiences, but in the meantime Kay sought to overcome her comparative isolation on their trips to Italy. Success, she discovered, was a mixed blessing.

"I found, quite soon, that speaking so much to Italian people began to improve my Italian enormously, and then I realized that Frank didn't like it because I detracted from him. We'd go to a party and suddenly a lot of people would be talking to me and that didn't go down well at all. But, still, I adored Italy, which was just as well, because we visited Italy at least once, often twice, a year. We stayed at the Hassler Hotel, at the top of the Spanish Steps, and Frank had two old aunts who used to come and have lunch with me while he was out. They were so cute and wonderful; two old ladies shriveled up like autumn nuts. They were as sweet as Frank's father, whom I met for the first time when he passed through the States after visiting Peru on a convention of some sort. He was a professor of law at Rome's university and he was tiny, much smaller than Frank—even 'Mamina' was bigger than he—and he was so sweet, just a charming, humble man. When we went out to dinner, I'd cut his meat up for him; he needed someone to take care of him. He was so unlike Frank that it was unbelievable."

Kay had learned in the very earliest days with Frank that if she was going to be a successful wife for an upper-class Roman, one of the prerequisites was a knowledge of how to eat fruit.

"It started one night in Baltimore when Frank announced that he was going to teach me how to eat grapes. I laughed. I said I knew how to eat grapes. 'Look, you pop one in your mouth'—I picked one up from the plate in front of us—'and chew-chew; no pips; it's gone.' I thought it was funny. Frank didn't think so. He just grabbed me, threw me down on the floor, tore off my clothes, and had sex with me right on the floor. It was not an act of love or even of lust. He was very angry. 'Now,' he said, 'get up and learn to eat grapes.'"

In time, Kay learned to eat all the fruits, and a large number of other foods, the Italian way, and when they got to Italy she understood why. As Frank's wife, she was on display; she had to perform every trick of table etiquette as if it came to her as naturally as the air she breathed.

"At the Chequer Club in Rome, for example—I think you have to be a member of an old Roman family even to join, and one of Frank's oldest friends filled that role—there is beautiful black and white decor; a long, ascending staircase of black and white marble; waiters attired as if to serve eighteenth-century aristocrats; and this silence—like a church. That's where I took my first test.

"We were the only table in the club—every other was empty—ten of us, and the guy on my right was from Germany, someone's husband, a real pain. And that silence! You could have dropped a match and everyone would have heard it; it was very intimidating. As I was the wife of the guest of honor, everything came to me first, carried by these waiters wearing white gloves. I could feel Frank's dark eyes on me and knew my responsibility.

"When the spaghetti arrived I knew I was the one who had to take the right portion, thinking, *Now, there're ten people and that's ten portions but how much do these people eat? And where do I put the spaghetti? Do I put it on this side or that side or in the middle or what?* Frank was across the table talking to some woman but he was not going to help me out, so all eyes were looking at me. I didn't know whether the waiter was going to serve me or I was supposed to serve myself, but I could sense that if I were to do the wrong thing, it was going to be Signora Sandiford is an ass—and I would never live it down. I felt that they'd love it if I were to cut it with a knife; if I'd done something like that, I'm sure it would have made the front page. I mean, I know how to handle spaghetti; we had spaghetti every night. But in Rome spaghetti is handled like the unleavened bread. Anyway, I guessed that the waiter couldn't hold that big bowl of spaghetti and serve me as well, so I figured it was up to me to do it. On the other hand, the serving pieces were not directed toward me; they were turned out, and to me that indicated that someone else was going to serve. So I sort of pretended I was talking, and everyone went on looking and the waiter wouldn't give up—he just stood there like a dummy—so I took a chance and took a great blob, and naturally all of the ladies after me took about a teaspoonful. But I ate it all. We had a fish course with a very light sauce, then veal and salad, then, of course, the fruit, which was always my Waterloo—positive deathsville.

"On this night the fruit was cherries. Frank had anticipated as much—cherries were in season—so I was prepared. In fact, I'd spent all day practicing eating cherries. I must have eaten two dozen cherries, and, boy, the technique! When the waiter comes around he has his fruit and the bowl; you have your water bowl to wash the fruit. You take the cherries out by the stems, and you take one more than you intend to eat, so if you want three cherries you take four; and you pick them up, rinse them, and put them on your plate. And you let them sit—you don't dive right in—you talk and whatever, but even if someone is still talking to you, you now take the plunge: pick up your cherry by the stem and hold it and then put it in your mouth. You place the stem delicately on the plate, carefully eat the meat away from the pip, put your hand to your mouth, cover your mouth with your index finger, slip the pip between your index finger and thumb, and place it on the side of your plate. Don't for heaven's sake drop it on your plate and make a scene. Then you swallow your cherry and smile.

"Peaches are all right so long as they're ripe; if they're not you're in trouble. But ordinarily you simply peel the peach. You don't go through the sectional thing; you just have bites.

"I was conscious every time I picked up a piece of fruit that Frank's dark eyes were on every movement. And what was amazing, during all this jazz, was that he was the one who would pick up a peach, wash it off, and pop it into his mouth, just to be different. He made a point of being a little vulgar, a little bit of a peasant, and I'm sure that appealed to the women. At the time I was not conscious that Frank knew all of the tricks about impressing women, but hindsight has made it plain that he did.

"Then we got to the sweets and I'd always take one, but a lady doesn't have to eat her sweet so I'd take one little bite and leave it. Then the men would go and smoke cigars and drink cognac and the women would go and sit and drink coffee, and I would think, *What I wouldn't do for a whiskey*.

"I really hated that side of aristocratic Italian society, much as I love Italy itself."

Frank had prepared for his and Kay's first trip to Italy with the help of two Italian acquaintances to whom Kay took an immediate dislike, because she recognized at once that they had nothing to do with the medical profession but were simply mercenaries drumming up trade for Frank. In fact, they were advance men, squeezing what percentage they could from the prospective patients by charging them for an introduction to the eminent heart surgeon from the States. At this time, Kay still clung to her belief that medical practice was a vocation, not a trade, and she was certain that this sort of behavior offended the ethics of her husband's profession. Frank did not seem to mind too much.

In any case, the two middlemen had spread the word very well. The telephone in the Sandifords' suite at the Hassler never stopped ringing, with patients requesting immediate consultation. After twelve hours of this a harassed under-manager disclosed that he had had to hire a second telephone operator to cope with the traffic. Kay recalled, "I was going frantic from morning till night, trying to play secretary in Italian, and then Frank having a stroke because I didn't speak good Italian and often didn't get the names right."

The Hassler Hotel was literally besieged. A line of prospective patients formed outside the hotel and encroached into the lobby. The hotel management put up with it very patiently; after all, it was a humanitarian thing the miracle heart surgeon was doing. What the other guests thought no one bothered to ask. Frank was charging around twenty dollars for each examination, and Kay was delegated at the end of each day to deliver the takings to the Hassler's cashier.

"I'd give him a handful of checks of various shapes and sizes, and he would cash them for me, but often when he sent the checks to the banks they bounced, and I caught on to the facts of life regarding Italian checks. Some were written on banks that didn't even exist; the check writers just printed fake ones. It was never worth trying to do anything about it; it was more trouble trying to find out who they were than just treating the whole thing as a loss, and Frank wasn't supposed to charge them anyway. So eventually Frank would take only cash.

"Then, of course, there was the phenomenon of the mothers who would bring their comely daughters along to be examined by Frank. There was nothing wrong with their hearts whatever, but they thought it was a great idea to meet the famous heart surgeon who would perhaps have opportunities to suggest to them.

"That entire first trip was eye opening. Frank soon moved his activities into a hospital but that didn't work out either because the hospital would not accept a straight fee, like a hundred or so dollars a day, for the use of their space; they wanted a percentage of every patient's fee, and they provided a granite-faced nurse who extracted the money before the patient was shown into the office. So eventually during the later trips Frank ended up examining patients in a cardiologist's office."

Kay, meanwhile, was employed as all-purpose aide-de-camp, a role in which she was not so much unqualified as simply doomed to failure. No matter what she did, it was wrong.

"But that didn't upset me at all. I knew I was wrong, and just believed every word he said. However, about the ethics of his behavior, I was very worried. I felt that in order to maintain his dignity and professional integrity he should follow the standard procedure in heart surgery and only take patients from referring physicians. I remember one occasion very well. We had just stopped our car outside the Hassler, and I suppose I must have had a drink, which blew all my usual caution out of my head. I said, 'You're associating with people who are not professionally of your caliber. It's not only unethical, it's dangerous. This running off at two in the morning to talk to these patients that these characters have dredged up. It's all wrong.' In fact, I got so worked up, I cried, 'What's the point of fooling around with all this nonsense? I'm going back to Texas!'

"Frank didn't just get hot under the collar; he went crazy. He simply took my head in his hands and started banging it backward and forward against the steel edging of the door, screaming at me never to interfere. Did I ever get him any patients? Never! Until I did, I was to keep my nose out of his affairs."

During all those visits to Rome, Father Georgi remained Kay's firm friend and mentor. She would arrive at the Hassler with Frank, their luggage would be carried up to their regular suite, and Frank would disappear. Invariably she would be left alone, and always she telephoned Father Georgi at the Civita Catholica, bubbling with laughter and suppressed excitement at the thought of meeting him again. She would hear his voice, happy at the reunion, and say, "Can I come around?" and he would reply, "Of course, you can, Kay, my dear! Come round at once."

Hardly pausing to brush her hair, she would scoot out of the Hassler and scurry down the Via Sistina and around to the huge door, to be scrutinized by the suspicious or worried little priests hurrying everywhere on the most mysterious of errands. Someone would lead Kay to Father Georgi's reception room. He would open the door, reach out two welcoming hands to draw her in, dismiss the acolyte with a word of thanks, close the door firmly, and give her a big hug, which she returned and amplified with a kiss on his cheek.

"We were so happy together, and we'd talk and talk and talk. It would be two hours at least before we stopped talking. He soon knew everything about me—that I'd been divorced, that Charles wasn't Frank's natural son—and although I didn't say much about it, I guess he knew pretty well that I was a loyal and devoted wife, trying to hang on to the coattails of the flying Frank. I suppose Father Georgi was twenty years older than I. He knew that Frank had been engaged to some Italian girl and broken off the engagement when he went off to seek his fortune in the U.S. Father Georgi was so wise and kind; he seemed to know everything.

"Occasionally he'd have dinner with me in the Hassler and we'd drink a bottle of wine together and go on talking. Frank was rarely there, but Father Georgi would cheer me up about Frank, rationalizing the situation, and always tell me I was right in what I was doing."

Father Georgi eventually urged Kay to become a Catholic, and for a time she thought about it seriously. Probably because of her Quaker upbringing, with its emphasis on service and simplicity, she faltered.

"I saw at the Vatican how well off they were. All the top echelon lived like kings—all those beautiful priests in their beautiful robes who drank beautiful wine. The superb food, the magnificent china, the table linen and napkins of the purest white...."

She viewed the scene with a suspicious eye. She was awed by what she saw but not overwhelmed. She expected religious devotion and found it; she expected an ageless tradition and saw it. But the Church of Rome was a society that seemed to her to have stopped growing centuries ago and never restarted, never reached the twentieth century. The esoteric indulgences worried her. "I had a funny idea," she said, "about them being servants of the people, servants of God; but you've never seen such well-served servants in your life. I suppose I was being overidealistic."

When Kay returned to Houston from that first recruiting trip to Italy, she discovered that much of the elitism and snobbery of the self-styled aristocratic Italian scene was evident in the expatriate Italian community in Texas.

"In Houston there were big holiday celebrations at the Italian consulate. We were invited to all of them and we generally went. I found them an uphill proposition, especially on one occasion. As soon as we arrived, this Sicilian woman came up. Frank was standing right next to me, and she said in a loud, snooty voice, 'You know, Kay, you really must stop wearing those cheap American clothes now that you're married to such a brilliant surgeon. You should start to wear Italian clothes; they have so much more style.' And we'd just arrived at the party! I should have been warned. When she came to my home she would criticize the way I made pasta: 'Oh, you *haven't* put sugar in the tomatoes?' Which I hadn't. But she was always making some derogatory remark that I didn't come up to *the* standards.

"But in the end, on this occasion she did me a lot of good, for when we got home Frank said, 'I want you to go out and get a decent designer and some good clothes.' So I started buying clothes costing a fortune—blouses three or four hundred dollars each, dresses a thousand dollars each. And I found Yves Saint Laurent and I really did like his stuff.

"And now, for the first time in my life, Frank was making enough money to contribute.

"He couldn't really tell me what to wear until he started paying the bills, but if he wanted to pay for that stuff it was okay with me, and I got to the point where my little Baltimore dresses disappeared and I was properly turned out for those Italian lunches and dinners. But *they* wouldn't have liked me even if I had walked in in Pope Paul's habit. There was no way they were going to take to me. Now I realize there was so much feeling about an American girl walking off with their top Italian heart surgeon. But I didn't care and everybody thought I was really chi-chi at last because I was running around in Saint Laurent clothes. So really I suppose I should say thank you to that Sicilian woman."

10

THERE were many things Kay disliked about Frank during the years at Wordsworth and Del Monte Drive, but there were many other aspects she liked, and in those days she equated "like" with "love."

What first attracted her to Frank, or what she really liked about him, was that he was excitingly male. She never quite put her thoughts into words, but she really liked his smooth olive skin and black-brown hair, which he brushed back from his forehead. He had a nicely shaped head, albeit it was almost too big for his body. His eyes were "kind of spooky"; she always felt they were too dark. His legs were great, strong and muscular and smooth. He told her that his legs were good because all his life he had ridden bicycles fast and furiously, but she decided he was just born with good-looking legs. He had good teeth, his smile was good, and he had a very sensuous mouth. He had very smooth lips, almost a feminine mouth, but women liked his mouth.

Kay also liked Frank's taste in ties, and she liked the way he acted in public, particularly with his patients. With them, his character changed: he was serene and quiet, almost humble, a manner very similar to that of Denton Cooley. Both men had a gift for reassuring patients.

In these early years of their marriage Kay thought Frank was wise and erudite, a veritable Encyclopaedia Britannica. She wanted to believe that, because Frank was her life. Everything was going to revolve around Frank; she was going to live in his shadow.

As the years passed, however, she realized that it was not wisdom that poured out of Frank, but knowledge, lots of diverting little trinkets of knowledge. He was full of good stories: the trouble was that after many repetitions she found it difficult to laugh at the punch lines.

Still, she was deeply aware of Frank's immense potential: he could, if he turned his mind to it, have become almost anything he wanted to. The trouble was he didn't know what he wanted to be. She was not even sure he wanted to be a surgeon, but he had started out in that field, and achieving that ambition had cost him so much in terms of time and effort that he was in far too deeply ever to be able to change. But Kay had no great belief in Frank's overpowering urge to be a surgeon.

Life settled down fairly quickly into a normal routine at Del Monte— if anything could be said to follow a normal routine with Frank around. He went off to the hospital every day and Kay played tennis with her group at Memorial Park. During the first two or three years she played tennis five days a week, mornings and afternoons. Two or three times a month on Friday nights, they entertained.

Frank frequently lamented the fact that he had learned to play the piano when he was a boy but had never been able to afford a good one; he had always wanted a Steinway. Now they bought one, a grand piano made of cherrywood, one of the last ever made by the original Steinway company. At the time they thought it was very expensive—over seven thousand dollars.

It transpired, however, that Frank's musical ability was very slight: he played only one tune, "Traumerei," so Kay was pressed into service. Playing the piano had never greatly appealed to her, because she considered herself to have so little real talent, but now she persevered. Frank saw to that. Moreover, he started choosing the music she should play and insisted that she practice for three hours a day. She would then record her interpretation and when Frank came home he would offer "constructive criticism." The point of his insistence was that she should play the piano for their guests after dinner. Somewhere down deep in his soul Frank craved the satisfaction that the Friday night routine could give him: dinner over, filled brandy snifters warming in their guests' hands, he would softly command, "Darling, would you play something?" Kay, rising gracefully from the settee, would reply equally softly, "Of course, darling."

Kay quickly discovered that none of the guests knew any more about music than she did, and she soon found that she could skip whole passages—all the difficult bits—without anyone's knowing the difference. She also understood that she was nothing more than a brief entertainment to allow the men time to drink their cognac and smoke their cigars. Then she was delegated to serve the coffee.

Preparing a dinner party took four days. There was linen to be washed, starched, and pressed, silver to be polished, a menu to be chosen: hors d'oeuvres served with pre-dinner drinks; then into the courses—never less than five—appetizer, soup, sometimes fish, entree, salad, cheese and fruit, sweets and wines to match. That took a lot of thought, a lot of shopping, and a lot of cooking, and Kay did all of it herself.

Frank always invited the same type of guests: patients or people he thought could help him. Kay often thought one thing rather strange. Their guests rarely invited them back. She once asked Jennifer about it. Jennifer explained that it was because the Sandiford dinners were so superb: no one dared compete. Thinking about it, Kay knew Jennifer was right: everything was so staged, from the sparkling crystal to the elegant candles, the starched apron of Ferrie Lee, the cutlery placed exactly one inch from the edge of the table, the napkins folded perfectly.

And, truth to tell, Kay was often grateful they weren't asked back to other people's houses, because of Frank's increasing eccentricity.

"Frank always managed somehow to put a distance between the new people we met," she recalls. "Frank's reactions to these people when they were trying to be nice to us, and I was trying to be nice to them, were inevitably the same: 'She was a prostitute; he was a queer.'"

Why did Kay put up with it when her whole upbringing revolted against such behavior? Because she was so in awe of Frank that she could not disbelieve him. When they went back to Little Dix Bay in the Virgin Islands for a vacation in 1978, she was certain that everything that happened was all her fault. They met Mike and Laura again, still living on their boat, the Reef Runner, but this time with another crew member.

"They had a little boy, named Billy," Kay recalled, "a precious, tow-headed blue-eyed little creature, and they were really happy because they'd both wanted a baby for years. Frank's reaction was nasty: 'It can't be Mike's baby because he's impotent!' I mean, what nonsense; how is Frank to know who's impotent or not? I thought it was just a downright cruel thing to say, to try and cut them down like that. They'd wanted a kid, they'd had a kid, and they were good together, all three of them.

"Anyway, we went scuba diving out of Caneel Bay with this great big guy who was in charge, a husky, blue-eyed fellow: four of us, a dentist from New York and his wife, Frank and me. I don't think the dentist was all that keen—I wasn't either, with my earlier memory of Frank and the sea—but when he heard I was diving, the male ego stuff appeared and he had to go down while his wife waited in the boat.

"We were down there with the big guy at about eighty feet, looking for black coral—everybody wanted black coral—when the dentist suddenly panicked, started hyperventilating, and ripped out his mouthpiece. That's not unusual when panic sets in, so the big guy grabs him, holds him, then he shoves his own mouthpiece into the dentist's mouth and indicates that he's going to take him up. It's the usual technique—a mouthful of air for you, a mouthful for me. And he manages to calm the dentist down. Then he signals very definitely for us to stay where we are and he would come back down for us.

"But is Frank going to stay? Not on your life. As soon as the other two are gone, he grabs my wrist and starts swimming off with me. I just didn't want to go at all. In the first place, when an experienced diver says stay, you stay! Especially when you're that deep. We were down eighty feet or lower, and it's not clear water; it's twilight down there, almost dark. And I wasn't an experienced diver, and just then I wasn't in the best condition—the dentist had frightened me, I was breathing hard, and when Frank towed me away I started breathing much too hard and taking in air faster than I should have. I was getting low on air and Frank had plenty, but he wouldn't let me go, and I couldn't get my hand away from him. I thrust my wrist gauge into his face to show him how low on air I was, but Frank just ignored the whole thing, and I was really scared. Then, thank heavens, the big guy came floating overhead and swam into my vision, and as soon as he was close enough I stuck out my free arm and he took one look at the gauge, grabbed my wrist, and started to try and haul me to the surface. But Frank wouldn't let go, and the big guy jackknifed down and literally tore my arm out of Frank's grasp and we went up.

"Frank stayed down a minute or two longer and then he surfaced too. And was he unpopular! The big guy roared at him, 'That was a goddamned stupid thing to do!' He really was very angry; I suppose he thought he might have lost both the dentist and me, and that would not have been good for business. He spouted water and went on, 'You're a stupid son of a bitch.'

"I think Frank decided not to hear that. Back in the boat the big guy calmed down; after all, we were customers. Frank was as smooth as silk—'No need to worry. I had things under control. She was perfectly safe.'

"And what was I doing? Being my usual submissive, apologetic self. It was all my fault, I told them, for being so stupid and breathing too much air. Can you imagine? I'd even rationed my air. Yes, I was so sorry; I'd breathed in too much air!"

Much, much later a long, hard look back at Frank's determined efforts to "improve her character" would eventually convince Kay that those efforts also went a considerable distance toward endangering her life. She was wearing only one weight belt. Frank was wearing two. If Kay had passed out he had only to fasten his second belt around her waist and she would have gone to the bottom, probably never to be seen again. And by that time Frank would have thought up an adequate way to absolve himself from all suspicion.

The trips, Kay feels, brought out the worst in Frank, especially the trips to Italy.

"Of course, on all those trips, unless I could be useful to Frank, for all intents and purposes I was locked in the hotel room, a prisoner, waiting for Frank's phone calls. And if I disobeyed his orders I was beaten up. He'd say, 'You stay here until I get back.' If I said I wanted to go out and see the monuments, he'd say no. And I was afraid of him. He'd telephone to check. If I went out and he found out, he'd come back and hit me: get me in a closet or come up behind me and twist my arm up behind my back, or knock my head against the wall, and say, 'Where the hell have you been? I called and you weren't there!' I remember on one trip to San Francisco, it was sunny downstairs and I paid the desk clerk ten dollars and said, 'If a phone call comes for this room, put the caller on hold and page me; I'll be right out here on the terrace.' So on that occasion I got to sit out on the terrace and Frank never found out. But if he'd found out that I'd been out of the room, he'd have hit me; no question about it.

"But, as I've said, the trips to Italy were the worst, because they were so unethical and I had to participate in Frank's cynical recruitment.

"When we were touring the small towns outside Rome, I wasn't present when he examined the patients. But after he saw the morning patients, a luncheon was always arranged; the mayor would be there and all the notables. These people weren't rich or poor; they were all middle class, all nicely dressed, all lovely, kindly people, and Frank didn't pay for a damn thing. These tiny little towns would be forking out for the visit of the great *'dottóre.'* His purpose, pure and simple, was to examine people and say whether they should come to the United States for an operation or not. But, of course, you can't just *look* at a chest, or *listen* to a chest, and say you need a triple bypass. You need a study done; you need to go to a cardiologist; you have to have an electrocardiogram. What Frank was doing and saying was commercial enough to be unethical: if they came to Houston and they wanted an operation, they could have one.

"Maybe it's the way these things are done in Latin countries, but I thought it was reprehensible—although I didn't say so. I'd made my protest on the first visit and nearly been slaughtered for having the temerity to do so. So I just stuck with the ladies. When I arrived in each town, the ladies' committee would take over Signora Sandiford. Typically I was given a tour of the town and a little book about its history, driven to the church, the square, and the school, and then taken to one of the ladies' houses for coffee and sweets, and then to another for lunch. No wonder I had a weight problem. Lunch was pretty predictable: always prosciutto and melon first, pasta, then meat, a salad, and a huge dessert, and, being Signora Sandiford, I had to eat the whole meal to please the lovely fat mama who was standing behind me saying, 'I made *that* especially for *you!*' So I ate it all up and prepared to explode.

"Frank could always miss a meal. I would always say, 'He's under such stress, he doesn't eat properly.' Frank could get away with not touching any of the food. Then he'd need a nap and he'd get up and go and have a siesta, and I'd be sitting there playing good Signora Sandiford and entertaining forty guests.

"After lunch Frank would go back and attend to another long line of patients, or sometimes go on to another town, where maybe there'd be a party with lots of wine. I always wanted to drink bourbon but Frank said that was unladylike; with him, you'd have to drink champagne or wine. If only Frank could have been nice, it could have been such fun. But, of course, at all these occasions I'd always do something wrong—I hadn't finished the wine; I had finished the wine; I'd insulted somebody's grandmother because I didn't eat all the lasagne she'd prepared; I didn't wear the long dress; I shouldn't have worn that short-sleeved dress in front of those ladies—that was not proper; and my hair's a mess! Hell, you walk around smiling at churches, shops, and babies in all kinds of weather; what do you expect?"

One of Kay's more delicate tasks in Italy was to explain to the anxious wives how their husbands would react after their successful heart surgery. There were usually postoperative repercussions, she told them, generally affecting the male psyche. One of them was a possibility that the patient might tend to exercise his renewed strength and virility by chasing young women—any woman, in fact. He was apt to show a marked increase in sexual desire, and the wife, who had probably given that up years earlier, would be well advised to beware.

"They'd been ill for many years and they hadn't made love for years, and it would probably have taken twenty years before they got to the point of heart surgery. Before that they had gradually cut out anything that was exhausting, and that meant activities in the bedroom. So the wife looked at her husband, postoperatively, as a patient who needed to be nursed back to health and treated with tender loving care. And the husband looked upon himself—after having been told that he could do anything he had done before he got sick, and more—as a new man, and was running around trying to prove that he *was* twice the man he'd been twenty years before. The wife would reject the husband because she didn't want to overtax a poor convalescent patient; the husband would reject the wife because the wife would not accept him. This was just something that had to be explained.

"So at luncheon parties we'd discuss mutual problems. I'd try to explain to the wife the little difficulties she might encounter with a convalescing heart patient. One understood what the wife was likely to go through; she'd spent five, ten, twenty years nursing the man she'd loved and cared for and who was the father of her children, and she had obviously grappled with the idea that he was on the brink of death, and ten days after surgery he's grappling with her in the bed; I mean, the poor woman didn't know what was going on. It was a great shock."

Kay's assistance had become quite valuable, but Frank generally took it for granted. "Living with Frank was like living on a live volcano, always smoldering and likely to blow. Loudly. I never remember seeing Frank quiet anywhere. I mean, if he went to bed he hit the bed like it was going through the floor, and when he woke up he was through the house in three minutes flat. There was never any peace; it was all so exhausting. Oh, sure, when there were other people around, he was *very* nice, always called me 'darling'—great husband in front of guests. But in his bad periods, he'd look at me and say, 'That color's not good on you!' And then we were in for it. I'd sit there and listen to the whole why-it's-not-good-for-me razzmatazz all over again. This is the way he used to operate: he'd excite himself; he'd have to get up, and he'd come over and say, 'This goddamn blouse!' And then he'd rip it...and once he'd touched me that would get him going, and once the blouse was ripped, then he'd slap me across the face, first with the palm and then back again with the back of his hand. Then he'd punch me. It depended on how upset he was. The bad times were when I was on the floor being kicked; they usually happened in the evening, never first thing in the morning. They happened on weekends. I don't mean that every weekend I was beaten up, but weekends could be bad, especially Sunday. I had no maid on Saturday or Sunday, and I used to hope he'd go to the hospital and work on Sunday, for Sundays were often awful. They were always a bad day for him; I think he got frustrated and angry at being around the house with no place to go.

"The whole time I was learning. I mean, getting beaten up is not all that bad—physically there's a pattern to it—when you know that there's a beginning and a middle and an end. This might sound crazy, but if you know it's going to end and you know what to expect, you learn how to shield yourself. When he started in the last ten months—just breaking me apart with words—that was harder. If he'd just kept on hitting me, I don't think I would have cracked. It was the psychological thing—the constant hammering at my mind—that was the worst.

"I suppose an outsider might have thought that one of those nights we slept in the Grand Hotel in Rome was funny. There's Mario, the manager, so proud of the fact that his bedrooms contain real antiques. And Frank comes home late from some Roman outing and he's so furious he decides to use one of Mario's antiques for his assault. It's an antique chair, a side chair, a really pretty chair; that whole suite was done in Italian antiques. It was over by the window and there was a chaise longue in front of the big bed. When Frank started on me, I had room to run. I didn't want to get in the closet because I knew if I got in that big closet he'd have me trapped. I suppose if you weren't in the process of probably getting your head knocked off it was really funny, because I was running around that damned chaise longue like a little chicken, while he kept trying to sideswipe me with the chair. I knew if I got on the closet side I'd be trapped, so I dodged back and forth. It ended when, in disgust, he threw the chair at me and it whizzed past and smashed against the wall. And I stood there puffed out but still ready to sprint.

"This sort of bout generally finished with him either slapping or kicking me. But if he'd exhausted himself, run out of steam, run out of anger, he'd slump into a chair and have a few drinks and that was the end of it. I'd go into the bathroom and have a shower and try to go on living.

"Some of these situations *were* farcical. I'd look at a room and consciously look for the best exit, the most handy piece of furniture to dodge around. At Del Monte the dining room was the best place to be. Upstairs wasn't too bad either because I could get around upstairs. But I certainly didn't want to be in the living room or in that little room at the far end because he could catch me and there'd be no way to get out; whereas in the dining room I'd have the back hall, the kitchen, three exits. And upstairs, as long as I was on the door side of the TV room, I'd have that whole upstairs to double around and back—a circle in which to get away."

11

THE year 1979 was catalytic—the year of the emotional upheaval that blew Frank and Kay Sandiford to smithereens.

Perhaps the greatest irony of that interlude was that here was a young wife aching to lend support and comfort to her husband—even though his conditioned reaction was only coldness and disdain—who, had she known how concerned he was, not only about his health, but about his career as well, might well have saved him. But Frank was too arrogant to accept her help.

The only person who knew about Frank's state was Denton Cooley. And at the time, never guessing what violence lay ahead, he bowed to the requirements of professional courtesy: silence, a silence necessarily abandoned when the explosions from Frank's Colt Python revolver on January 29 shattered the peace.

The year didn't start too badly. Kay devised a regimen to keep from going crazy. "I've always tried to keep physically fit," she said. "It's a thing with me. I've always thought that the mind and the body have to work in harmony, and Frank and I were not getting on. For a long time we were not getting on, and I got to the point where I couldn't leave the house. He didn't want me to play tennis at all, and I had gained weight—about fifteen to twenty pounds just sitting around doing absolutely nothing. And that Christmas of 1978 I made a New Year's resolution: Frank wouldn't let me play tennis, which had filled so much of my time, but I could creep up to the University Club, and Ferrie Lee would cover for me, and I'd start jogging. Everybody jogged. Why couldn't I jog? So there I was on the fifth-of-a-mile track around the top of the Galleria, in running shorts and a T-shirt, and I didn't know a soul, and I started to trot and I puffed and panted and I couldn't even get around the circuit once, not even half a circuit.

"But there was this nice guy who was out there running, and he paused briefly beside me as I dropped to a walk, and I can tell you I felt more like crying than talking, and he said, 'Oh, give it a few months and you'll be flying around.' And then he obviously saw the look on my face and the tears gathering and he said, 'Tell you what: I'll walk with you.' And he walked; he walked with me a whole mile. He didn't know me from Eve, but he knew I was dying, dying inside, at least, and if he hadn't done that, I know I would have stopped and never tried again; I would have been too disappointed. So when I got home, I had accomplished something. I said—not to Frank, of course—to me, I said, I have walked one mile today. And from that point on I would go up there every day for an hour or two. I'll never forget when I completed running my first mile. Again it was a guy who came along after I had completed four laps, and he said, 'I'll pace you.' And he made me finish that first mile. Now, I know it sounds silly, but it gave me such a sense of achievement. It didn't matter to anybody but me, but it mattered to me like swimming the Atlantic. I wasn't the useless failure Frank said I was. I *had* run a mile! Isn't that silly? Nobody could take it away from me. I had run a mile!

"Well, within that year I was eventually running eight and ten miles a day; but then I sort of checked myself and I said, 'Now, wait a minute.' My whole life was revolving around that mileage—I was living to run, not running to live—and I said, 'Wait a minute; this is getting out of control.' And I didn't want that. I wanted to do it, but then I had to get it into perspective.

"Remember, I wasn't storing up hatred against Frank. I have to repeat that time and time again. I loved him. I was at his side, doing his books, planning his trips, being a loyal and faithful wife, and thinking I probably deserved all the tears and beatings.

"Frank in his terms never made a mistake. I accepted that I was the

Kay, age three, 1943

Kay, age five, and friend: Atlantic City, New Jersey, 1945

Kay, age twelve, astride Cherokee, 1952

Kay, age thirteen, in confirmation
dress, 1952.
UDEL BROS., BALTIMORE, MD.

Kay, age eighteen, 1957: graduation
picture, Friends School, Baltimore, MD.
UDEL BROS., BALTIMORE, MD.

Kay, age nineteen (1958) in her wedding dress. UDEL BROS., BALTIMORE, MD.

Kay, age twenty-six, 1966: Central Park, New York

Kay with Charles, Connecticut, 1966

Kay with Charles, New York City, 1966

Wedding day,
marriage to Frank,
June 1968

Wedding reception,
Baltimore Country
Club, July 1968

Frank becomes an American
citizen, August 1969

Frank

Frank the heart surgeon, Texas Heart Institute

A trio of heart surgeons—Frank Sandiford, Chris Barnard, Denton Cooley—and Kay

Kay's famous tomato crop

Kay, 1978

Kay at twentieth high school reunion with Frank as guest

Kay and Frank on
holiday cruise

Kay and Frank upon arrival in Italy

Kay talks to the press in Rome

The papal meetings: Frank in audience with Pope Paul VI

Kay in audience with Pope Paul VI

Kay and Frank with Pope John Paul II, Vatican Square, 1979.

Holiday in Corsica

Frank with friends in Italy

Italian party, Sicily: Kay is served the fruit course

Fishing trip in Sicily

Frank lectures, Caracas, Venezuela.
MARCO FILM, CARACAS, VENEZUELA

Frank alone in Italy

Shattered night of January 29,
1980: Kay photographed at the
Houston Police Department

Kay attends sculpture class, 1981

End of trial, February 1981: Kay, Charles, and Marian Rosen

one who made the mistakes, like the time he wanted the lights in the garden fixed.

"Once or twice a year we used to give really big parties, invite all the people from the Texas Heart Institute...big bars, food, dancing, everybody spread out in the house, the garden, and around the pool.

"But the garden and pool area weren't very well lit, so Frank decided we had to illuminate them better.

"That morning Frank told me exactly where he wanted the lights placed in the trees, and, being Frank, he wanted them placed in the trees *now*—'now' being by the time he returned that evening. He wanted to reach out a hand, turn on a switch...and low and behold...light!

"I called the electrician, Skip, and he came out with his mate, and I guess I worked harder than the workmen worked—making sure it was *exactly* the way Frank wanted it. And Skip was really nice; he and his mate dug up the grass very neatly to conceal the cable, because I knew that if Frank saw his lawn had been disturbed there would be hell-fire and damnation. So I pleaded, 'Please, don't leave a mark!' And they were so sweet about it—remember, they were electricians, not gardeners—and I remember I went over it after they had finished, patting the turf and sweeping bits of dirt away. Everything was perfect.

"That night Frank arrived home and I knew immediately that it was a bad night. The first thing he wanted to do was have a drink outside, and off he went to switch on the lights, and then he started to have a fit! I mean a real fit!

"'What the hell do you think you've done? What's that light doing in that tree? That's *my* tree. Don't you ever hurt that tree. That tree is sacred. It's worth twice as much—no, three times as much as you are. Do you know how long it took that tree to grow? What have you done, you poor, stupid idiot, you crap American peasant?'

"By then I knew what was coming—a back-hander across my face, which knocked me into the azalea bushes. I get up and I'm already apologizing. 'Frank, I misunderstood. I didn't understand where you wanted the light placed...'

"'You didn't hear me!' he screamed. 'You didn't do what I told you to do. Now you've ruined the pine tree. You've ruined the whole damn garden. And you get this stuff out of here tonight, and I mean tonight!'

"So he just went on following me around the pool and knocking me down, and each time I'd get up, because at this stage of my punishments he was kicking me harder and that hurt a lot. But even then, I knew, or thought I knew, that he wasn't hitting me because I was me, but because he was angry and he couldn't hit his damn tree; so he hit me. But on the other hand, I was being knocked down on concrete and that hurt. I started crying. I mean, you get hit two or three times and you're upset because you've done the wrong thing one more time, and you want him to calm down, and you don't want the maid, Ferrie Lee, finding out what's going on . . . and I'm not really brave about stuff like that. I was crying and apologizing.

"So when he stopped and went in to dinner, I called Skip, because he'd been real sweet. I think he knew from my voice that I was in trouble—that morning he'd said, 'Mrs. Sandiford, if you ever have any electrical problems, even over the weekend, sure, I'll come around and fix it'—but he explained that he couldn't work in the dark and that he would come around first thing in the morning.

"Ferrie Lee brought the coffee tray into the garden and Frank went on throwing things at me—the coffeepot, the cups, the dessert—and wouldn't allow me to enter the house again that evening. I had made a mess of the whole thing; I could spend the night in the garden and tell the electricians what to do when they arrived."

Kay did as she was told. She sat in a chair all night. She felt that she had made another mistake, and she vowed to do better. That was her eternal hope, that she would stop making mistakes and begin to please Frank. She hoped her gardening enthusiasm would please him, for Kay loved growing herbs: parsley, rosemary, oregano, and marjoram. Therefore it was not surprising that she should try her hand at tomatoes. From the nursery she bought eighteen healthy-looking plants, each nine inches tall, and carefully installed them in the border in front of Frank's cypress trees. Each day she watered them, and at regular intervals she gave each one a ration of plant food and talked to them as lovingly as a junior Mother Earth. They grew so fast and tall that eventually and sadly she had to sacrifice six plants to allow the other monsters to expand. By the end of June they were five feet tall, strongly staked, and bearing fruit: ripe tomatoes, larger, rounder, more fabulously shining and scarlet than any tomatoes she had ever seen before.

Her girl friends, who crept in while Frank was away, decided she was a gardening genius. Even Ferrie Lee came out and made admiring murmurs. Frank never even noticed them.

It was during the month of July that an Italian magazine sent a small team of journalists—editor, writer, photographer—to Houston to do a feature article on the famous heart surgeon, Frank Sandiford, his work in the hospital, and his life.

At the hospital they took photographs of Frank, green-gowned, serious-faced, scalpel in hand, engrossed in a heart operation; Frank monitoring the dials on special equipment as he peered through the glass screen at one patient in the intensive care unit; Frank cuddling a cute little black girl on his knee while she played with his stethoscope.

Arriving at Del Monte, they took pictures that Kay knew would end up captioned "Dr. Sandiford, a patron of the arts, lovingly watches his wife play one of his favorite melodies on their Steinway piano," and "Dr. Sandiford is never far from a telephone in case one of his patients should need him," and "Dr. Sandiford takes a short rest on the Early American armchair in the living room of his spacious River Oaks home, while his wife arranges flowers picked from their garden."

Having completed their work and asked all their questions, the team, at Frank's suggestion, proceeded with Kay to the garden and sat around the pool while he mixed the drinks and brought them out.

In the garden they made admiring remarks and noted the wickerwork basket full of tomatoes that Kay had picked that morning. That interested them. She had grown these herself? That was remarkable!

They had never seen tomatoes so round and fat and luscious. The wife of the great heart doctor possessed unsuspected talent. To grow tomatoes of such size needed what were called "green fingers," yes? Flattered at this sincere Italian admiration, Kay blossomed. She was delighted. When Frank carried out the tray full of drinks, she cried, "Frank, they love the tomatoes. They want to take a picture of you and me admiring them!"

By the slight stiffening of features on Frank's face, Kay knew immediately—even though the Italians did not even suspect—that Frank did not see himself in this role. And that Frank was furious. That his wife should replace him in the "admiration limelight" was utterly humiliating. Kay, now observing the fixed, film-star smile—a little jagged at the edges—as he allowed the photographers to snap pictures of both of them among the gargantuan plants, knew she had made an error. She knew as they photographed Frank holding two enormous tomatoes and made allegorical Italian compliments about scarlet fruit and human hearts and sensitive surgeon's hands that he would cheerfully have strangled her.

Nevertheless, he played his part, took them all on to a tax-deductible dinner at the Doctor's Club, said good night in the usual flamboyant style to his Italian guests, and drove Kay back to Del Monte in his huge red and white Buick. He entered the house with her, made his usual telephone call to the hospital, and turned to her with the usual news that he was needed there and had to leave immediately. What he did for the rest of the night—when or if he came home—Kay did not know. But the evidence of one thing he did was quite plain.

When she went into the garden at ten or eleven the next morning, every one of her giant tomato plants had been torn up and thrown onto the concrete path. Her entire crop of slowly ripening tomatoes were ruined. Kay wept. Even Ferrie Lee was upset. Kay knew that she had made yet another "mistake."

Several months before, she had decided that Frank was working too hard, becoming much too irrational and irritable: he needed a place to relax. It was with that thought in mind that she bought the lake house near Huntsville, some seventy miles to the north. What better birthday present, on his forty-seventh birthday, than a little getaway where he could forget all his cares? And maybe understand that Kay really loved, understood, and cared for him.

"I knew it had to be a place within an hour, an hour and a half, two hours at the most, from Houston to be feasible as a weekend house or a place to go overnight. It had to be either Galveston, on the Gulf, or somewhere to the north in the green, rolling, lake country.

"I knew Galveston quite well, and I really wanted to buy a house on the beach because I love the sea. I found some pretty houses on the bay side, but the thought of having to go down to board up every time there was a hurricane warning put me off. And there were other disadvantages—many more people, transient people; and the cost was twice the price of the lake properties.

"I loved the little house I found on the lake near Huntsville. I fell in love with it as soon as I saw it. It was a great secret that I shared with Jennifer. She already lived up there, and she'd like it too.

"I bought the house and got in touch with a builder and he gave me an estimate. I gave him the go-ahead to knock out a couple of walls and reorganize various bits, while I planned the furniture. He worked hard because we had a deadline, and I had it all planned to go up the weekend of Frank's birthday ostensibly to see Jennifer and Bob. Of course, I might have guessed what would happen. Frank wouldn't go. Drive seventy miles up north just to see Jennifer and Bob! No way! He could see them anytime in Houston. So eventually I had to tell him, appeal to him. 'Please come, if only for a couple of hours. I've got a surprise for you. Frank, I've worked on this thing for three months. Please come just for tonight. If you don't want to stay we can drive back.'

"I'd hoped desperately that he'd like it, but when he walked in and saw it, well, I realized that he wasn't real wild about it. It was all right, but just all right.

"My idea was that he should come home from the hospital on Friday night and we'd go up to the lake and spend two nights up there... but as it turned out, he never wanted to go. We used it perhaps three or four times and the last time was horrific.

"It was my birthday, September ninth, and he started giving me bourbon at seven in the morning, in my coffee. I didn't want it, but he made me drink it, and he kept making me drink bourbon all day long... I don't know why. He was also drinking it. In the evening it was champagne, a sort of mocking celebration, and then he started throwing things at me, the green glass shades from the table lamps. One hit me in the head and the others smashed against the wall, and all day he'd been horrible, just telling me what to do... you take this and drink it... I told you to drink it... do as you're told. And he'd stand over me until I drank it... and that was my fortieth bithday. Then he fell asleep. He woke up and wanted pasta—I remember he wanted pasta—so I made pasta for him. But that was no good either so he threw that at me... a big bowl of pasta, thrown at me. Just what I wanted: bourbon and pasta for my birthday."

Roberto arrived in Houston in the fall of 1979 with his quiet but attractive little wife, Piera. He was on a NATO scholarship to work at the Texas Heart Institute. He was twenty-eight years old and very Italian looking. Not very tall, he wore his pale blond hair quite long and had light brown eyes. Because his English was minimal at first, he was put under Frank's tutelage and in his operating theater to learn the trade.

However, although Roberto worked under Frank as a fellow and a student, he was a full-fledged doctor, earning a salary in the hospital of between five and six thousand dollars a year. Undoubtedly both men were drawn together by their work and their Italian background and they became firm friends, with Frank undoubtedly the dominant and senior partner. Kay could never quite understand the intensity of Frank's relationship with Roberto.

Kay thought of Piera as a very quiet and sweet girl. Apparently when they first arrived they told Frank that they had tried to have a baby but had not been successful. Could Frank help? Certainly he could. He passed the problem on to Kay: she had to find an expert in gynecology. Kay asked Jennifer and a couple of her friends and discovered—with a certain ironical twist—that her own doctor was the very person they wanted. Kay arranged Piera's first appointment, and Piera soon became pregnant.

Kay didn't expect a medal, maybe just a little friendship, but Frank closed her out. Roberto and Piera often came to Kay's house but Kay was invited only once to theirs. Frank made his position plain to Kay: he decided she didn't like them; she looked down on them. If she joined him on the visits he made, they would know that she looked down on them; therefore she couldn't go. Moreover, Piera was a real woman; she was having a child, an accomplishment Kay was quite incapable of performing.

That transparent lie hurt Kay deeply, as did the knowledge that when the child was born, Frank was going to be asked to be its godfather. She would not even be invited to the christening; she had nothing in common with these fine young people.

Roberto and Piera also, and obviously, knew all about Frank's meeting with Liza, the young Italian cardiologist from northern Italy, and his growing relationship with her. In fact, it was they who first brought Liza to the Del Monte house and witnessed the painful scene there.

They were all in the small room where drinks were served—Roberto and Piera, Liza, and Frank—while Kay was busy mixing drinks and serving small hors d'oeuvres, which was her usual duty. The conversation seemed quite friendly and innocuous, especially when Liza prefaced a remark to Kay with, "Oh, *Signora* Sandiford..."

The impact on Frank was unbelievable. Even now Kay can remember his noisy intervention: "Frank just had a fit. He burst into her conversation and just turned a torrent of hate on me. How I acted as if I were a queen when I was nothing but an American peasant, and always would be an American peasant.

"The others looked at him in surprise, but remained silent. He berated me to the point where I burst into tears and had to leave the room. Frank had done this to me a hundred times before, but never in front of our guests. I couldn't understand that. And never for a moment did I suspect that it was all because he was getting involved with the charming young cardiologist, and that the trigger to his emotional outburst had been her innocent reference to *Signora* Sandiford."

That November another incident occurred that Kay found rather strange. If Frank had had girl friends, they'd certainly never rung him at the house. But now there was a woman's voice on the phone, asking for Frank. Thinking about it long afterward, Kay realized that the woman could not have been Liza, because this woman's English, although accented, was good. Also, Frank was then speaking Italian as much as he could, and when called to the telephone he began his long and loving conversation in English: "Yes, darling, I love you too. Yes, of course, we shall meet at Thanksgiving. . . ."

Kay sat in her chair slightly stunned. Never in their whole married life had Frank talked in front of her like this before. She was so taken aback that she didn't even walk out. Yes, she was aware that Frank always said contemptuously, "Sure, women are crazy about me, always following me around. You'll have to get used to it." And she had got used to the Frank Sandiford admiration societies. But never before had she thought in terms of a *reciprocal* relationship. And she was hurt. In some distress, she said, "Frank, if you want to carry on like that, at least don't flaunt it in front of me."

Frank was immediately angry. "If you don't want to hear it, you can leave. You can leave, do you hear?"

Kay had not wanted to go to Italy on their last journey, in October 1979. She told Frank there was no point: when they got there he was never with her anyway. She was always left behind, locked in the hotel room. And the trips often lasted four to six weeks. It was always a bad scene, with him down on her. Why, then, didn't he just take off alone?

No way. Frank wasn't prepared even to discuss the matter, and Kay knew why. He had arranged for an audience with the new pope, John

Paul II, no doubt in continuing pursuit of his private ambition to become one of the pope's physicians, and on this occasion would bear a gold-plated brass heart and a book of photographs and text commemorating the work of the Texas Heart Institute for presentation to His Holiness. Protocol demanded that his pious little wife be at his side.

Kay remembers the occasion as one of the most bizarre of her life. From the time they'd awakened in the apartment at the Hassler, Frank as usual had been on to her and kept on to her.

The papal audience was set for eleven in the morning in Saint Peter's Square. Apparently Pope John Paul did not believe only in private audiences; on this occasion he instructed that his throne be brought out of the Vatican into the open air. But that situation, as far as Frank was concerned, was all Kay's fault, all her fault that they were not being seen in the pope's private chambers. In vain Kay tried to point out that Father Georgi had set up his audience, and if the pope preferred to hold it in the square, there was little she could do about it. Frank ranted on. Even as she stumbled across Saint Peter's Square in her long, hot, black dress, wearing her long, hot, black veil and carrying the heavy, solid brass heart that Frank was going to present to the pope on behalf of the Texas Heart Institute, he berated her: she looked dreadful; she was the only woman in the audience; she had no right to be there. He couldn't stop.

It was October 31, All Hallow's Day, the celebration of the dead, and ever since Kay has wondered how prophetic that was to prove. She listened to the pope's blessing of the dead in seven languages, and three months later, almost to the day, she shot Frank Sandiford dead. But that morning in the heat and dust, it was her own survival that she doubted.

The score or so of people who were to receive the papal blessing sat in a double line of chairs in front of the throne. The sun was very hot. The crowd, kept back by barriers from the central area of the square, was huge. The pope approached and, seeing a woman in his audience, walked to where she sat to talk to her first. Both Kay and Frank stood up. Frank took the brass heart from the velvet case in Kay's hands and presented it to the pope. The pope thanked him and handed the gifts to a secretary who stood at his side, then extended his ringed hand to Kay. She bent low to kiss it, as she had learned to do from her previous audience, and the pope extended both arms to lift her to her feet. But as he did so, she felt Frank's shoulders heave her out of the way, so that she stumbled out of the pope's arms and Frank was there instead.

For a split second she saw consternation darken the pope's face as he held on to Frank. But she rationalized, "I guess he was used to people crowding and pushing in on him while photographers were clicking away. Still, it was such a shocking moment. And I thought, *There's something really wrong.* I know the pope's not my pope, but at the same time anyone who could do that—push me out of the way while the pope is actually lifting me up with his hands around my shoulders, so that he will get the blessing and I will not—must be very strange. But then Frank frightened me practically all the time on that visit."

Then, suddenly, for the first time in their dozen journeys to Italy, Frank declared that he had to go off alone. Claire, a former patient of his, was going to take care of Kay. Claire, an attractive, intelligent woman in her fifties, was going to take Kay to Lugano, where she had an apartment, and then, together, they would take a trip to Zurich, Geneva, and back to Milan, where Frank would join them. Kay had no option but to agree.

The trip took four days. In Lugano they saw an exhibition of fourteenth and fifteenth-century painters and dined at the Oasis. In Zurich they stayed at the Baur au Lac Hotel and walked around the town. Ordinarily Kay would have felt stimulated and excited, but now she was drained of self-confidence.

"I had disintegrated," she said. "Leaving Lugano, I felt I couldn't make a move; I didn't have enough guts to get myself into a taxi. And this was *me*, who used to charge across to Switzerland to see Charles and stay in a hotel and make friends with all the visiting parents. Frank seemed to have numbed even my will. When I look back, I find it unbelievable. In Milan—and Frank wasn't there when we arrived, only showed up in Rome much later—I couldn't get a taxi to go to the airport and catch a plane. I had to have a friend go with me. I had shriveled into a little, helpless American girl who sat in her hotel bedroom in Milan, eating a little bit of salami and drinking half a bottle of wine, because she didn't have the confidence even to go sit in the hotel dining room."

Later, when she had had time to reflect on that trip, Kay was disappointed with many of the Italian women she had thought of as friends.

"Some of them were wonderful—still are to this day. But many of them knew all about Frank, and knew that he was off with Liza during that period. I'd been sitting there on all those journeys through all those years, thinking that they were my friends—listening to all that chitchat about how crappy their husbands really were, and I'm denying the very idea of Frank behaving like that—and they're chuckling behind their hands at this dumb little American wife.

"I was so defensive and supportive of Frank it was like a mania. I knew Frank *must* succeed Denton eventually as head of the Heart Institute; I thought he was the finest surgeon in the world. I was fanatical about his getting ahead and becoming a great success; I was fanatical in the way I praised him. But that was the way my deep unhappiness relieved itself; everything about me on that trip was fanatical.

"In a few days Frank arrived back in Rome—he'd been off looking for patients in the south, he said—and the lonely pattern of days and dinners returned. Frank took me out alone to dinner one night and we spent less than an hour together before he said he had to leave, returning me to the hotel so he could go out. The intensity of his emotions was steadily increasing. When he was telling me what to do or say, he would grab my arm. Those big, strong surgeon's hands would grind a thumb up into my armpit or knuckles into my side, and it hurt like hell. And I was scared to death of him by this time. Sometimes he'd grab me by the throat. Sometimes he'd find a pressure point and knock me out. And I would do whatever he'd say: you know, 'I'll do it, I'll do it, but don't touch me; please don't hurt me again.'

"I couldn't go out with my eyes all puffy from crying. I'd cry all day long. I couldn't stop crying. And Frank would start on me every time he was with me—how worthless I was, that I didn't have any reason to live, and why did I take up his time when he'd done all he could for me? He never stopped. The fact that, consciously or unconsciously, he was trying to destroy me never entered my head. At that time I thought, *I guess I really am worthless*, and I cried because I was worthless, though I tried so hard to be something.

"Then, of course, the 'packing' syndrome didn't help my condition. Oh, God, we'd start out from America with nine suitcases and come home with fourteen; you can't imagine the garbage we collected. And Frank wanted to take it all home, but at the same time he wanted to go through and decide what was useful and what he could give away as gifts to people he knew in Rome—forty or fifty gifts: the plants, the handmade baby clothes, the bottles of wine, the tablecloths, Etruscan art.

"We'd come down to the morning when we were to leave; we're staring a dozen more suitcases in the face, plus the fact that we've still got ten people in the room left over from last night waiting to see Frank. I mean it was like holy hell. He'd be talking to these people and smiling at me—never screaming at me in front of them—and then he'd take my arm, grab me, and lead me into the other room and that's when he'd start: 'Why aren't you packed?' How could I pack when he didn't want me to pack? I couldn't make a move. There was no way of satisfying Frank. I'd manage to get myself packed; then he'd get these friends to pack for him and I'd stand there like an idiot. Then he'd take me into the closet or the bathroom or bedroom, hit my head against the wall, shake me, and I'd be hysterical, I'd be like a zombie. I'd stay in the closet for maybe thirty minutes, sobbing soundlessly. Everyone must have known that I was absolutely strung out. Don't tell me it passed over those people. And it was constantly like that at night for three or four days before we left; the twenty-four-hour day, maybe two or three hours' sleep at most, not being able to communicate, never being able to do anything right, never being able to make a move. If I made a move I was open to attack. It was like: I should stand here, but if I stand here I'm going to be shot down; but if I move I'm going to be shot down also. So there was nothing I could do but take it. And the whole point of it was that there was no way to control or change the situation or have any influence over events. It was just a Roman nightmare. These last two trips to Italy were the worst—the trips in 1979. The last one was the end. You see, I'd gotten into a crying state; I literally cried the whole year. I'd burst into tears almost anywhere, and that year I didn't really see many of my friends."

But Frank, Kay now believes, was disintegrating as rapidly as she.

"For the last few months of the year, and especially after Christmas, Frank began talking to himself. That was when I really began to lose contact at any level with him, because I could never catch his eye; he wouldn't look at me. If I could catch his eye, I could sort of tell where he was at. I couldn't tell what was going to set him off, but if I could catch his eye, I could sort of feel if he was building up to something, and I could try to take evasive action.

"Always he started out verbally; he didn't start out slugging. He started with 'constructive criticism' but the slightest thing could set him off. And, strangely, in those last months he rapidly regressed into Italian. It really was remarkable; even in Houston he reverted to his native language. He wouldn't speak English unless he had to, and all his patients were Italian, so all his time was spent with Italians, and he became more and more Italian."

At this time also, he began to terrify her with his threat that he intended to murder Denton Cooley. Denton stood in the way of Frank becoming head of the institute. Frank intended to smuggle in a gun from abroad and kill him. Seeming almost as unreal was what Kay went through for Roberto and Piera that Christmas. Every time he saw her Frank nagged her about them: "'They must be given presents. Don't you realize that, unlike you, she's having a baby? They need flowers, books, wine...you get them.'"

Frank wanted her to buy the complete baby layette: clothes, feeding utensils, cradle, toys—all to be presented by the loving godfather. Kay told him that the whole idea was ridiculous; the chances were that the two young people would return to Italy before the child was born, and to carry all the material he wanted to give them would be a burden. Reluctantly, Frank accepted her reasoning: "'Well, then, for Christmas they must have things for the immediate present: the best wine money can buy; flowers—lots of flowers.' Why should he do this for Roberto? Because at last he'd found a partner in the operating theater who'd stand up for Frank Sandiford—against all the lunatic doctors, administrators, nurses, technicians, and all the members of the staff who'd balked him at every turn, and had done so for the last God knows how many years."

One day about a week before Christmas, Kay drove to her favorite wine store, loaded wine into the car, and drove home. It was exactly the brand of Italian wine, the correct vintage and importer, that Frank had specified. When he came home it was arrayed on the kitchen table for his approval. He seemed to be in a reasonable mood. They were going out for dinner. She had to go up and get dressed. She knew what he liked her to wear. Pleased, she went upstairs and dressed in a white silk blouse and a black gabardine skirt—sensible and right for any occasion. As she came down the stairs, she could hear first one, then two, then a third bottle smashing out in the garden.

"He was livid. 'This isn't the wine I told you to get, you idiot. This is crap, you incompetent fool. What's the matter with you? Can't you even do the simplest task?' The note specifying the wine, in his handwriting, lay on the kitchen table. I pushed it nervously toward him saying, 'But, Frank, it's written down here. It says—'

"But Frank wasn't listening to any reasoning. 'You can't expect us to go out to dinner after a thing like this!' he shouted. 'Go back upstairs and take those clothes off. Don't waste those clothes. Go and take them off.'"

Obediently Kay went upstairs again and changed back into her ordinary clothes. Coming downstairs, she could hear him telling Ferrie Lee what a wonderful cook she was. That stung a bit. The only thing Ferrie Lee ever cooked in Kay's house was okra, fried tomatoes, or fried chicken.

The adoration of Robert and Piera went on for approximately two weeks. Frank's next gift was to be poinsettias, individual plants, set in attractive Roman clay pots. The sooner Kay bought them the better. So Kay went around to several nurseries and collected the most beautiful poinsettias she had ever seen—red, pink, white, every color of poinsetta known to nature. She carted the plants and pots back home, planted each flower with loving hands, tied a ribbon around each to match the color, and inscribed neat little cards.

"Frank came home, took one look at my collection, and off he went again. 'You idiot, you fool, you useless piece of humanity. This is crap-crap-crap...' He emphasized each 'crap' by kicking over a plant and smashing the pot to pieces."

There was no pleasing Frank that Christmas, but in the past there had often been occasions when there was no pleasing Frank. She always remembered the time when Charles was home on a school holiday and they were having dinner: Kay tried her best to avoid having dinner with both him and Frank around; inevitably Frank vented his rage against either her or her son.

"That particular night Frank decided to pick on Charles," she said. "'What did you do at school today? How's your Latin? Terrible, as usual, I suppose.' Charles mumbled a reply, not in an offensive way, but he knew, as I knew, that no matter what he said he was going to be wrong. So bang—down goes Frank's fork; the salad sails across the table. I mean, Clochette often got a treat because Frank would thrust his plate on the floor saying it was only fit for the dog: 'Clochette, eat that!' And she'd trot over and eat his dinner off a china plate.

"Anyway, that night he got absolutely livid. And even though we knew Frank, when he got up furiously and stamped upstairs, we had no idea that he was rushing up to get, of all things, a gun—a thirty-eight revolver. He always kept it at his bedside, loaded and very often cocked. Charles and I went on eating and I remember Charles saying, 'Heck, I hope he cools off and watches television,' and I said, 'Oh, he's just blown his top again. Get on with your meal, that's a good boy.' And then, my God, from where I sat at the end of the table, I could see through to the hall stairs, and there's Frank rushing down brandishing the thirty-eight. I yelled at Charles, 'He's got a gun!' Charles leaped up and started running around the table, with Frank shouting at him and pointing the gun at him. Charles tore out through the back door, with Frank after him yelling his head off, but Charles was too quick for him and shot down the drive and disappeared along Del Monte. Frank stopped running then, but went on screeching, 'That son of a bitch! That young bastard! That no-good layabout!' I was terribly upset, crying, 'Frank, you can't do this. If you go on doing this I'll call the police.' Of course I didn't—never would have. But I was terrified. He was trying to kill my son! I wasn't worried about his yelling. Nobody hears anything in that neighborhood; you could die and go to heaven and no one would hear the noise. So Frank stormed back into the hall, shouting, "I don't want that no-good kid in the house again. I want him out of this house for good.' And he slammed upstairs to drink and watch television for the rest of the evening.

"I sat down on the front step. I was nearly hysterical at first, and then I slowed down to tears, just waiting for my son to come home. I couldn't call people; I didn't know what to do. So I cried and cried until I heard him in the drive, about two hours later—must have been close to midnight. We hugged and kissed. Eventually we sat down in the garden, under the magnolia tree, and Charles said slowly, and I've never forgotten his words, 'Jesus, Mom,' he said, 'why do you stay with that son of a bitch? Get out from under it. I'm not going to be here forever.' But, as usual, I was making excuses for everybody and everything. 'Charles, you know we've got to hold the family together, have to make everything look right. Once everything with you is settled, then I'll think about it.'" But even as she said it she knew she could never explain to Charles. When you're married it's for better or worse. Until death do us part. She was a wife. A loving wife. She had convinced herself of that. There was no walking out on that. Now or ever.

12

Kay Sandiford watched Angela approach and, her voice slightly reproving, ask, "Mrs. Sandiford?"

Kay was chatting with Victoria on the settee in the solarium. She inclined her head toward the attractive receptionist. "Yes?"

"Your husband is on the phone." Kay remembered the firm admonition given to her on her arrival: telephone calls from *anyone* were not welcome; Main Chance was *your* chance to abandon boyfriends, lovers, or husbands, especially husbands. Forgetting your (not necessarily) nearest or dearest was part of the protocol and therapy.

"I'll come at once," Kay said.

She glanced sideways at Victoria, who was raising her eyebrows.

Victoria, sixty-five, looking forty-five, slender as a bamboo shoot, elegant as only the vast fortune left by the loving and alas "late" husband could make her, was that not-so-rare creature at Main Chance, a merry widow. She smiled. "Don't forget, Kay, we're in wax in ten minutes. I love being a fly in aspic."

Kay followed Angela toward the reception area. In expiation of her transgression, she asked, "I wonder how he found out. Did he say where he was calling from?"

"No, he didn't," Angela replied politely. "Would you take it in that booth over there, Mrs. Sandiford?"

Her spirits sagging, Kay picked up the phone, turning on her bright public voice, the same voice she used countless times after Frank had twisted her arm until it nearly came off and then pushed her through the door to welcome the guests. She thought, *What am I, good actress, fake person, or just survivor?* "Hello, Frank," she said.

The voice was distant, but clear and, as usual, unfriendly. "Where are you?" he demanded.

She decided on flippancy. "You know where I am; you've just rung me. Are you calling from Italy?" He was too far away to hit her. She could chance being playful.

"It doesn't matter where I am. What are you doing there?"

"Remember, Frank, I told you about Main Chance and we told everybody we were going to Arizona on vacation. I thought I'd better show up so I'd have something to talk about."

"Don't be funny with me," he snapped and then added suspiciously, "What is this place you're at?"

"I told you but you didn't listen. It's called Main Chance—a beauty and health spa in the middle of the Arizona desert near Phoenix. Very exclusive. Hard to get a booking. A friend had her reservation made six months ago and then had to cancel. She offered it to me. That's why I'm here."

Frank's voice was harsh. "I want you home."

Why didn't she say, "I'm not coming home?"

"Okay, Frank. When are you arriving back?"

"I'm back on January twenty-second. I want you to meet me with the car at the airport. Understand?"

"Yes, I understand, Frank. I'll be there. Ring me with your flight number and time of arrival."

She put down the phone, conscious that she was shaking slightly. The twenty-second gave her time to finish her stay on the twentieth, as planned, and get back to Del Monte two days before he did. She drew in her breath sharply, a cold wind of remembrance bringing back fear. "The gun. God! Will he bring back the gun?" She stood in the booth for a second, giving herself the lecture: "You're having a great time here. Therapeutic! Healthy! Relaxing! Go out and face the world." She smiled at Angela as she went past. "Thank you. Sorry he rang."

Angela smiled back, showing her beautiful teeth. "Think nothing of it. He sounded great. What a voice! You're lucky."

Kay thought, *Even from three thousand miles away Frank can exact his tribute of female adoration.* What was his recent angry contemptuous boast? "If they're good for my career, I'll sleep with them." "Yes, I suppose I am," Kay said untruthfully, and went to join Victoria, who would already be immersed in her weight-reducing basket of hot wax.

Maybe, Kay thought as she retraced her steps toward the solarium, her determination to go to Main Chance had had something to do with the unconscious rebellion that had prompted her on Christmas Eve to strike Frank in anger. Kay hated to admit it, but during the past year she had been much happier when Frank was out of the house rather than in it. However, Christmas Eve was a special occasion and she loved special occasions. Charles was home, and it would be a small family celebration. Kay had cooked the meal; Ferrie Lee would serve it. They would all try to have a really good time.

But practically as soon as they'd gathered at the table Kay had known all her hopes were in vain. Over the past few months Frank's habit of talking to himself had increased, and during the main course he'd started doing it again. First he was addressing himself to the food. "This food is terrible. It's uneatable. Who cooked this terrible crap? Is this supposed to be the sort of food anyone would want to eat on Christmas Eve? And look at this napkin. Doesn't anyone know how to fold a napkin in this house? These napkins look like washrags. And this silver. This silver's never been polished. Nothing's been done in this house, nothing."

Kay had sat throughout it, silently listening. She knew better than to utter a single syllable. But she was worried about Charles. And she was bitterly disappointed. Just this one evening was all she'd asked, and now. . . .

Meanwhile, Charles had seized an opportunity, a small break in Frank's monologue, and slipped away to the kitchen, where he could take refuge pretending to help Ferrie Lee.

Frank thereupon had gone upstairs, and after a while Kay had followed him into the TV room, where he was standing up drinking Petrus out of the bottle. "Just one dinner with Charles and me, was that asking too much?" she'd blurted out.

And he'd turned to her, taunting: "So why don't you do something about it? Why don't you show some backbone? Haven't you got any guts?"

It was the first time she'd ever struck him in her life, and as soon as she had, he'd gotten that dark look in his eyes that terrified her. And he'd beaten her savagely. And during it she'd never made a sound.

Kay now also pondered Frank's recent threat about the gun, the most sinister threat he'd ever made. He was going to kill Denton Cooley. He'd gone to Italy professedly to collect a revolver from some friends, and either he or they would smuggle it home. He was going to kill Denton Cooley for several reasons: first because Denton was very jealous of Frank's skill as a heart surgeon and for that reason did not intend to advance Frank's career; secondly because Denton had a son-in-law working as a heart surgeon at the institute and no doubt would try to assure the son-in-law's succession; thirdly because Denton was getting too old to do the job and he, Frank, was the only one who could possibly replace him.

As with Frank's other threats and fantasies, Kay did not know what to believe. She knew—or, rather, she knew from what Frank had told her—that he hated Americans, in particular Denton Cooley. But was he just fantasizing, or was he trying a new way to terrorize her? Frank was so crazy she couldn't possibly know.

But Frank's craziness was getting to her too. Several months earlier it was Frank's utter fascination with guns that had prompted her to buy the .357 Colt Python revolver from Oshman's sports shop in Houston. Frank had been conferring with a neighbor of theirs, who was a great sportsman and an excellent shot. He owned a .357 Colt Python, and Frank, handling it, thought it was the greatest weapon he'd ever seen.

To Kay, purchasing it, it looked like the biggest revolver in the world. Not even in old Westerns had she seen cowboys wielding guns as big as this. It frightened her. But Frank had dropped all the hints, and Kay, "to take the heat off a bit, and perhaps make him relax with a new toy," had gone out and bought it.

And then, impelled by that same vestige of rebellion that had driven her to strike him, she'd seized her opportunity and headed for Main Chance.

Little did she suspect as she rejoined Victoria in their skin-cleansing wax treatment that her third and last rebellion, now less than two weeks distant, would blow Frank and his fantasies away forever.

Three

THE
TRIAL

13

SPRING in East Texas is rapturous, and it was a good spring the year between Frank Sandiford's death and the trial, when Kay Sandiford needed it most. Practically every weekend she took Highway 45, heading north for Huntsville and the lake house, returning only when she had vital commitments in the city.

She remembered that year as one of profound self-examination—and relief. She hadn't realized how unbearable life with Frank had been.

Past the Woodlands on 45, on a Friday afternoon in early June, she reached Conroe, which marks the end of the residential overspill from Houston and the beginning of the gentle, green, rolling East Texas countryside. For more centuries than local historians can count, Indians, nomadic and pastoral, lived and hunted in these hills. Their disappearance is not mourned. In Texas the destruction of men, forests, and land and their replacement by real estate and industrial development are considered healthy signs of prosperity and growth. So, except for a few reservations, the Indians are as remote today as the cloud shadows that pass over the lakes lying in the hollows between the hills. Yet they were present in their hundreds when Pleasant Gray, adventurer and pioneer from Alabama, located his Indian Post here about 1830 to mark the beginning of Huntsville.

Today, despite the fact that the Texas penitentiary for both male

171

and female prisoners lies on its periphery—a disquieting fact that Kay could hardly miss as she neared the town's outskirts—it is a quiet and pretty town, with a museum and close associations with Sam Houston, after whom its university is named, and it retains its own distinct flavor and friendliness.

To Kay, during that year preceding the trial, when she tried to close out pressures and retain her sanity, the house near Huntsville provided both a refuge and a restorative.

Her feelings of guilt continued unabated. No matter how her friends tried to cheer her by saying, "The case will never go to trial; you'll never go to prison," the trial itself was not in the forefront of her mind. Fixed there was the stigma of her worthlessness; she felt she was as marked and repellent as a leper doomed to a life of ostracism and despair. So she would park her car and hide herself in the cottage on the lake.

Marian Rosen knew all about Kay's fears and tried to counter them. She knew that when Charles returned to school at the end of the summer, as inevitably he must, Kay would insist on living in the big house on Del Monte again. That resolve was fixed in Kay's mind with desperate intensity, perhaps because of Frank's brutal and abrupt attempt to force her out of it.

Before summer's end, therefore, Marian, anticipating what bad memories might be reawakened, was anxious to get someone close to the Del Monte house, someone Kay could turn to in the event of a crisis. The double garage at the back of the house offered a potential solution. On the upper floor was space that could be converted into a small apartment. Marian looked for a volunteer and found one in a young law student, Michael Von Blon, a graduate of the University of Texas, who worked in Marian's office. Sure, he'd like to live in the garage apartment, especially as he was certain to be involved in much of the legwork leading up to the trial.

Michael was twenty-five years old, tall, sensitive, serious-minded, and sympathetic. He had a quick and ready smile and an engaging, youthful attitude toward life. What he did not realize, when he agreed in the spring to undertake the task of becoming Kay's guardian, was how deeply he would become involved in her predicament himself.

Michael liked the idea of living in a comfortable neighborhood and a free apartment, because he was still putting himself through law school. But he had second thoughts when he went around to meet Kay. He had been told to go to the back door, because that was the only door she would answer. But even then, she wouldn't let him in. Even though she had received a phone call from Marian Rosen's office telling her that he was coming, she called through the door that she had no intention of letting any man, especially a strange man, into her house.

Michael was patient. Michael was kind. Eventually Kay opened the door. And after listening to his story, she took him across to the garage apartment, which still awaited its alterations.

There was a lot of old junk there and Kay began to fuss with it. She came across a pair of surgical gloves, which she fastened onto as if they were jeweled gauntlets, instantly recalling that they were the gloves Frank had used in performing his first open-heart operation.

She turned appealingly to Michael, asking if he thought she should donate them to Denton Cooley or some other medical organization because they were terribly important, weren't they?

Michael soon discovered that Kay had emerged from the nightmare in January believing absolutely that she was guilty: she had not understood Frank; she had not done her duty by him; she had been a terrible wife; she had deserved to be beaten; she had squandered the life of a great human being; and even though she couldn't recall the faintest suggestion of the crime, she accepted without question her culpability. Michael realized that Kay was still very much attached to Frank, and that the year elapsing between Frank's death and the trial would be filled with anxieties and forebodings.

"Kay had retreated into a little womb of helplessness," he recalled. "She just never went out of the house, never looked out through the curtains—just stayed inside what she called her 'mausoleum.'"

It took Michael six weeks to cajole her into venturing out into the garden. The lawn needed watering and Michael had to know how to turn the sprinklers on. He remembered Kay standing on the front lawn looking at a passing car as if it were the first one she had ever seen. Three weeks later he discovered her opening a curtain to let the daylight in.

Kay avoided the dining room on Del Monte as if it contained a monster. Then one day she opened the door and looked in, then walked in and touched the table, which had once belonged to her parents. And so, slowly, week by week her confidence returned, and Michael was there to reassure her.

Kay still thinks of Michael as a "treasure," such a good friend in her time of need. "I kept calling him a little boy and Michael was polite and sweet enough to accept it. There was no way I could stand any man—especially a man around the house. I'd call the River Oaks police and tell them when I was going to the lake, and I'd say, 'But it's all right; the little boy will be here to look after it.' And they'd sound puzzled and say, 'Oh, you mean the *young man* who lives in the quarters?' and I'd say, 'No, the *little boy* who lives in the quarters,' and they'd realize I was a bit nutty and say, 'Okay, ma'am, that's all right.'

"I was adamant that Michael remain a little boy. He went to the office every morning about eight o'clock and he came home every night about six thirty, and we'd have dinner probably once a week, but he was around and that's what I needed.

"During the first weeks I was home, the DA's office or the police department were always coming to take samples of paint or look at the carpet, all sorts of stuff, and I'd insist that Michael be with me when they came. I needed *anything* to cling to. I was walking a thin line, and life didn't mean a damn thing to me. It really didn't. I mean, the whole idea of getting up there in a courtroom was impossible.

"I was not ever going to say anything about my life. It was so awful and so ugly, and as Frank had said, 'Nobody will ever understand our relationship. You can't ever get out of it, you can't ever tell anybody, because nobody has had a relationship like we've had; nobody has done the things we've done.' I had this in my head, and not only in my head—it had seeped into the bones and tissues of my being.

"I had done ugly things with Frank, things you'd not have dreamed existed, and I was guilt-ridden about them, guilt-ridden to the point of self-destruction, but especially over the fact that I'd shot him. Although I didn't or couldn't remember it, I knew I'd done it. People told me I'd done it. So it seemed in those weeks I'd never reach the trial.

"There was a time in those first few months when I was drinking like you wouldn't believe. Whatever anybody put into my hand I'd drink. I had to keep moving; I had to do something or the world would spin away from me. So if I got three invitations for drinks and two for dinner the same night—and for a period there I really did—I'd go to somebody's house and have a drink, and then I'd go to somebody else's house and have another drink, and I couldn't handle all that liquor. I'd never drunk seriously before in my life.

"Then it hit me. I realized that in all this fake sort of social scene

I was really a freak, the woman who'd shot her husband—what a giggle—
and it pulled me up short. I knew then that I had to sort out who were
the real friends and who were just the morbidly curious, the name drop-
pers, the sensation seekers. And I needed to make a few quick decisions.
The first was obvious: stop drinking. Which I did. Overnight.

"But many people were marvelous: my neighbors, in particular, and
my tennis friends. I found out later that a group of them had arranged
among themselves that I wasn't going to be left alone for a single evening,
and they worked out a rota to make certain that it happened."

The turning point in Kay's purgatory occurred on the nineteenth
of June, a Thursday. Marian Rosen arranged for Leonore Walker, an
expert psychiatrist from Denver, to come to Houston and talk to Kay. It
was only after those two days of conversation and gentle interrogation
that the black mental barriers that Kay had erected began to come down.

"It was after talking to Leonore and reading her book on battered
women, and then starting to read other books on that subject, that I
began to see a glimmer of light and could begin to believe that perhaps,
after all, I was not a freak, that other women had experienced the same
sort of hell I had. At first I couldn't believe it, I couldn't take it in; it was
like finding a new continent. I didn't know such things as battered women
existed. But here were all *my* experiences, all my symptoms, written
down.

"During that spring I'd been seeing a lot of women, through the
University Club, through tennis, through jogging. They knew I'd shot
Frank and I suppose they'd seen the newspaper reports, which mentioned
the beatings. Several began to cultivate me; they wanted someone to
unburden to, someone who perhaps understood... some of my own
friends, a wide variety of women.

"Sometimes on weekends I used to jog on a dirt track over at Lamar
High School, not far away from Del Monte. One Saturday I was jogging
around and this girl cruised up alongside. I didn't mind when girls came
up and talked to me, but I just hated men approaching me. She asked
if I was Kay Sandiford, and I said yes. 'Can I talk to you?' she asked,
and I said, 'Sure, but let's just go on jogging.' So around we went and
she told me that she had been married seven years and had two kids,
and that her husband used to beat the devil out of her every Friday night.

"It was the classic pattern: pay night; he gets drunk with the guys,
comes home, realizes he's spent too much money, and takes out his

anger and aggression on the nearest object—his wife. She probably goads him with, 'Where've you been? Who've you been with?' which doesn't ease the situation.

"This girl said she couldn't stand much more of it and wanted to know what to do.

"I said, 'Do you have anything in your name?'"

"'No, I don't,' she said.

"'Do you have any money of your own?'

"'No, I don't; he gives me about eighty dollars a week.'

"I told her that if she really wanted a divorce, she'd have to plan for it. She had to plan collecting his back tax records, copies of them, which she was perfectly entitled to do. And this wouldn't take only a couple of weeks: it might take as many years.

"She said she hadn't been happy since the birth of her first child or shortly thereafter. It was a regular pattern of beating; it might stop for six weeks, then it would occur four weeks straight. I told her it wouldn't get any better—because by now my reading was getting extensive, and I was becoming knowledgeable on the subject. Sometimes also I was almost stupefied by how so many of the cases duplicated my own. I'd always thought, as so many women do, that I was the unlucky oddball who got hit. I'd thought I deserved it, that it was my own fault. Never for a second did I realize I was just one of countless women getting this vicious treatment.

"We jogged and talked through three or four sessions after that, and suddenly she failed to show up. I guessed what had happened. With two young boys, she'd had to accept the tough option and stay with him, taking the same old stuff. Women get to the point where they believe they can make that big first step of separation, but when they have to consider finances, social standing, making a living—not in the sense of a financial living, but of being an entity, a person, an individual standing on her own two feet—it often proves too hard for them. For a woman to go out on her own, one who has never worked—maybe gone to college, maybe not—it's too much. Her identity reposes in her home and her family. And to throw that all up and suddenly become a nonperson . . . it's frightening.

"It's frightening for her to even think of having to compete outside. In the house she is the kingpin, like being the head of a department, and to be suddenly thrust out and find herself trying to earn a living as a salesgirl—sometimes it's impossible to cope with the shock of such a change. So she figures, well, he only beats me once a week, or maybe only once every two months if I'm lucky.

"But, my God, I know, and they know, what that attack, that cruelty, does to your soul. It's crucifying!

"Of course, sometimes I had to go down to the court for what they called motion hearings, when tricky points of law were argued out between defense and prosecution and the judge made various rulings about what could and could not be done. Most of this went over my head. I could come to grips with the knowledge that I must go down to the court and sit there, and how very important it was for me to be physically present, but the matter-of-fact attitude of the law and the people concerned with it was very distressing to me; it took me a full day to get over having to go down to the courthouse."

It was in the spring, azalea time in Houston, when Kay made her first small attempt to appear at a social event. It was the time of the Azalea Trail, when people with big houses and beautiful gardens open them up so that flower lovers have an opportunity to admire them. Every house that opens needs a few helpers to steer people around, and a friend of Kay's asked her to help out. So, nervous but smiling, Kay stood in the garden telling people which way to go. It worked for a while. But she noticed the look on the faces of certain people she hadn't seen for some time; she saw their faces change as they saw her, and she didn't like what she saw. So she tried to hide behind an azalea bush, but that didn't work either, so she went back to her post and tried smiling again. It was not a successful return to society. The next attempt went better.

"In November one of Denton Cooley's daughters was getting married, and I was invited to the wedding. Michael and Charles and a bunch of my friends were also invited. It was a very big affair, and I agreed to go if they all promised they wouldn't leave me alone. It was at the Houston Country Club and about two thousand people were present. And as soon as we arrived and the dancing started, Denton made a point of asking me to dance, and I danced several dances with him, and I've never fogotten his chivalry and understanding in leading me out on the floor and giving me his moral support and friendship...though he scared me to death with his first question, when he said casually, "Kay, where've you been keeping the body?" I went almost rigid. Body? I wasn't hiding the body...then I realized that Denton was referring to the black turtleneck dress I was wearing; it was the only slightly sexy dress I had, because Frank always wanted me properly covered up. And I relaxed; I managed to squeeze out a laugh, but it wasn't a very loud one."

The only really cruel and cold rebuff Kay Sandiford received at that time came from a woman she'd once thought of as a good friend. A friendly acquaintance had tried to effect the reintroduction: "Kay, she would like to see you; she's told me so. Send her a note and she'll reply and you can meet." So Kay wrote a small note and on impulse, instead of posting it, took it across to the other house to pop it in the letter box. As she drove in through the gate and halted in the driveway, she saw that a River Oaks patrol car stood just outside the house, and she saw the woman in question chatting with the policeman. The woman glanced at Kay and then leaned forward and said something to the policeman. He paused, then turned and came toward Kay. Kay rolled down her window in order to hand him the note she had written, whereupon the policeman, plainly very embarrassed, said quietly, "I'm sorry, Mrs. Sandiford, but she's just asked me, will I please tell you to get off her property."

At the trial a few months later, the same woman's husband was to appear as a witness and deliver a devastating piece of testimony against her. Kay could never understand why.

Up at the lake, meanwhile, no one was ever cruel or unkind, and in her innocence Kay always thought it was because no one knew who she was or what she had done. It was strangely ironical, she thought, that the cottage she had bought for Frank's salvation now turned out to be her own.

There were four cottages built in a row in weathered gray pine. They stood apart at one end of the lake in a small semicircular bay where a small stream filtered in from higher ground. A narrow jetty no more than a foot above the water pushed out into the lake. Sitting on that narrow veranda, Kay could see more than a mile of shining water enclosed by the rise and fall of forested hills.

She thought of herself and her cottage as part of the lake, denizens of its watery environment. On the water-lily pads that tilted their sails in the wind, baby turtles no bigger than small egg yolks struggled across the small green fields in search of food, or balanced precariously on pieces of floating wood. Giant dragonflies zoomed in, paused in whirring flight, examined the water with the thousand facets of their eyes, and swept away again. In the lake she knew there were catfish, black bass, and perch, for out beyond the area of lilies, a great blue heron maintained his regular patrols, standing as still and silent as a tree reflection in his chosen place, then striking so quickly that all Kay ever saw was the silver toss of the fish as it slid down his throat. Occasionally a flight formation of cormorants would arrive to fish the lake, balancing on tree stumps to hang out their wings to dry. She didn't like them. Their snakelike necks and thin black bodies were too predatory for her. Once she saw a water moccasin swim past her porch and didn't like it either, although she recognized that it had as much right to inhabit the lake as she had.

"At first when I arrived up at the lake house," she said, "I slept with all the lights on. I was afraid to be in the dark, and I really didn't sleep much at all. I'd lock the doors and pile furniture against them, and I'd panic at any noise. Often I'd just curl up in front of my open fire and snooze off because I was frightened to go upstairs.

"Jennifer was so good to me at that time. She'd help me plant aspidistra and moneygrass outside the cottage and she'd come and talk to me. And my neighbors were very nice to me too. Tom, in the end cottage, was always glad to see me, and he'd say, 'Now, is there anything we can do for you?' No one said a word about the shooting, and as I got a bit of confidence back, I went up to the tennis courts, and these lovely tennis ladies got me playing tennis with them, and then got me into their competitive league to play matches, and I'd come up on Thursday and stay through until Mondays. Sometimes I'd come up for the whole week, and gradually I got to the point where I could sleep with only five lights on, instead of having the house lit up like a Christmas tree."

There was, to be sure, the occasional gaffe, as when in a mixed doubles match she missed an easy smash and her partner snapped, "The trouble with you, Kay, is you don't have the killer instinct!"

To Kay, East Texas, green and pastoral, was made up of reassuring experiences and warm, homespun people. The elderly proprietor who had developed the estate was very kind and supportive. He put his arm around her and kissed her on the cheek. She wasn't afraid of him as she was of most men; he was kind and avuncular.

"Then there was Janet, my little Catholic neighbor. As I was always up before four o'clock every morning, I was glad to have someplace to go on a Sunday, and it was an excuse for her to leave the baby for her husband to look after for a couple of hours. So off we'd go to early morning service—an Episcopal church actually, where the preacher was very good, and we didn't really think that God would mind us mixing up our faiths a bit. Afterward we'd stop for coffee and a doughnut and we'd sit and talk, and we became real good friends.

"Then there were Jill and Steve, other neighbors, and without knowing it—or perhaps they did know it—they helped me to become alive again. Every Friday night we'd take turns providing steak and wine, and perhaps Janet would make the veges and salad, and we'd have a barbecue and talk till three in the morning. Then sometimes on Saturday night Steve would take Jill and me off dancing: country dances, barn dances, miles off the beaten track away from Huntsville. That was great. You'd take your own bottle. The guys would have to put their guns on a side table as they went in, then you'd go sit at your table and start drinking bourbon and water. Everybody danced with everybody else. It was a marvelous atmosphere. The gentleman would come up and introduce himself: 'I'm Jim Jones from Abilene'—he's addressing himself to Steve— 'May I please dance with this young lady?' Then Steve would say yes or no, and the young lady would say yes or no, and off you'd go bounding around the room, and when the music stopped he'd return you, panting and breathless, to your table and say thank you. It was all very family; daddies would dance with their little daughters and small boys with their moms, and there were dances that women could do together. I enjoyed it all immensely.

"Only once up there did I have a bad experience. I was jogging a couple of miles away in the country all by myself, and you get sort of hot and sweaty after two miles. I came up over a hill and down to this grassy area; it's a sort of big field that separates the lake property from the prison territory. There were three people there; one a prison guard on horseback with sunglasses, Stetson hat, cowboy boots, rifle crooked across his arms, slouched down in the saddle. I'd jogged this route two or three times and the field had always been empty, so I was surprised, but I jogged on. I could hardly turn back.

"These two black prisoners were chopping wood with axes. One of them saw me as I came over the hill, and he stopped and watched me, and then the other prisoner saw that his partner had stopped and he looked up too. Then they both stood up and looked toward me as I came jogging down the hill on the other side of the barbed wire fence. I could see that the black guys were as hot and sweaty as I was; they were black

blacks, not brown blacks, and they wore white shirts and white pants, usual prison stuff, and I could see the sweat on their skin.

"Anyway, the guard spoke to them. I saw him straighten up in his saddle and speak to them. The first guy turned back to chopping wood, but the second one just stood there, axe-head on the ground, staring at me. By this time I was about fifty yards away from them, and instinctively I felt a communication between us. The second prisoner raised his hand in a small salute, and the palm of his hand was white, and I waved back. Then the next thing I saw was the butt of the rifle coming down on his head, and I saw the blood pour down and stain his shirt. My mouth went dry with shock. I just kept going, but it was dreadful, dreadful! I'd forgotten I was in the Deep South. But I hadn't forgotten that it was the woman's version of that prison where they'd put me if they found me guilty. If they caught me alive, that is."

All through the long hot Houston summer Marian Rosen and her associates had been preparing for the trial. Plea bargaining between the judge, who would try the case, and the district attorney's office, which would conduct the prosecution's case, had produced only negative results. Marian drew her own conclusions about what lay ahead: "I suspected what the judge would do. He would not give Kay probation, because he could have given her probation during the plea bargaining and he wouldn't do it. He said he didn't have the authority to do it, but I did not fully agree with that." The district attorney would not accept probation, saying the shooting was a premeditated crime.

And so it went. Summer drained slowly from the fields and woods of East Texas, the leaves along the paths turned russet, and around the lake the strident chorus of bullfrogs and cicadas gradually died down. The tiny green chameleon that patroled the rail along Kay's jetty, periodically inflating the small red bag under its chin to threaten Kay's indolent and elderly black poodle, Clochette, became now a rare visitor, for temperatures can rise and fall dramatically in a single day. Along Highway 75 the roadside stand that sold luscious, scarlet, Texas-size tomatoes shut up shop. Kay could still buy tender rib-eye, rump, and T-bone steaks from Sherill's on the edge of town and sizzle them over charcoal on her little hibachi grill, but now she spent more time in front of her fire, reading and thinking and seriously wondering what life had left for her. She didn't let anyone share her loneliness; loneliness was at least a place to hide. The lake was her security: the progression and pattern of its myriad life forms from birth to death—often only in a few hours—made the sense of timelessness coherent. Its circle of seasons, its resistance to change, brought reassurance. Sometimes the wind roared and whipped its surface into angry waves. Occasionally driving gales of rain blotted out its shape. But the next morning, with sunup, there it would be, restored and shining. Kay Sandiford felt at peace with the creatures of the lake, felt herself part of their pattern of existence; she sensed their fatalism, their continuity and submission. Sometimes she thought she also might slip beneath that shining surface back into the warm slime of Creation. Who then would mourn her passing?

14

CASE number 309472, *The State of Texas* v. *Kathleen Sandiford*, opened session in the District Court of Harris County, Houston, at nine in the morning on January 15, 1981. Sitting in the dock looking vulnerable, small, and neat in a dark gray flannel suit and blue turtleneck sweater, Kay appeared hardly a fair match for the whole state of Texas.

To Marian Rosen there was a disturbing coincidence in that the trial of Jean Harris, headmistress of a fashionable girls' school in Virginia, was taking place in New York State at the same time as Kay's. Nor did it help that there were odd similarities between the two cases. Jean Harris's lover, Herman Tarnower, the author of the best-selling *Scarsdale Diet Book*, had, like Frank Sandiford, taken great pride in climbing the social and professional ladders to success. Both were immigrants, Tarnower the son of an Eastern European; Frank, Italian. Both were doctors engaged in the heart business; Frank a cardiovascular surgeon, Herman Tarnower a cardiologist. Both had managed to provoke their own executions with similar weapons by driving their loved ones to temporary but lethal mental collapse.

In Marian's terms the similarity ended there. Jean Harris had to drive up from Virginia for several hours to shoot Tarnower, proving at least that she had had a long time to think about it and suggesting premeditation, whereas Kay, Marian contended, had shattered in one blind second of mindless fear and fired instinctively and in self-defense.

Nevertheless, although the Harris trial ended *after* Kay's, and resulted in Jean Harris's receiving fifteen years in prison, and therefore could not reasonably be thought of as influencing the Sandiford trial, it was not beyond comprehension that a jury—especially one drawn from the Bible Belt—might well feel that firm measures were needed to curb a growing tendency toward an "open-season" on errant husbands and lovers. Certainly the prosecution would do its best to discover parallels.

Prosecutors rarely suffer from inhibitions. Their job is not concerned with understanding or compassion; such luxuries are the prerogative of the court. The prosecution's task is to secure a conviction, in this case for murder, and the prosecution planned its tactics accordingly. It would do its utmost to anticipate the defense's arguments and to destroy them; it would lay traps for the unwary defendant, spring surprises to convince jurors; it would manipulate evidence not to establish impartial truth but to prove pervasive guilt. Justice? Who said anything about justice? As the famous attorney Clarence Darrow once declared: "There is no such thing as justice—in or out of court."

The prosecution also knew it had a hundred-yard head start on the defense, burdened as the defense was with an accused who had all but proclaimed from the rooftops that she had killed her husband.

The defense was led by Marian Rosen, with Carol Vance as associate attorney. Carol had been a highly respected district attorney in Harris County for fourteen years, admired for his fairness, tolerance, and dedication. Marian's contention was that the defense needed a male attorney on its team; it must not be suspected of being a women's lib front, trying to defend a woman's right to dispose of a difficult husband. Carol would add experience, weight, and dignity to the cause.

One other, and more serious, responsibility on Marian's mind concerned Kay Sandiford's life. Kay had made it quite clear to Marian that the outcome of the trial would determine whether she lived or died. Kay was convinced that she had paid all her debts to herself and society during the twelve years of fear, humiliation, and brutality with Frank, and she was not prepared to spend a year, a day, an hour, in a prison cell. She had in the past tried to commit suicide on two occasions, and even though she now accepted that these attempts were possibly no more than protests against Frank's domination, she was certain that she possessed the determination and the means to kill herself. Moreover, she carried the means with her in her handbag wherever she went.

Kay felt that her plea of self-defense was altogether correct. Frank had driven her to the edge of despair, intending to drive her over the edge. Through the intensity of his hatred he had aroused in her a sudden, instinctive recoil so violent and desperate that he had made *her* his own executioner.

Marian accepted Kay's reasoning. She also accepted Kay's deal that she promised to forewarn Kay of any jail term in time for Kay to carry out her plan. Marian knew there might be ways of talking Kay out of her decision, but she also said, "There are times when you know someone's mind is made up and you know that you are not going to move or alter them. Kay said to me, 'I have thought it out and I have made my decision. I must live my life with dignity, and you must allow me to choose. I can't live my life with dignity if I'm incarcerated in a prison cell.'"

So Marian went into the District Court knowing that nothing less than Kay's life depended on her skill and judgment; if the jury brought in a verdict of guilty and decided that imprisonment was called for, it would effectively be sentencing Kay Sandiford to death.

Texas law gave the defense various options regarding what part the jury should play. The defense could opt for a trial by jury with the jury responsible for the verdict alone, the presiding judge taking responsibility for the sentence. Or it could opt to have the jury decide both the verdict and the punishment.

Marian and Kay elected the second course: both verdict and sentence entrusted to the jury. Marian favored that course because, although she believed the judge was a humane and compassionate man, his early legal career had been spent as a prosecuting attorney. She felt that, considering his background, if the verdict went against Kay, he would inevitably impose some term of imprisonment.

Better therefore to go to the jury, even though she was well aware of the inherent dangers. She could not agree with Mark Twain's opinion that "The jury system puts a ban upon intelligence and honesty, and a premium upon ignorance, stupidity, and perjury." But when the jury was finally selected, from a panel of sixty citizens, Marian Rosen was far from happy with its composition. There were too many questionable individuals aboard. Past legal experience sent a small warning current through her bloodstream.

Marian had been born in New York City and moved to the South in her teens. She had graduated from law school there and married Freddy, her tall, easygoing, Texan husband. Between a series of eventful cases she had produced two children, both now in their twenties. She had practiced for a while in Florida, where one of her first clients had been Ora Lee Price, a young black woman arraigned on charges of murdering her entire family and best friend in order to collect half a dozen small insurance claims. Ora Lee appeared hell-bent for the electric chair, and to this day Marian is not quite sure how she managed to get her off with a life sentence.

Now, in an effort to provide the best possible defense for Kay, Marian had decided—and it was the first time either she or the prosecution had used the tactic—to employ a professional in "jury research." The professional was a young woman named Cat Bennett, and it was Cat Bennett's job to build up a composite picture of the right sort of person the defense wanted on the jury, and key that information into a series of questions that Marian would put to members of the panel. Conversely, Cat Bennett would also try to assure that both Marian and Kay made good impressions on the jury.

Cat breezed into Houston like a hurricane, a bundle of energy, immensely likable, concerned, and expert; she grooved on hard rock music, she traveled extensively, and she knew her job. After one look at Kay, she decided she could have dropped dead. That hairstyle! That blouse! The color of it, scarlet! God Almighty, did she want the jury to think she walked the streets? And Marian! That leather suit. Sure, she knew it was expensive, soft and feminine. But its effect on the female jurors? Unknown. Therefore take no chances.

"Cat," Kay said, "decided *exactly* how I should look in the courtroom: I should wear pastel shades, soft sweaters and skirts, and I should wear my hair in a headband: that was really the only thing I hated, and I've never worn one since. No gold Rolex wristwatch—that would identify me as the spoiled little rich bitch—no lipstick, which I hardly ever wore anyway. But I had to borrow clothes. Although I love bright colors, I'd always had to wear dark colors with Frank because that was the way Frank wanted me. But Cat thought that what had been okay for Frank was too somber for the courtroom: I'd be buying the role of the heartbroken widow. My best friend lent me some of her things, and so did her sixteen-year-old daughter, so I collected, altogether, half a dozen outfits."

It was Kay's friend, incidentally, who came up with the last useful idea. She foresaw that Kay would find the courtroom experience an emotional ordeal and she would probably cry from time to time. Therefore, she must have the "Bambi treatment"—her eyelashes dyed. Nothing would look worse to the jury, she said, than a defendant with her face perpetually streaked with mascara.

Trial days started bleakly. Inevitably they followed mostly sleepless nights. After two or three hours Kay would lie awake, staring dry-eyed at the ceiling, waiting for daylight to seep through the shutters, then she'd get up with relief to shower and dress in the prescribed "outfit for the day." In the TV room, sipping coffee, nibbling a biscuit, she would wait for Kathy, her friend's daughter, who had volunteered to drive her back and forth to the court every day. She arrived about 8 A.M.

That January the weather was awful—gray skies, almost incessant rain. The trips downtown were worse: trees along Del Monte desolate and sad, Allen Parkway hissing with tires spraying water, windshield wipers opening pie-shaped views of downtown Houston's tower blocks wreathed in mist. A left on San Jacinto and a series of traffic lights leads to a crummy area checkered with parking lots; an occasional drunk sprawled in a doorway; a tableau of spooky people; the dreary edges of derelict areas: old hotels, run-down cafes, bars—the red light district. Everywhere are dilapidated warehouses, abandoned since the days when ships and barges plied the Bayou from Galveston, steaming in the Gulf heat—now sad places of paint-peeled, sun-faded brick.

The Harris County Courthouse is vintage 1950, beige brick, a tired cement facade, a terra-cotta entrance framing a row of heavy glass doors admitting and inviting their daily flow of humanity.

Inside, scores of people come and go, scampering up the wide staircase, waiting for elevators, gathering in little whispering groups, suggesting that in this starkly functional building a great deal of starkly functional legal business is going on, a suggestion reinforced at every floor as the elevator stops to spill out a part of its burden.

Rarely is a glance directed at Kay and Kathy as they make their way to the fourth floor, turn right, walk fifty yards, and go in through the heavy wooden doors of Court 284.

188   KAY SANDIFORD AND ALAN BURGESS

The room is comparatively small—sixty feet by thirty-five. The judge's bench rises at the far end, the jury dock at its left side facing a large oblong table surrounded by chairs shared equally by defense and prosecution. The prosecution pointedly has left one chair empty, the chair reserved for Frank Sandiford, the late Frank Sandiford.

The responsibility for directing the case for the prosecution was borne mainly by Assistant District Attorney Mack Arnold, assisted by Jesse Rodriguez. Arnold was thirty-six years old, big and broad-shouldered, a good-looking, easygoing six-footer, affable, a bit macho, a man's man. During the trial he sucked cigarettes constantly, inhaled deeply, and occasionally startled Kay by seeming to swallow the smoke. He also adopted attitudes: the bull about to charge; the gunman about to fire. She felt that he would have been more at home in blue jeans and a cowboy shirt than in the dark suit, white shirt, and silk tie that were his ordinary attire in the courtroom. An article appearing in the Houston press during the trial confirmed Kay's guess that he had been born and reared in East Texas, rode bulls on the farm, became a high school coach, got drafted and then used the G. I. Bill "to make himself a lawyer," and he did not believe *mean* was the proper word to describe his sometimes harsh questioning; he saw himself as being "direct."

Kay had observed Arnold closely during the first two days of jury selection and had been suspicious of what she saw. From the moment he greeted his cute eight-year-old daughter arriving in court one afternoon, taking her by the hand and occasionally bouncing her on his knee, so that the panel could see what a simple, down-to-earth family man he was, she had been unimpressed. As Arnold was at the time divorced, or in the process of getting a divorce, Kay thought this performance a deceit.

Judge "Pete" Moore was in charge of the case. He had thinning gray hair, parted on the left, and a bronzed face. He often wore a pale gray suit with a dark tie, and he peered through gold-rimmed glasses. He smoked incessantly, a cigarette perpetually poised in his left hand. He was an elusive man, reserved, a man hard to understand.

Nevertheless, for the layman to see him operating from his bench on a busy day, dealing with a series of offenders—most of them young, many wearing the white trousers and shirts of prison detainees—was to observe a professional in action. His pleasant, even voice droning on in the microphone would be directed at each defendant: "The charge against you is grand larceny—to wit, that on the twenty-fifth of December, shortly before your arrest while proceeding north on Highway Forty-five, you stole a 1978 Buick from Smith's Garage. Which way do you wish to plead to this charge? If you plead guilty you are liable to a fine not exceeding a hundred dollars and/or a term of imprisonment not exceeding five years. . . ." Ten cases are dealt with in this manner within half an hour.

To the onlooker it appears that justice, although swift, is balanced and impartial. The judge projects an image of understanding and compassion. The law appears just; there is no feeling of hatred or contempt. This is the law; these are the penalties.

Many people in the courtroom during the trial of Kay Sandiford were also aware that Judge Moore carried his own personal burden into the court, the knowledge that his twenty-six-year-old son was dying of cancer—and indeed died a few months later.

The events of the evening of January 29, 1980, as presented in the police reports, were quite clear. At nine thirty that evening Patrolman C. Dennis and Sergeant S. Gribble, patrolling River Oaks in their River Oaks police car, received an urgent call on their radio: a shooting had taken place at the home of Dr. Frank Sandiford on Del Monte Drive. All cars were to investigate at once.

Several police cars reached the Sandiford house within minutes of that call, but Patrolman Dennis and Sergeant Gribble were on the scene first. The front door of the residence was open, spilling light across the lawn. The two policemen got out and loosened the revolvers in their holsters. Houston's violent crime rate dwarfs those of most other cities in the United States, and Houston's policemen are aware of the risks.

The maid, Ferrie Lee Potts, was standing in the front driveway. She seemed quite calm. "The missus has shot the doctor," she announced.

"Where is he?"

"He's in there, lying on the kitchen floor."

"Has she still got the gun?"

"No, she's gone upstairs. The gun is in the kitchen."

As the entered the house, they could hear the sound of a woman crying, and occasional screaming coming from the second floor.

They found Dr. Sandiford lying face down in a pool of blood near the bottom of the back stairs, among pieces of broken glass, no doubt shattered by his fall. He was wearing hospital greens and a thin, dark blue sweater. He appeared to have been shot a number of times, and there appeared to be bullet wounds in the buttocks. A .357 Colt Python revolver rested on a countertop about two feet from the body.

Several vital pieces of evidence were recorded during the first minutes of the police investigation. Sergeant Gribble recorded that, as he hurried upstairs to try to talk to Mrs. Sandiford, he walked past a tennis racket lying on the upper landing.

Other policemen were now arriving. It took a small posse of them to catch Kay Sandiford—who, with instinctive experience in dodging Frank, was aware that she could race from her own bedroom, around by the corridor to Charles's back bedroom, and then through his bathroom, a guest bathroom, and a dressing room, and into her own bedroom again. Eventually the police managed to cut her off and hold her. One, Patrolman Maywald, tried to convince her that they were not going to harm her and that she could calm down and tell him what happened. Just tell him about the shooting downstairs. Mrs. Sandiford said, "I shot him. I shot him. Oh, my God, I shot him."

"Why did you shoot him?" Maywald asked.

"My husband, I shot him. Oh, why? Why?"

"Why did you shoot him?"

"He told me to get out...to go..."

"To go where?"

"He told me to go. But I knew in December."

"What did you know in December?"

Kay did not respond to that.

"What happened downstairs tonight?" Officer Maywald continued.

"He got the racket."

"What racket?"

"The tennis racket, the tennis racket. Why did he do it? Why didn't he stop? I loved him. I wouldn't have. He knew that. I shot him."

"What was he doing with the tennis racket?"

"Beat me. I can't take any more; he beat me."

"Did your husband beat you?"

"Yes. I just couldn't take it anymore. I loved him. Why didn't he stop? I wouldn't have done anything. He knew that. Oh, I've shot him...Ferrie Lee...Ferrie Lee..."

Patrolman Maywald added, "Sergeant Linney was present during most of Mrs. Sandiford's remarks," and, "At this point Sergeant Linney stated he wanted 'to get her outside and into a patrol unit, get her hands bagged or wrapped and get her transported to the homicide division.'"

Patrolman Maywald and Sergeant Linney then got Mrs. Sandiford up from the chair she had been sitting in and led her out to 17461's unit and put her in the car for the ride to Central. Mrs. Sandiford's hands were wrapped with newspaper, which was secured with rubber bands.

Sergeant Linney's report said simply, "The white female was nervous and crying. Upon getting closer to this female, I heard her making statements in regards to a shooting. The white female was identified as Kay Sandiford; Mrs. Sandiford was stating, 'I've shot Frank. I've shot Frank. I just don't understand why he was hitting me with the tennis racket. I've killed him; I know I've killed him.'"

A third document of importance was provided by Patrolman J. H. Binford of the Houston police, who on arrival was assigned the task of taking a statement from the maid, Ferrie Lee Potts. He wrote: "I spoke with Mrs. Potts and learned that she had been an employee for about six years and during that period of time she knew that Dr. Sandiford *had beat his wife often*. She heard them fighting, and saw Kay Sandiford go upstairs, followed several minutes later by the doctor. Ferrie Lee said she then kept busy and then heard some gunshots and looked to the staircase and saw the doctor coming down the stairs. She could not see Kay but she did see fire coming down the stairs from a gun, and that she ran outside into the garden and the little black poodle ran with her."

In the garden Ferrie Lee heard two more gunshots and went back into the kitchen and found Kay standing over the doctor crying, with a big revolver in her hand.

Patrolman Binford also reported: "Ferrie Lee repeated over and over again that she hoped she would not get into trouble with 'Kay' or any of the doctor's friends because of talking to the police. A sworn statement was taken from Ferrie Lee Potts and was sworn to and notarized."

Patrolman Binford's report concluded: "Mrs. Potts read the statement with minor difficulty and said it was the truth. She stated several times she did not want to get anybody mad at her because she really liked her job."

Reading Ferrie Lee Potts's statement, one could not help feeling sympathy for her, because the job "she really liked" was now blown away. Nevertheless, reading the statement taken from her so soon after the shooting, when one would have thought events were clear and vivid in her memory, and bearing in mind her attachment to Kay and her job, it is a little difficult to understand why she eventually appeared in the court as a *prosecution* witness.

15

IN Marian Rosen's opening address to the jury she outlined the defense's case. Frank Sandiford, she said, was a man who, physically, emotionally, and psychologically, abused his wife throughout their marriage, but she, in return, both loved and feared him. The defense was not denying that she killed him, but not every shooting was a case of murder. In this case it was self-defense.

There was no doubt, either, she continued, that Dr. Frank Sandiford was a brilliant heart surgeon, but he often used his medical skills and his powerful surgeon's hands to abuse his wife, and he could abuse her and beat her without leaving any physical traces.

To Frank Sandiford, she said, position in society was of paramount importance, and his wife, Kay, had to protect the image he conceived for her, and he was determined to train her for that effect. Kay Sandiford was the one with the money and Frank Sandiford was determined to use it for his own benefit. It was *he* who had insisted that they move into the wealthy residential area of River Oaks, where she provided seventy-five thousand dollars toward the purchase price.

"He saw the house," Marian Rosen said. "He knew it stood no more than a few hundred yards away from where Denton Cooley, the head of the Texas Heart Institute, lived, and he was determined to live in the same style."

Their marriage, Marian Rosen went on, became a strange relationship, with Dr. Sandiford imposing his will on his wife until she became little more than his servant.

All this she would prove to the jury.

Mr. Arnold, after hearing the evidence from the policemen who had arrested Kay Sandiford at Del Monte, began calling various officers he referred to as "expert police witnesses."

Kay Sandiford found their testimony puzzling and confusing, and it did not seem to her to arouse much interest among the jury members either.

No doubt, however, both prosecution and defense had their reasons for wishing to establish a "ground plan" acceptable to Judge Moore and giving guidelines to the jury.

With gentle southern politeness Mr. Arnold started his examination of Patrolman Murray of the Houston police department.

"Officer Murray, let me show you what has been marked for identification purposes. It's State's Exhibit Number 25. Do you recognize that, sir?"

"Yes, sir. That would be a diagram standing on the stairwell looking at the north wall to the residence on Del Monte."

Officer Murray's instantaneous and collaborating reaction created a small frown on Marian Rosen's brow.

"Standing on the second floor?" prompted Arnold.

"Yes, sir, the second floor."

"And although it may not be to scale, does it fairly and accurately depict the area as it appeared on the night in question?"

"Yes, sir, it does."

Judge Moore now decided it was his moment to enter the dialogue. Addressing Arnold, he said, "Can you compare that to one of the photographs that have already been taken so that you can orient and the jury may orient themselves to this?"

Arnold was happy to cooperate. "Yes, sir, I believe we can do that."

The jury leaned forward and tried to look interested as Mack Arnold guided Officer Murray through diagrams and photographs of the house and then continued, "Officer Murray, I'm not trying to block you, but let me show you State Exhibit Number 26. Can you identify that?"

Again Patrolman Murray was on the ball: "Yes, sir; that is an artist's sketch of the upstairs area showing the doorways."

And so on through more drawings and photographs, which Patrolman Murray cheerfully confirmed were true and accurate representations
of the scene of the crime, until Mack Arnold was able to plead, "At this
time, Your Honor, the State would ask permission to use these before
the jury."

Judge Moore agreed to this suggestion. Marian Rosen took exception. Quiet and assured, her mouth set in a firm line, she turned toward
Patrolman Murray.

"With reference to State Exhibit 26, Officer Murray, what is the
scale that was used in connection with that layout?"

Murray's certitude flagged a little: "I do not know, ma'am."

"Did you prepare that yourself?"

"No, ma'am."

"Someone else did it?"

"Yes, ma'am."

"So there is no way that you can tell the court what scale was
utilized in preparing that layout of the exhibit? And there is no way of
knowing what is the exterior line of Exhibit 26 or what it is supposed to
reflect?"

"That just represents the end of the wall."

"But you have no knowledge as to whether it is or is not the wall;
that's just a presumption on your part."

"Yes, ma'am."

Two minutes later, as Patrolman Murray's testimony was being
quietly demolished by Marian's unrelenting cross-examination, Mr. Arnold admitted defeat.

"I don't want to interrupt, but just as a matter to speed things up,
this attempted use of State's Exhibit—whichever this one is—26? . . ."

Marian Rosen knew which one it was. "You're withdrawing this as
a State's exhibit completely?"

"Yes."

Without a change of expression Marian Rosen turned back to the
hapless policeman. "Now let me show you what has been marked as
State's Exhibit 24 and again ask you. . . ."

Kay tried to look interested, and the jury did their best to concentrate, but really only Marian Rosen, Mack Arnold, and Judge Moore
knew the vital significance of the evidence concerning those stairs and
doorways, exits and entrances. It could decide whether Kay Sandiford

had fired at her husband in self-defense, or, coolly and abominably, had hidden herself behind a door and shot a defenseless man to death.

"The overwhelming feeling I had," Kay recalls, "was that I didn't think it was me there. I was strangely removed, but then I've felt removed most of my life. I've never really been part of my reality; I've always lived something different from what really was. I guess that's part of my romanticism. I don't know how to put this—it's just that my life for such a long time was unpleasant, and I pretended that it wasn't. I pretended that things were better than they really were; that's how I got through life with Frank. I kept a smile on my face, I kept going, I kept fixing dinners, whether he was there or not. And that same attitude got me through the trial. I kept going. I never thought in terms of it all being over; I projected myself into that scene every day. I did what I was told; I did it as well as I could. I didn't smile, I didn't show emotion, I sat barely breathing for all those weeks; but I'd been doing that for so long with Frank that it was easier on me than on somebody who had not lived all those years behind a false facade."

Later that afternoon Mack Arnold got around to Frank's body, and photographs of Frank's body, and enlisted Patrolman Murray's help in explaining details to the jury. Here, in this photograph, was Officer Owen holding a steel tape from a bullet hole in the wall indicating the path of a bullet that had nicked the bannisters on its downward journey into Dr. Sandiford's body, fired from a spot where Kay Sandiford had allegedly stood about one or two feet outside the upstairs study.

Mr. Arnold dwelt at length on the exit and entrance wounds and turned to State's Exhibit Number 5, which apparently contained evidence that should surely interest the jury. Could Officer Murray tell them about Exhibit 5?

"It's a photograph of Dr. Sandiford as we found him and observed blood, and what appears to be bullet holes through trousers at the lower end of the photograph. . . ."

"Were there any bullet holes in the front of his body?"

"Yes, sir, there were."

Kay listened stoically. After all, if five bullets out of six had hit Frank, there were bound to be bullet holes all over him. She would have thought a child could have understood that.

"How many?" Mr. Arnold asked.

"There was a bullet hole in the right shoulder or right arm area, and a bullet hole in the left chest area."

Mr. Arnold then explained that the police had visited the morgue, where they had been able to examine all the bullet wounds on the body, and again Mr. Arnold went into the question of exit and entry wounds with Patrolman Murray.

At this point Marian Rosen objected to the witness's testifying because he was not an expert on entrance and exit wounds. Judge Moore, with a certain reluctance, sustained the objection, but allowed the witness to state "what he saw."

Mr. Arnold then established that this witness had spent three and a half years on the Houston police force observing bodies with bullet holes in them, and as Houston, Texas, had a far larger number of bodies with bullet holes in them than most other U.S. cities, he could claim to be something of an expert on body bullet holes.

Mr. Arnold, no doubt in search of jury indoctrination, seemed fascinated by the wounds. "Okay, sir," he said genially, "let's take the wounds, one by one, and I guess I'll use my body—okay?"

"Yes, sir."

"Could you step down here, so I can just kind of stand here, and you can show where they were."

Marian Rosen objected to this piece of theatrics and was overruled.

Patrolman Murray explained that the bullet wound in the shoulder—the right shoulder—had passed through the body, and Mr. Arnold elaborated on how it went in and how it came out and what bones it had broken.

Kay thought the whole performance both ghoulish and irrelevant.

When Marian Rosen's turn came to cross-examine, she discovered that Patrolman Murray covered as many as fifty homicides in a year. It was a year since Frank Sandiford had been shot. Did he mean to tell this court that a year later, even with the help of his notes, he could offer a fair and accurate picture? And if he didn't think that, what about this reference in the State's evidence to "the kichen steps"? Did he realize that there were not steps of any kind leading in or out of the kitchen?

Marian Rosen was still fine-toothing the State's evidence, still inquiring who had turned over the body before it was taken to the morgue, when the judge intervened and decided it was time to adjourn for the day.

"The afternoon session would usually be the longest," Kay recalls. "Judge Moore would let it go until five o'clock; sometimes it would go later. Sometimes he'd break at four thirty; sometimes Marian would want to talk to me, and sometimes she'd meet me at the house later in the evening.

"If we got home and it was still light, we'd jog, Kathy and I—that was one thing we'd try to do, and it worked out pretty well, and sometimes Michael would jog with us, because we all needed physical activity. And then, of course, every Friday I'd get in the car and head north for Huntsville and the lake house, which was such peace, and I'd come home Sunday night. So that was the way it went for those four weeks."

On Friday, January 19, the court was still listening patiently to evidence about bullet trajectories, wound entrances, and bloodstains; and, as Mr. Vance for the defense was cross-examining Robert Warketin, a chemist and toxicologist with the Houston police department, it looked very much as if one or two of the jury were taking refuge in naps.

Mr. Warketin pointed out that his day-to-day work could be anything from examining glass and paint samples to soil comparison, fiber or hair examination, gunshot residue determination on clothing, and toxicological examinations of body fluids to determine the presence or absence of heavy metals, alcohol, drugs—things of this kind, which everyone knew must be very interesting.

It was also known to everyone present that justice must be done, and also must be *seen* to be done. But to many observers, this repetition of forensic evidence that seemed only to substantiate that Kay Sandiford had fired six bullets, five of which had hit and killed her husband, seemed endless, confusing, and pointless. By now Kay herself had reached certain conclusions: that the criminal justice system was an infernal machine, with policemen giving evidence like ritually clicking clocks, Mack Arnold advancing one step further in his chosen career, and Judge Moore logging one more case toward retirement—and Kay Sandiford caught in between.

After both prosecution and defense were through with Mr. Warketin, Leonard Lee Cooper, a police latent-fingerprint expert, was called by the prosecution. He explained that he had worked in his division of the Houston police department for ten years, and had worked daily with fingerprints. He said he had received in his laboratory for fingerprint examination one Colt Python .357 revolver, one bottle of Chianti wine, one empty bottle of Fontana Candida wine, one box of Dunhill cigarettes, and six empty .357 cartridges. The conclusions drawn from Mr. Cooper's investigation were that there were no fingerprints on the .357 Colt Python, no prints on the packet of Dunhill's, no fingerprints on either bottle, and one was left wondering why Mr. Cooper had bothered to come at all. On cross-examination Marian Rosen elicited the information that, although the tennis racket that was State's Exhibit 30 had a surface that could have been fingerprinted, the tennis racket had not been submitted for fingerprint identification.

The next witness called was Ferrie Lee Potts, the Sandifords' maid. Although she appeared as a prosecution witness, there was no doubting that she was of crucial importance to both prosecution and defense, because she was the only person who had witnessed the shooting. She had made two statements, one to the police at 10:20 P.M. on the night of the shooting, the other to Marian Rosen in her office the next morning, both duly signed and witnessed. Two days later a third statement was made, in the presence of Doug Shaver, an assistant district attorney, and Duke Bodisch, an investigations officer at the DA's office.

Ferrie Lee Potts was forty-eight years old and had six grown children, none of whom lived with her. Mr. Arnold's opening questions established that she had been working for the Sandifords for six or seven years, that she cleaned and did the washing and ironing and sometimes a bit of cooking, and that during the past few years she had worked from twelve noon to nine or ten, sometimes even eleven o'clock at night. On the day of the shooting she had arrived at noon, as usual, and found Kay there with her friend Jennifer.

Mr. Arnold said, "She told you that Dr. Sandiford had called her and threatened her, and that she was going to leave the house."

"Yes, sir."

"Did she pack her bags and leave?"

"No, sir, she didn't." Ferrie Lee then described how Kay had left with Jennifer. "She said she was going to see about a divorce, and when she got back at four P.M. she had seen Mary Rose."

Ferrie Lee's gaffe broke up the jury, which from that moment on referred to Marian Rosen in their discussions as Mary Rose.

Ferrie Lee went on to say that Marian Rosen had told Mrs. Sandiford to stay in the house, but that she, Ferrie Lee, had advised her to leave.

"To your knowledge there wasn't anything preventing her from walking out of the house at that point in time, was there?" Mr. Arnold asked innocently.

Marian Rosen immediately objected that the question called for an opinion on the part of the witness, and Judge Moore sustained her objection, instructing the jury to disregard the question.

Ferrie Lee went on to describe how Kay ate her dinner and then went into the far room to drink her coffee, and how Dr. Sandiford arrived home about eight, still in his hospital greens.

Mr. Arnold inquired, "What does he do when he comes in the house, Mrs. Potts?"

"Well, he always comes in the kitchen, you know, and asks me how I'm doing, if it's all right."

"Comes in and hugs you?" suggested Mr. Arnold with a clairvoyance that seemed a little surprising. "Is that what you said? And did he do that that day, come in and hug you and ask if you were all right?"

"He did; he did that every time he would come in."

Ferrie Lee said that when she took Dr. Sandiford's food into the dining room that night, there seemed to be an argument going on, but she went back into the kitchen, ran the water for washing up, and turned on the exhaust fan so she couldn't hear what was going on. The next thing she heard was the sound "of shooting going on." She heard one shot, came out of the kitchen into the breakfast room, turned left into the corridor that led to the back stairs, and saw that the doctor was coming down the stairs with Mrs. Sandiford behind him firing a gun.

"Then I see two more shots when she shot him twice."

"Did you actually witness those two shots?"

"Yes."

Ferrie Lee also testified that Kay was holding the gun in both hands, that the doctor didn't say a word, that he came into the breakfast room and fell between the breakfast room and the kitchen, and that Kay followed him into the breakfast room and stood behind the table, when Ferrie Lee "hollered at her, 'Mrs. Sandiford, you done shot Dr. Sandiford! Put that gun down. You done shot Dr. Sandiford!'"

But, far from putting the gun down, Ferrie Lee testified, Mrs. Sandiford had pointed it at her, and she had run out of the house through the kitchen door, accompanied by the Sandiford's poodle, Clochette.

Outside in the back garden, Ferrie Lee said, she heard two more shots, and when she went back into the house Mrs. Sandiford was still standing beside the table. Several times, Ferrie Lee said, she tried to call the police on the kitchen telephone and get an ambulance, but Mrs. Sandiford kept pushing down the button that cut her off, saying it was *her* job to call the police.

"Did you eventually quit trying to call the police?" asked Mr. Arnold.

"Yes, sir, I did."

"What happened then?"

"And then he stopped breathing. I got down on him and I felt his pulse and I said, 'Poor old Dr. Sandiford is gone.'"

What had Mrs. Sandiford done then?

Ferrie Lee replied that she had gone upstairs and called her lawyer in Baltimore.

Marian Rosen objected and the judge sustained her objection. Ferrie Lee went on to say that she herself then went upstairs and heard Mrs. Sandiford saying to her lawyer, Mr. Steadman in Baltimore, "I done killed my husband Frank." Then she, Ferrie Lee, had spoken to Mr. Steadman, and he had told her to call the police immediately, which she did.

On examination by Mr. Arnold, Ferrie Lee also testified that she had seen neither a copy of *Time* magazine nor a tennis racket on the stairs as she went up; the only thing she had seen was a wine bottle.

"Could you have seen this tennis racket if it was up there?"

"Yes, sir, I would have."

"But you didn't see it?"

"No, sir."

Ferrie Lee testified further that she saw Mrs. Sandiford crying and becoming hysterical only when she herself went upstairs, and that Mrs. Sandiford had told her that if only she had listened to her, Ferrie Lee, then Dr. Sandiford would still be alive.

Mr. Arnold then elicited the astonishing information that Ferrie Lee had never seen Dr. and Mrs. Sandiford arguing or fighting, which information, however, clearly contradicted her first statement to Patrolman Binford.

"No kind of pushing, shoving, beating, anything like that?" Mr. Arnold asked.

"No, sir."

Mr. Arnold then turned his attention to the previous Christmas Eve. Had Dr. Sandiford and Mrs. Sandiford had an argument then?

"Well, she *said* they had an argument on Christmastime," Ferrie Lee answered.

"You weren't there?"

"I was there in the kitchen, me and Charles, and she told me they had argued that night, but I didn't—you know—I didn't hear them."

Both Marian Rosen and Kay raised their eyebrows in disbelief, especially as, in the signed statement made in Marian Rosen's office before a notary public the morning after the shooting, Ferrie Lee had testified:

> I was working on Christmas Eve night and heard a commotion. Charles Sandiford, the son of Dr. and Mrs. Sandiford, was home from school for the Christmas holidays. He came in the kitchen with me and was eating in the kitchen when the commotion got worse. We heard arguments and noise between Dr. and Mrs. Sandiford. The following day, Mrs. Sandiford told me about Dr. Sandiford beating her and kicking her.

> Over the last few months, it looked like Dr. Sandiford's looks had changed and almost like he had death on his mind. He had become very nervous. On Christmas Eve night, he beat a lighter on the table. On Monday, January 21, 1980, he beat a cake plate on the table until it broke. Afterwards he told his wife that he didn't know why he broke the cake plate. He had become extremely nervous over the last few months and also looked drowsy and tired all the time. He would fall asleep after only two minutes and went to sleep as soon as he laid down. Everything about him seemed extremely nervous over the last few months and he seemed to be a different person. Dr. Sandiford had taken to talking to himself and on at least one occasion he was upstairs talking to himself and answering himself. I felt like this was very bad and that something was wrong with him. This started some time around October or November of 1979. His nervousness had become so bad that I felt that something bad was going to happen.

When Ferrie Lee went on to testify that Charles had only *told* her—*told* her—that Dr. Sandiford had once chased him with a gun, Kay felt her heart sink. After all, Ferrie Lee had been there in the kitchen when it all happened; she must have been deaf and blind to have missed such a dramatic scene.

When Marian Rosen stood up to cross-examine Ferrie Lee, there was a touch of asperity in her attitude. Like Kay, she knew that when you're poor and female and black, and you've got children who can also come under pressure, and you live in the Deep South and the law wants you to testify on its behalf, your options are strictly limited.

Coldly she asked if Mr. Duke Bodisch, the prosecution's chief investigator, would stand up. Mr. Bodisch, in his mid-thirties, stocky, dark-haired, moustachioed, dressed in a blue blazer and gray flannels, and smoking a pipe, stood up. As Kay had never known him to look directly at her or anyone else, she didn't know whether his look registered concern or innocence.

Marian Rosen directed her attention to Ferrie Lee. Did Mrs. Potts know Mr. Duke Bodisch?

She did.

When was the last time she spoke to Mr. Bodisch?

It was last week, in his office.

How long did she spend with him?

Not long, about half an hour.

Did he go over her testimony with her?

No, he didn't.

Did he ask her any questions?

Ferrie Lee couldn't recall that he had.

What was he talking about for thirty minutes then?

Ferrie Lee couldn't recall.

"You can't recall anything he said to you during that thirty-minute conversation last week, is that right?" Marian Rosen asked in a slightly incredulous voice.

"He just wanted me to talk as anybody else would," Ferrie Lee answered.

Judge Moore intervened. "Did he talk to you about this case?"

"Just about this case, that's all," Ferrie Lee answered. "Just about this case."

On further cross-examination Ferrie Lee admitted that she had seen Mr. Bodisch "quite a few times."

"And now about the statement you gave the police on the night of the shooting," Marian Rosen continued. But Ferrie Lee didn't recall much about that either. Marian Rosen persevered: "Mr. Arnold asked you about how many written statements you gave, and you said you gave three written statements that you signed; do you recall saying that?"

"I just can't recall," Ferrie Lee answered.

Ferrie Lee Potts didn't recall many of the things that she had said that night of the twenty-ninth of January.

Marian Rosen helped her out. "In other words, there was a lot that was going on that night, and you were very upset about everything. Is that right?"

Ferrie Lee could only remember one policeman that night.

Marian Rosen pressed her on that point: "Those first officers that came out there, do you remember telling the police officers that Dr. and Mrs. Sandiford had been arguing for some time? Do you remember telling them that?"

"I told them that they were arguing at the table."

"And do you remember saying that Mrs. Sandiford was very afraid of her husband?"

"Well, she was, she was."

"And do you remember also saying that Dr. Sandiford had struck his wife in the past and said Mrs. Sandiford was afraid he would do so again. Do you remember saying that?"

"I did not say that. I have never told you that, told nobody Dr. Sandiford—I never have seen him . . ."

"And if the offense police report said that, you would say it was correct?"

"That is not correct, but I never have . . . she can tell you that I have never seen her . . . seen him strike her."

"Do you remember stating to one of the police officers that although you were present in the house at the time of the shooting, you did not actually witness the incident? However, you did hear a number of explosions which sounded like gunshots. Do you remember telling the police officers that?"

Ferrie Lee Potts had now been in the witness box for nearly two hours, and both her concentration and her security were deserting her. She began to mumble to herself between answers, on the verge of tears.

"No more than Mrs. Sandiford . . . shots . . . the onliest time . . . because he did not have no gun, so he could not . . . could not have. . . ."

Marian Rosen repeated, "Do you remember telling the police officers that?"

"The only shot I heard was the one, the first one, and that's when I came and see what's going on." Ferrie Lee now broke down and started sobbing.

Marian waited patiently until her sobs had subsided. "If the police offense report stated quite categorically that you, Ferrie Lee, did not see the incident, that was *not* correct," she persisted.

"It is not correct," Ferrie Lee cried.

Marian Rosen then asked the judge if she might approach the witness and was given permission. She held up a piece of paper and asked Ferrie Lee if the signature at the bottom of the page was hers.

Ferrie Lee said she did not recall "none of it."

But was it her signature? Marian Rosen asked.

Ferrie Lee didn't remember seeing this paper.

Marian Rosen tried again. "Does this look like your signature?"

"I don't remember this," Ferrie Lee repeated. "I have never seen this paper before." Ferrie Lee maintained that she did not recall signing such a thing, and "whoever put it on there, it's not the truth at all." Ferrie Lee Potts then slammed her hand down on the witness stand, exclaiming, "I'm tired of going over and over it, I'm tired—" She burst into tears once more. On that total rejection of her signed and sworn affidavit, the court adjourned for the day.

The next morning Marian Rosen did not at first return to the subject. She turned, instead, to the subject of what Ferrie Lee did to help in the Sandiford household. She helped to fix the food for the dinner parties, right? Helped to serve the food, right? And Mrs. Sandiford would try to have everything right at those dinner parties; she wanted to make everything nice for Dr. Sandiford. Right? They all tried hard to please Dr. Sandiford.

Often Dr. Sandiford wouldn't be there when she got dinner ready, Marian Rosen continued. And Ferrie Lee would leave the food in the oven for Dr. Sandiford when he got home. Right? And both Dr. Sandiford and Mrs. Sandiford were good to her. Right? In fact, the Christmas before this happened they even gave her an automobile for her Christmas present. Right? Right.

So it went, with Marian Rosen questioning Ferrie Lee on the shape and size of the house, and which doors from the kitchen she kept closed and which open, and determining that Ferrie Lee would not be able to hear much that was going on in the dining room or the rest of the house. Then Marian Rosen turned back to the subject of the fighting.

Did Ferrie Lee ever remember going into Mrs. Sandiford's bedroom and finding her crying there?

Yes, but Ferrie Lee didn't ask her why she was crying; it was none of her business.

Marian Rosen then asked Ferrie Lee about the lights that were put up in the garden. Did she recall telling people that Dr. Sandiford had a hot temper?

No, she just couldn't recall that.

And that Christmas Eve, did she remember that Mrs. Sandiford had told her Dr. Sandiford had attacked her?

"Well, she told me he had knocked her down and kicked her or something," Ferrie Lee replied. "Well, she said he had kicked her; that's all she told me."

Marian Rosen then got around to the subject of her previous day's interrogation; it appeared to her that Ferrie Lee's signed statements and her evidence given in court were totally conflicting:

"At the time you gave that statement in the police station, everything was fresh in your mind?"

"Well, it was."

Marian Rosen read the statement to the jury:

I have worked for Dr. Sandiford and his wife for about six years. During the period of time they have argued and argued. I have heard them fighting and from the sound of the fight I came to the idea that he had hit her, many times. She has told me that he kicks her on her hips. I have never seen him hit her but I think he has and that she is telling the truth when she told me about getting kicked. Dr. Sandiford has always been nice to me, in fact he treats me better than he treats his wife.

Both the doctor and Kay drink that old wine a whole lot. Kay is a good woman and stays at home and all. Kay told me that on Christmas Eve the doctor beat her up pretty bad. I remember hearing the fight but I stayed downstairs and did not want to get in the middle of it.

Anyway, tonight [January 29] I cooked dinner and was working in the kitchen. Kay had eaten and was seated at the table talking to the doctor while he ate. They started arguing, I think over another woman, but I'm not sure. The doctor told Kay to get out of the house. I tried to get Kay to leave and go to a friend of hers, but she would not listen to me. After a while Kay got up from the table and went upstairs. A few minutes later the doctor got up and went upstairs and I heard a bunch of shooting. I don't know how many shots I heard but it must have been three or four. I saw him, the doctor, coming down the stairs and then he grabbed his hand or arm and she was in back of him. The doctor got to the bottom of the stairs and I heard her shoot again and I saw the doctor fall. I took off and went outside and heard two more gunshots. After a little while I went back inside and Kay was screaming and all and I told her put the gun down and she did. The gun she had was a big revolver, not the kind of gun that you put the bullets in the grip, but a revolver.

I have been asked if the doctor had anything in his hand and when I first saw him after the first group of gunshots he did not have anything in his hand. I saw him grab his right wrist with his left hand. When he got to the bottom of the stairs he fell, I saw him fall, with his head laying next to the telephone in the breakfast room. I remember seeing fire come from the gun as he was running down the stairs. I was scared. I don't know if she meant to hurt him or not but she was real upset. When I came back into the house she was crying over him and that's when I told her to put the gun down. The doctor lived for a few minutes and then quit breathing. After it was over I saw some bottles that I do not know where they came from.

I like Kay and I don't know what happened between her and the doctor and I sure wish that this had not happened. I do know that no one else was in the house tonight, just the doctor, Kay and me. I had been there since about noon.

I called the city police and they called the ambulance, I guess. The policeman asked me what happened and when he found out that I was there when the shooting was going on they brought me to the police station.

I have completed the eighth grade and can read and write and understand the English language and this statement is true and correct to the best of my knowledge.

Toward the end of Ferrie Lee's cross-examination Marian Rosen had obviously decided that the time for pussyfooting with her was over. She prefaced every question with a terse "Do you remember?"

"Do you remember making the statement, 'It looked like Dr. Sandiford's looks had changed and almost like he had death on his mind'?" she demanded.

Ferrie Lee didn't remember.

"Do you remember having made the statement to me, 'Everything about him seemed extremely nervous over the last few months and he seemed to be a different person'?"

"Well, you know, just like I say, he was a nervous person; he worked so hard."

"Do you remember having made the statement to me, 'Dr. Sandiford had taken to talking to himself'?"

"Well, he was—he was sick that night and just like I think he had a fever or something and he was sick that night."

"Do you remember having made a statement to me, 'His nervousness had become so bad, I felt something bad was going to happen'?"

"Well, just like I said, that Tuesday, that something was going to happen, that Tuesday when I came to work."

Ferrie Lee denied saying that Dr. Sandiford called Mrs. Sandiford and said he was going to kill her, but she admitted saying that Mrs. Sandiford was afraid of Dr. Sandiford. She admitted it was strange, "him eating a whole potful of cauliflower off the stove" the night of the shooting.

Marian Rosen contended in closing that the two statements given by Ferrie Lee Potts—one to the police not much more than an hour after the shooting, and the second to Marian in her office the next morning—told the truth, the *real* truth: that when she said she knew Dr. Sandiford beat his wife, she was telling the truth; that she was telling the truth when she said, "Mrs. Sandiford looked like her hair was standing on end, her eyes were wild and she didn't know what she was doing. She looked like she was out of her mind. She pointed the gun at me and I ran outside. I heard two more shots while I was outside. I then came back in the house and told Mrs. Sandiford to put the gun down and she laid it down. I really don't know how it happened because I was downstairs in the kitchen and they had gone upstairs." And she was telling the truth when she said, "Mrs. Sandiford didn't know what she was saying or doing. After the shooting, I told her Dr. Sandiford was dead and she kept saying, 'My husband is not dead.'"

16

IN bringing Kay Sandiford to the witness stand so early in the trial, Marian Rosen was taking a calculated risk; she knew that there were various critical areas that she would have to clear up for the jury as quickly as possible. Her client had made no bones about confessing that she had indeed killed her husband. Kay had also taken out very large amounts of insurance on him, dating back eight years to the time of her father's death, admittedly, and she personally had purchased, many months before, the revolver with which she shot him to death.

"I knew that in the jury's minds," Marian explained later, "there were so many points they would want answered. What the prosecution did basically was read the indictment and begin putting in its witnesses without much of an outline. The prosecution's case, in effect, was that Kay premeditated the shooting; that she was furious because her husband said he wanted a divorce, and that there was another woman involved and Kay was very jealous; that she had purchased this gun earlier and that she had premeditated his killing and that it was cold blooded.

"I thought they were going to go into the insurance money, but they didn't go into that much, and I really think I beat them to the draw on that, so to speak, by bringing that out at the beginning, and I tried to defuse the importance of that. But the prosecution's implication was if she couldn't have him no one else was going to have him.

"The jury wanted to know: Why did she marry him if she was so afraid of him? Why didn't she leave him, especially as she had no little babies at home? She had money. She was intelligent. Why didn't she just walk away from him? Why did she stay there? Why did she take this constant abuse and beating? Where were the pictures of the bruises? Why didn't she report this to the police? Why didn't she report it to a doctor? Even to her friends? It was only a couple of months before Frank died that she talked about it, and then it was just a casual comment. It wasn't a case when you have reports of a woman going to the hospital or to the doctor, or there are pictures of bruises and scars. It's fine if you can produce evidence showing X rays and you show a fracture of the leg; it's something a jury can see. But when you introduce evidence of psychiatric or psychological trauma, the jury can't see it; it's all subjective and that's very difficult to prove.

"You see, Kay kept everything to herself. She is a very closed person. She was raised in such a way that you don't tell people your troubles. You don't confide in people. Even I had to spend a long time drawing her out and, even when I had her on the witness stand, I would ask her a question many times, especially about their sexual relationship or about her abortion, and her reaction was like: 'Do I have to tell about that?' It was really out of fear, and because of her privacy, that she feels so strongly about such things; and being such a private person, she's very shy about those things. It really took a great deal of drawing her out to make that clear.

"The other main task of the defense," Marian Rosen continued, "was to develop damaging character testimony about Frank to the fullest extent possible. And there we were in difficulty because a lot of it we guessed the judge would not permit before the jury. He would exclude it from the jury because it wasn't Frank who was on trial; it was Kay. He'd say it was not material, relevant, or germane to any issue before the jury, and that sort of thing. But I had to argue that we must try Frank for his character, because that was crucially relevant to what went on in Kay's mind."

Marian Rosen also decided at the outset to call Jim Claghorn, Kay's psychiatrist, to the stand before she introduced Kay herself. He had interviewed Kay within hours of the shooting, and his testimony, both medical and psychological, would be invaluable.

She questioned him first about Kay's condition at that first meeting.

"She was in a state of shock," replied Dr. Claghorn, "extremely agitated, confused, having difficulty recalling events of the recent past. Just at first glance, you could see that she was reacting very, very severely to the stresses she was under. Her face literally would flush a bright red, blanch white, and flash red again in an extremely dramatic way."

What about Kay Sandiford's *feelings* shortly after the shooting? Marian Rosen continued.

"Well, I think at that point she was overwhelmed with tremendous feelings of guilt, of anger at herself. And there was a tremendous feeling of hopelessness that she expressed, that something terrible had happened, that there was no way to resolve the dilemma she faced or to deal with the overwhelming feelings she was experiencing, and I think at times people such as those abandon all hope and usually don't value their own life and their own survival and she didn't.

"She was totally focused on the events of the night before and she expressed a tremendous sense of despair, dismay, and loss at the death of her husband. She was just totally overwhelmed by the events. She characterized him as a wonderful man, whose death was a great loss to the community, and she expressed her love and affection for him. She was extremely overwhelmed at that point. She also expressed great fear and terror of him, and described the events leading up to the evening. . . .

"She had tried to create as harmonious and as pleasant an environment around that evening's experience as she could. She had warned people that there would be tension; she had prepared a list of phone numbers for Ferrie Lee to contact other people who might help if there was any stress. She had advised Ferrie Lee that it was extremely important that a calm and pleasant evening meal be the order of the day, and the turn of events that had sent her running up the stairs was still foremost in her mind. One had the sense of someone who had been forced into a situation that couldn't have been anticipated, and that was motivated by total terror.

"The reaction I saw in Kay was extremely profound and was far in excess of the reactions that would ordinarily be seen, even in such a situation. She was under tremendous stress. So no part of this pattern was just simply an overreaction . . . that is, this was not somebody who just gets agitated and goosey whenever any little thing goes wrong. This was a stoic person, who struggled with her feelings ordinarily, who had for years kept secret the discord in her home and the misery that she was experiencing, so she was a pretty tough lady in the sense she certainly wasn't somebody who went around and cried on people's shoulders about things that happened, and here she was experiencing this extreme and profound change in her personality.

"I believe her greatest distress over the long run came from Frank's name-calling, the criticism of her intelligence, the constant 'I've got to make you over from this American peasant into the Italian noblewoman that a man of my stature should have.' Part of his personality was to make these unreasonable demands of himself, and of other people, and so he continued to force her into a mold that he shaped. It was the verbal abuse that caused her to feel humiliated and injured . . . much more than his violence."

About Frank's drug-taking, Claghorn said, "I thought the rubber band was about to break. I don't see how he could possibly have gone on much longer. Kay was, and still is, deeply fascinated by this very compelling man's personality," Dr. Claghorn continued, summing up. "He was very dramatic, forceful, in some ways, technically, a brilliant man, and there was a sense of great importance about what their life together had meant, even with the pain that accompanied it."

In cross-examining, Mr. Arnold looked very thoughtful. Had Dr. Claghorn attempted to discuss with Kay Sandiford what really happened on the night of January 29, 1980?

Dr. Claghorn replied that his main concern had been to deal with her immediate pressure and loss of self-esteem, her grief and mourning. At that point, to try and force her to relive moment by moment the events of that night, might have been enormously harmful.

Mr. Arnold allowed Dr. Claghorn's rational approach for a few more seconds, but he was not going to let his vital question be submerged under a veil of medical compassion.

If Dr. Claghorn could be so certain about diagnosing Mrs. Sandiford's feelings after the shooting, retracing her actions, analyzing her emotions, then surely he could bring out the most important thing that concerned this court . . . those important seconds just prior to, and after, the shooting.

Dr. Claghorn's reply was reasonable. He felt that her therapeutic interests would not be served by his causing her to return to those particular moments of hell.

"Okay," Mr. Arnold retorted. "But it serves her therapeutic interest to go back through two abortions, numerous beatings... what has been described—this is my terminology, not anyone else's—and referred to as rapes and emotional battering...." Mr. Arnold's voice was now scornful. "I mean, just a list of things that you are well aware of in the history of this lady...?"

Jim Claghorn was not perturbed. "Yes, I am."

"And it serves her therapeutic interest to bring all that out and make her remember all that, all these terrible, terrible, terrible things that have happened to her, but it doesn't serve her therapeutic interest to bring out, so everyone can know, what happened on January 29, 1980?"

He had a good point. The jury, judging from the attentive look on their faces, thought it was fair. After all, we were all into psychology now; everyone saw this sort of thing all the time on television: the miracle return of memory under hypnosis or psychiatric treatment.

Dr. Claghorn, however, was not buying. "The battering that she experienced over those years, most of it, was a fairly remote memory," he explained carefully. "It has a lot to do with the fact that she doesn't think much of herself, doesn't feel that she can function without her husband. In her mind, all beating was terrible; that made her feel that life was not worth living. That made her feel helpless, inadequate, useless— all those bad things. It was necessary for her to look at all that through someone else's eyes. It made no sense to her. Here she'd been doing all this, and in retrospect, I think she wonders now why. How it happened. At the time she was so totally caught up in it, it seemed that it must be what life is—that must be what everybody goes through."

It was not an evasive answer, but it needed thinking about. Pausing for a second, and exhaling a rather exasperated breath, Mr. Arnold turned again to the attack.

"Okay, are you asking her to face reality, then?"

"Reality as I see it?" Dr. Claghorn countered. "Yeah. You know the commonplace... people come in to see a psychiatrist, and they tell him their story, believing that the story has never been heard before, that no one has ever heard that story. The truth is that often the story is commonplace—many people are experiencing it—and it falls into the category of those forbidden things that go on in people's desperate lives, things they don't share with anybody. And they're made much worse, much more painful, much harder to deal with, by the fact that they're not shared. In fact, people don't know until they talk to somebody else that what they're going through is something that other people have experienced before."

"Something similar to a lawyer who tries murder cases?" Mr. Arnold said coldly. "You are very good at explaining yourself, but I still missed the 'yes' or 'no' concerning whether or not you're trying to get her to face reality?"

"Yes."

"And the fact that she killed her husband is part of her reality?"

"Yes."

"And eventually, someday, you are going to ask her to face that, aren't you?"

"Yes."

"You were aware that the trial was coming up?"

"Yes."

"And did the fact that she was going to have to testify in this trial play any part in your work?"

"I'm a psychiatrist, not a lawyer," Jim Claghorn said. "I work with people to deal with their mental health problems. I leave the law to somebody who's got a degree in that."

Mr. Arnold decided this was mere verbal fencing. "I'm not concerned so much with the law, as I am with if you were aware she was going to testify and how that might affect her. Not from a lawyer's point of view."

Jim Claghorn tried to make his position quite clear. "From my point of view I wanted her to be able to withstand as much stress as possible. I know her to be a person who handled stress before all this happened. She's gone through a maladaptive period because of a great increase in the intensity of the stress and I wanted her to be back where she was before—able to handle the stresses of trial. To that extent the answer is yes."

Mr. Arnold was now a little terse. "Did you need to prepare her for facing that reality that she refuses to remember or you don't ask her to remember, whichever it is?"

"I heard two questions in that, but I'll answer that in round words. No, I didn't get her ready for trial."

"That's not what I'm asking. What I'm asking you is concerning your treatment and evaluation of her when you knew she was going to be faced with the reality of all this evidence concerning January 29, 1980.

Was it not important to attempt to make her remember what happened
so that she could face the reality herself and *know* what happened, as
well as see it being presented in the courtroom?"

Dr. Claghorn thought about that, and answered clearly. "The answer to your question is no. And my comment is similar to what it was
before. My concern was for her to be as nearly her normal self as possible,
as calm and relaxed in a general sense as she could be as she faces the
ordeal she has to face. With confidence that she'll tell it like it happened.
She's an honest woman who is going to tell her story, just exactly the
way it happened. My concern was for her to be able to do that."

At the end of his cross-examination Mr. Arnold put his own interpretation on Dr. Claghorn's evidence. Plainly Dr. Claghorn had based
all his opinions about Kay Sandiford on what Mrs. Sandiford herself had
told him. He had also based what he thought about Frank Sandiford
again on what Mrs. Sandiford had told him. It surely must have occurred
to Dr. Claghorn, he continued, that the major source of his information—Kay Sandiford—was really quite interested in not being found
guilty of murder, and therefore must have told him only, and exactly,
what it suited her to tell him. After all, Mr. Arnold continued with
exaggerated rectitude, Dr. Claghorn was receiving payment for giving his
evidence, was he not? A matter of seventy-five dollars an hour, wasn't
it? And yet Dr. Claghorn was prepared to call this a professional opinion?

Claghorn had had ample previous experience with attorneys who
found it expedient to try to impugn his judgment or denigrate his motives.

"I feel comfortable with the conclusions I've reached," he replied
mildly. "I've deliberated over them carefully. I'm not apologizing at all.
And furthermore," he added, "I wouldn't sell my judgment for seventy-
five thousand dollars an hour."

Mack Arnold decided to begin the prosecution's examination of Kay
with a little calculated flippancy. "Mrs. Sandiford," he asked bluntly,
"before we get started on any questioning, is there anything at all that
you have left out that you want to say about Frank Sandiford—anything
else that's bad. Please, take this opportunity to say it."

Marian Rosen immediately objected to the question, but Judge
Moore overruled her objection. Kay simply said quietly, "Frank wasn't
all bad."

That one of the crucial points of the trial would turn on the reason why Kay had not simply walked out on her husband was clear to both Marian Rosen and Mack Arnold. Marian's opening examination of Kay had clarified her client's reasoning.

Mack Arnold, however, was operating on a jury that needed convincing. *Why* couldn't she walk out?

"Do I understand your testimony to be that the very first time you ever met Frank Sandiford, he attempted to rape you in a public swimming pool or in a swimming pool . . ." Mr. Arnold asked.

"I didn't say rape, I don't think."

The prosecutor raised his voice. "Well, he attempted to have sexual intercourse with you against your will?"

"Yes."

He was now bullying. "Is that correct? And your reaction to that was that you were frightened; you were afraid; no one had ever treated you like that before. Is that correct?"

"Yes."

There was a sneer now, a complete lack of belief. "Yet you started seeing him on a daily basis?"

"It wasn't just seeing him. He started calling me on a daily evening basis and coming to see me."

Mr. Arnold was back to benign innocence. "Was your first reaction to him something to the effect that you'd never see him again?"

"It was a strange attraction, I think."

A pause. A new thought.

"Oh, you were attracted to him?"

"I did not go to see him; he came to see me. He came to see me."

"You had people at hand at that time, though, did you not? If you chose not to see him, you could have told him you did not want to see him and more or less enforce that, couldn't you?"

"I probably could have said that and I probably did say that, but Frank always did what Frank wanted to do." She knew it was an ineffectual reply, but how could she explain Frank?

"Weren't some of your friends there in Baltimore, your friends, family friends, weren't there some pretty rich and influential people involved there who could have interceded on your behalf?"

"They were friends . . . friends, not all those other adjectives . . . but friends; they weren't involved in the relationship."

"But what I'm asking you, Mrs. Sandiford, is that if you had been told...at that point in time...the end of this relationship...?"

Kay interrupted. "I didn't see the end. I saw only a very small periphery. A very intense small viewpoint. I don't know if you understand that."

Mack Arnold was not going to be interrupted and patronized. "No, ma'am, I don't," he retorted loudly. "You received part of your education in Switzerland? Also—I believe you testified too, did you not?—though I may have misunderstood this: you traveled to Switzerland and came home and discovered you were engaged?"

Kay, realizing that Mr. Arnold had confused education with her travels, corrected him primly. "I don't think I said that specifically."

Mr. Arnold recovered immediately. "I'm sorry, I may have the wrong country." But he was still not going to let her slip out of anything. His question was casual: "Where was it you got shipped off to and then came home and discovered you were engaged?"

"Shipped off?" Kay asked indignantly.

Mr. Arnold smiled. "Well, where was it you got sent off on a trip to come home and discover that you were engaged?"

Kay was still cold. "I went to France, Italy, and Germany."

Mr. Arnold paused. "Have you made other trips abroad?"

"Yes."

"You've attended two different colleges?"

"Yes."

"You've been married once, suffered through all that man put you through; you've been engaged once; you've been through two abortions—you've done all this and you can't see beyond your own little circle? You have a degree in Russian history from one of America's major universities, but you can't see beyond this little small circle, is that correct?"

Kay did not agree, and Mr. Arnold moved on. Referring to Marian Rosen's questioning, he said, "You made the statement that you had to resign yourself to things in life, to 'go on.' You said that—in response to one of Mrs. Rosen's questions—about why you put up with all these beatings and this abuse. What do you mean by that?"

Kay thought about it. The only instruction Marian had given to her before the trial was: listen carefully to the questions and answer them truthfully. The difficulty, as far as she was concerned, was precisely that the answers were never simple or easy. Life with Frank had never been simple or easy; it has always been complicated.

She replied, "I think that when you find yourself in a situation like that—and you know it's not something that will change—you try and pull things together and think positively."

"Was that your attitude when you tried to commit suicide in 1966?"

Kay tried not to be perturbed. "I don't know at which point I was in 1966. I've changed a lot. I'm not like I was then."

. Mr. Arnold proceeded to another point. "In describing one of your beatings at the Wordsworth house, you said he came in, he was slamming things around, he was talking to himself, you were in bed. He came up to the bedroom and he knocked down the bedroom door. Is that correct?"

"Yes."

Mr. Arnold quoted from his transcript. "'He jumped on me, started hitting me,' and that is, I believe, the first time you described his ritual of hitting you in the head, chest, and somewhere. Is that correct?"

"That wasn't one of the typical times. He did that if I was standing up. In the bed, it was different. At that particular time I remember in bed he was kicking me."

"You described him as, 'He jumped on me and started hitting me. He hit me with the side of the hand and the flat of his hand until he got tired. I learned how not to get hurt so much....'"

Kay nodded equivocally, and Mr. Arnold, possibly pretending to help her, summed up:

"So, to go back to an earlier point in time—prior to your marriage— you had been beaten, a man had killed your mother, had done terrible things to you, sexually assaulted you in ways that amounted to being beaten, embarrassed you in every way, and prior to that you had had a husband who had beat you and done some of the things, same things to you and you still married him. And still put up with him all these years. Is that correct? And you still have no explanation for it other than that you thought things would change."

"No."

Mr. Arnold went on to a different subject.

"At that point in time," he said with deceptive casualness, "Mrs. Rosen asked you if you knew some lady—a Mary Ann something?— who lived across the street on Wordsworth. Was there some importance to Mary Ann something?"

"Mary Ann lived across the street from us, yes, and she worked in the hospital."

"Oh, he was having an affair with Mary Ann. How did you find out about that?"

"After my husband died, I learned that about Mary Ann."

"How'd you find out about it? Did she come up to you and tell you?"

"It seems that it was general knowledge at the hospital."

Kay knew she had been dumb, stupid even, not to have known about Frank's affairs; but the truth was that for the last few years of their marriage she wouldn't have cared if he was having affairs or not because it would have kept him away from her, and in the early years she had been brought up to believe that once you got married, you remained loyal to your partner. Throughout the trial Marian Rosen brought out the fact that Frank had never been averse to an affair with an attractive woman, and, with hindsight, Kay also realized that only too clearly. But at the time she hadn't suspected, and didn't want to suspect, her husband.

Mr. Arnold turned to testimony introduced by Frank's sister, Maria, who had married an American and lived in Washington.

"Do you recall leaving Maria's house when you were about to drive to Houston, you and Frank, you were leaving?"

"No...I mean, it could have been. I just don't remember."

Kay could not remember because the question was untrue. They had left for Houston from a friend's house.

"You don't remember Maria asking Frank why do you need such a big car for just you and Kay and the boy? Do you remember having a big Oldsmobile station wagon?"

Kay thought this was pure invention—inaccurate invention, at that. "No, it was a Buick. My father bought it."

"Buick station wagon?"

"Yes."

"You don't remember that you were sitting right there beside him, and Maria asked you in front of Frank Sandiford, who with a grin that wide, said we're going to fill it up with kids."

The thought of Frank wearing an American-sized grin, the thought of him being pleased at the idea of a car full of kids, was simply ludicrous to Kay; to her, these questions were so far removed from the truth that she could scarcely believe they were being asked.

"No, I don't remember."

"And it's your testimony that this was a philosophical thing concerning his profession—that children got in the way, they interfered with progress in his chosen profession?"

"That was part of it."

"Okay, give us the rest of it."

"He said I wasn't good enough to bear his children. . . ."

Mr. Arnold did not pursue the subject further at the moment. But he did not intend that his premise—that it was Kay and not Frank who did not want children—should escape the jury's attention. Thus, when he asked Kay, with an air of beguiling innocence, quite out of the blue, about the abortion she had had in Sharptown Hospital, in the suburbs of Houston, in 1976, Kay sat bolt upright in her chair. But it was not the reaction of a woman with a bad conscience; it was utter surprise.

"An abortion in Sharptown Hospital in 1976?"

"Yes, here it is in the hospital records." Mr. Arnold waved a photocopy and continued affably, "An accurate, testified entry that Mrs. Frank Sandiford received an abortion in that year."

Kay was hostile. She remembered that her sex life with Frank at that time had been nonexistent. She replied that most certainly she had "had no abortion in a hospital in Sharptown in 1976 or at any other time."

Kay's cold denial of the accusation caused Mr. Arnold to pause. Indeed, there appeared to be an air of some confusion on the prosecution's side of the table as the magnitude of the error began to seep in. The hospital records certainly revealed that the devious Frank had supplied a Mrs. Frank Sandiford with an abortion. But it was a *second* and bogus Mrs. Sandiford.

The prosecution dropped the subject with the speed of light, and as Kay observed, "At the time we were all puzzled . . . you can't falsify hospital records. So we wondered at the time who the mysterious Mrs. Sandiford could be."

17

THE prosecution naturally made the most of what the defense referred to as the "little rich bitch from River Oaks" theme.

"Did you ever make the statement to anyone that your husband could never have gotten into River Oaks because he was Italian but for you?" inquired Mr. Arnold. "You got him into River Oaks."

This was, as far as Kay Sandiford was concerned, an insinuation without the slightest basis in fact.

"I don't know that I ever said that. I don't know that I ever had that kind of discussion."

"I'm not talking about a conversation with your husband. I'm talking about with anyone."

"I don't recall that. As a matter of fact, I think there are a number of Italians living in River Oaks."

She could have added that she had been an admirer of Italy and the Italians generally ever since she had first visited that country.

Kay was in the witness box for the prosecution's examination most of one whole day. And Mr. Arnold saved his most intensive bout of cross-examination for those vital few minutes before she shot her husband.

"Before you went upstairs to show Frank that you had been doing the taxes on the evening of January 29, it is my understanding that the only—absolutely only—thing you remember about is Frank coming up the stairs with a tennis racket and telling you 'I'm going to kill you.'"

That needed immediate correction. "He didn't say, 'I'm going to kill you.'"

"Okay. What'd he say?"

"He said, 'I'm going to *get* you.'"

"'I'm going to get you.' You remember him coming up the stairs with a tennis racket. You remember him saying, 'I'm going to get you.' And you don't remember one single thing that you did after that?"

"No."

"Can you explain to the ladies and gentlemen of the jury where . . . how this *Time* magazine got there with a bullet hole through these, every page but the first one?"

"No, I cannot."

"Can you explain to the ladies and gentlemen of the jury how this broken wineglass got up there near the landing?"

"No, I can't."

"Can you explain to them how this wine bottle got up there?"

"No."

"These Dunhill cigarettes?"

"No. I cannot."

"Can you explain how that tennis racket got there?"

"Frank picked it up."

"Okay. So there is no plausible explanation for anything being there but the tennis racket because that's what he was coming after you with. Is that correct?"

"He may have had other things. They may have been up there already. I don't know."

"Well, that's rather a large handful of stuff to be carrying. He's coming up there really prepared, isn't he?"

"Prepared for what?"

"Well, to read, to beat you up, to have a drink, smoke a cigarette— all the things a person does when he goes upstairs to beat his wife. Does it make sense to you, if he had been coming up those stairs to beat you with a tennis racket, that he would have been carrying a magazine and a glass of wine?"

"He was carrying a tennis racket."

"How'd the rest of the stuff get up there?"

"I don't know."

"There is absolutely no explanation for it being there, then?"

"Do you want me to have an explanation?"

"Well, no. You've already told me that you don't."

"I don't."

"Okay. If he were walking up those stairs, having eaten at least some portion of his meal, and he was gonna have a drink, smoke a cigarette, and read the *Time* magazine, isn't it logical that he would not be carrying a tennis racket?"

"I have no idea if it was logical or not. Depends upon who you're speaking about."

"Well, we're speaking about Frank Sandiford."

"What do you want me to say?"

"The truth is all I want."

"What was the question?"

"Is it not logical to you that if he were going up there to smoke, drink, and read, that this is what he would be carrying and he would not be carrying a tennis racket."

"That evening he was going to do something else."

"So he was going up there to smoke, drink, and beat his wife up?"

"I have no idea."

"Did you see anything else in his hand, in the hand that was carrying the tennis racket? Now, we know you saw it. You remember it."

"Yes, I remember the tennis racket."

"Okay. Did he have anything else in that hand?"

"Not to my knowledge."

"So then he had to be carrying all of this in his other hand."

"I don't know what was in the other hand. I don't know."

"Was he carrying the tennis racket in his right hand?"

"Yes."

"And when you saw him coming, where were you when you heard him say, 'I'm going to get you'?"

"I was inside the study getting the papers."

In her own mind, Kay had gone over the events of that night a thousand times. She could recall that she never varied her routine. "I was not allowed to have people over. So at six o'clock I'd watch Walter Cronkite on the news and have one bourbon and water. I was wearing corduroy trousers and a burgundy sweater. I went to the beauty parlor twice a week, so my hair was immaculate: Frank always wanted it back and set; he never liked it loose. I never laughed at anything on the news; I only laughed in public, never in private, there was nothing to laugh about. I usually read a book or magazine or something during dinner, because almost invariably I ate alone; but I was there, all ready, if Frank happened to show up. Dinner was at seven thirty and it was chicken. Frank, during the last month, only ate chicken, so we had chicken every night he was home. So I had salad and chicken, and I drank Perrier water. Ferrie Lee would bring in the salad and then the chicken. I used to take my little Sony TV out of the dining room across the hallway into the living room, and into the little morning room we used as a bar and look at TV sometimes. It was comfortable. Two large windows, armchairs, a sofa, and a little bar. I'd curl up on the sofa and Ferrie Lee would bring me coffee and I'd read or watch TV. I'd read and by nine o'clockish I was ready to go upstairs, take my bath, and go to bed. Ferrie Lee would be tidying around and leave before midnight.

"On the sad nights, I'd get to my bathroom, and I'd just sit on the floor and cry and cry until I fell asleep. If he came home, and that was rare, he'd sleep on the couch, so I'd just shut the doors, lock the doors, cry myself to sleep, on the yellow and green rugs, and I'd wake up and find I was still on the floor and still crying. It wasn't a good time: a sort of half life, and though now I look back I know I was in deep despair. I was always trying to maintain some sort of normality—as if everything was all right, as if there was no one screaming in my dreams. I had to make it work; I couldn't let the whole thing break down. It's just amazing how I managed to go on. I mean, I was choking on food, but I was just going to get the goddamn stuff down just to keep up appearances, not just for somebody else, not for Ferrie Lee, but for me: I had to keep going. It was a matter of survival. . . .

"I was in the far room having coffee when Frank came home that night. When he arrived he always had a drink, usually a bourbon, and ate Genoa salami sandwiches, on my bread—the bread I made. Ferrie Lee made them up for him. A big stack. He always complained about being hypoglycemic and, as a matter of fact, during that year waiting for the trial I was reading everything I could about men who beat up their wives, and I found a couple of articles in magazines. They reported a cycle about when men like Frank get all riled up. It suggested it had a lot to do with lowering of the blood-sugar level. It was very interesting to me, because many of the things they mentioned related to Frank. Apparently, these beatings up, these cruelties against a woman, came on a cycle-type thing, almost like a menstrual cycle—a chemical reaction in his metabolism. I really feel that he had an illness that was mainly physiological.

"Frank got me started on diuretics—they get rid of water in the body, and they drain you in more ways than one. Frank used them all the time to lose weight, and he'd come home having taken these things, absolutely unable to move, and angry at the world. He'd drink bourbon— he always drank sweet drinks, never gin, vodka, Scotch; had to be bourbon, Campari, sweet vermouth, Punt E Mes, always the sweet things— and eat Genoa salami with the bread and salt and butter. He couldn't wait. As soon as he came in the door he slammed into the kitchen and began to wolf them down, wouldn't even bother to change his clothes, and he'd have dinner in these bloodstained hospital greens.

"That night I went back into the dining room with him and sat there while he ate. I sat there listening to him and he went on. I remember he was on about Roberto and Piera, as usual, on and on and on, never looking at me, his voice getting more sibilant—picking up his wineglass and swilling it down, not wiping his lips, missing the place where he was putting the wineglass down. I could feel the tension growing, I'd got it so many times before. I could feel the violence growing inside him, feel the thing building. I wanted to show him that I was going—really going, leaving the house, as he ordered me to. I knew he was going to be mad, be furious—I hadn't done what he said, I hadn't left; I'd disobeyed him. I'd been sitting over in that little morning room trying to act as if the world was all very nice and everything was all right, and 'Hello, Frank, did you have a good day?' and inside me there was building this enormous, all-pervading terror, and I was holding it all inside me—now I look back and I'm trying to understand it—but I'm certain that is what was happening.

"I expected he'd march straight in and smash me down. That might have solved the problem; that might have settled it for me. But the worst thing was he didn't, and he didn't look at me. When somebody won't look at you, there's no contact, there's nothing, there's no communication, there's no language between you, and there was no language between us that night—except that he went on with this growling recital of hate.

"I was expecting something to happen. At that point—well, he'd beaten me up on Christmas Eve and his mood had the same sort of menace that evening and I thought if I showed him I was really going, if I showed him I had done all the tax work, that I had an appointment with the man looking after our tax affairs the next day, then Frank couldn't grumble. If I told him I'd worked myself to death Sunday and Monday, because usually I didn't have them ready until the end of February and that was the end of January. I wanted to say, 'Frank, look, I can't go to Reno that quickly. Sure, I'll go, but you can't just close up a house after six years; there are procedures to be followed.' And what did he mean 'housekeeper'? Frank didn't even know what a housekeeper was. He was going to move in with 'his housekeeper'? But I was too frightened to say any of those things. I could feel my panic growing—trying to show, to convince him that I'd been desperately trying. . . .

"So I said, 'Wait here, Frank. I'll just go get the tax forms to prove that it's all done.' So I hurried away and I was fumbling around on the desk when I heard his footsteps coming up the stairs. Not slow, not peaceful, but as if he was coming up two at a time. I turned back to the twin doors that open to the landing and I saw he'd reached the top of the back stairs where they join the main landing and he had two more stairs to climb.

"All I remember were three things: he held my tennis racket, the unstrung one in its heavy wooden press, and he had it lifted up and I heard him say, 'I'm going to get you!' But neither of these two things made as much impression as his eyes . . . they were black, steely black, and they stared at me."

"He's there on the landing on the steps?" Mr. Arnold inquired incredulously. "He's right here?"

"Yes. Coming up those steps," Kay replied.

"Were you seated and you could see out the door, or what exactly was your position when he says, 'I'm going to get you' with the tennis racket and stuff in his hands?"

"I can't tell you my exact position, but I was not seated."

"Okay. You were standing up, then, I take it?"

"Because I was getting the tax papers and the bills. I was going to take them down to the table and show him."

"So then you were standing over the table that's pictured . . . you're

standing over the table that is pictured in State's Exhibit Number 16?"
He took her through "where the furniture was, which wall was which;
where was the bookcase?" She was standing where?

"I was in the vicinity of the table, because I had gone there for that
purpose."

"Okay. So from the point in time that he told you, standing up
here on the landing, 'I'm going to get you,' we know, do we not... I
mean the gun was hidden over here, wasn't it?"

"It was under the pillow on the sofa."

Mr. Arnold now raised his voice, his finger pointing accusingly.
"There's the gun! Under the pillow on the sofa! So we know, do we not,
that, in order for you to get that gun, you had to come from this vicinity,
general vicinity, over to here, wherever you were, and I'm not trying to
pick a particular place in there; but you had to go there to get the gun,
didn't you? Whether you remember it or not."

"I had to get the gun."

"You had to take the gun and walk back to this doorway, didn't
you? Or run back. However you got back. Okay? And during those few
seconds, Frank Sandiford just stands there, doesn't he?"

"Frank Sandiford was coming for me."

"He was coming for you. Where was he when you shot him the
first time?"

"I don't know."

"Well, the physical evidence would tend to indicate that he was
standing right there when you shot him, would it not?"

"I don't know if that's conclusive or not."

"Well, you've heard all the testimony that's been elicited so far,
have you not?"

Marian Rosen objected: "Your Honor, I submit it's improper to ask
the witness about testimony of other witnesses. Your Honor, that invades
the province of the jury."

Judge Moor overruled the objection and Mrs. Rosen registered her
exception to the ruling.

Mr. Arnold pressed on. "You don't deny that a shot was fired that
passed through the railings and into the wall, do you?"

"No, I think that it's been said that they were there, yes."

"Ample evidence of that, is there not?"

Again Marian Rosen objected. "Your Honor, I submit that that's improper. Now he's asking her not whether she heard testimony, but her opinion on interpretation of testimony of other witnesses and it's totally—"

The judge said, "That's sustained."

"Thank you, Your Honor."

Mr. Arnold returned to his theme. "Well, you've been back out there and looked at the scene, have you not?"

"Have I?"

"Yes, ma'am."

"When I saw it, a great deal had been removed. I didn't look at it."

"Has anyone removed the hole in the fifteenth bannister? Have you seen it?"

"I don't recall seeing it, no."

"And I'm sure you don't recall seeing one in the fifth or fourth?"

"I don't recall any bannister damage."

"Do you recall, happen to recall, this hole in the wall?"

"There were holes in the walls."

Mr. Arnold was scathing about her memory lapses. "Where have you been living for the past year, by the way?"

"In my home on Del Monte."

"Has any of that been repaired? Have you had it repaired?"

"Yes, it was repaired."

"Did you hear Dr. Jachimczyk say that it was highly unlikely for a person to, who was carrying a magazine, to have been hit in the shoulder and still be carrying it?"

Dr. Jachimczyk was the Houston city coroner who had testified earlier.

"I don't remember all that Dr. Jachimczyk said. If he said that, it would be in the testimony I don't recall."

"Wouldn't that indicate to you that the first shot that was fired was the one that traveled through the fifteenth, the fifth, the fourth, through the mazagine as evidenced by the paper on the floor back here and into the wall?"

Exasperated, Marian Rosen objected again: "Your Honor, I object to that as asking this witness what she thinks of another witness's testimony and invades on the province of the jury."

The judge didn't think so.

Marian asked that her exception be noted.

Mr. Arnold went on. "Wouldn't that indicate to you that that was the first shot?"

"I don't know."

"You don't remember?"

"No, it's not that. I don't know about those things."

"Wouldn't the fact that blood and sweater fibers are right up here on this wall indicate to you that the man was standing fairly close to this wall when he was hit with the shot that went in the shoulder?"

"I personally am not able to say how that sort of thing occurs and how it was determined."

"If down these stairways was found a spent copper jacket with pieces of wood in it, wouldn't that indicate that that is the copper jacket that had been through here and that copper jacket flew off and went down the stairs? Got down there somehow, didn't it?"

The purpose of that long full testimony by the experts at the beginning of the trial was now revealed.

"It got down there, I guess, if it's from there. I don't. . . Mr. Arnold, I don't know about those things."

"Would it not indicate to you that the copper jacket with blood and tissue on it, and the bullet with blood and tissue on it that was found a little further down, or maybe further back up, is the bullet that went through his shoulder and then it ricocheted down into there, 'cause it could not penetrate that wall?"

"I don't know about that. I have no way of knowing."

"And certainly you don't remember pointing the gun at Ferrie Lee down at the bottom of the. . . in the bottom portion of the house."

"No, I do not."

"Okay. You don't remember standing over Frank Sandiford and pumping two more bullets into him after that, do you? You just can't recall anything that happened other than he had a tennis racket and said, 'I'm going to get you.' Just any iota that you may remember that might help this jury determine whether or not you committed murder or you committed self-defense."

"I remember Frank when he came home. I remember. . ."

Mr. Arnold charged on: "You understand that it's absolutely necessary to a self-defense charge that you be in fear of your life and someone is threatening you at the time you shoot him. You understand that, don't you?"

Marian Rosen objected that that was an improper question, an improper statement of the law. The objection was overruled.

Kay returned her attention to Mr. Arnold. "Excuse me. What did you say?"

"You understand that self-defense . . . you must show that you were in fear of your life, that someone was attacking you with some type of deadly weapon and threatening you?"

Kay thought about that but Mr. Arnold was not waiting for an answer.

"Don't you think it's very convenient the only two things you remember are the two things that will establish that?"

"My memory's not convenient."

"Don't you think it's rather unusual that that's the only two things you remember?"

"I don't think unusual is applicable."

"Just happens to be what you remember."

"It's what I remember."

Thirty seconds later Mr. Arnold was back on his theme.

"Well, if your husband is standing right here when he says, 'I'm going to get you,' and you have time to walk over here, or run, however you got there, from this area, get the gun, come back, fire one shot across there, and he's still right here on the landing and then you fire another shot at him from four or five feet, doesn't that indicate to you that you've now moved out of here and you're over in this area somewhere?"

"I don't know that he remained on the landing. I was under the impression at the time he was coming at me."

"Well, everything he dropped on the landing, didn't he?"

"That's where it was. I don't know if he dropped it."

"Well, that's where the tennis racket was, wasn't it? And we do know, we do remember the tennis racket. That's one of the things we remember. This deadly weapon here."

"I remember the tennis racket in his hand. I don't remember being on the landing."

"Then whether or not he had anything else, we know he dropped the tennis racket on the landing, don't we?"

"I . . ."

Again Mr. Arnold wasn't waiting. "And if you shoot him the second time from five feet, who is attacking who? Is he attacking you or are you attacking him?"

"I have no memory of that."

"Okay. And then the man takes off down the stairs and you don't remember pumping those bullets into him going down the stairs either, do you? Ma'am, one of the things you've used to describe your husband is that he was one of the world's greatest heart surgeons. Is that correct?"

"Yes."

Mr. Arnold was now poised for the attack. His voice was raised, his manner threatening; he itemized his accusations, leading toward his theatrical climax.

Kay Sandiford refused to be intimidated. She listened carefully to his questions—when they were questions and not merely rhetoric—and she did not try to score points. She answered truthfully even when Mr. Arnold's next question was rather involved.

"In describing him in other ways, you describe a person almost by definition; you never used the name—like we discuss sadist—and you agreed, I think, eventually, that what you had described was a sadist, did you not?"

"I don't believe I agreed to that," she said.

"Okay. But your testimony would tend to indicate that, would it not? I mean, the things he did to you. Riding crops, beating you over the head with this, that, and the other."

"Depends. It could have been that. It could have been something else. It depends upon where, what was motivating him."

"So today you have accused him of, by implication, at least, being a member of the Mafia. Is that correct?"

"I don't believe I've accused him of that."

"He was a social climber. Wanted his house over on Del Monte. You hadn't used that term, but that was your description, wasn't it? He wanted to move up in the world?"

"I think that social climber is not the correct word. It depends on how you look at what you're doing. You can say also that he wanted to progress in his career."

"Okay. He was a blackmailer, but you didn't use that term. You gave us your description of the abortion kit and why he kept it around.

If you got out of line he was going to tell everybody. That's blackmail, isn't it?"

"If that's the word . . . it could be. There are other ways of describing it."

"He's a pill pusher also, although you don't use that terminology. You say he gives me pills. To make me fat, to make me thin. I don't know what they were. He just gave me pills."

"I don't think pill pusher is . . . indicates . . . the terms you're using are so derogatory."

"Ma'am, I'm trying to understand what you're testifying about. You're the one who gave us the broad general definition, but you don't use the word. You've indicated to us that he was a sex maniac, assaulting you at restaurants, bathrooms, parking lots."

"I didn't use that word."

"You've indicated to us he's a racist. He hated Jews."

"I didn't use that term."

"You've indicated to us he was a drunkard, at least in his last days, didn't you?"

"I did not call him a drunkard, no."

"You indicated to us he was a dope addict. He took injections. He ate Valiums."

"I have not said that. I have not called him a dope addict."

"We've already discussed sadist, have we not? Except you don't use that terminology. Have you indicated to this jury that he's a sexual deviant? He did strange sexual things while you were tied to the bed. Did you indicate that . . . ?"

"I did not say he was a sexual deviant."

"You indicated he was a smuggler. He smuggles guns into this country and out to kill people with."

"I believe I explained. . . . You asked me a question about his project, about what was to occur, and I told you what he said to me."

"Yeah, and what you said to me was he was smuggling a gun in and out of the country. Isn't that right? In so many words without using that terrible word smuggler."

"I don't know if he himself was going to do that."

"Basically, the man you've described is . . . by any definition, would be a lunatic certainly, wouldn't he?"

"I think he had a great number of problems. He was very—"

"And without saying so, you've labeled him a liar."

Marian Rosen interrupted. "Would Mr. Arnold please let the witness answer. She was right in the middle of a word."

Mr. Arnold was elaborately polite. "Please, go ahead."

"I mean, Frank was very . . . very confused and very ill. He was having a great deal of inner problems and all the things that happened were things that he couldn't control. I don't think a normal person would have done those things. A reasonable, rational person."

"You've indicated to this jury that he was a liar, have you not? Concerning your first marriage, concerning whether or not Charles was adopted, where you got married?"

"Again, I feel that when you say liar . . . he wanted a certain image and told untruths."

"You've indicated to this jury that he was some type of suicidal maniac, having you put a gun to his head and all that, have you not?"

"He was concerned with suicide later, the last months."

"You've indicated he was an unfaithful husband to you."

"I didn't know that."

"You accused him of being an abortionist on two different occasions, have you not?"

"He did not make a profession of it, so I wouldn't say that you would call him an abortionist. He performed those operations twice. That I knew of."

"He was a wife beater on many occasions, wasn't he?"

"Yes, he beat me; yes, on occasions."

"He was a child abuser."

"He hit his son, yes."

"And he was a killer. He poisoned your mother, he attempted to drown you . . . he was gonna kill Dr. Cooley and attempted to virtually aid you in suicide on the night of January twenty-fifth, didn't he?"

"He was . . . he was very ill."

"You don't deny you killed him. I'm not going into why or anything, but you don't deny that you killed him back on, in January of 1980, do you?"

"I shot him."

"Okay. You killed him. At that point in time all that was left of him was his good name. Do you realize that you've killed him again here in January of 1981?"

Marian Rosen objected immediately to the rhetorical flourish of Mr. Arnold's closing observation. But it was too late. He had passed the witness.

18

MARIAN Rosen's defense against the prosecution's reiterated accusation that Kay Sandiford admitted unreservedly that she had shot Frank Sandiford rested upon the contention that Kay was defending herself against a brutal attack, and moreover that this brutality had been a continuing evil for many years—that, cornered and about to be attacked, she had seized a handy weapon, then, possessed by a paroxysm of terror, killed unknowingly and in self-defense. To bolster that defense Marian had recruited, first, Jim Claghorn, and then, Professor Leonore Walker, a psychologist from Denver.

Marian Rosen knew that a defense resting purely on psychological grounds was not the best one. Juries often disliked and distrusted such evidence; it collided with their common sense; it went over their heads; they just didn't like headshrinkers—albeit that was a risk Marian Rosen knew she must take.

Anticipating Leonore Walker's testimony, Mr. Arnold had already taken precautions. Examining Kay earlier, he had initiated the following exchange:

"You know a lady named Leonore Walker?"

"Yes."

"Have you had occasion to talk to her?"

235

"Yes."

"She's going to testify in this trial, is she not?"

"I believe she is."

"She's an expert on the battered wife, battered woman. She wrote a book called *The Battered Woman*. Didn't she?"

"Yes."

"You expect her to come in here and tell this jury that you are the perfect example of the battered woman, don't you?"

Marian Rosen objected. "Your Honor, I object, as it is an improper question to ask one witness what another witness may or—"

"Sustained."

"Thank you."

"You've heard of the battered wife syndrome before, had you not?"

"No, I had not."

"Never in your life heard that."

"Do you mean before the incident?"

"Yes."

"No, I had not."

"It is something that has received a great deal of publicity over the last several years. Are you now aware of that?"

"Yes, I'm aware."

"But you had never ever even heard of the battered wife syndrome prior to January twenty-ninth of 197 . . . 1980."

"No, I don't believe I had."

Thus prepared, the court now gave its attention to Professor Leonore Walker.

Beginning the examination of the witness, Marian Rosen sought to acquaint the court with the "battered woman" syndrome.

It appeared that one of the prime areas of Professor Walker's concern had been to investigate the psychological pattern of what she termed "a battering relationship." She divided the pattern into three phases: the tension-building phase, in which submerged stresses build toward open conflict; the "period of inevitability," the phase in which something is going to happen and does, either an emotional or physical explosion, when the man is most out of control; and the phase of contrition, in which he avers "it will never happen again." When it does happen again, Professor Walker explained, the woman is considered "battered."

In these battering situations, Professor Walker continued, investigations were now able to assess *before* the situation became desperate the "risk of lethality," that is, the risk that someone might be seriously injured or even die, and they were attempting to predict if the man was more likely to die than the woman, assuming the couple did not terminate their relationship.

One of the great difficulties in her fieldwork, Professor Walker admitted, was separating the "serious" from the "normal." With all couples and all relationships, she explained, there exists a certain amount of abusiveness and angry feelings—that is quite different from "serious psychological harassment." If the woman believes that she will die, or could die, or the man threatens to kill her, that is considered "serious," and that threat is often thought more serious than physical abuse.

Professor Walker then went on to talk about a subject she called "learned helplessness." Until fairly recently, she said, many psychologists believed that women stayed in a violent relationship because they somehow believed they deserved it—masochistic women who believed this was their lot in life. But recent research had tended to show, she said, that these women were disabled from protecting themselves.

"I think that it may be a vulnerability which is set down in childhood, that makes it difficult for women to learn how to cope with violence when it occurs—the role stereotyping: Little girls are taught that they are supposed to be ladies and never fight back. There seem to be two sorts of influences present in childhood: if battering is commonplace at home it seems to recur in their own relationships; at the other end there is the girl treated almost as if she is a china doll, sheltered from almost all forms of violence, or it can be a very strict home where a child is told what to do and if it doesn't it is punished.

"Our clinical work," she continued, "had indicated it's more difficult to end subsequent marriages [to the first one], even though it's very hard to end the first one too. Ending one marriage, they lose some of their self-esteem. They also learn that it's much harder to be single in our culture and particularly to be a single parent than to be married, even if the marriage is not the ideal marriage that they dreamed about. And so it becomes more difficult to end [marriage] a second time or a third time."

Marian Rosen asked the witness about the characteristics of a battered woman.

Referring to her fieldwork, Professor Walker replied, "Battered women

also have specific characteristics that we have isolated after they have
been battered for a while. Again, low self-esteem is the most critical one
and the one that's most obvious. They're also traditionalists, like the men,
and so they believe that their role is to be in the home and to serve their
husbands in whatever way they can. They believe it's their job to make
life as smooth as possible for them... that nothing happens to them.
They really control what happens for the men, so that it prevents them
from getting angrier. Battered women also fit the batterer's need to blame
someone else. Battered women tend to assume all of the responsibility,
and all of the blame.... They also tend to feel very guilty and they tend
to deny most of the battering. These women minimize rather than ex-
aggerate what's happened to them and they rarely will report to outsiders
what has been happening."

"Why is that?" Marian Rosen asked.

"Most of the women feel that nobody can help them—that, in fact,
outsiders are going to make it worse. In our study, the very first study
that I did for the book, we found only ten percent of the women had
even called the police or reported to them because they felt that if the
police came, they would only leave again."

Listening to Leonore Walker, Kay Sandiford knew she was listening
to a playback of her own past existence.

"Were there any patterns as to whether a battered woman considered
herself to be a battered woman? Have you done any work on that?" Marian
Rosen asked.

"Most battered women do not consider themselves battered women.
They don't put that label on themselves and that, of course, makes it
even more difficult for them to get help."

How did she evaluate Kay Sandiford? Marian Rosen asked.

"We took the very first incident that Mrs. Sandiford could remember
and that was an incident, as I recall, that occurred in a swimming pool,
where Dr. Sandiford forced her, or attempted to force her, into sexual
activity... which was something that was not something that she wanted
to engage in, and that was the first time that she recalled he was really
cruel and he was abusive and he really pushed at her to do something
she did not want to do. After that event, she realized that he did have a
mean streak in him but she also felt there were a lot of positive, good
things in this behavior. My guess is that his persistence in pursuing her

was a very important factor in the beginning. For example, she was engaged to someone else at that time and would go on the train to see him frequently and when she would come back, Dr. Sandiford would pick her up at the train station. He would send her flowers. He would be very charming. That's the charming part of the two sides of the personality that was very strong at that time. And I think that Mrs. Sandiford had been flattered by that attention and really enjoyed the charming part of him. That was very rewarding for her and so she continued to see him. Now, the violence was not continuous. It happened sporadically and it's only in hindsight... that we fit it into a cycle. The people involved in this violence don't see the cycles at the time they are going through it. But, of course, after that period of the loving contrition, again another incident would occur and we had several other small incidents until the time of the first abortion, which was a very significant event for Mrs. Sandiford."

"Why?"

"Well, at the time, abortions were illegal and so women who became pregnant, again for Mrs. Sandiford, that meant that she was engaging in sexual activity without being married, which in her background was an embarrassment for her to have done.... And then having a doctor perform the abortion illegally at that time, and putting that in the context of the values of that time, was a very clandestine and embarrassing event for her. The fact that Dr. Sandiford did it for her was something that almost bonded them together in a way—that they both engaged in something illegal together—and that was very significant. She agreed. His price for doing the abortion was that she was to give up her engagement to this other man and agree to marry him. And she agreed to do that in exchange for it. So that was another very significant event."

"Could you expand on that a little?" Marian Rosen asked.

"Well, then we took into account several other events up to the second abortion that he performed. That was the one that I would probably use as the second battering incident and I use it as such because it really sets the pattern.... She did not want the abortion the second time. She wanted to have this baby. And Dr. Sandiford forced her to lose that pregnancy and again did the abortion on her in their own home and in a clandestine manner so that no one else knew about it. At this time— it was when Kay reported all of the events that occurred there—that was the most critical event for her in really losing her will. It was as though he had terrorized her or brainwashed her in a way that she believed he had total control over her and she just gave up at that point. In retrospect, it looked to me as though she had suffered from a serious psychological depression at that time—which really made it impossible for her to make any kind of clear decisions about her life. And he was willing to do it. She had recently lost her mother. Her mother had died and this was . . . all of these events together just forced her into the final learned helplessness process, if you will."

Exploring Kay's predisposition to the "learned helplessness" syndrome, Professor Walker testified:

"I think we have to look at Kay Sandiford's childhood experiences. She grew up in what I would consider a fairly typical traditional upper-class home, where she was treated . . . much more like the Dresden doll . . . the china doll. She was the little girl who was raised to be a lady, and learned all of the values of those days in what it meant to be a lady. She was not taught about violence in the world; in fact, she was over-protected and secluded from it. And even her family, when she complained to them about the abuse in her first marriage, really did not deal with that as though it could be true. So she had a lot of history of not even believing that men could be that way to a woman. She was raised in a different value system that does not understand that. And I think that was very important for Kay Sandiford because she constantly denied it and did not psychologically deal with the fact that there could be that violence that would come from that man and, consequently, believed it must be something in her . . . if she could only do something better, then all of that would drop away. And that was a very important reason for her particularly—that childhood experience and all of the traditional upbringing that she had so that she didn't know how to deal with the abuse at all."

Marian Rosen asked if Professor Walker could compare Kay Sandiford's case with others she had worked on.

"I think that the psychological abuse was far more life-threatening than the physical abuse to Kay Sandiford at most times. This is a woman who attempted to kill herself several times and she was not successful, not because of intent but because some of the medication that she used was probably outdated and not sufficient . . . she didn't take it in sufficient quantities. But she certainly was at that depth of despair."

"Couldn't we talk about suicide... her state of mind that night...?" Marian Rosen asked.

"Kay Sandiford was convinced that Dr. Sandiford wanted her to die. Certainly the suicide attempt on the Friday preceding that Tuesday night was an indication of that. She had told him at that time that she took enough medication to die and, instead of using his ability as a doctor to pump her stomach or take her to an emergency room or save her life, he had laid her down and covered her, and said you have done the right thing, dear, good-bye.... He had continuously told her that he thought suicide was a better way out than divorce, and that she should commit suicide, and other people should commit suicide. In fact, he fantasized his own suicide, which is very common in these cases where the lines between life and death get blurred between the men and the women...."

"... fantasized suicide?"

"There were some events that were reported where he had her practice, both verbally describing and actually practicing with holding the gun against his head and teaching her how she could make it look like a suicide and kill him by actually pulling the trigger. He talked a lot about death. He was fairly obsessed with death and dying. He used guns in his backyard in a neighborhood where certainly using guns would not be tolerated or permitted and he did talk about killing Dr. Cooley. He had an obsession, I would call it—in retrospect, of course—with death and dying, and that's very common with other cases in which I have worked where somebody has died, whether it be the woman or the man. Kay Sandiford believed that he was capable of killing her and, in fact, the use of guns to terrorize her would further prove in her mind that he could do it."

"And about that last few seconds before she shot him?"

"She is also very frightened of him. His eyes... that she reports his eyes and the fear in his eyes, the change in the way he looked at her and in his eyes, as being a critical event in terrifying her, and of all of the other battered women where there has been a lethal incident involved, that's exactly what they talk about. They talk about this change in the man's eyes. The change in their ability to be able to control his behavior. The lack of predictability. So she believes she had no more control to work with him and he came at her upstairs that night—I believe she was just terrified. That was just the point at which she just... it all climaxed, it all came together for her, where she truly believed he was going to kill her at that point."

It was a dramatic statement with which to close, and Marian passed her witness.

Standing up to cross-examine, Mr. Arnold began by attacking Professor Walker's methods.

"So far as you *assume* that Dr. Claghorn talked to people," he observed, "and you *assume* that Marian Rosen talked to people and you have *assumed* that Kay Sandiford is telling you the truth, is it correct that now you are telling all these people that the Gospel is based on your *assumptions?*"

"I used the tools that psychologists are trained to use," Professor Walker answered mildly. "I spent a lot of years learning how to do that and I am telling people the best that I can given the training and the tools and the understanding that I have."

"And one of those tools is assumptions, is it not?"

"I think you are using words—"

"I didn't use words...you did," Mr. Arnold interrupted. "You did a lot of research concerning lethality, I believe...when the situation becomes lethal."

"That's part of my research."

"...however much time you spent with that research, you managed to determine that...two people who—and I'll use my own words; I don't have a psychology background—people who fight, two people who fight with each other, are much...have much more potential for lethal action than two people who don't fight. Was that basically correct?"

"Yes."

"Restatement of what you said earlier?"

"Yes."

"Don't you think you could have asked any barfly in Houston that question and got the same answer?"

"I don't know what a barfly would say in Houston."

"How much time did you spend determining the accuracy of the information Kay Sandiford gave you?"

"I did the normal and standard procedures that I have done with all of the women with whom we've interviewed. We have some checks and balances in our interview. We look for consistencies. We look for patterns, and I spent the appropriate time that was necessary to check that out to the very best of the state of art of our profession at this time."

A little later Mr. Arnold inquired, "Do I understand you to mean, then, that...let's take Kay Sandiford...that here's what Kay Sandiford told you. Okay. Are you taking that and basing it on...are your patterns derived from your prior experience and everything, is that correct?"

"Yes."

"Okay. So in order to determine whether or not Kay Sandiford is telling you the truth, you compare what she has told you with what a bunch of other people, that you don't know whether they have told you the truth or not, did, in fact...is that correct?"

"Yes."

"In other words, there is no basis for this whatsoever. There is nothing you can go to and say A will happen every time if you do B. Because it is all based on what someone told you, and your system of checks and balances to determine whether someone is telling the truth is based on false information?"

Professor Walker replied that Mr. Arnold was oversimplifying a scientific process—every accusation he made was an oversimplification.

The prosecutor was mocking. He returned to the swimming pool incident: "First impressions obviously are false.... Well, don't you think that human nature would indicate to us that no matter how charming or delightful a person was, if the very first day you ever met him, he tried to rape you in a public swimming pool, you would probably just not want any more to do with him?"

"I think it depends upon the psychological state of mind of somebody when that occurred in their life. I don't think you can judge, make a general judgment about it, unless you put it in the context of somebody's life."

One had the feeling that Mr. Arnold was enjoying matching a legal brain against a scientific one: "And, as I recall, it was and...just virtually everything you have testified to with the exception...to details that Kathleen Sandiford told you of her life, are in your book?"

"Well, they are not quite in the same way that I have talked about them here today, but many of the details are. And we have a lot more research results, and it's hard for me to know which ones are the newer research results, and which ones are from the older ones. That book, although it came out in 1979, was written about a year earlier than that."

"My next question is when was it published?"

"It was published in 1979."

"Okay. Uh . . . you are aware of when this killing occurred?"

"Yes."

"January twenty-ninth, 1980, and you were contacted in April of 1980."

"Yes."

"And you first saw this lady in June of 1980?"

"Yes."

"Did you find . . . well . . . I'm sure you must find it very pleasing to find the textbook case, the lady you wrote about, sitting right here. Didn't you?"

". . . if you read my book, you will note that there is really . . . they are all textbook cases . . . that most of the cases with which I have worked, the patterns are fairly similar. In fact, they are strikingly similar and so I was not . . . I mean it was not a great joy certainly to find people who have been so seriously battered and so seriously harmed in their lifetime." Professor Walker's voice was cutting.

Mr. Arnold, rolling with the punch, was at once penitent. "Let me say this: I admire your work and I'm not in any way disparaging that there are battered women. Don't get that idea at all. What I'm concerned about is, and what we are all here to determine, is what happened at nine o'clock at night on January twenty-ninth at Del Monte Drive. All of your opinions of Mrs. Sandiford's state of mind or whatever are based—I mean, concerning what happened there—based on her word that she saw her husband coming up the stairs with a tennis racket and said, 'I'm going to get you.' I mean, doesn't it all boil down to that and that's what we're here to try and determine? Are your opinions based on her statements . . . ?"

"Yes."

"Okay! If the evidence were to show that it didn't happen the way she says at all, that at the time she shot Dr. Sandiford, that Dr. Sandiford was walking up the stairs . . . had arrived at that landing and he had a glass of wine, a bottle of wine, a *Time* magazine, and a package of Dunhill cigarettes and maybe or maybe not a tennis racket—but for the sake of your opinion, let's assume he did have the tennis racket—would that be indicative to you of a person who is going up to beat his wife with a tennis racket?"

Marian Rosen strenuously objected that the question was leading, and the judge sustained the objection.

Mr. Arnold smiled. He'd made his point. It was all in a day's work. "Well, let me make it very, very clear. Assume with me that this is what the evidence shows, if it shows... is this a man who is going up to beat his wife?"

"Based on all of the information that I have gotten, I would think it would be a reasonable perception on Mrs. Sandiford's part that he was coming up to hurt her, and because of the angry footsteps, the arguing the night before, the reign of terror as I described it for the three nights prior—three days or four days prior—to that Tuesday, she was so frightened that she even gave her maid a list of people to call and telephone in her perception that she feared he was going to come up and hurt her."

"Even though he's carrying all these items as if he were going upstairs to have a drink, to read a magazine, smoke a cigarette?"

"Well, you are asking me a question that would assume whether she was able to perceive reality or whether a reasonable perception to her as to whether or not he was going to hurt her and, based on what her evidence was, her state of mind, her frame of reference, based on everything else, it was indeed, in my professional opinion, a logical conclusion based on where she was at, what she knew about him."

"Assume with me for a moment," Mr. Arnold said patiently, "that this lady has lived through this reign of terror, and she's standing over here in this area at the table. Assume that this is the doorway, that you can see out to the landing; she's standing here and she sees him coming up; in this frame of mind she's in she's scared to death because she sees a tennis racket. She has to go some distance, whatever it is, probably not very far, lift up... or at least... or stick her hand under a sofa, to get a .357 Magnum, walk back to the door, and he's still in the same position. He's still over there on that landing. Was her state of mind such that she cannot perceive that this man is not attacking her?"

"I don't think she was capable of perceiving that."

"Then, no matter... are you telling us that at this point, no matter what happened, Frank Sandiford was a dead man, wasn't he?"

"No, I think Frank Sandiford was coming up to hurt her, and that she was accurate in her perception. That's my professional judgment based on what she has told me and what I have looked at, the ways I have put the things together. Now I understand what you are saying, but my perception is not in that way."

"Let's say this: you are on Kay Sandiford's side. That's fair to say, isn't it?"

"That's a hard question for me to respond to."

". . . You have. You are on Kay Sandiford's side?"

"I think I am trying to tell what I know in the way that I know it."

Mr. Arnold was using exactly the same technique on Leonore Walker that he had used on Jim Claghorn. "But all you know is what Kay Sandiford has told you, now isn't that correct? And if she's wrong, you're wrong. Isn't that a fact, or will psychology accept that?" It was a tactic that might work with a jury suspicious of experts.

"I don't see that as a fact."

"All right. Thank you, ma'am. I pass the witness."

19

I F anyone uncovered the root and reason of Kay Sandiford with clarity
and perception, it was Leonore Walker. And to a different degree, if
anyone revealed the essence of Frank Sandiford, his fears and fallacies,
it was Denton Cooley.

Before Denton Cooley appeared on the witness stand, however,
Marian Rosen called several other witnesses.

Three nurses who had worked alongside Frank at various periods
in his career, and volunteered to give evidence on behalf of the defendant,
were allowed to testify in open court but *not* with the jury present, Judge
Moore ruling that their evidence "did not have sufficient bearing as to
Mrs. Sandiford's guilt." The only nurse's evidence the jury was allowed
to hear was a fragment that Marian Rosen was allowed to extract in re-
cross-examination.

Reporters from the local newspapers were in court, however, and
the judge's ruling did not bind them in any way whatever. Their daily
headlines made the most of the suppressed evidence: "Sandiford Known
as 'Frantic Frank'" and "Sandiford Often Acted Bizarrely, Nurse Tells
Court."

Naturally, despite the judge's constant admonition that members of
the jury were not to read, discuss, or be influenced by matters other than

the evidence they heard in court, the jury members returned to their homes every evening—except at the end of the trial, when they were sequestered to consider their verdict—no doubt to be interrogated by wives and husbands. Patently, one needed to be a very strong-minded individual to avoid that "suppressed evidence" reported in the papers and on television and radio.

One nurse testified that Frank got his nickname Frantic because he often became very upset over small things and was inclined to lose control in critical situations, especially when the operation was not going according to plan and a patient had to be reopened. In his haste Frank would then hurl sutures and blood clots in all directions, sometimes hitting members of his surgical team in the process; she had never known any other surgeon to behave in this way. The same nurse also testified that if one of Frank's patients died during surgery—a rare occurrence— he was likely to call his nurses "murderers and killers," and therefore all new recruits to the wards had to be warned about the volatile Dr. Sandiford. Frequently, he would call a nurse a murderer when a patient wasn't dead, while on other occasions he'd told the nurse who was testifying that she might as well tell the nurses to "bring guns to work and shoot the patients," which did not amuse them at all. Indeed, he allegedly wrote on one chart: "Do not kill this patient!" Also this nurse never succeeded in getting him to stop smoking in the intensive care unit, where perhaps thirty or forty patients would be recovering in oxygen tents and there was danger of an explosion. As far as he was concerned, rules of that kind did not apply to him. None of this evidence was allowed to reach the jury, however, except the fact that the "doctor was not considered to be a peaceful man by those who worked with him" and his reputation among the other doctors and nurses was "bad."

When Denton Cooley appeared on the witness stand, Marian Rosen went straight to the subject that most concerned her.

"Did you notice any change in Dr. Sandiford for approximately one year prior to his death?" Marian asked.

Denton Cooley was clear, concise, and authoritative. "Yes. He would come to me and talk to me about his illness."

"What illness was that . . . ?"

"Well, of course, his first illness that he related to me was hepatitis. And then the second illness was arthritis. He was quite concerned about the condition of his hands. He had some swelling and pain in his hands and some type of reactive arthritis. And he was concerned that this would prevent him from carrying out his career and also he thought it might shorten his life if he had to continue to take cortisone."

"Were you aware that he was taking steroids?"

"Yes, he told me that. It was obvious from his appearance that he was taking steroids."

"What did you observe about his appearance?"

"Well, his face was demitic, sort of moon-face appearance—cortisone—and he had gained weight and had developed enlargement of the abdomen; muscles appeared softer and his color was generally poor."

"Did he seem to be overconcerned with the thought of dying or loss of life?"

"Yes, he was older than most of the young associates that I have, even though he had just finished his resident's program. He was in his mid-forties at the time, and I thought that he had a shorter time in which to distinguish himself or become successful in his career. He seemed quite anxious to get on with his achievements."

"Would you explain that, please?"

"Well, he, of course, like many cardiovascular surgeons, sought recognition for his contribution, and it seemed to me that he might be more impatient in that regard than some of the other young men who had finished residency. He seemed almost frantic to move ahead in his own career."

"Was there anything significant about his age...older than some of the other men...?"

"Well, I don't have a specific answer to that. I do know that it wasn't but a few months before his death that he requested that I lighten the work load that he was carrying, that he didn't feel up to carrying the amount of work that the other associates do."

"Was that attributed to his health...?"

"Yes. He said he just didn't feel as strong as he had in the past, and I think it characteristic of patients on cortisone that they don't have the physical strength to carry on activities that are considered normal."

"Did you observe in him anything which you might define as paranoid?"

"Yes, repeatedly. He would talk to me about the people who were preventing him from getting ahead. This included cardiologists, administrators of the hospital, some of the anesthesia staff, the intensive care nurses, and so forth."

"Did you ever have occasion to consider the problems he was reporting to you?"

"Yes, I did discuss with him these problems and I tried to advise him, tried to calm him down in some of these periods of anger that he had. It was my advice to him that he should look for work elsewhere."

"Why is that?"

"He obviously wanted to be the chief of the service and he wanted to be the director and I told him that, so long as I was active and so long as I was in charge, that he...his best...that he could hope for would be second in command, and maybe third or fourth. But that I was still very active and I planned to be so for another fifteen or twenty years and that if he wanted his own service, he ought to go to another hospital, and I suggested to him that since he did have friends in Italy, that he return to Italy and try to develop his own institute, such as we have developed in the medical center."

Moving on, Marian inquired, "During the course of your relationship with Dr. Sandiford, did you recall any incident involving a gun and some teenagers?"

"Yes."

"Would you tell the jury what you recall about that?"

"Well, he came into my office one morning before work and was in a state of high emotional reaction and told me...about some teenage boys who had driven up on his lawn and that he had gotten his pistol and had shot at them."

"Did you make any comment...?"

"Yes, I expressed my alarm over this reaction. I told him that was a terrible, hideous thing to do. Suppose you had hit one of the boys, probably the son of one of your neighbors—never live down such a crime."

"Why did it alarm you so, Dr. Cooley?"

"Well, I guess I am a peaceful man and I have children of my own and I know what children do...pranks of that nature...youngster myself at times, but to think of something so awful as risking a child's life over something as minor as that was completely uncalled for—showed a serious lack of self-control."

During her questioning of Dr. Cooley, Marian avoided emphasizing Kay's anxieties about Frank's plan to kill the director. With as convincing a witness as Denton Cooley batting for the defense, she knew she could leave that ball to be thrown from Mr. Arnold's side of the court and see what he made of it. Marian simply asked Dr. Cooley if he believed that Frank Sandiford would ever have got a gun and attempted to kill him. Dr. Cooley replied that he did not disbelieve that Frank had told his wife such a story, but he did not think that Frank Sandiford had the courage to carry out that intention.

When Mr. Arnold's turn came to ask questions, he wanted to know much more about this preposterous story, plainly invented by Mrs. Sandiford. To start with, if Dr. Sandiford had succeeded in killing Denton Cooley, who then would have taken Denton Cooley's place?

Dr. Cooley was cool, collected, and sure of his ground. Without hesitation he replied, "More than likely, Dr. George Reul."

"Would that have been fairly evident to almost anybody there in the Texas Heart Institute?"

"Yes."

"Certainly to Dr. Sandiford, would it not?"

"Probably not."

Mr. Arnold was surprised. "Why not?"

"Well, as I say, Dr. Sandiford was a very self-assured man. He was the oldest. . . ."

Mr. Arnold incredulously: "He was *unable* to see what was very, very evident to everyone else at the Texas Heart Institute?"

"Yes."

Mr. Arnold moved on a bit more cautiously. ". . . I believe you stated you don't really believe that he actually intended to do that."

"No, I don't."

"Then you made a supposition as to why he would have told his wife that—in other words, lied to his wife about it?"

"Yes."

"Trying to frighten her?"

"Yes."

"Could you give us a little supposition about why that statement would have been made if Mrs. Sandiford is not telling the truth about the doctor making the statement. Why would *she* say that?"

"It would be a rather farfetched story for her to make up. I guess anything is possible, but it would be an extremely bizarre type of story and, for that reason, I accept the story as truth; but I think the purpose Dr. Sandiford may have had in mind was not to actually have me destroyed, but to frighten his wife."

"Okay, Dr. Cooley, I'm sorry, but you've repeated the supposition you're making about that. Are you just totally unable to accept the fact that she might have made that up?"

"I believe I am."

"Okay. Well, let me ask you this. Wouldn't it be logical that that might aid in and assist her in her defense here and paint him out to be the monster he's been painted to be? Do you see a little logic here that she might have some reason to be telling this story?"

"I can understand that possibility."

"You don't accept it obviously?"

"No."

But Mr. Arnold remained unconvinced that a man of Denton Cooley's intelligence could believe there'd been a plot against his life, even a capricious one, and that Frank Sandiford would try and kill him.

Dr. Cooley corrected that assumption.

"I don't believe that he'd make any serious threat to my life. I was something of a father image to Dr. Sandiford. I befriended him when he had been turned out."

"Turned out?" Kay Sandiford opened her eyes at that. So Frank's story that Dr. Cooley had stolen his valuable services away from Dr. DeBakey was untrue. DeBakey had obviously fired him.

Mr. Arnold tried again.

"By the way, Doctor, had you heard about this alleged plot on your life by Dr. Sandiford before or after he died?"

"After."

"And who told you about it?"

"I think Mrs. Rosen told me."

Mr. Arnold nodded and paused. "You've been in contact with Mrs. Rosen from time to time since Dr. Sandiford died."

"Yes."

"Were you made aware that part of the alleged plan that where he was going to do this thing is the basement of the hospital here."

"Yes."

"Wouldn't that be a rather ridiculous place to do it and plan to get away with it?"

"No, I think it's as logical as any place. It's a place that's relatively uninhabited. My hours are such that I'm down there at ten, eleven o'clock at night. No one else is there. I arrive in the morning at six thirty. Not many people there."

"Okay. Y'all do have security there, though, don't you?"

"Yes."

"That basement, that's where you park your car, isn't it?"

"Yes."

"And isn't it a fact that that entire area is monitored by television by these security guards?"

"Yes—well, I'm not sure. The elevator is."

"Well, certainly that wouldn't be a very good place to kill someone and expect to get away with it on television, would it?"

Dr. Cooley was not commenting on a hypothetical supposition. "Not my specialty," he replied.

Mr. Arnold pressed: "Well, just could you use your common sense and apply it to that and tell us whether or not that'd be true?"

Dr. Cooley was equal to the task. "I'm sure that there are areas in the basement that are not covered by television cameras. There's one camera over the elevator, but I'm not aware of any other cameras in the basement."

"The area we're concerned with is where you park, where you park there over to the elevators, isn't it? You're not going to be down on the other end where it's dark?"

"Not unless somebody walks you around the dark area."

"Yes. Isn't there a security office just about maybe, say, thirty yards from where you park your car and that's where a security man is twenty-four hours a day."

"I think they just opened that office—October, November."

"Have you always had security down there in the basement?"

"No."

A little later, referring, to a eulogy that Dr. Cooley had delivered at Frank's funeral, Mr. Arnold asked if the praise expressed then was not inconsistent with his present attitude. Dr. Cooley didn't think it was.

"I had pity for Dr. Sandiford," he said, "and I had pity for his family, and I like to cherish the good memories that I could hold. I think that this was an opportunity for me to express some of those good sides of his life, and I didn't feel hypocritical at all about saying some complimentary things about him, and express my sympathy to his wife, Kathleen."

Alluding to an allegation that Frank Sandiford stole other surgeons' patients, Mr. Arnold drew Dr. Cooley's attention to a letter that one of the institute's surgeons had written to Frank, and Frank's letter of reply. Mr. Arnold then read aloud that part of Frank's reply which he thought relevant:

Bob, I am exhausted, frustrated and embarrassed by circumstances such as these, which suggest that some professional staff of the Texas Heart Institute is not an interactive team of cardiovascular physicians and surgeons and who may not hold in high regard the ethics of the practice essential to harmony among ourselves with not the best possible care for the patient...

Mr. Arnold paused and looked up from his brief. "Now, doesn't that indicate to you that he *did* have concern for his patients, and what frustration in things he had, he had because of what was going on at the hospital. Not what was going on at home?"

Denton Cooley was not accepting that line of argument either. "I think that's very presumptive and assuming a lot of things which are not in that paragraph. What does that have to do with his home?"

"That's what I'm asking you," Mr. Arnold said politely. "If he was exhausted, tired, et cetera, doesn't it appear that that was because of what was going on at the hospital, not what was going on at home."

"I still don't follow you. I don't see how the two things are related the way you put the two. I know that these things were of concern to him in the hospital and a frustration—"

Mr. Arnold quickly interrupted: "It'd be a concern and frustration for any good doctor, wouldn't it, sir?"

Dr. Cooley remained unimpressed. "It might be that he was embarrassed by the exposure."

Mr. Arnold turned back to Frank's letter. Kay wondered who'd written it for him. Frank couldn't use phraseology like this.

In keeping with our philosophy we should not be airing our problems publicly, but rather should seek personal and internal resolve. I sincerely hope that we can measure up to this responsibility and ask that you counsel your associate accordingly. I in turn will continue to relate to our Italian referral patients substantial interest to both of us in the best proper manner. If I fail to do so, your criticism will be well received if constructively offered. In my personal view I do not feel that exchanging letters which imply aberration or suggest competitive concerns for the referred patients is appropriate. If we cannot wholly abide by our understanding and function on a mutually exlusive basis, then we need to make amends or meet with Dr. Cooley together, accept his counsel or discern his wishes.

Mr. Arnold paused, his voice deferential. "Does that not indicate to you that he was willing to go along with whatever you wanted him to do?"

Dr. Cooley's disagreement betrayed itself in his emphasis: "That's his *written* word, yes."

Mr. Arnold continued to quote:

As you know and as everyone knows, I'm only trying to do my best to develop my practice in an honest, productive way in order to achieve more experience with a variety of cases. I never had nor have the intention to compete with Dr. Cooley or with you and I do not try to take Dr. Cooley's place in our institution.

Mr. Arnold looked up with an innocence born of much legal experience (as the woman juror said later, "Well, Mack is a good ole boy and smart"): "That's what it says there, but you don't agree with what he says?"

Dr. Cooley's reply was succinct. "No!" he said.

"You agree with me, though, that that's his only chance to say it."

"I don't know that. He was there full time. . . ."

Mr. Arnold quickly moved in on this reply. "Well, let me say this." A slow glance at the empty chair on the prosecution's side of the table emphasized Frank's absence. "Since January twenty-ninth he's no longer . . . he's not going to get to take the stand or anything, so that's his word."

Marian Rosen was enraged. "Your Honor, I object to that—"

But Mr. Arnold, ignoring the objection, continued, "Whether you accept it or not."

Marian raised her voice. "Your Honor, I object to that as being improper questioning."

The judge was obviously enjoying the encounter. "Well, does he accept it? That is his word. Overruled."

Mr. Arnold sped on, reading the letter:

No response is really required to this letter although I would certainly welcome discussion. What should be done is readily apparent. We should recognize too that others, be they patients, associates, volunteers or personnel unintentionally or otherwise, that referral is the primary physician relationship. Were you and I to have a more positive association and give some quarter to mutual respect which I have for you and your significant role in the institute program, these unproductive distractions would lessen or disappear. Sincerely, Frank.

Not overplaying his triumph, Mr. Arnold looked up. "Doesn't, really, that letter indicate to you a man who has some concern for his patients, for the hospital, and for you personally?"

To Denton Cooley it did not indicate any such thing. "That was the *intention* of the letter. It is not the feeling that I have for the letter. He showed me this letter, I believe, before he sent it to his colleague and I tried to dissuade him from sending it to him because I thought it was the height of hypocrisy and showed a definite paranoid trend. *This is not the type of correspondence that goes between doctors in our hospital.* We've never had this type of... this doctor has been there twenty-five years without a single conflict. This is a culmination of repeated infractions of what we consider good medical ethics. This just happens to be an overreaction on the part of Dr. Sandiford to what was apparent to everyone else—that he had been trapped doing these types of unethical things which he'd been accused of."

These were strong words and Mr. Arnold, possibly realizing that the behind-the-scenes realities of medical ethics were more complex than he thought, asked mildly, "Just recruiting patients?"

Dr. Cooley answered with finality. "Visiting another doctor's patients and telling them that he could perform the services better than the doctor who's seeing them, that's considered unethical. You don't go in the patient's room unless you are invited by the doctor or specifically invited by the patient or a relative."

Re-examining on this point, Marian Rosen turned to screw a little tighter: "With reference to the matter of the problem that existed between Dr. Sandiford and the other doctors concerned, there have been two exhibits—these letters—that have been admitted into evidence. Would you expand on what you understand that problem to have been, please?"

"Well, I think it was a matter of professional jealousy. The conflict grew out of the fact that one doctor had established a clientele from Italy and suddenly an individual came along, namely Dr. Sandiford, and Dr. Sandiford told the patients untruths about the surgery program."

"What types of untruths?"

"Well, he would state that if a patient came to me that I was incapable of doing that type of surgery or that I wouldn't do it myself and other less capable surgeons would take over."

Dr. Cooley tried to be polite in his answers. It was not in his nature to denigrate a colleague. But when Marian Rosen returned to the subject of Frank's medical articles, a subject that had been raised earlier by Mr. Arnold, Dr. Cooley clearly was feeling a little terse about Frank.

"Would you explain," Marian Rosen asked, "why you consider, although there are ninety publications, that Dr. Sandiford is not well published."

Dr. Cooley was quite clear. "Well, I had concern about Dr. Sandiford in the last five years of his life that he was not making a contribution to medical literature, and there was a great deal of clinical material to study and do research on. But a good many of these papers which Dr. Sandiford's name is on, I or one of my associates had written in English; he translated them into Italian as his own."

Marian went on: "Do you find that in his last years, in '78 and '79, that these indicated papers are on the decrease?"

"This is what we call a *padded report. Padded bibliography.* Every little opportunity had to speak is included in here as publications and it seems that in the last two years of his life, according to this, he published nine, ten papers of which he was senior author in two."

It seemed, in fact, that Frank was a plagiarist of a rare order. Not only did he take factual material from other sources and include it in his own papers as original material; he calmly translated *entire* manuscripts of other doctors into Italian and attached his own name as the author.

20

THE evidence given by Paul Moris—whom she had visited in great confusion the Saturday before the shooting—by itself seemed innocuous and not of special significance. However, its manner, timing, and—as far as the jury was concerned—its apparent disinterested truthfulness made it one of the most damaging statements in the trial. Its effect on the collective mind of the jury was immense, coming, as it did, just before the final summations.

The effect was achieved by the prosecution through the cumulative impact of three pieces of evidence: an effusive testimonial to Frank by a planeload of Italian notables and former patients; a letter Frank had written to a friend supporting the contention that he had fallen in love and was about to leave his wife; and, finally, the evidence given by Moris himself.

Among the Italians who testified was Frank's young friend and associate, Roberto. Speaking through an interpreter, Roberto confirmed that he had worked with Frank almost every day for many months, and that Frank had told him of his plans to marry an Italian woman named Liza. Roberto also said that Frank had confided to him that Kay had told him she could not have any children because she wanted Frank to concentrate his affection on Charles, her nineteen-year-old son.

Frank had also reportedly told Roberto that he was planning to go back to Italy and that friends there were preparing a hospital clinic in Milan for Dr. Sandiford.

In passing, Roberto also made one allegation that, true or not, probably nevertheless broke Kay Sandiford's heart. Cross-questioned, Roberto said that Frank had intended to marry Liza "within this year." Asked if he could be more specific, he replied in Italian to his translator, who said, "No, but he knows that Dr. Sandiford told him that he had already told Liza to talk to a priest that was supposed to perform the wedding...Father Georgi."

For Kay, it was the worst moment of the trial. She didn't stop to consider whether Frank might have been lying or that Father Georgi may never have been approached. With Italian enemies arrayed against her, she simply took it at face value and tried to hide her acute distress.

The high point of the Italian revelations, however, came in a letter Frank had written to a wealthy ex-patient and friend during his last flight back from Italy, and the Houston papers made the most of it: "Letter Detailing Dr. Sandiford's New Love for Italian Doctor Introduced at Trial" came out in the morning and "Slain Doctor's Letter Tells of New Love" in the evening.

"You see, I have given you life with my work as a surgeon," Frank wrote, "and you have created this new life for me." Apparently the friend had been responsible for introducing Frank to Liza, the twenty-seven-year-old cardiologist from northern Italy, and they had met during a visit she made to Houston accompanying a patient to the Heart Institute in July 1979.

"I have lived through the most beautiful week of my life," Frank continued, "and I want you to be the first person to know that I fell desperately in love and in a total, and, I think in a definite way with a unique and marvelous woman, Liza. She is an exceptional girl, and the most beautiful girl, inside and out. She is adorable, classy, terribly in love, very intelligent. I intend to marry her and to have children with her, at least three. She makes me feel twenty years younger, but mainly she has helped me discover a new world, complete and complex, that in all my forty-seven years I had only hoped to find. . . .

"You have known a Frank," he admitted to his friend, "very limited and shabby in his feelings and realizations, compared to what I am now and what I will be. I will find many difficulties because of my decision: an American divorce, a very difficult change of life and a future in which

I believe with the heart of an Italian immigrant. Maybe my future will be in Switzerland, or maybe it will be in Houston. However, it will always be with Liza as my wife and mother of my children.

"I do not know what will happen to Kay but for a long time she has not participated in my professional and sentimental life and a separation has been considered for many years without, however, the hope of a new life which I now have with Liza."

Kay listened incredulously until the prosecution had finished reading, increasingly convinced that the letter could have been the product of another of Frank's fantasies. For one thing, she doubted that Frank was honestly contemplating a divorce, fraught as that was with danger to his reputation in Italy and especially in papal circles. For another, divorce was unreconcilable with Frank's image of himself: divorce meant failure; it meant he had chosen mistakenly, and Frank never made mistakes. No, Frank had other ways of getting rid of her, and they had almost succeeded.

Finally, Mack Arnold put Paul Moris on the stand, bringing him in at the last moment as a prosecution rebuttal witness.

Regarding Kay Sandiford's condition when she arrived at the Moris house, Mr. Arnold asked, "What was her state of mind? Was she upset or calm or whatever?"

"She was upset," Moris answered, "but under control."

"Did she relay to you why she was upset?"

"Yes, she told me that Frank had asked her for a divorce."

"Why did he want a divorce?"

"She said he has been having an affair with some young Italian girl."

"In discussing this did her mood change?"

"Well, she was crying when she talked about the girl. Very sad. And she also said then that he wanted to move to Italy, and I kind of pooh-poohed the idea, and that he was having an affair, and that he was in love with another girl, and that was impossible, and you've known that he has wanted to move to Italy for some time; besides, living in Switzerland wouldn't be so bad. But she became upset about living in Europe, and particularly living in Italy."

"Did you say she . . . went from just being upset and crying or getting angry?"

"Yes."

"Furious?"

"Yes."

Moris then said he had talked with Frank on many occasions about "the clinic that was to be built in Europe," that at one time he himself had "considered being involved in the financing" but would have preferred the clinic to be built in Switzerland because "setting up a clinic in Switzerland had many more tax advantages."

On cross-examination Moris insisted that Kay had become very angry.

"But she was crying and sobbing," Marian Rosen protested.

"Yes, I said she was sobbing and crying when she was describing the affair, and when she discussed going to Italy the mood changed. She got very angry and had very unkind things to say about Italians in general."

Kay candidly admits that she remembers very little other than the broad outline of her conversation with Paul Moris. But she is adamant that, since she knew nothing about "some young Italian girl," there is no way she could have discussed such a girl with Moris. Many people were surprised that Moris appeared for the prosecution as a rebuttal witness, especially as he had earlier assured Marian Rosen that he expected to be out of the country throughout the trial.

Paul Moris, replying to Marian Rosen's questioning, went on to testify that he did not believe Frank was having affairs. "I do not think he had enough time at the hospital to have an affair," said Paul Moris, "and I remember telling you that hospitals are small institutions, and that if he was having an affair with someone in the hospital, everyone in the hospital would know about it."

It was an observation that Marian Rosen would find difficult to understand, particularly as, within a few hours, a telephone call from a distraught young woman would prove conclusively the opposite.

The prosecution may have planned Moris's appearance as a big surprise, but as far as the defense was concerned, the bombshell surprise was the telephone call that occurred the morning after Frank's letter was published in the press, and indeed on the very last day of the trial, and too late to be of use in the trial.

Before eight Marian's phone rang, and she heard the voice of a young woman with a faint but attractive foreign accent sobbing out her story. No, she could not give her name. No, she could not give her address or phone number. She only wished to say that the stories in the newspapers were untrue. She had lived with Frank for the past four years—yes, he had written her letters like the letter that appeared in the newspaper—and something must be wrong.

Did anyone at all know about this? Marian asked. Had she talked to anyone at all. Yes, she had talked to a Mr. Bodisch. He knew all about her story. She rang off.

When court proceedings opened that morning, a curt Marian Rosen requested permission to bring Duke Bodisch to the stand, explaining that she had just received a telephone call from a young woman and that not only could the woman's testimony be important to the defense, it had apparently been suppressed by the prosecution.

Mr. Bodisch, the picture of innocence, acknowledged that he knew a young woman who fitted Mrs. Rosen's description and had talked to her, and he offered to supply Mrs. Rosen with the woman's telephone number. But owing to some mistake, the young woman, whose testimony might well have altered the outcome of the trial, was not located until the trial was over.

Marian, therefore, had to make her summation to the jury in the teeth of Paul Moris's testimony that Frank, although he may have been contemplating divorce and another marriage, clearly could not have been having an affair with anyone else.

"You've got to place yourself in the defendant's position," Marian said, seeking to enlist the jury's understanding. "It's not going to be a question of what you might have done, or what I might have done. You've got to put yourself in Kay Sandiford's shoes because she is the only one who could know, based upon everything that had transpired from her background, from her first marriage, from the continuous beatings, from the hearing of the feet pounding on the staircase, and her husband telling her that he was going to get her, that he was going to teach her a lesson, having told her the day before that he was going to kill her!

"Not every killing is murder," she insisted a minute or so later, "or voluntary manslaughter. The law provides for justification and self-defense. That is the law in the state of Texas and the law in every state in the United States. Kay Sandiford, under the law, had a right to defend herself and that's what we're talking about in this case."

Marian went through the evidence, scene by scene, incident by incident.

"Mack Arnold will undoubtedly argue to you that Frank Sandiford wanted to have children, and that Kay Sandiford didn't want to have children, that Kay Sandiford was a terrible mother, that she got rid of her son, Charles, by sending him off to Switzerland to school. I don't believe that's true and I'm sure that if you considered and weighed all the evidence about the kind of person Kay Sandiford is, you'll agree she was sending her son, Charles, off to school in Switzerland for a good education. And if you'll recall her testimony on the witness stand that she wanted a child, particularly the child of the second abortion. It was Dr. Sandiford who did not want to have a child prior to the day of marriage, so, therefore, he used the same instruments of torture to perform a second abortion. Dr. Walker said, and I quote from testimony, 'that was the most critical event for Kay Sandiford in really losing her will. It was as though Frank had terrorized her, or brainwashed her in a way, so that she believed he had total control over her. She just gave up at that point.'"

Marian knew that the jury would certainly boggle over one point as she began: "You know I asked and if you recall, I asked Kay Sandiford, 'Why didn't you walk away? Why did you stay?' And this is what she said and I want to read it to you: 'I thought about that a lot. I know that I was frightened of him and I know that I thought he knew a lot more than I did. I mean, he did, but he was much smarter, and I wanted to please him, and I guess that's why. I don't think that's an easy question and I don't know if I'll ever know the answer.' And when I asked Kay why did you marry Frank Sandiford, if you'll recall, she said that she promised him: 'I would marry him and I loved him. Love is strange. It's a strange word that means different things to different people, I think.'"

Concluding, Marian said with conviction, "I submit to you that Kay Sandiford is not only *not* guilty...she is also innocent. She is a victim in this situation, which has been a tragic one for all concerned."

Marian Rosen now made a point about which she felt deeply, and which she thought of paramount importance. "In my opinion I tell you that if Kay Sandiford had not shot that .357 that night to defend herself, someone else might be on trial here today and Kay Sandiford would have been dead. That's something vital to take into consideration. And when Mr. Arnold gets up here—and he's going to talk to you about the conscience of the community and that if you acquit Kay Sandiford it's going to be open hunting season on husbands... well, that's not so. Kay Sandiford is a member of this community and she has legal rights also. She has a right not to be battered and beaten by her husband. She has a right to defend herself, just as you have a right to defend yourself, whether you're male or female, against attacks from someone else. The fact that she happens to be a woman, the fact that she is a battered woman, the fact of her psychological problems and the stress that she was going through—those are things you should also take into consideration. But she has the rights that need to be defended also. The word verdict is a Latin word: it tells us to speak the truth. And I know that you'll speak the truth, and when you come back to render your verdict it will be not guilty."

Marian returned to her seat and Mack Arnold approached the jury. In his closing address, he still maintained his plain, simple approach. His instruction to himself, he informed the jury, was always the acronym "KISS—Keep It Simple, Stupid."

The defense plea that Frank Sandiford was going to kill his wife, that he was coming after her with a tennis racket, he said, if the jury believed that, then they should find her not guilty by virtue of self-defense. "But if she stood there and waited for him to walk up those stairs," he continued, "and boom, boom, boom, and a couple more booms... then that's assassination."

Speaking only for himself, he opined, he did not accept the defense's theory of a madman pounding up the stairs to attack his wife with a tennis racket.

"The normal thing that a man who just got through putting in twelve or so many hours a day at the hospital doing three operations might want to do is sit down and relax, have a drink, smoke a cigarette, read a *Time* magazine. Some of you may not drink. I'm sure that a bunch of you don't smoke, but the general idea of all this is, you want to relax. That's what the evidence shows you that the doctor intended to do.... She took that opportunity to assassinate him. The evidence is there. That's what the evidence is!"

Mr. Arnold also opined that, as a sharpshooter, Mrs. Sandiford had demonstrated more than simple beginner's luck.

"If you believe her," he said, "the very first time she ever picked up a gun she proved she was a good shooter. She's a natural shot. Five times at a moving target. I'm sorry; three at a moving, two at a dead target. I don't know if she took shooting lessons or not. I guess I could have gone out and scoured the whole United States and try to find some gun ring that she had been shooting at, but that's a little too much, you know; I just have better things to do than scour this whole country to prove that.

"Mr. Paul Moris is the key to this case," Mr. Arnold continued. "There's no doubt. If you don't believe him, then forget the whole thing. And what reason does he have to lie? And nobody said he was a liar or had a bad reputation. A retired president of an important industrial company. You don't get to be president of an organization like that by being a liar. The man came down here and told the truth, for the sake of the truth, and that truth indicts Kay Sandiford. It gives her the motive that she claims not to have.

"Mrs. Rosen said that I would classify the defendant as a jealous woman," Mr. Arnold said toward the close of his address. "I don't think she was a jealous woman at all. I think she could live with him running around on her, having affairs with other women. But I think the thing she could not live with is this: she does not have a pleasant life. She has made many, many sacrifices. And in no way are we denying that. Her money bought the Wordsworth house; her money bought the Del Monte house. We are not denying that. She made sacrifices. She stayed home and she gave these parties because it helped him. I think she did it because she loved him. I sincerely believe that. I don't think she was jealous. She had settled into this role of life where she didn't see her husband very often. But all of a sudden the doctor's going to divorce her and he's going to move to Switzerland. And that totally destroys her world over there at Del Monte Drive. That's what she couldn't live with. The fact that she had made these sacrifices. She had done these things and helped him get where he was and now he is destroying all of her work, all of the things that she has done. That's why she killed him. I don't think jealousy enters into it. It wasn't because he was divorcing her for another woman; it was simply because he was divorcing *her*. And destroying the things that *she* had worked and helped him to get. Was she compelled to murder her husband in self-defense, through 'her instinct to survive'? When he used to beat her up and kick her and do to her much worse, terrible things, her 'instinct to survive' never popped up then. She never told anyone, not even the police."

Mr. Arnold placed his hands on the back of Frank's empty chair and stared sternly at the jury. "Frank Sandiford was a human being," he said, "with human weaknesses. No one said he was a saint, but he was certainly not the demon the defense tries to make him out to be. And Kathleen Sandiford assassinated him. She assassinated his body in 1980 and his character in 1981."

21

As candidates for jury foreman, two individuals stood out because of their experience and seniority: Bill Norton and Richard Devane. They liked each other, shared a room at the motel when the jury was sequestered overnight, and got on well. The one thing disturbing their relationship was that they totally disagreed about Kay Sandiford's guilt. Bill Norton decided for murder, Richard Devane for self-defense—acquittal. Each respected the other's view. Both were strong-willed and determined. If Norton carried the jury with him, Kay Sandiford would spend the rest of her life in the penitentiary; if Devane won, she would be free. In the vote for foreman, aided by Devane's statement that he felt the older Bill Norton to be the better equipped man, Norton was chosen.

Bill Norton was fifty-nine years old, of medium height, squarely built. There was an authority about his presence, a sureness in his manner of speech. Married, with three grown children and one grandchild, he was the manager of engineering at a metal fabricating firm and lived in a pleasant bungalow in a tree-shaded lane some distance from the center of Houston.

Bill Norton was a God-fearing man. "I believe in capital punishment, if the crime fits the punishment," he had said. "I believe that's what the Bible teaches, and I have no qualms about that. I want to be fair and impartial, and I want to hear both sides of the story."

Now, after listening to a month of evidence, and after much soul-searching, Bill Norton was convinced that Kay Sandiford was guilty, and his vote and weight of opinion would back that belief. He stood for life imprisonment. He also believed that if Kay Sandiford was committed to prison she would not survive incarceration for a long period and would probably die in jail. He would regret that, but he stood for the old biblical maxim, "An eye for an eye, a tooth for a tooth."

"Right," Bill Norton said. "First thing is for us to take a vote and see what we think the verdict should he. Our decision has got to be unanimous. We take a secret ballot. Write your verdict on the slip of paper, fold it, and pass it up to me."

One of the other jurors, Jeanine Donaldson, asked him to redefine what options were open to them. Yes, she knew the judge had already explained this to them, but a little extra clarification would be of help.

Bill Norton recapitulated the three verdicts among which they had to choose: murder, voluntary manslaughter, or self-defense. If they found for self-defense, it meant innocent—immediate release. Murder, the most serious charge, entailed a long prison sentence. Voluntary manslaughter could also mean a prison sentence, of up to twenty years, but with the possibility of probation.

The jurors listened to Bill Norton's explanation and he verified that they all understood what they had to do. Each of them marked his or her slip and passed it up the table. Bill Norton scrutinized each in turn and put them in three separate piles. There were six votes for a verdict of murder, four for voluntary manslaughter, and two for self-defense.

Many jurors played an important part in that jury's decisions, but none more than Joe Poole. Joe was fifty-five years old. He drove a '73 Impala and a '74 Ford van and worked as a fitter. He was married and his wife also worked. They owned two poodles, a toy and a miniature— though one got the impression that they were more his wife's indulgence than his—and a ranch house in what Cat Bennett's researchers had denominated an "interracial area."

Joe was short and taciturn. He didn't waste a lot of time with words, but nothing slipped out of his mouth without his being well aware of what he meant. He chewed gum, and very often, listening to evidence, he closed his eyes. Indeed, the defense would have been prepared to testify that Joe Poole slept through seventy-five percent of the entire trial.

They were all totally wrong.

Behind those closed lids, Joe listened to every word of the testimony and took it all in. He was friendly and polite at the coffee and lunch breaks, but betrayed no hint of his feelings.

Jeanine Donaldson, a teacher of English as a second language, was a perceptive and observant juror. Her husband jokingly accused her of being more interested in the psychology of other people than she had any right to be, and it was true; she found her fellow jurors fascinating. She admitted, "You are all in the same boat, and you probably say things and tell each other things that you wouldn't tell your family, and not even anybody."

To her, jurors themselves were often surprising. They were not supposed to discuss the case while it was going on, but to a certain extent such a ruling was untenable. Nevertheless, they maintained standards: they never discussed the subjects that would concern them when they reached the jury room; they made no prejudgments about guilt. Therefore, when it came time for individual decisions, it was strange to see which way they voted.

Jeanine Donaldson, enjoying herself on her small psychology trips, paid scant attention to Joe, and was therefore totally surprised when on that first afternoon of jury deliberation, when it appeared that the whole jury was against the defendant and ready to impose the most severe penalties, Joe Poole popped his two cents' worth into the discussion by saying quietly: "I've listened to all the evidence that has been offered, and I know that she shot him, all right, but there's nothing I've heard that makes me feel she's guilty of murder." He opted for the manslaughter verdict. Richard Devane agreed with Joe Poole, but went even further, calling it self-defence... acquittal.

That sparked a little gust of outrage, especially from two of the ladies. Joe closed his eyes, leaned back, and for the time being, said no more.

Devane was forty-seven years old, dark-haired, good-looking, with clean features and a pleasant smile. An ex-army sergeant of artillery, he had served in the armed forces for five years and seen action in Korea. He liked fishing and the outdoors. He was a self-employed brick contractor, and when asked if he had anything against people who lived in River Oaks, he'd smiled and answered that he did a lot of work for people who lived in that area, and he had absolutely nothing against people who helped provide him with a living.

There was one aspect of Devane's experience that could have influenced his thinking, and which he related to Jeanine Donaldson during one of their off-duty discussions. His sister, during one period of her life, had been married to a wife batterer and a brute, who on the last occasion had left her with a broken leg, and unable to move.

In all, the jury consisted of four white women, the oldest sixty-nine, the others in their forties, all of them married; two black men, a postman and a stockclerk, both in their early thirties; and six white men, three middle-aged, three in their twenties.

By now they all knew one another well, were on a first-name basis, and got along together. In their coffee and lunch breaks and during those periods when the judge confined them to the jury room while he decided if the evidence of various witnesses should be admitted, they had a lot of time to talk. Considering their verdict, they now had to translate that chatter into a hard decision.

They discussed every aspect of the trial beginning with Kay Sandiford's first meeting with Frank and the swimming pool incident.

Grace Nash spoke up first. She was the oldest juror. A widow, she had two sons, both in their late twenties, one of whom had been an army captain in Korea. She still worked from her office behind the house. She was a strong, down-to-earth matron with a hearty laugh.

She said, "I never could see any reason why she just couldn't get up and walk away. I couldn't see why she had anything to do with him in the first place. The first time they met, they went up to the swimming pool and he tried to rape her... why did she ever have anything to do with him after that? I would have said bye-bye...."

Mrs. Nash could not go along with the "battered woman" theory. She just couldn't accept the fact that there was such a thing.

Every member of the jury thought that Paul Moris's testimony, coming so late in the trial, was very damaging. Richard Devane was quite certain about the impact it had: "It changed a lot of opinions right at the last. A lot of them who thought she was not guilty—after his testimony—thought she was lying. There was a very definite change."

One of the jurors in whose feelings there was a major change was young David Ryan. Twenty-six years old, with a sparse, straggly, blond beard, he arrived in the courtroom every day wearing a bandanna around his head, and usually a colored T-shirt bearing such messages as "Legalize" and alongside it a colored drawing of a marijuana plant.

During the first three weeks of the trial David's sympathies had been consistently with Kay and Marian. He made this clear to the other jurors. His dramatic change was clear to all of them. Joe Poole remembered his reactions:

"This boy was absolutely messed up. He was saying 'Not guilty' all along until this happened. Then he said: 'She lied to me!' And he cried. And he protested then: he wore a black bandanna to protest, and he turned his chair around so that he had his back to the judge as a protest. He was mad at Mrs. Sandiford and mad at Mrs. Rosen. Now he was for murder. A life sentence."

The arguments, followed by voting, continued. It was plain that if they wanted to reach a verdict and come together on common ground, the common ground would have to be that held by the four jurors favoring voluntary manslaughter. Reluctantly Richard Devane and twenty-two-year-old Evan Baker, a superviser in a supermarket, a nonpracticing Catholic with a steady girl friend, changed their not guilty plea to voluntary manslaughter. Everyone moved to the middle position—except young Ryan. He wasn't changing his verdict of murder for anybody. Eleven to one and the jurors talked to him and reasoned with him. No, he was sending out a note to the judge to inform him that he was not changing his mind.

Judge Moore received the note and sent back his reply. Apparently it said in essence that the jury, including David Ryan, would stay where it was until it *did* reach a verdict.

At three thirty in the afternoon on Thursday, February 5, 1981, the jury returned to the courtroom. Bill Norton handed a slip of paper to the clerk, who bore it to Judge Moore. The judge read it and folded the paper. "Guilty," he said quietly, "of voluntary manslaughter."

To Kay, the word *guilty* meant that her personal world had been blown to bits, and she disintegrated. All though the trial, even during the worst moments, she had hung on to the faces of the people she knew, knowing that if they "looked good" or "reasonably hopeful" then she was all right. When she was giving evidence, Michael had sat behind Marian and she could tell by his face if she was coming through. Even before the jury came in, she had been searching around the courtroom for one of her "faces" to hang on to. And now all her "faces" were bleak: Kathy was crying; Marian's face was wet; Michael wasn't crying but looked as if the sky had fallen in on him. There was only one "face," only one positive, hanging-on face, she could see. It belonged to her son, Charles. But by that time she was on the brink of collapse.

"I was just hysterical," she said later. "The only reason I got up there on the witness stand and faced the trial was to try and explain, to try and make twelve decent, honest people understand what I've gone through; to reach through to them and make them understand. At first in those pretrial months I was just not going to appear on that witness stand. I wasn't going to talk about myself. I was going to die. I felt no good would come from trying to explain to a whole courtroom of people — all those reporters who fill the television screens and newspapers — what life with Frank was really like. No good would come from it. No one would ever understand, because I hardly understood it myself. I couldn't believe the whole thing was happening. I mean, sometimes when I'd drive up to Huntsville I'd be in the car by myself and I'd think, *How did this happen to me? How did I get mixed up in this?* It was like it had happened to somebody else.

"So I was going to die. That was it. It was no big deal: you're born, you pay taxes, and you die; it's just a matter of when. If I went a little early, that was my bad or good luck. That's the way I felt after Frank."

Now Kay had to cling to one simple determination: to keep herself pulled together. She had the pills in her handbag and she had to get time to use them. She had to talk to Marian and make certain that Marian saw to it that she had the time.

That evening on their car radio commuters listened to the voice of a woman newscaster sketching in the background: "Kay Sandiford broke down in the courtroom, crying in the arms of her son, Charles, for a long time. She would not talk to reporters. She was taken to the back offices where she continued crying. I tried to talk to her but one of her constant companions since the trial started held me back, saying, 'She's in shock; she'll poop out if you try.'

"Finally, after hearing more testimony from character witnesses, the jury will assess punishment. Voluntary manslaughter carries a sentence from probation to twenty years in prison and a fine of up to ten thousand dollars."

What the newscasters could not report was that Kay Sandiford, driven home still in shock, was trying desperately to hold herself together and remember what she had to do that night.

In a vague way she was surprised to see that Jim Claghorn was at the house; it was the first time she had ever seen him at Del Monte. Holding out a couple of pills and a glass of water, he smiled and said, "Now, Kay, I want you to take these. They'll give you a good night's sleep, which is just what you need."

Instinctively Kay did as she was told. Kathy led her off to bed, then kissed her on the cheek and left her in the quiet darkness of the room where she had waited for Frank's return on so many sleepless nights. She fought against sleep, for she knew this might be her last chance to make her own decision. On the bedside table stood the handbag containing the drugs. Confused, she thought about that terrible verdict . . . now what should she do? Marian had said she would give her time, but what if there was a slip-up? She remembered nothing more; the sedatives had robbed her of her will. She fell asleep.

The verdict of voluntary manslaughter was a terrible blow to the defense. However, in the interval before the jury retired for a second time to consider what sentence it should pass, the defense had the right to offer extenuating and mitigating reasons for mercy, could bring to the stand witnesses who would testify to Kay Sandiford's good character. The prosecution meanwhile could drive home the argument that voluntary manslaughter must entail a lengthy and deterrent sentence in the women's penitentiary at Huntsville.

Marian Rosen, Carol Vance, and Michael Von Blon spent all that evening until after midnight telephoning people they thought would want to come forward as character witnesses, and asking them in their turn to call other people who might wish to testify. In effect, it became a sort of chain-telephone appeal.

When Judge Moore reconvened the court the next morning, the results of their efforts were staggering. The court teemed with character witnesses. There was standing room only. There were so many that Judge Moore swore them in like a cowboy posse, asking that all who anticipated "being witnesses in this case, please rise and raise your right hand and swear to this effect. . . ."

Michael Von Blon remembered, "Everybody in the whole damn courtroom raised their hands. It was awesome."

Marian Rosen made one other dramatic move. She had been outraged by Paul Moris's last-minute testimony and, accordingly, had called him at seven fifteen that morning, telling him she thought the least he could do was to appear as a character witness. He had agreed to think about it and now, to her astonishment, he stood among the multitudes, ready to testify on Kay Sandiford's behalf.

Kay was slightly bleary from her sedatives when she and Kathy arrived at the courthouse. Even so, she immediately sought out Michael and informed him that she had to speak to Marian. Marian plainly expected her, and led the way to a back office where they had privacy.

Kay said, "Marian, remember our deal. How are you going to get me the time I need... those six hours?"

Marian took Kay's arm. "I'll get you the time," she said. "But, Kay, if they're going to send you to jail, I tell you I'm coming with you. I've got my case packed, and I've told Freddy what I'm going to do. I've never felt like this about anyone I've ever defended before, and I've never been to jail before, but if they send you to jail, so help me God, I'm going to go right along with you."

Taken by surprise, Kay blinked back her tears.

Not long afterward, Marian, in her closing plea, said, "Kay Sandiford is not a hardened criminal. She is a loving, caring, kind person— a person who will go out of her way to help other people, and has always done that. She is not the kind of person who belongs in prison. Frank Sandiford's death was the result of unique circumstances.... If the purpose of imprisonment is to deter future crime, remember Kay Sandiford, who, until this incident, had never committed a crime in her whole life, will never again commit a crime; therefore I ask you, the jury, to arrive at a sentence which will allow Kay Sandiford to avoid imprisonment."

That Marian Rosen was more moved than at any time in her career was revealed when Kathy, who had driven Kay to the courtroom for a month, and protected her with an eagle's vigilance, testifying to Kay's character, broke down on the witness stand and began to cry, and the court was treated to the unusual experience of witnessing the defense lawyer joining in the tears.

Carol Vance guided Marian gently back to her chair and took over. "I have worked on the prosecution side of the law for twenty-two years," he said, "and I can stand here before you now and truthfully say that I have never seen a case with so many mitigating circumstances. Kay

Sandiford was pushed to the absolute limits. She is a 'battered woman.' 'Battered women' come down to the complaint desk at the police station every day. Kay Sandiford has never come down to that desk, never would come down to that desk, but to the police she *is* a 'battered woman.'"

When it was the prosecution's turn, with a trace of compassion Mack Arnold admitted that Kay Sandiford was in all probability, usually, a law-abiding citizen. But it must be remembered, he said, that she had killed her husband and should not escape punishment. "I urge you to send her to the penitentiary for a number of years," he said. "When she gets out she can pick up her life with all the advantages she had before. And when she does that, Frank Sandiford will still be dead."

It was Friday morning. The jurors were nearing the end of their near month-long stint. If they came to a quick and unanimous decision, they could all be home with their families in time for lunch, freed at last from a responsibility that, without exception, they all found onerous and acutely difficult.

They had spent the night in strange beds, and several had not slept very well. Some of them had prayed. And they were no nearer a unanimous decision than when they had started their considerations at noon the day before.

Two of the women jurors were still strongly against Kay. They thought she should receive a sentence of twenty years in prison. It was not because they were savage or vindictive women; both simply felt that she had transgressed too seriously to be automatically forgiven.

The jurors' positions, in terms of sentencing, had hardened: five advocated a long sentence, four a term of imprisonment of not more than ten years, and three—because Joe Poole had come across to join Richard Devane and Evan Baker—a suspended sentence with probation, which meant Kay would go free.

Again, they reviewed the case. Again, they argued. They took votes. They got nowhere. They reiterated their arguments and Bill Norton presented a powerful point of view. "I just can't follow this 'battered woman' theory. I think she had so many times when she could have left and got away from Frank Sandiford. That's the part I don't understand. I know that the psychiatrist testified to that—the battered woman gets to the point where for some reason she can't seem to leave—but I have a hard time understanding that because, to me, she had a number of times when she could have left. She was independent, wealthy; she had her own money, and she could have left and taken care of herself. My personal opinion, if you want that, is that Kay Sandiford was married to a heart surgeon who was going to become very famous possibly, and she was very hesitant about giving up that part because it was a place in society for her; and I think she held on to it to the point where she couldn't stand what was happening anymore, especially when she found out that her husband was going to leave her possibly to go back to Italy and marry a woman doctor there. And I think she just kinda went off the deep end when she found that out and just couldn't cope with it, and that was the only way she saw out. Now, whether or not she finally intended to commit murder or just went off the deep end and did it, I don't really know that. Now, the evidence that was presented in the trial I believe shows that she planned the murder, because some of the things that were brought out I don't believe could have taken place in the time span that the defense tried to make it look like they took place."

Joe Poole was having none of this. Yes, he'd voted for voluntary manslaughter as the proper verdict. He was firm about that. But he was equally firm about what should happen now. "I know she is guilty of shooting her husband. That's plain. But under what circumstances; that's what this trial has been all about. There's never been any violence in her life before. After her marriage she had a good moral record. No violence. So why send her to the penitentiary: that'll do her more harm than good; that's not for reform. She'll never do anything like this again as long as she lives. She's not a violent person. She just went off the deep end, and I think he drove her to it."

Back and forth they went, going over every aspect of the trial in search of convincing evidence that would support each juror's hypothesis. The prosecution's constantly expressed conviction that on that Tuesday evening Frank was just the quiet family man, yawning his way upstairs, carrying his bottle of wine, his glass of wine, his packet of cigarettes, and his *Time* magazine, carried a great deal of weight for many of the jurors.

The defense's contentions carried weight for others—that items for later collection were often left on the flight of wooden stairs leading up from the kitchen and breakfast room, items such as *Time* magazine; that Frank always carried his cigarettes in the waistband of his hospital greens; that Frank in an angry mood might well have made for the stairs carrying a bottle of wine and a glass, but had then spied the tennis racket screwed into its heavy, butterfly-bolted frame; that, putting down the glass, he had then gone on up the stairs, also putting down the bottle on his angry journey, and carrying the racket as his instrument of punishment; that Kay had seen it—almost the last thing she remembered seeing—as he reached the top landing and heard his threat; that the bullets fired from the .357 had driven Frank back down the stairs, where on his downward path he missed the bottle but kicked over the glass.

The jurors went over this scene many times, in as many arguments:

"The man was supposed to be barefoot," Bill Norton argued.

"Wearing socks," one of the other jurors corrected. "The police reports said wearing socks."

"Okay, okay. But the defense attorney talked about angry footsteps. How can footsteps be angry . . . in socks?"

"On *wooden* stairs you'd have heard them all right," Devane declared.

Bill Norton was convinced. "If that man was running up the stairs intent on beating his wife, I don't think she would have time to run back and get the gun and still catch him on the landing—"

"Bill," Devane interrupted, "she could have seen him from where she was standing at her desk through the open door. The guns were under the cushions a stride away. She grabbed one, turned, pointed, and fired. You've been in the forces. You know with a revolver if you point and shoot at close range, you hit—"

"I believe that she went upstairs," Norton said emphatically, "and she got that gun immediately. I believe she'd put that gun under the couch cushion in the first place for that very purpose. If she didn't intend to kill him, why did she follow him down the stairs, shoot him in the back, and then, when he'd fallen on the kitchen floor, pump two more bullets into him?"

"Because at the time she just didn't know what she was doing," Devane retorted. "Her mind had reached boiling point. It had all come to a head. She just went over the edge."

Jeanine Donaldson concurred. "I've got to agree with that. I think once she started shooting she absolutely blanked out. Once she shot him that first time, she could have shot twenty times if there were that many bullets in the gun."

It was Jeanine Donaldson who recalled a little sadly, "I always thought these votes should be anonymous, and they were at first, everyone sitting there and handing in their slips of paper. But then when things got heated during that punishment phase, and there was so much diversity of opinion... you know: 'Tell me why you feel that way. What part of the evidence convinced you to say that?' So it got to scenes where the jurors were cross-examining each other. And people started giving in. 'I'll give in here if you give in there'— that sort of negotiation went on. No one wanted to come back on Monday; they wanted over with it, and that's rather tragic. But then maybe we would have gone on arguing forever and never reached a unanimous agreement."

Bill Norton's arguments were persuasive, but Joe Poole and Richard Devane were equally powerful and convincing. And they were not changing their beliefs come hell or high water.

Joe Poole observed: "I said, ten years suspended sentence. Ten thousand dollars fine. And *probation*. I wasn't changing my mind for anyone, and I could live with it."

Richard Devane said, "One thing was absolutely certain. I wasn't going to guilty. [If we had to stay there for another year I wasn't going to guilty.] I definitely didn't feel she was guilty and I definitely wasn't going to vote that way just to get out of there. I didn't feel that was fair to anybody, and as a matter of fact the sense of responsibility was very strong amongst everyone, very strong. I agree one or two of them said, 'Come on let's get together, so we can get out of here.' I said, 'This woman's life is at stake more or less'—I mean it wasn't a matter of the death penalty, but [the years in jail] would have meant the same thing. Joe Poole was sticking good too. He said, 'My mind's made up and I'm not changing it.' He just sat back and relaxed and closed his eyes." Young David Ryan in his black bandanna retired to the men's room and stayed there a long time. He declared that he needed to concentrate by himself. When he returned he was in tears because of possibly having to change his vote of guilty, entailing a life sentence, to something less severe.

Richard Devane recalls that it was Jeanine Donaldson "who first came across to join us."

It was Jeanine Donaldson who observed, "It was strange how, when we first started out in the jury room, practically everyone stood for the letter of the law, the principles—justice must be done. But then as we went on arguing and talking, more and more the humanities, the compassion, became apparent."

Michael Von Blon remembered those hours waiting for the jury to return as the longest of his life. And when they filed back into court, he remembered looking at them with deep distrust. *God*, he thought, *I misjudged them yesterday, when I was certain they would bring in self-defense; what are they going to do now?*

"I stared at them," he recalled, "trying to get the smallest indication . . . of . . . something. I thought, *For God's sake, one of you do something. Cry, smile, anything.* Then one of them—I can't remember which one—let out a half-smile, but I refused to believe that; they'd let me down yesterday.

"Eventually the slip of paper was passed to Judge Moore. He adjusted his glasses. On oath, I swear it took him twenty minutes. Then he said that magical word, 'Probation.' A probated sentence of ten years in prison, and a fine of ten thousand dollars. She was on probation. It meant we could drive her home. Out under the sky. Free!"

EPILOGUE

F
EBRUARY 15, 1983: Kay's last appearance at the Probation Center, Court Annex 21, San Jacinto, in downtown Houston. A renovated warehouse that had once been derelict, it stood one empty parking lot away from the Harris County Court.

On the sixth floor she stood in line to pay her fifteen-dollar probation supervisory fee, then descended to the fifth floor and the waiting room. It was small and utilitarian: half a dozen tubular steel chairs with plastic seats, a table to match bearing three dog-eared copies of *Time*, *Newsweek*, and *People*.

From the front cover of *People*, "lovely Dud"—Dudley Moore, slightly dwarfed by his tall and beautiful girl friend—exhibited twin rows of exquisitely crowned teeth in flashing smiles. The three probationers waiting with Kay had no dentistry to admire and did not smile. Nobody smiled much along those thin corridors paneled with cheap white sheetrock. The tall, thin white man with a gaunt, pinched face wearing an orange baseball cap, worn brown slacks, and a scruffy raincoat, leaned over toward her and said "Pardon me" as he expertly peeled off the top copy from the block of Probationer's Monthly Reports. His grimace, unlike that of the radiant Dudley, smelled strongly of eucalyptus, and Kay could make a good guess at his drinking problem. The other two were not quite so simple to read. The pasty-faced, overweight youngster in the black coat and black trilby hat, and exhibiting a Manchu mustache, probably spelled drugs, but the good-looking black guy in the corner, this time wearing a baseball cap divided into blue and white segments, leather windbreaker, jeans and rubber boots turned over at the top, was a puzzle. He sat with head bowed.

Kay Sandiford sat clutching her handbag, demure and earnest. She expected that they looked at her in the same way as she looked at them, and wondered what secret crime or strange craving had placed her outside the law.

For the past two years, obeying the conditions of probation—"that the ends of justice and the best interests of the public as well as of you" would be served—she had "committed no offense against the laws of this or any other State of the United States," avoided injurious or vicious habits, places of disrepute or harmful character, reported faithfully to her probation officer, worked at suitable employment, and supported her dependents, and had driven up the 45 to Huntsville, her cruise speed level at 55 while huge trucks roared past at 65, with never even the hint of alcohol on her breath. And had hated—deeply hated—the fact that probation deprived her of the right to vote.

She had also, following the last two lines of the probation order, "sincerely tried to obey and live up to conditions of probation," so that, "her attitude would improve to the benefit of the public and herself."

And what had she learned in her two years of redemption? More about God? No. More about life—oh, yes, certainly. More about Frank? Oh, yes, *most* certainly—from the moment the telephone rang for a second time in Marian Rosen's home, the day after the trial ended, and the same young woman with the attractive foreign accent began to talk, saying she was now ready to make a sworn statement before witnesses and a notary public.

"Alma was twenty-nine," Marian Rosen recalls, "quite a lovely young woman. She was divorced, had a son of nine from that first marriage. She came from a wealthy family and was very honest and straightforward."

Alma had first met Frank Sandiford in 1975, at the Texas Heart Institute, when she came up from South America accompanying two Italian friends, to help them with the language. They brought with them their second child, who had been born with a heart defect. Frank advised them to bring the boy back later for heart surgery, when he would operate. It was just a casual friendship. In January 1976 Alma returned to Houston and the affair with Frank began. When she went home after that, he began to write her letters: "beautiful letters that would resemble enormously the famous letter in the paper. You would be surprised how similar they were to the ones he wrote me," Alma said. In the autumn of 1976 Frank told Alma that he loved her, that they must make the relationship permanent, and that she must move to Houston. She did so and eventually they got an apartment there, and they were able, if not totally to live together, at least to spend a lot of time together. As Frank was never at home, but always "on call," Kay Sandiford could vouch for the truth of that statement.

Kay Sandiford could not have counted the times in the evening when Frank would make his phone call and then search her out—in the kitchen, in the lounge, upstairs doing the bills—kiss her perfunctorily on the forehead, and say, "Darling, I have to go." And that absence might last for a few hours, a few days, or a few weeks—oh, yes, interspersed with a few phone calls and a few visits to the house, usually when she wasn't home, to collect fresh clothes.

Was Alma aware, Marian asked, that when Frank made trips to other countries he was going out with other women? Oh, yes, Alma understood that perfectly. She knew that his wife, Kay, accompanied him, but overseas she would always prefer to stay with her own friends and leave Frank to his own devices. She knew he had affairs with other women; she found letters and photos they sent him. But Frank had always brushed such things aside. It was "no big deal," he'd said. "You know the type of thing that two weeks later you barely remember her name."

Alma knew nevertheless that her own relationship with Frank was safe and secure. Certainly they had discussed marriage, but both felt there was no hurry. Frank needed to sort out his family problems first; he had to provide his son, Charles, with a stable home, and Charles couldn't leave until he had reached a more mature age. The divorce would have to wait for these reasons. But for the record, only a few weeks before Frank died he told Alma that he now felt the time had come to make a decision. In that December of 1979 he had made it quite clear that within a very short time he would get his divorce and they would be married. He even informed their mutual Italian friends, saying, "At last we are going to have a peaceful family life. We shall settle down and have a family." He was telling her the same thing until three days before his death.

Did she know something about his affair with the young Italian cardiologist, Liza? No, he had never even mentioned her name. These trips to Italy and these other women had happened before. They meant nothing. There was a continuity about their love: "He felt so comfortable with me. I understood him and knew him so very well. He could just think out loud and not have to worry, just be really at ease."

And what about his moving to Italy to open a hospital there? Absolutely ridiculous, she said. For this type of work, he always said, there was no way of operating or organizing such things in Italy.

What about Kay Sandiford?

She had met Kay twice and was "uncomfortable in her presence." But Alma never thought Kay Sandiford cared enough about Frank to be jealous. They had drifted apart. He seldom spoke about her.

Did they talk about having children?

Oh, yes. He had always wanted little girls. Their favorite name was Elizabeth, but they had dozens of names picked out.

Who had contacted her from the district attorney's office?

She had been interviewed by Mr. Duke Bodisch. They had met many times. He had even rung her twice when she was at her parents' home in South America. On one occasion he had said jokingly, "Are you ready to testify?" and she, taken aback, had replied, "What! No! No!" Bodisch had laughed and said, "I'm just kidding. You know I promised to keep you out of this."

As a good case could be put for Alma—from her place in Frank's life, probably knowing him as well as any woman ever did, and very assured in her statement, which she repeated in an interview some two years later, that in her opinion Kay was certainly not "a jealous woman" and did not care enough about Frank to be "jealous of him"—it is interesting to speculate on what the jury, swayed by the Paul Moris and "Liza letter" evidence, would have made of Alma's revelations delivered from the witness box.

It is also fairly simple to understand why the prosecution, which, through Frank's secretary and other friends, had located Alma within a matter of hours, forgot to mention her existence.

It was about three days before it was convenient for the defense to pry into Frank's office, and by then the cupboard was bare.

Kay always wondered whatever happened to the expensive diamond, sapphire, and pearl earrings that Cartier had rung her about from New York a few weeks before Frank's death. They hoped they were not disclosing a secret, but Dr. Sandiford had been very particular about the design, and they needed a little information. Kay helped them all she could. As Frank had "borrowed" ten thousand dollars from her shortly before then (months later she was to discover that he had borrowed ten thousand dollars from another friend, presumably for the same purchase), Kay was hopeful that perhaps a surprise Christmas present was in the offing. After nothing appeared, she wondered if perhaps Liza was the recipient? Or perhaps the lucky girl had been named Joan, for a gold ankle bracelet inscribed with that name had arrived at Frank's office two weeks after Frank's death.

Alma still thinks the defense's attacks on Frank's character were appalling, although she could understand and not condemn the reasons for making them. Frank, in Alma's opinion, was a warm, loving, considerate, kindly man who would never have hurt a fly. This talk of cruelty and "battering" was preposterous. Certainly both Frank and she were "Latins" and understood the passionate nature of "Latins," but to libel him in this manner was abominable. "Ask his friends—ask his patients," she said.

Liza, also generously answering a request from this author, wrote sadly from Italy that Frank was the most wonderful and important man she had ever known; that she had loved him with all her strength and soul and still loved him. She did not feel herself guilty because of this love, "because I made him happy for some months, full of life, loved as he had never known love before." And she was tired of words, trials, and uneventful things made in "that terrible, ugly, stupid, racist false world of vulgar cowboys that is called Texas, in particular Houston." All her story was in her mind and heart forever.

Kay sat in the waiting room of the Probation Center on San Jacinto looking at the tall, thin man who smelled of eucalyptus, and remembered the coffins. The conversation was between Ernest Steadman and Marian at a time when Kay was still paralyzed by doubts and fears. What should be done about Frank's body? Where should it be buried—Houston or Italy? And all she could think was, *Bury him, for God's sake, just bury him.*

Someone, probably his sister and mother, tilted the scales for Italy. And the succession of coffins began: coffin one, in which Frank was laid out at the funeral she attended; coffin two, which was apparently necessary for the memorial service (which she did not attend) but was too big to be crated and placed aboard the aircraft bearing the corpse back to Italy; coffin three, which made the air journey but would not fit into the family crypt near Rome; and coffin four, the final resting place. The Italians certainly were into coffins, she thought: one body, four coffins. She sat in the probation office hoping that Frank, now interred, was finally at rest. The bills when they had arrived had come to more than $30,000.

Funny how hindsight provided such sharp eyesight. She was pretty sure now that during those last few years when Frank was making large sums of money, which he spent as if it would never end, and he no longer needed the financial security she gave him, he had tried to kill her. Certainly the scuba-diving incident was one occasion. And it was odd that she had never considered the Mojave Desert incident in the same light, until, while she was waiting for trial, Cat Bennett had urged her to visit California, and she had replied, "Not on your life. I was out there... and I didn't like what happened." And then it had all come out. She and Frank had been at a conference in Palm Springs, and Frank just had to see the Mojave Desert—this close, they mustn't miss it. So Frank had hired a car and a few hours later there they were right in the middle of the blazing desert, in the middle of the afternoon; just one little road with the immensity of boiling desert on either side—no cars, no people, no air, just a great brazen sun occupying the entire sky.

Frank suddenly brakes to a halt and barks, "Get out!"

Little, submissive Chinese wife, wondering for a second what he's up to now, but obedient as ever, gets out. Frank leans over, pulls the door shut, and whoof—he's gone. Immediately she thought: the character-building caper again. But it was so hot, so breathlessly hot, and she in a short-sleeved dress and no hat, and the car engine dwindling, and then silence. She would swear the silence made a sound against the boiling asphalt, as if it were vibrating. She'd die if she walked. She'd die if she sat down. And there was nowhere to go. She was conscious that already her arms were burning, that she had a headache, was losing track of time, feeling everything blurred and muzzy; and knowing later that she must have passed out, for she didn't hear the car come back, but was suddenly vaguely aware that a big black wheel was near her head. She remembered Frank coming around, picking her up, and putting her in the back of the car. She was half conscious; she didn't remember the drive back or going to bed.

Kay also remembered that last time in Atlanta, only a few weeks before the end. It was another medical conference, this time at the Hyatt Hotel. The first night Frank had been acutely difficult: he wanted sandwiches, then he didn't want sandwiches; he ordered a bottle of bourbon and immediately started drinking it out of the bottle—Wild Turkey, one hundred and one proof. Then the usual screaming accusations—useless, childless—and the brutal blows.

The next night he'd been worse. He'd come back late, aloof and very distant. He said they must go to dinner, but Kay, remembering the night before and all the uneaten sandwiches, had made no arrangements and knew nothing about Atlanta restaurants. They chose one of the many restaurants in the hotel. But no sooner had they ordered their meal than Frank had to go to the bathroom. Weeks later—after his death—Kay realized what had taken him so long: the charge for that date on the telephone bill was for a call to Liza in Italy.

Returning after she had finished her meal, and ignoring his own, Frank threw his credit card on the table. He waited for her to settle and led the way to the elevator. Climbing to the twentieth floor, Kay realized something was terribly wrong; Frank was different, brooding, on edge. Even his bulk—for he'd put on a lot of weight recently—threatened her.

They got out on the circular walkway that rings the atrium above the lobby. Kay disliked the walkway. Only a foot or so of bricks and a waist-high bannister protected one from the drop. They could have taken a short route to their room, but Frank insisted on taking the long, counterclockwise route. And now, as they walked along, Kay was aware that his heavy body was pressing her against the bannister... not pushing, just pressing. Another chilling thought struck her: she was suddenly conscious that the extra inches of her high-heeled shoes put her hips level with the top of the bannister; her entire center of gravity was above the height of the railing. One quick shove could plunge her into the abyss.

She was intensely aware of his mood. The blackness that had enveloped him the night before, when he'd beaten her, still gripped him. That frightened her. Usually, once he'd screamed at her, punched her, kicked her, his anger diminished. Now, to her horror, she knew it was still there, festering. There was not another soul on the walkway, and

Frank took her upper arm, hurrying her footsteps. As he tugged her along she thought desperately of the options open to her, and could think of only one. She bent lower, trying to reach down to her shoes, protesting, "Frank, stop. I think I've broken the heel of my shoe." He pressed on, even when she struggled in his grasp, trying to stoop lower. "Frank," she gasped, "let go of me!" And as she spoke, with enormous gratitude she saw a door open a few yards ahead and the most wonderful man she had ever seen—middle-aged, bald-headed, wearing glasses—emerged. He carried a plastic bucket on his way to collect ice from the dispenser.

He glanced at them and said, "Hi!"

Frank, as if emerging from a trance, flipped back to near normal. Kay acknowledged the man's greeting as Frank snapped, "I want you to get ice too."

Kay unlocked their bedroom door. She grabbed the ice bucket and was outside the door again almost before Frank had entered. Shaking, she took at least five minutes to collect the ice. When she returned, Frank was lying on the bed drinking Wild Turkey out of the bottle and watching television. Kay went into the bathroom and turned on the taps. She took a two-hour bath that night, and when she emerged he was asleep.

During those two years on probation, before her parole record could be reviewed and she could be set entirely free, Kay often sat on the lake house veranda looking at the dark, shining water and thought that this must be how an aquatic creature must feel, freeing its wings from a clinging underwater sac and spreading them to dry in the sanity of the sun.

It was in those first few months of 1980 that she had been convinced by Marian Rosen, Jim Claghorn, Michael Von Blon, Leonore Walker, and a few others that she could stand up and face a trial.

"Not for women's liberation or anything 'principled' like that. I've never been into that sort of activity. But just for *women*, the ones who get a raw deal, the ones who get kicked and beaten in a variety of ways—and I don't mean just physically—and go on with their lives and care for their kids and don't make any sort of fuss about it. For those were the ones who supported me that year. Women, strangers I'd never even met, would telephone me out of the blue that year and wish me luck. Women I met in stores would support me with smiles and encouragement, not because they were going to be witnesses, but because they could understand what had happened. That kind of reinforcement made me go on to the witness stand and tell the truth.

"Marian said to me once, 'The strength was in you.' But I didn't really go along with that: the strength was from others—the support I took from all around me that year; those friends who took it in turn to see I was never alone in the evenings; the support that didn't know anything about the other support, which came from the telephone, someone coming up on the street, padding alongside when you were jogging."

Once she had got through the trial, Kay remembered what her friend Julia, who organized Family Outreach, had said to her. "I feel really strongly that one of the answers to child abuse—if there is an answer—is to get the community more involved, to involve people as volunteers, especially people who have had life experience, especially people who have got their act together and will make an effort to help others in need."

Kay felt she had had "a life experience" all right, though she wasn't certain if she'd got her act together. But at least she could try.

That's when she went to Family Outreach. At first she had thought she might be of some help in some organization concerned with abused women, but the idea of having to confront the belligerant male batterer was too much for her; she'd experienced years of that and knew she was far too emotionally involved and too subjective to be of any assistance.

But Julia's organization was different. Its personnel worked closely with the Harris County Welfare Department, and when they heard of a child being beaten, starved, or otherwise endangered, they had the right to move in and, if necessary, move the child to a temporary home. Family Outreach dealt with the whole family group, trying to help parents who had abused their children, or felt the potential for abusing their children.

"I really love that bumper sticker," Julia had told her, her bright eyes shining enthusiastically through her spectacles, "that says: 'Don't have a child until you're through being one.'"

"And that's the really important point," Julia went on. "And if only everybody listened to that advice, I'd be out of a job, and that would be a good thing. You see, people get out and have sex, and they want love, and it's so cute having a precious little baby. And once they've got one they just don't know how to handle it or what to do with it. And if they haven't got a good strong family behind them to get them through this sort of crisis, then that baby's at risk, and it's a wonder more children aren't abused than already are."

Kay had attended the training sessions and had eventually got herself qualified as a field counselor, which meant she was equipped to help a family unit deal with its problems. Her first job had been sitting in the office doing three-and-a-half-hour stints on the telephone trying to answer the various questions that pour in and sometimes trying to console someone in distress. She knew she wasn't doing very much. But it had been a beginning.

The female voice calling "Kay Sandiford?" toward the waiting room stirred her out of her reverie and reminded her that she herself, to a certain extent, was still "in distress," and that it was her turn to see her counselor, her probation officer. Jeannie was twenty-eight years old, pretty, petite, intelligent, and Kay often wondered what turned her toward such a demanding profession. Jeannie said, "Hi, Kay," as Kay handed her the receipt for the supervisory fee, and Jeannie made the appropriate note in her ledger. "How are you getting on with the kids?"

"The kids" meant Family Outreach. Jeannie knew about it and understood. She'd got permission for Kay to put one of their posters in the waiting room. Now they chatted and discussed Kay's future, because Jeannie always said that she'd found Kay an exemplary probationer and her request for release from parole would almost certainly be granted.

When Kay stood up to leave, they both found themselves in tears, and gave each other unembarrassed hugs, and a few days later the letter arrived:

> It appears to the Court after considering the recommendation of the defendant's probation officer, and other matters and evidence to the effect that the defendant has satisfactorily fulfilled the conditions of probation... the indictment against the defendant be and the same is hereby dismissed and the Judgment of Conviction is hearby set aside, as provided by law.

Much later Kay said, "Angie Brown, who worked with Leonore Walker and talked to me a lot, always said, 'You are going to go through a period when you really hate Frank.'

"I never really believed her. I never hated him through the trial; I lost my guilt but I never hated Frank. But after the trial I really hated Frank. I really hated him for the seventeen years I thought he had stolen from me. I just didn't want to hear his name. But I'm not that way now.

"Sometimes I think I'm lucky to be alive because the psychologists engaged in this field are convinced that a man and woman locked in a serious 'battering' situation will advance inevitably towards a clash resulting in the death of one or the other . . . unless they terminate their association.

"And I think there are a great number of women in the world who at this very second are unaware of the danger they are in.

"The U.S. Government recently recognized that this epidemic of family violence is a covert evil in our society, and the President gave the Attorney General the go-ahead to take legislative steps to curb it.

"People still say to me, Why didn't you get out? Walk away? There was never any chance of my walking away. I never even considered it. I didn't want to. I had convinced myself that I had fallen in love with a great and good man. Whatever he did was right. I made all the excuses, I was always in the wrong. I was a self-indoctrinated prisoner believing I was truly in love, and had no other standards to judge by. I was going to be a good and faithful wife and stay if necessary until I died.

"I don't think it's a case of Frank guilty or Frank innocent. I feel that Frank was an extremely sick person—especially during that last period—both mentally and physically ill. Now I have compassion for Frank. What's done is done. I do believe, as I've said before, that from the time he married me he planned at some time to do away with me. But I don't blame him for that, because I think he was sick and I think he was driven. He was never in control of himself; he was searching from woman to woman for a reason he didn't understand; I can see that in hindsight now.

"I don't think the man would ever have found peace. Frank was never at peace. I couldn't give it to him. He couldn't give it, or find it within himself."